the
affair

Amanda Brooke is a single mum who lives in Liverpool with her daughter, Jessica, two cats and a laptop within easy reach. Her debut novel, *Yesterday's Sun*, was a Richard and Judy Book Club pick. *The Affair* is her seventh novel.

www.amanda-brooke.com
@AmandaBrookeAB
www.facebook.com/AmandaBrookeAuthor

Also by Amanda Brooke

Yesterday's Sun
Another Way To Fall
Where I Found You
The Missing Husband
The Child's Secret
The Goodbye Gift

Ebook-only short stories
The Keeper of Secrets
If I Should Go

the
affair

AMANDA BROOKE

HARPER

Harper
An imprint of HarperCollins*Publishers*
1 London Bridge Street
London SE1 9FG

www.harpercollins.co.uk

A Paperback Original 2017
3

A catalogue record for this book
is available from the British Library

ISBN: 978-0-00-811655-2

Typeset in Sabon LT Std by Palimpsest Book Production Limited,
Falkirk, Stirlingshire
Printed in the United States of America by
LSC Communications

Find out more about HarperCollins and the environment at
www.harpercollins.co.uk/green

For Jessica Valentine, who made the task of bringing
up a teenager surprisingly easy

Scarlett

You might as well know from the start, I'm not going to tell on him and I don't care how much trouble I get in. It's not like it could get any worse than it already is. Well, actually, it probably could get a whole lot worse, which is why I'm not doing it.

I can't. Don't ask me why, I just can't.

It's so unfair.

1

The Accusations

Monday, 22 February 2016

Nina sat alone at the breakfast bar as the sun began its slow ascent over the quiet Cheshire town of Sedgefield. The watery light had an ominous red tinge as it crept into the darkened kitchen of the pretty townhouse she shared with her husband and two teenage children. By rights, she should be unloading stock at the shop by now after an early morning trip to the flower market, but Nina was still in her dressing gown, her blonde hair pulled back in a butterfly clip, her face unwashed and her blue eyes dull and empty.

Nina had inherited a strong work ethic from her father, along with the family floristry business, and it had been going against everything he had taught her when she phoned her assistant Janet to say she wouldn't be in. There were a handful of orders that Janet would do her best to complete from the slim pickings what would be left at the market by the time she got there, but Nina had told her not to worry and to turn down new business if she needed to. In truth, Nina didn't care, and she had no idea when that situation might change. She wondered what her parents would make of the sorry mess she was in. She was almost glad they weren't around to see it.

Ever since Scarlett had dropped her bombshell on Saturday night, Nina had been in a state of shock, and more than twenty-four hours later, she was still struggling to work out how she was meant to react. It didn't help of course that Scarlett had barricaded herself in her bedroom. Nina had tried to reason with her, she had spoken gently to coax the truth out of her daughter, and when that had failed, she had yelled and made threats, only to be met with equal success.

With nothing except the most meagre of information to go on, Nina had no option but to sift through the minutiae of her life and question everything she had thought to be true. The returning answers were ones she didn't want to hear, but she couldn't ignore them, not any more, not when her fifteen-year-old daughter was pregnant.

And of all the questions she had, there was one that scared Nina most. Who the hell was the baby's father?

2

Before

Nina pulled up outside the house and paused for a moment to savour the new life she was slowly adjusting to. Something both marvellous and momentous had happened over the summer holidays: Nina Carrington was no more. The ever so slightly bitter divorcée who had brought up two children singlehandedly, vowing never to be financially or emotionally dependent on any man ever again, was no more. She blamed the Welshman.

She had met Bryn Thomas at a New Year's Eve party thrown by one of Sedgefield's most renowned citizens who happened to be Nina's best friend and confidante. Sarah Tavistock and her husband Miles knew how to throw a good party and Sarah had high hopes every year of finding a suitable candidate for the vacancy in Nina's life.

Yet despite Sarah's valiant efforts, for the previous eight years Nina had been left feeling distinctly underwhelmed. It was going to take someone exceptional to persuade her to forsake the independent life she had become accustomed to, and, to everyone's surprise, that someone had been the taxi driver who had dropped her off at the party.

Within six months, Nina couldn't imagine life without her Welshman and by August, Nina Carrington had officially moved out, making room for Nina Thomas, the forty-two-year-old, newly married wife of Bryn. Nina's second husband was a year younger than her, and as far removed from her first husband as she could hope. Where Adam Carrington had been a smooth operator, Bryn was quietly charming. He was attentive, he was eager to please, and he was gentle in spite of his muscular frame. Bryn did his best to keep in shape despite a job renowned for late nights fuelled by junk food, but he was by no means vain, which was perfect because Nina hadn't been looking for an Adonis. She had been looking for someone who wasn't expecting to be noticed, and when she had found him, the speed of their relationship had surprised them both, as it had her family and friends.

When Nina Thomas put her key in the front door, she pitied her former self, who would have been about to step quietly into an empty house. It was Liam and Scarlett's first day back at school and Nina would normally be the first one home during term-time. What wasn't normal, or at least not yet, was coming home to the aroma of home baking.

'You've been busy,' she said as she stepped into the large open-plan kitchen.

Bryn picked up a flapjack from the cooling rack and held it temptingly towards her. 'Like to try one?'

Nina walked over and with her hands behind her back, opened her mouth while suppressing a smile. Bryn held the flapjack at a tantalizing distance so that Nina had to snatch a bite. When she bit down on the delicious mix of sweet, golden oats, toasted hazelnuts and juicy raisins, she groaned. 'You're deadly for my figure.'

'I'd say it's your figure that's deadly,' Bryn said, replacing the flapjack with a kiss.

'You won't be saying that after I've had a year of your home cooking.'

'The recipe is low-fat and I've only used natural sugars. Besides, a little of what you fancy does you good.'

'And what happens if you have too much of a good thing?' Nina asked.

Bryn patted his stomach. 'If I'm anything to go by, you won't be gaining weight.' There was a note of pride in his voice, but then a thought occurred. 'But that's only because I was turning into a bit of a couch potato before I met you. I'm not suggesting you need to lose weight.'

Nina gave a soft laugh. 'Don't panic, I know what you meant, but I could stand to lose a few pounds. Believe it or not, I was once as slim as Scarlett.'

'And she has you to thank for her looks,' he said, sounding serious all of a sudden. 'You are without doubt the most beautiful woman I've ever met, Nina.'

When she held his gaze, Nina felt such a rush of love that it took her breath away. She knew they were still in the honeymoon period and there would come a time when they would settle into a comfortable life but, right now, she wanted her husband and he knew it. The air fizzed between them.

'The kids will be home soon,' he said.

Letting out a frustrated sigh as she took control of her

desires, Nina said, 'I know. So what else have you been up to? I hope you've had a chance to get your head down.'

'A few hours, once I knew the kids were off OK.'

Bryn worked the late shift for a local cab company and was out from early evening until the small hours. Before taking on the responsibilities of a family, he would have returned home and gone straight to bed, not rising until midday.

'How were they this morning?' Nina asked, having set off for the market shortly after Bryn had come home.

'I wouldn't go as far as to say they were raring to go,' he said, 'but they were both up in time to eat breakfast, even if Scarlett did have to rush to catch the bus. Liam was his usual leisurely self, so if he was running late, I didn't notice.'

Nina scrutinized Bryn's slate-grey eyes. He was painting a picture of average family life that didn't quite fit with her household. For most of their young lives, her children had endured an absent father and an overworked mother who had either dragged them out of bed to stay with a child-minder, or more recently, left them to their own devices in the mornings and hoped for the best.

Liam was the oldest at seventeen and Scarlett two years younger, and despite the challenges of single-parenting, they had all been happy enough with their unremarkable lives. Nina wasn't sure if her children had ever considered the possibility that she might find a new man; Bryn had been her one and only serious relationship since her divorce. Their reaction to his sudden appearance had been muted, and while they hadn't gone as far as refusing to accept Bryn into their lives, neither had they welcomed him. Liam had continued with his usual routines, which rarely involved leaving his room; for the most part, his acceptance had been less tangible. Scarlett, on the other hand, was more aloof than hostile. Nina had watched anxiously as her daughter attempted to work out how, or even if she should, acknowledge Bryn's intrusion into the family.

Aware that the idyllic family life of her dreams was still a work in progress, Nina asked, 'Did you actually see them?'

'I piled a plate high with toast to tempt them,' he said in a low hush as if he were a naturalist out in the field waiting for a glimpse of some rare species. 'Using a news-paper as a hide, I heard the female approach. The fridge door opened, orange juice was poured and there was the distinctive crunch of toast. When I looked up, the juice had been discarded and the creature was cursing under her breath as she slammed the front door.'

'And the male?'

'He was far more elusive, and I must have become distracted by the sports section, because the next thing I knew, the last of the toast had been reduced to crumbs, and with a gentle click, the front door closed again.'

'Did either of them actually speak to you?' Nina said, her playful tone replaced by one of exasperation. When Bryn winced in response, she added, 'Not even a good morning, please or thank you?'

'It's the first day of term, what did you expect?'

'A bit of gratitude wouldn't have gone amiss, given how you stayed up to make them breakfast.' She looked at the flapjacks, and added, 'And I suppose those are to make their homecoming more welcoming?'

'I enjoy baking. I enjoy having a family to look after.'

Nina slipped her arms around her husband's neck, which was quite a stretch. She was the shortest member of the household and even Scarlett towered over her these days. 'Well, if my self-centred children don't appreciate you, I do. I really did get lucky when I phoned for that taxi.'

'Oh for God's sake, get a room,' someone said from behind them.

Rather than pull away from the embrace as Bryn intended, Nina drew him closer for a kiss, not caring that it would intensify her daughter's mortification. If she couldn't convince her children to accept Bryn, she was going to make it absolutely clear how important he was to her. Marrying Bryn Thomas was not the symptom of a midlife crisis, as Sarah had suggested on more than one occasion. There were simply times when something felt right because it was right.

By the time Nina was ready to face her daughter, Scarlett had turned her back on them and was inspecting the contents of the fridge. Gone were the days when her daughter looked cute in her new uniform. Her plaid skirt had been rolled up at the waist so that it was a couple of inches higher than the regulatory knee-length, although thankfully still longer than most of the outfits she was inclined to wear these days.

When Scarlett picked up a half-eaten bar of chocolate, Nina said, 'Why don't you try a flapjack?'

'Chocolate's good for you,' Scarlett said, snapping a piece from the bar.

Nina tutted. 'You do know that's just a myth? There's no scientific evidence behind it.'

Scarlett popped the chocolate in her mouth and beamed a smile. 'I'll take my chances.'

'The flapjacks will keep, I'll put them in a container,' Bryn said. 'They're only a hundred calories each, and they have slow-releasing energy.'

Under her mother's withering glare, Scarlett's conscience was pricked. 'I suppose I could take some out tonight for my mates.'

'Out? Tonight?' Nina repeated. 'I don't think so. Summer holidays are over and you have your GCSEs this year. No socializing during the week and only once at the weekend.'

Scarlett's jaw dropped. 'You can't do that!'

'It's not open for discussion, Scarlett. That's how it is. And by the way,' Nina added, dropping her gaze to Scarlett's hands, 'when I told you last night to take off your nail varnish, I meant take it off. You know the school rules, and by my reckoning you're breaking at least half a dozen.'

'But, Mum, nobody cares. Everyone wears makeup and nail varnish, and the teachers don't say a thing. If you're that bothered, I'll put nail-varnish remover in my bag and, if any of the teachers freak out, I'll take it off.'

'No, do it now.'

Scarlett shoved another piece of chocolate in her mouth before returning the remainder to the fridge. 'If I do, can I still go out tonight? It's not as if school's started properly.'

In the midst of their negotiations, Liam had appeared like a spectre only vaguely aware of the world around him. Without uttering a word, he grabbed something from the fridge and wedged it between two slices of bread before disappearing.

'I give up, honestly I do.'

Scarlett's face lit up and she ran over to give her mum a dramatic hug. 'Thank you, Mum,' she said, scurrying out of the kitchen before Nina realized her daughter thought she had been talking to her. Nina was going to have to up her game if she were to avoid being outmanoeuvred by her children in the coming year.

Nina stood on the landing staring at two firmly closed bedroom doors, and as she listened to Bryn preparing dinner downstairs she could feel her frustration get the better of her. She accepted that they were all in a period of adjustment, but was it too much to expect Liam and Scarlett to at least acknowledge the efforts their stepfather was making, even if they chose not to reciprocate? Her marriage could be a great opportunity for them to have a male role model in their lives at long last, if only they would recognize it.

Liam and Scarlett's dad worked on the North Sea oil rigs and lived a single life in Aberdeen as far as Nina was aware. His children rarely had contact with him and it had been a year or two since either of them had made noises about going to stay with him. Nina had been a lone parent in every sense of the word and, despite heroic efforts, there had been limits to the advice and support she could offer her children, not to mention time. Bryn could bridge the gap. He *was* bridging the gap, and while Nina wasn't quite ready to drive the point home forcefully, she wasn't averse to helping things along.

She tapped on Liam's door and, after receiving no reply, pushed against the doorstop her son used to deter unwelcome visitors. The door opened only a fraction, revealing a darkened room thick with stale air. A flicker of blue light suggested Liam was using some form of electronic device to communicate with his virtual world.

'Liam?'

When she received a grunt in response, she asked, 'How was your first day back?'

'Fine.'

'Dinner won't be long. Bryn's trying out a new recipe.'

Nina hadn't posed a question so received no answer or acknowledgement.

'Have you made plans for the weekend?' she continued, and although it was a question this time, an answer wasn't necessary. If Liam had friends outside school, they rarely met, not in the real world at least. 'Sarah's suggested we all go out for Sunday lunch. I'd like us all to go.'

There was a hiss of annoyance, but not an outright refusal.

'OK?' she asked.

'OK, Mum. Is that all?'

'Great, lovely. I'm so looking forward to having quality time with my family,' she muttered under her breath as she closed the door and turned her attention towards Scarlett's room.

Of the two adolescents Nina had to contend with, she held out most hope for Scarlett. At fifteen, she was still young enough to want to please her mum, or at least Nina hoped that was the case. She tapped lightly on the door and walked in.

Scarlett was sitting at her dressing table absorbed in the task of applying dramatic sweeps of eyeliner to accentuate violet eyes that were already guaranteed to draw attention. She had always been a pretty child and undoubtedly she would become a beautiful woman one day, but at that precise moment she was somewhere in between and it didn't rest easy with Nina. Her daughter had plenty of friends who were boys and one day, perhaps soon, she would break someone's heart and most likely have hers broken in return. The best Nina could hope for was that Scarlett wouldn't follow her example and leave it until middle age to find *the one*.

'Scarlett!' Nina shouted loud enough to be heard above the music being channelled through headphones and assaulting her daughter's eardrums.

Scarlett jumped and the delicate flick of black she had been applying zigzagged towards her temple.

'For f—' Scarlett began, only to check herself. 'Flipping heck, Mum. What did you do that for? You scared the sh—, the life out of me!'

Try as she might, Nina couldn't keep a straight face. 'I think you need to redo your makeup.'

Scarlett turned back to the mirror and examined the damage. 'Oh great, now I'll have to start again. I'm going to be late.'

'Late out, but not late back,' Nina told her. 'Where are you going anyway?'

'Only Eva's.'

'To do homework?' Nina asked hopefully.

'On the first day back? Not even *my* teachers are that mean.'

'How was school?'

Scarlett pulled a face. 'Mrs Russell has left. She got a better job in Chester.'

'Good for her,' Nina said. Scarlett owed much of her academic success to the woman who had been her form tutor for the last four years. Whenever there had been a suggestion that she was becoming distracted or disheartened,

Mrs Russell had managed to get her back on an even keel. 'You're going to miss her, aren't you?'

Scarlett shrugged. She preferred not to admit to liking any of her teachers and Nina had to read between the lines. 'So who's her replacement?'

Wiping her eyelid with a dampened cotton bud, Scarlett appeared disinterested in both the question and her answer. 'Mr Swift.'

'Ooh, isn't he that good-looking English teacher?'

The soiled cotton bud was cast across the dressing table. 'Urgh, if you're into ancient relics.' A smile began to form as she drew her dazzling violet eyes away from her reflection and towards her mum. 'He's about to turn thirty and the whole of our form convinced him he's losing his hair. He's probably gone home to ask his wife if he really does have the massive bald spot we all swore we could see.'

'The poor man.'

'Linus said he's going to bring in one of his granddad's caps as a birthday present.'

'Ah yes, Linus. Will he be at Eva's tonight?'

'Probably,' Scarlett said as she began reapplying her eyeliner.

Scarlett had spent most of the summer helping her best friend Eva convert her parent's garage into a crash pad. She had stayed over so often that Nina had felt obliged to send groceries as a contribution to Eva's parents' burgeoning shopping bill. According to Eva's mum, they had a strict no smoking and no drinking policy in place, and thanks to an internal door that meant an adult could barge in at any moment, Nina was reassured that they weren't up to anything else either.

15

'I hope you behave yourselves.'

There was a split second where Scarlett might have been about to ask her mother what she meant, but they had already had that conversation and Scarlett was in no hurry for a repeat. 'We will.'

Having remained on the threshold, Nina looked over her shoulder towards Liam's closed door. 'Boys might seem a mystery to you now, but, believe me, it doesn't get any better.'

The comment had been directed to herself as much as it was to her daughter, and Scarlett chose not to respond.

'You do know you can talk to me about anything, don't you?' Nina continued.

Scarlett huffed, suggesting she didn't quite agree.

'What?'

'I would have thought you're too loved up to be bothered about what's going on in my life any more.'

'Just because Bryn is here, it doesn't mean I haven't got time for you, Scarlett,' Nina said carefully. 'I know you're getting to an age where you can make your own decisions, and I trust you to make the right ones, but sometimes it helps to talk them through with someone, and not only me. Maybe Bryn can give you the male perspective where I can't.'

Scarlett put down her eyeliner. 'OK, Mum, is this conversation about me, or could it possibly be about Bryn?' she asked.

Nina felt her heart being pulled in two opposing directions. She and her children had made a formidable partnership over the years and she didn't want that part of her life to change. 'All I ask is for you and Liam to give him a chance. He's not trying to foist himself on you as your new dad. We both know you'd only resent him if he tried.' Nina left a pause in the hope that Scarlett might tell her she was worrying for nothing, but her silence told her all she needed to know. 'Please, Scarlett.'

Scarlett bit her lip. This was another conversation they'd had many times before, right up to the eve of her wedding, in fact. Both Liam and Scarlett had needed some convincing that Bryn wasn't a con artist preying on a lonely woman who just so happened to have a house and a business. It didn't help that Bryn had made the mistake of mentioning to Sarah that he had been made bankrupt in a previous life, and so Sarah had sided with the children. Nina had told them to trust her judgement, and although that argument hadn't been completely won, she clung to the hope that one day Scarlett and Liam would come to love Bryn as much as she did.

'I'll try,' Scarlett promised.

Leaving a pause that was thick with disappointment, Nina asked, 'What time are you planning on coming home?'

'Eleven.'

'Ten.'

'Ten-thirty?'

'If you're expecting me to pick you up, it has to be ten o'clock, Scarlett. Some of us have to get up at five.'

'I could walk. It's not far.'

'Not at that time of night.'

'I'll get a taxi.'

'Bryn will be out then, I could ask him to pick you up?'

The refusal was already forming on Scarlett's lips, but with her promise to her mum still fresh in both their minds, she managed another shrug. 'I suppose.'

'Great, so that's settled. And like I said earlier, don't think this is a regular occurrence. As of next week, studying begins in earnest. You've worked really hard to get this far, don't fall at the last hurdle, Scarlett.'

'Mum, it's the first day, at least give me a chance to mess up before you go into nag mode,' Scarlett replied before returning to the task of putting on her makeup.

Rather than leave, Nina crept deeper into the room until she was standing behind her daughter. She waited for Scarlett to stop what she was doing and look at her mum through the reflection in the mirror. Nina kissed the top of her head. 'Sorry. I should have more faith in you,' she said.

'No arguments from me,' Scarlett said with a smile and the kind of assured tone that Nina was convinced would see her daughter achieve the A-star grades her teachers were predicting.

Sunday, 6 September 2015

There was a varied selection of restaurants in and around Sedgefield, and if it were up to Nina, she would have been happy enough with the local pub for Sunday lunch, but Sarah had other ideas. The two friends had known each other from childhood, back when Nina had helped out at her dad's shop and Sarah had faced a similar plight in the shop next door. Unfortunately for Sarah, her father had been a butcher; she would often sneak off to help Nina with her flower arranging, if only to avoid the smell of blood and guts.

Despite the similarity in their backgrounds, Sarah's life had taken turns that neither of them could have imagined. Sarah would say she had more of an incentive to turn from the paths their parents had led them towards, but it also helped that she had a driving ambition. She had gradually taken over the management of the butcher's and introduced new product lines until the business was as well known for its delicatessen as it was for fresh meat. When she had married Miles, he had encouraged her to diversify into property management and goodness knew what else. Nina often wondered what she might have made of herself if she had hated flowers as much as Sarah hated raw meat. Would she have gone on to explore new and exciting opportunities instead of being satisfied with business as usual?

As things stood, Nina lived an average life with average expectations, while Sarah had become accustomed to a certain level of service. Pub grub would not do and a table had been booked at the Stone Bridge, a restaurant that overlooked the Bridgewater Canal and was on track for its first Michelin star.

'Are we happy with the table?' Miles asked, pulling out a chair for his wife.

Nina had already taken her seat and felt Bryn's hand on the back of her chair in a clumsy attempt to follow Miles' example. 'It's a lovely view,' she said.

'Hmm,' Miles said, glancing out of the window only briefly. They were on the upper floor of the restaurant, which had a grand view of the dense Cheshire countryside that had yet to be touched by autumn's scorching fingers. Sarah's husband was more interested in checking the distance between their table and those on either side, which were both occupied. Even if he had wanted to move, which he was obviously considering, the restaurant was almost full and their options would be limited. 'I suppose it will do.'

'I hope you're all hungry,' Sarah said, 'and I don't want to hear anyone suggesting we skip starters.' She was directing the comment towards Scarlett and added, 'You can always give dessert a miss if you want to watch your figure.'

Scarlett blushed fiercely but said nothing.

'She doesn't need to watch her figure. She's perfect as she is,' Bryn said.

His tone had been light but there was no mistaking the defensiveness in his remark and it made Nina smile. He was protecting her family, but judging from Sarah's expression she wasn't reading it that way.

'You think so?' she said, raising an eyebrow.

Nina held her friend's gaze long enough to let her know she should keep her thoughts to herself. The only reason she had gone along with Sarah's suggestion that they all have lunch was because she saw it as a way to cement her new husband's place amongst her friends and family. It was not another opportunity for Sarah to sit in judgement of Bryn, and she had told her as much.

'Of course it's perfect,' Sarah continued, with a small nod of apology to Nina. 'You're turning into quite a stunner, Scarlett. Your mum's going to have to keep her eye on you.'

Scarlett slunk lower in her chair, threatening to disappear and never return.

'How's business, Miles?' Nina asked, to divert attention. After all these years she still wasn't sure what exactly Miles did, other than he was something big in engineering and the demand for his skills took him all over the world.

'Busy as always,' he said, 'and it doesn't help that my darling wife has a habit of jumping from one new project to another while expecting me to sort out the paperwork for what is meant to be *her* company.'

'But you're far better at it than I am,' Sarah said with a playful smile. 'And there's so much to do.'

'Which means I should be back at home sorting things out, but you insisted, and what Sarah wants, Sarah gets.'

'Well, we're glad you could make it,' Nina answered, 'aren't we, Bryn?'

'Most definitely. I know how work can take over your life.'

Miles gave a disinterested nod and it was Sarah who asked, 'Have you never thought of starting up a business again?'

Bryn seemed to consider the possibility for a moment, only to shake his head. 'Printing was all I knew, but the industry changed so fast. I wouldn't know where to begin these days, and I wouldn't want to try. Taxi-driving suits me fine: not as much stress and more time to spend with Nina and the kids.'

'Have you been working this weekend?' Sarah asked.

'Yeah, and I'll probably go out for a few hours tonight, although it's hardly worth the effort on Sundays.'

Scarlett stopped gazing out of the window and turned an arched eyebrow towards Bryn. 'Could you pick me up later?'

'Pick you up from where?' Nina demanded.

'Eva's,' Scarlett said, as if it were obvious.

'You were there last night and it's school tomorrow.'

'Oh, let the girl live a little,' Miles said. 'Is there a boy on the scene by any chance?'

Nina was about to come to her daughter's rescue again,

but this was a question she had asked often enough and it was refreshing to hear it from someone else.

'No.'

'How about you, Liam?' Sarah asked.

All eyes turned to Nina's eldest, who had kept his head down and his eyes fixed on his smartphone throughout the entire conversation. Nina had warned Sarah not to make any remarks if he insisted on using it during their meal; it had been part of the deal to get Liam there in the first place.

'Yes, Liam, are you seeing any boys?' Miles said. He was the only one to laugh at his joke.

Nina was about to say that it didn't matter which of the sexes her son preferred provided he was happy; but saying such a thing would only expose the fact that this was a possibility she had considered. She really didn't care if he was interested in girls or boys, just as long as he was interested in someone with a pulse. She had shared her concerns with Sarah and suspected her friend had continued to speculate on Liam's sexuality with Miles.

Liam lifted his gaze and fixed it on Miles. Her son didn't speak often but when he did, he used his words to full effect. 'Sorry, Miles, you're not my type.'

From the corner of her eye, Nina knew Bryn was trying not to laugh, which made it doubly hard to suppress her own smile. She would have liked nothing better than to high-five her son.

After placing their orders, it was Sarah who kept the conversation flowing. And while she was busy telling Bryn how her company supplied the hummus he had ordered for starters, Nina let her mind wander. She looked at her children in turn and wondered how the next critical years in their lives would play out. She was hoping that her marriage would add some stability to their lives; although they weren't quite there yet, Scarlett appeared more comfortable in Bryn's company of late, possibly because she had worked out that she had a chauffeur at her beck and call. Except she didn't look comfortable now, Nina realized when she saw a deep blush rising in her daughter's cheeks.

'What's wrong, Scarlett?' Nina asked quietly.

'Nothing.'

Scarlett pressed her chin to her chest. Her sleek blonde hair fell over her shoulders and partially obscured her face while she played with her hands.

Liam was first to locate the source of her embarrassment. 'It's Mr Swift,' he said, tipping his head to the far side of the restaurant.

Scarlett's form tutor was even more handsome than Nina remembered and, in contradiction to his students' teasing, his thick dark hair showed no signs of thinning. On the few occasions she had spoken to him at parents' evening, she had been almost tongue-tied, but it was Mr Swift who looked lost for words at present. He was with a small group consisting of two women and a young child, and was as yet unaware of the attention he had drawn from their table, being fully preoccupied with the two helium balloons that had been tied to the back of his chair. A large silver number three and a matching zero.

'I remember him, he was one of Charlotte's teachers,' Sarah said. 'Why didn't we have teachers like that in our day, Nina?'

'Maybe we should go and say hello,' she suggested.

Scarlett snapped her head towards her mum. 'Don't you dare!'

'She's only teasing,' Bryn said. 'Even your mum wouldn't embarrass you that much.'

'I think the embarrassment is all his,' Miles said. 'I spent my thirtieth in New York having a whale of a time.'

'Would that be the business trip you were forced to take while I was at home caring for our baby girl?'

'Ah, yes,' Miles said and cleared his throat. 'When I said a whale of a time, what I meant was because I was working so hard, dearest.'

Nina bit her tongue. Unlike her oldest friend, who would jump at the opportunity to scrutinize the cracks in someone else's relationship, Nina preferred to focus on the positives. Sarah's marriage might have its faults, but it had been strong enough to endure an affair, and if Miles had strayed since, he was a brave man indeed. By contrast, Nina's first marriage had disintegrated at the first hint of a problem, and Nina would be eternally grateful to Sarah, who had stopped her falling apart by convincing her she could go it alone.

'Thirty is *so* old,' Scarlett was saying.

Sarah choked on the sip of wine she had been taking. 'God knows what she makes of you then, Miles.'

'Fifty is the new forty.'

'And twenty years more than thirty,' remarked Scarlett.

When the starters arrived, the English teacher and his family were all but forgotten as the grown-ups focused their attention back on their own table.

'So what are you up to, Liam?' Sarah asked.

'Not much.'

'Have you picked a university yet? I'm sure it was around

this time that Charlotte dragged us all around the country for countless open days. Typical of Charlotte, she opted for the first one we'd seen.'

'She's at Liverpool, isn't she?' Bryn asked.

'Yes. I can't believe it's her final year so soon, and now the little madam has her mind set on a career in advertising. If I'd known she wouldn't be coming home to work for me, I might have thought twice about paying for all that extra tuition that got her into uni in the first place.'

'It's a different generation,' Nina offered.

'Maybe, maybe not,' Sarah told them. 'By hook or by crook, I'll rope Charlotte in eventually. I know I take advantage of Miles, but we can't go on as we are. It's only going to get busier in the next year.'

'I can't imagine convincing any of mine to become florists,' Nina said, confirmed by the expressions on her children's faces. 'And I wouldn't want them to. I'd like them to go off and explore the world. Liam came up with a long-list of possible unis over the summer, but I suppose we do need to whittle it down. Isn't January the deadline for getting applications into UCAS?'

'It doesn't matter any more,' Liam said. 'I've changed my mind.'

'Pardon? What do you mean, you've changed your mind?'

'Not everyone has to go to uni.'

'I know,' Nina said slowly to keep her temper in check, 'but up until now, it was what you wanted. And if you don't go, can you please tell me what you do have planned?'

'My company has a very good apprenticeship programme,' Miles offered. 'Or failing that, there could be opportunities with Sarah's new housing development. It's still going through planning, but once we get the green light, I'm sure we could persuade one of the contractors to take you on. What kind of career were you thinking about?'

Nina was struggling to keep up with the pace of the conversation. 'Hold on, can we rewind for a minute. We haven't ruled out university yet.'

Rather than answer, Liam returned his attention to his phone. The argument was closed, for now at least, and perhaps that was for the best. She didn't want Miles mapping out her son's life for him, she had managed well enough on her own so far.

'I'll be out this evening and, by the sounds of it, so will Scarlett,' Bryn said. 'Maybe you two could have a chat about it later?'

'Good idea,' Nina said, admonishing herself for forgetting she was in a partnership now. The conversation she needed to have with Liam might be better alone, but it felt good knowing she had backup.

While everyone had been concentrating on Liam, Scarlett became disengaged from the conversation. She had finished her starter and was looking absent-mindedly around the restaurant. Taking her lip gloss from her purse, her mouth open in a pout, she stroked the wand across her lips in soft, sensual strokes.

'A word of advice, my lovely,' Sarah said, her note of caution laced with a hint of envy. 'Don't do that in public unless you want to attract the attention of every hot-blooded male in the room.'

Bryn and Miles remembered themselves and looked away from the fifteen-year-old schoolgirl.

Scarlett

I used to think I could tell Mum anything, but not now, at least, not everything. Actually, not even close.

I know all this is driving her crazy, but it's not like I meant to cause so much trouble. It just happened, and it happened so bloody fast. It was like, one minute I hadn't spoken two words to him, and the next, he was the only one I could talk to. I'm not saying I didn't know it was wrong, but I honestly couldn't help myself and neither could he. You have no idea what it was like. We fell truly, madly and deeply in love and it was like we became addicted to each other.

And do you know what really annoys me? People won't take my feelings seriously. Like, they assume because I'm technically underage, I couldn't possibly know what real love is like. I'm sorry, but what does a date on a calendar have to do with anything? I was in love. I still am.

I know I shouldn't say this, but it was actually funny looking back at how I acted. I didn't have a clue he was interested in me, not in that way. I'm sort of used to people staring at me and I don't want to sound vain or anything, but I know I'm pretty. It doesn't matter how big a group I'm in, people always look at me first. I used to think it was because I was the tallest, but now I get it. It was always the men who looked at me the longest.

I've been told that I could hypnotize men with my dazzling violet eyes, but the person who said that was interested in a lot more than my eyes.

'That mouth of yours is going to get you into trouble one of these days,' he told me.

I bit my lip and said, 'I don't know what you mean.'

To be honest, at the time I wasn't sure if he was talking about all the backchat I'd been giving him, but when he glanced at my mouth, I swear to God, it was so obvious he was wondering if my strawberry lip gloss tasted as good as it smelled. But the next minute he was laughing.

'OK,' he said, 'if not you, then most definitely me.'

3

The Accusations

Vikki Swift didn't know why she had been lying awake all night worrying about Scarlett. It must be so awful for Nina, but teenage pregnancies were a sad fact of life and Vikki had been little more than a teen herself when she had had Freya. Of course the difference was that Vikki had been married by that point, but who was to say Scarlett wasn't in a loving relationship? Except that seemed extremely unlikely, if what Scarlett had said was true. How was this man she was involved with going to explain himself to the world in general, and more especially to his wife?

Refusing to dwell on the subject, Vikki turned on her side and slipped an arm around her husband. She reminded herself how lucky she was to have Rob. He was her one and only love, and even though she was still only twenty-four, she couldn't imagine life without him. She held him tightly as she thought about everything they had been through, and how much growing up she had had to do. She might be a teacher's wife and a mother, but up until six months ago they were simply labels she had collected, certificates she had acquired without actually passing the exams. She had always depended on other people to make sure she didn't mess up, and although she was trying her best to think more for herself these days, it was still so hard. There were some things that she could never have been prepared for. It was scary how life could change so quickly.

'What's wrong?' Rob whispered.

Vikki was surprised that he had been awake enough to notice her clinging to him. Or was there something keeping Rob from sleep too?

'Nothing,' she said.

'Are you sure?'

'Hmm,' Vikki said, which was as near to a lie as she was prepared to go.

The truth was, she wasn't sure of anything all of a sudden.

4

Before

Sunday, 6 September 2015

As thirtieth birthday parties went, having lunch with your wife, mother-in-law and daughter was not how Vikki thought the occasion should be celebrated, but Rob had insisted that he didn't want a fuss. Reluctantly, she had gone along with his wishes, although she had been a tiny bit naughty. There were two helium balloons tied to the back of his chair which he obviously hated.

'Sorry, is that annoying you?' she asked when a balloon hit Rob in the face as he turned to fill her mum's glass.

'It's fine,' Rob said. There was a smile on his face and a glint in his eye when he added, 'Who wouldn't want to be assaulted by an inflatable number three. It could be worse; I might get my head stuck in the zero.'

When Rob leant over and gave her a peck on the cheek, she relaxed; she had done the right thing. Smiling, Vikki pushed back a rogue curl that had escaped the hair grip pinning back her dark golden curls, leaving only a select few tresses to fall over her round face in an attempt to lengthen her features. She often wished it were as easy to lengthen her petite figure, which was also a bit more curved than she would like since the birth of her daughter.

'Maybe we could re-tie them so they're floating higher above your chair,' Vikki's mum suggested helpfully.

Rob was still smiling when he said, 'Great idea, Elaine. There are probably people at the far end of the restaurant who haven't realized I've turned into an old git yet.'

'If you're an old git, what does that make me?'

'Have you never heard of the term Cougar?' Rob asked.

Elaine had stood up to rearrange the balloons and swiped him across the head. 'Yes, I have, and I think I'd prefer to be called an old git.'

Vikki's mum was technically middle-aged, but only just, and she was both flattered and annoyed whenever people refused to accept that she was a grandmother. Her husband, who had passed away four years earlier, had been much older and Elaine's youthfulness had been a sensitive issue for her. Despite the teasing, she didn't mind getting old, certainly not as much as Rob did. She loved being a grandmother, and that was something Vikki was counting on as she let the waitress take their orders before dropping the first suggestion about her plans.

'I've seen a couple of jobs I think I'm going to apply for, Mum. It's only general admin work, but it'll give me a chance to get my brain back into gear.'

'Oh.'

'I keep telling Vikki she's selling herself short,' Rob said when Elaine offered no further response. 'Anyone can see she does a brilliant job of looking after Freya, and me too. I'm sure she thinks that because she isn't earning a wage she doesn't contribute to the household. Your daughter's too proud for her own good.'

'But with Freya starting pre-school, I thought that's what everyone expected me to do,' Vikki said.

Before answering his wife, Rob shared the briefest look with Elaine. 'I support you one hundred per cent, Vikki,' he said, 'but I don't want you to feel pressurized into going out to work. I know we had this vague plan about you restarting a career, but plans can change. You shouldn't feel obliged.'

Vikki wasn't sure she did feel obliged. She liked the idea of finding a job that would take her interests beyond home, although, if she were being honest, she didn't exactly have a career path in mind. She wasn't even sure how employable she would be these days, which was why she needed someone to give her that final push. Rob was being too nice about it, and that was why she had raised the subject in front of her mum.

Her parents had had their hearts set on Vikki going to university after her A levels, and had only agreed to her taking a gap year because she had found herself a job she loved with a local estate agent. The gap year turned into two, and marriage and motherhood followed in quick succession, putting an end to her plans for university and her job, but Elaine still had ambitions for her daughter – it was what her late husband would have wanted and her support was assured.

'I'd only need to find a childminder for the afternoons, if I needed to . . . '

Vikki let her words trail off deliberately. This was where her mum was meant to speak up. It wasn't as if Elaine hadn't already hinted that she would be willing to take care of Freya if ever Vikki were ready for a career. Except, now that Vikki was ready to accept such an offer, her mum remained silent on the subject.

'Honestly, Vikki, now isn't the time,' Rob said, rather harshly, which made Vikki feel all the more confused. She didn't know what she had done wrong.

Elaine searched under the table for her bag and grimaced as she picked it up. 'Here you go, Freya, look what I brought for you.'

All eyes turned to the little girl who had inherited Vikki's curls. Freya's eyes lit up when she spied the colouring book. 'Me draw smiley faces now.' The three-year-old reached out and wrapped her hand around an orange crayon but when Elaine moved closer to help, Freya shook her head. 'No, Daddy do it.'

Rob was more than willing, if only to dodge the awkwardness of the conversation mother and daughter were avoiding.

'Where is that waitress?' Elaine asked, and a moment later cursed under her breath. 'Oh good lord, is that Sarah Tavistock? That's all I need.'

Vikki twisted in her seat to get a better look. Fortunately, the group of diners who had caught their attention were too involved in their own conversations to realize they were being watched. Vikki had briefly attended the same gym club as Sarah's daughter, Charlotte; although the age difference meant they had never been friends, Charlotte's parents were hard to forget.

'I had a letter from the planning department the other day,' Elaine said. 'Her company's bought the land directly opposite the house and she wants to build on it.'

The house in question was the home Vikki's parents had bought on the outskirts of Sedgefield when her dad had taken early retirement. Combining his skills as an architect and her mum's love of home-making, they had converted an old outbuilding into two holiday cottages; the intention was that this would provide enough income to allow them to take life at a slower pace. Unfortunately their plan for a perfect semi-retirement had lasted less than twelve months. Without warning, her father had collapsed and died from a massive heart attack, leaving his family bereft. It was an unspoken truth that Vikki and Rob's decision to have a baby had been a reaction to the family's loss. Freya's arrival was by no means an attempt to fill the void in their lives, but she had given them all a new focus, her mum included.

'Build what?' asked Vikki.

'Houses.'

Vikki watched as Elaine rearranged the cutlery in front of her, having decided there was no further discussion necessary.

'And you're not bothered about it?'

'There's not a lot I can do, Vikki.'

'Have you seen the details? Do you know what the plan is?' Vikki asked. Her alarm was magnified by the lack of response from her mum.

'It's a small development of luxury family homes.'

'How small?'

'Sixteen houses.'

'Someone wants to build a housing estate opposite your countryside cottages, and you're not bothered? Dad would have had a fit! He would be camping out on the site in protest until they changed their minds. Dad would—'

'Your dad isn't here!'

Elaine's raised voice drew Freya's attention away from the picture of a clown she and her daddy had been colouring in. She frowned until her grandmother gave her a reassuring smile, but when Freya returned to her drawing, Rob's attention remained with Vikki and Elaine.

'Fine,' Vikki said, folding her arms across her chest and doing her best not to pout like a petulant child. 'You might not want to do anything about it, but I will. I'll start a campaign.'

'Don't, Vikki,' Elaine said quietly. 'Now isn't the time, trust me.'

'How can it not be the time?' Vikki asked. 'If there's a planning application then there'll be some sort of time limit for you to object.'

'Please, Vikki,' Rob said as he leant over to touch her hand. 'Even if you did know how the planning process worked, do you really think it would do any good? People like the Tavistocks always get their way.'

'We'll see about that. Maybe I should go over there now and have a word with them,' Vikki said. Wanting to be taken seriously, she moved as if to get up, but they all knew she would never have the nerve to confront the Tavistocks. Rather than look at Rob or her mum as she settled back in her seat, Vikki cast a withering look in the Tavistocks' direction, only to lock eyes with the young girl seated at the table. Even from a distance, Vikki could see the look of alarm on her face when she realized she was being watched, and they both dropped their heads.

'Oh great, today's just getting better and better,' Rob muttered before adding, 'See that young lady over there pretending not to be looking at us? She's in my form and there'll be hell to pay in class tomorrow. I wouldn't put it past her to take a photo of the balloons and plaster it all over Facebook. If she hasn't already.'

For the remainder of the meal, they all did their best to ignore the other diners. They kept to safe topics of conversation to smooth over Vikki's spat with her mum, but an awkwardness persisted. After the main course had been cleared away, Rob made an excuse to leave the table, but before he left, he placed a hand on Elaine's shoulder. They shared one last look which filled Vikki with a horrible sense of foreboding.

'What's going on, Mum?'

Elaine was playing with her napkin and wouldn't meet her daughter's anxious gaze. 'I want you to know that I would love nothing more than for you to have a successful career one day, Vikki. You're a very capable young woman, and stronger than you give yourself credit for.'

'But?'

'Look what I did, Nanna,' Freya said, waving her latest work of art in the air.

When Elaine looked back up, Vikki was shocked to see tears welling in her eyes. 'Mum? Please tell me what's wrong.'

'What's wrong, Nanna?' Freya repeated. She had picked up on the anxiety in Vikki's voice and copied the frown that had appeared on her mother's brow.

Elaine stroked the side of Freya's cheek, making the little girl giggle, but the smile on her own face was heavy with sadness. 'I found a lump,' she whispered. 'Under my armpit.'

A cold chill ran through Vikki's veins, but her expression remained fixed. She wouldn't let her fear show. 'Have you seen a doctor?'

'Yes.'

'And?'

Rubbing her shoulder, Elaine said, 'When I went to visit friends last week, I wasn't exactly being honest. I was in hospital having a biopsy.'

'Oh, my God,' Vikki said softly and resisted the urge to put her hands over her ears. 'It's cancer, isn't it?'

'It's been caught at an early stage,' Elaine told her, 'and it's nothing I can't handle, I promise, Vikki.'

'But . . . ' Vikki said, looking around the restaurant and wondering why no one else was reacting to this earth-shattering news. She searched for Rob, wanting him back at her side so he would tell her how they were going to deal with this, and that was when a thought struck her. 'Does Rob know?'

'Yes, he does. I had to put someone down as my next of kin and we both wanted to spare you the worry until we knew the results.'

'You should have told me.'

'I wanted to protect you – isn't that what every mother does? It was Rob who insisted I tell you today, but I so hate spoiling his birthday.'

Vikki fought off the urge to rush into her mum's arms and release the sobs burning her throat. 'What happens now?'

'I'm waiting on a date for the mastectomy, which shouldn't be too long. The consultant is keen to operate as soon as possible.' Leaning over to her daughter, Elaine stroked her cheek as she had done with Freya, but couldn't raise a smile so easily. 'It's going to be OK, sweetheart. I'm going to be fine and so are you.'

Vikki nodded obediently as everything began to make sense; her mum's reaction to the new housing development; the reluctance to look after Freya; not to mention Rob's lacklustre response to her ideas about going back to work lately. In the space of one meal, her whole life had been turned upside down, and they hadn't even had dessert yet. Any minute now, a waiter would arrive with the birthday cake Vikki had ordered as a surprise, complete with the requisite number of candles. Rob would hate the fuss, especially with one of his students looking on. She had made a stupid mess of it all, as usual, and now she couldn't stop the tears slipping down her cheeks. Her mum was wrong about her being strong. She wasn't even good at pretending.

Tuesday, 15 Sept 2015

Vikki was kneeling against the back of the sofa as she looked out of the window with her chin resting on her hands. She was peeking through a gap in the vertical blinds so she had a good view of the empty space on the driveway next to her Corsa. From the corner of her eye, she could see Freya mimicking her, although her little girl had to stand rather than kneel to see out of the window.

'Where's Daddy?' Freya said with a whimper. They had been waiting for at least ten minutes and the toddler had lost patience after the first two.

'He'll be home soon,' Vikki said, and not for the first time. She was getting impatient too.

'No, tell Daddy to come home now,' Freya insisted as her cupid's bow lips began to tremble.

Turning her head towards her daughter, Vikki felt some of the tension that had been building over the last week or so slip away. Becoming a mother at twenty-one had been overwhelming and still was, but she would love and protect Freya until her dying day, just like her own mother had always done with her, and please God, would continue to do.

When Vikki's lip began to quiver too, Freya asked, 'Mummy want a cuddle?'

'Yes, please.'

Vikki held back the tears and began blowing raspberries against Freya's neck.

'We do tumbles now, Mummy?' Freya asked when their giggling subsided.

Vikki narrowed her eyes. 'Let's see if you can do this,' she said and shuffled backwards to give herself enough space. In one flowing move, she was standing on her head, her back brushing against the sofa cushions and her legs pointing to the ceiling. Using one hand to keep her balance, Vikki helped Freya into a vaguely similar position.

Despite being out of practice and out of shape, Vikki held her position with relative ease while the little girl toppled over and tried again. There had been a time when Vikki thought she might have made a half-decent gymnast, but her dad had convinced her that her greatest potential lay in academia. She had achieved success in neither, and as Vikki considered what a disappointment she would be to her dad now, she failed to notice Rob's old Ford Focus pulling up outside, or hear the clatter of keys being dropped on the radiator shelf by the door.

'Don't you think you're a bit too old for that?'

'Daddy!'

Freya tumbled off the sofa, tipping Vikki over in the process as she ran into Rob's open arms. Vikki got to her feet and waited patiently with her arms behind her back until Rob had balanced Freya on his hip and beckoned her towards him.

'I've missed you,' she said, stepping over so he could wrap his free arm around her. 'And I'll have you know there are top gymnasts who are my age and still winning gold medals.'

'For balancing upside down on the sofa? I dread to think what Freya will be telling her nursery teachers about your antics,' he said, before giving her a curious look. 'And what's with all the makeup?'

'I've got to keep up with the other mums on the school run.'

'Don't be silly, you don't need to compete. You're leagues above them all.'

Vikki wasn't convinced. She might be younger than a lot of the other mums, but for the last three years she had felt frumpy. She didn't know any of the others particularly well, and she desperately wanted to fit in. 'I wanted to make myself feel good, that's all,' she said.

He kissed the top of her head, 'Especially today of all days,' he said. 'How are you doing?'

She could only shrug. 'How was your day?'

'Still getting to know my new form,' he said, scrunching his nose. 'It's not easy when most of them are counting

41

down to leaving in the summer. I would have much preferred Year 7s.'

'It only proves what faith Mrs Anwar has in you,' she said. She would never get used to calling the head by her first name; Nadia Anwar had been deputy head when Vikki had attended Sedgefield High, and she still felt like a student whenever she was in her company.

'I suppose,' Rob said. 'She's certainly set me a challenge, although I think I've got a couple of allies in class who will keep the rest in check.'

'I bet you have them wrapped around your little finger.'

When he kissed her again, his daughter demanded attention. 'Frey-ya too,' she said and planted a sloppy kiss on her daddy's lips.

'Hmmm, blackcurrant-flavoured.'

'My juice!' Freya cried and began wriggling until Rob put her down. She raced back to where she had abandoned her sippy cup on the windowsill.

Rob took the opportunity to pull Vikki closer. 'If you won't tell me how you're doing, maybe you could tell me how your mum got on.'

'The operation went well,' Vikki said, surprised that her voice could sound so matter of fact. Everything had happened in a blur and Vikki almost wished Rob and her mum had kept their secret that bit longer. She would happily trade blissful ignorance for sleepless nights and restless days, and today had been the worst so far. 'I'll find out more later, but the nurse I spoke to said something about the surgeon taking more surrounding tissue than they were planning.'

'That might be a good thing, less chance of leaving anything nasty behind.'

'But longer for Mum to recover from the operation,' Vikki said. 'She's going to struggle on her own for a while.'

'Is there any chance Lesley could help out more?'

Lesley was a friend of her mum's who helped out with the holiday cottages during the busy season. She would do all she could, but it wouldn't be enough. Besides, it wasn't the suggestion Vikki had wanted Rob to make.

'I doubt it, she has so many other jobs to juggle.' Vikki clung tighter to Rob, as if it would squeeze the correct response from him.

When she bit her lip, he must have guessed what she was after. 'If you're asking if you should stay with her when she gets out, then say it, Vikki.'

'No, I don't want to leave you. Unless you could come with us . . . '

'The three of us in one bedroom and your mum in the room next door? What do you think?'

'If I did go, it wouldn't be for long, maybe just a week,' she said.

Rob didn't look completely convinced. 'But are you sure you could cope with looking after your mum, and Freya too?'

'I . . . don't know. But I'd hate to look back and regret not helping her more.'

The only time Vikki and Rob had spent apart since they were married had been following her dad's death. She had gone to stay with her mum for a couple of weeks under the guise of offering support, but it had been Vikki who had needed her mum as much as anything, and Rob had probably been relieved that someone else had to cope with her bawling her eyes out every two minutes. Vikki wasn't so sure she would cope any better now, and from the look on Rob's face, he was thinking the same.

Rob's body sagged a little when he sighed. 'Yes, of course you should stay with her.'

His answer should have made Vikki feel relieved, but she burst into tears. 'I'm sorry,' she said, burying her face in Rob's shoulder. 'I'm a rubbish wife and a rubbish daughter.'

'Of course you're not. You're doing amazingly well,' he whispered. When her sobs subsided, he lifted her chin so she was looking directly at him. 'I won't say I'm not going to miss you, but stay as long as you need. Don't worry about me.'

'Are you sure?' she asked, and with one small hiccup, swallowed the last of her tears.

'Yes, Vikki, whatever you want. You're the boss as always. I'm yours to command.'

She gave him a tentative smile. 'In that case, do you think you could do something else for me?'

'Hmm,' he said, raising his eyebrows. 'What are you after now, Victoria?'

'I've had a go at writing something and I need you to check it for me.'

Rob laughed. 'That wasn't exactly the suggestion I was expecting,' he said. 'What is it?'

'An objection to Sarah Tavistock's planning application,' she said, and then, seeing Rob's expression, added, 'Will you look at it? Please, Rob.'

'But why bother? Elaine doesn't think it's worth it, especially now you know all the details.'

Vikki's original assumption had been that the land in question was in the green belt and should be protected. She had been dismayed to discover that it was classed as a brownfield site and had been in industrial use up until fifty years ago. It had been an old pottery and when the buildings had been demolished, the land had been soiled over rather than cleared, which explained why it had been left fallow for so long. The new plans included the removal of all the industrial waste, which would actually improve the land.

'I still want to try. It's what Dad would expect one of us to do, and obviously Mum's not up to it. So will you?' Vikki asked again.

'OK, OK, if it keeps you out of trouble.'

When Vikki hugged Rob tightly his hands moved gently over her hips and bottom.

'So there was something else you were after,' he said in a hushed tone.

Sex couldn't be further from Vikki's mind, but she responded by pushing herself against him. 'I love you,' she told him.

'And I love you,' he replied, before pulling away with a groan. Freya had been watching them quietly. 'But I'm afraid some of your particular gratifications are going to have to wait until bedtime, or this one's bedtime at least.'

Despite the shadows hanging over her, Vikki felt a small sense of victory as she watched Rob scoop Freya up into his arms.

Scarlett

I remember the first time I realized exactly what effect I had on him. No way was I expecting him to, you know, get excited and I swear I didn't know what to do. When I think back, it was so embarrassing. I was such a child.

Mum had dragged us out for Sunday lunch with her friends Sarah and Miles. I didn't want to go, but sometimes it's just not worth the argument. I was the youngest there, so obviously they all treated me like a kid. Miles actually asked me what I wanted to do when I grew up.

When – I – grew – up?

I'd already grown up, for God's sake, and I'm pretty sure he'd noticed. Sarah definitely had. She made some comment about everyone looking while I was putting on my lip gloss in the restaurant, as if I hadn't worked that out for myself.

Anyway, after our main course, I sneaked off to the Ladies so I could put on more lip gloss without Sarah's bitchy comments, and after that I went outside to escape for a while. The restaurant backed on to the canal and had an outdoor dining area, but it was teeming down so luckily it was deserted.

I stayed close to a wall that had an overhanging roof to give me some shelter, and the sound of the rain hammering against the tiles was so loud I didn't hear him come outside, not until he'd sneaked up next to me.

'Looking for an escape route?'

I was looking out over the canal, watching it trembling in the rain. I was trembling almost as much, if I'm being honest, and I wouldn't look at him when I said, 'You too?'

'Yeah, this kind of thing is my idea of hell. I could do with a stiff drink.'

'So could I,' I said. OK, maybe I was only trying to sound older, but I really could have done with a drink.

'It's school tomorrow.'

'Don't remind me.'

'Your schooldays will be over before you know it, Scarlett. And in spite of all the stress with exams, I bet it'll be one of the best years of your life. It was for me.'

'You can remember that far back?'

He laughed. 'You're growing up fast, aren't you?'

It was a comment I'd heard loads of times, usually from older men who were staring at my boobs, but he just looked out across the water. I can remember wanting him to look at me. I took a deep breath so my chest would stick out more, and made a pout. 'Who says I'm not already?'

'Fed up being treated like a child?'

'Or ignored completely. Everyone's too busy worrying about Liam.'

'Oh, you're not ignored, Scarlett.'

'You think? For the last hour it's been all about Liam and how he should get out more. I'm sure Mum thinks he's going to hack into some government network from his

bedroom and bring the country down. Either that or she's worried he'll never leave home and she'll be stuck with him for ever.'

'He'll be fine.'

'I know he'll be fine,' I said through gritted teeth. 'The point is I don't care.'

'So what do you care about? What would make you happy, Scarlett?'

I liked the way he talked to me, like he was really interested in what I had to say, like I had an opinion that mattered. I could have told him that what I wanted most was to be noticed instead of gawped at all the time, but I'm pretty sure he knew that.

I didn't actually get the chance to say anything because just then a gust of wind caught the rain and blew it towards us. I turned to the side but he stepped in front of me, like he was protecting me. When I turned back to face him, I was too scared to look up.

'Are you getting wet?' he asked, whispering the last word.

He'd put his hand on the wall next to me, blocking me in and I had no idea what to do next. I'd had boys making crude comments before, but this was way different. For one thing, I most definitely wanted the attention this time. OK, I knew it was bad and Mum would be horrified if she knew, but I'd been dreaming of being this close to him. And in my fantasies we'd gone way further. But I wasn't expecting it to happen for real and that's why I panicked. 'I'd better go,' I told him.

'That's a shame,' he said. 'I thought we were kindred spirits for a moment, Scarlett. My mistake.'

He lowered his arm and trailed a finger down my arm,

which sent this weird electric current through my body. It felt so strong that it seriously made me flinch.

'Sorry,' he said quickly. 'You should go.'

I didn't move, and I suppose I was curious more than anything. It was like I had this power over him. He was tempted to do something he shouldn't, something that was very, very bad, and it was all because of me.

I looked up and whispered, 'Or I could stay.'

I was actually daring him to move closer and I couldn't believe it when he did. He pushed against me and it wasn't the first time I'd felt someone with a hard on, but that had only been Linus and I don't think he had a clue what to do with it. This was a man and he definitely knew what to do. He took hold of my hand and later he told me exactly what he had been tempted to do, but at the time he was being the perfect gentleman. He kissed my palm. 'Run away, little girl,' he said.

And I did run away, but I can't tell you how much I regretted it. I played that scene over and over again in my mind afterwards and I swore that next time, I wasn't going to let him off so easily.

5

The Accusations

Nina's head was throbbing but she didn't have the energy to move from the breakfast bar to search out painkillers. Rubbing her temples, she suspected the intense pressure around her forehead had been caused by all those months of sticking her head in the sand. How had she not seen this coming?

There had been plenty of signs that Scarlett was heading for trouble, if only Nina hadn't been so preoccupied with proving to the world, and Sarah especially, that everything was fine. If she had been worried about anything, it had been Liam and his complete withdrawal from society. She couldn't have named one of his friends, whereas she had met most of Scarlett's, or the girls at least. Her daughter had been more circumspect about introducing her male friends, but as it turned out, Scarlett hadn't been as interested in boys as Nina had presumed. At what point had she fallen for this man who had got her pregnant, the man who had *abused* her? Had Nina met him? Did she know him? According to Scarlett, he was going to support her, just as soon as he had told his wife.

Groaning, Nina dropped her head on the counter. *His wife*. She knew what Sarah thought, but what she was suggesting was unthinkable. She was wrong; except, no matter how many times Nina repeated this mantra, a seed of doubt had taken root in her mind and it was growing at an alarming rate.

She reminded herself that she was still in a state of shock. It was going to take a day or two for the news to sink in, and whatever happened next, it would ultimately be Scarlett's decision. Her daughter would need to know what support her family, and Nina in particular, were willing to offer. Bryn had given no view on what Scarlett should do, but he didn't disagree when Nina had said any ideas Scarlett might have about keeping the baby were utterly ridiculous. But this was an alien world she found herself in and stranger things had happened.

She had wasted too much time the day before, paralysed by fear while Scarlett and Liam hid away in their rooms. Bryn had been at a loss how to help, but had eventually got the message that his wife needed space too, and she had been relieved when he had gone out to work on Sunday evening. But the moment he had returned that morning and slipped into her bed, Nina had got up. She didn't want to talk to him, she didn't know what to say and, more tellingly, she hadn't wanted him to touch her.

Was she really as blind as Sarah seemed to think? Had she been taken for a fool and willingly put her family at risk? Was everything her heart had been telling her a lie?

With her head spinning, Nina tried to straighten up and as she did, the overhead spotlights blazed into life. She wasn't sure who was more shocked, her or Bryn.

'I thought you'd left for work,' he said when he had caught his breath.

Nina rubbed her eyes as she adjusted to the light and then looked at her husband. She searched in vain for familiar features, but her vision was skewed and her eyes refused to focus.

'I'm taking the day off,' she said.

6

Before

After parking her car behind Bryn's taxi, Nina rubbed the back of her neck. It had been an especially long day at the shop which had been transformed into a witch's coven for Halloween. After spending hours perched on top of step ladders draping gossamer thin spider's webs across shelves stacked with autumnal wreaths and papier-mâché pumpkins, she was looking forward to a long soak in the bath, but before she could get out of the car, her phone started to ring.

'Sorry I haven't called. I know it's been ages,' Sarah began, 'but I've been ridiculously busy.'

'It's all right,' Nina said with a twinge of guilt. She hadn't exactly gone out of her way to contact her friend either.

'Anyway, I've got a spare five minutes and thought I'd check on things in the Carrington household.'

'Thomas household,' Nina corrected.

There was a pause. 'Are you OK, Nina?'

Sarah's remark hit a nerve. After barely two words, her friend was ready to assume Nina's life was in freefall, which was why she had been less than eager to phone her. From the moment she had started dating Bryn, a lowly taxi driver and a bankrupt to boot, Sarah had been convinced Nina was going through a full-blown midlife crisis.

The question alone made Nina check her reply, but she felt confident when she said, 'I'm fine. A bit tired, that's all. It's been a busy day at the shop.'

'You should see my desk. I'm snowed under with paperwork and Miles has gone on strike. He has some major project at work that's slipping, so he's never here. I've got planning objections to deal with and, to top it all, the delicatessen has just secured contracts to supply another two restaurants.'

'And that's bad news?'

'Oh, you have no idea how draining success can be.'

'Couldn't you simply hire someone to help?' Nina said.

'You mean the job I had in mind for my darling daughter until she decided to betray me and turn her back on her heritage?' Sarah asked. 'I told her the other day that all this pressure will put me or her dad in an early grave, but she wouldn't listen, said I was trying to manipulate her.'

'I'd be happy to swap you one career-minded student for a teenage cave-dweller.'

'Ah, so that's what's bothering you,' Sarah said. 'I knew there was something. Did you have that talk with Liam?'

'In a fashion,' Nina said. 'He wants to do something in computers but I have a suspicion he thinks he's going to invent some amazing new program that will earn him millions without ever having to leave his room.'

'Maybe the problem is he doesn't want to leave home, as in, leave you and Scarlett.'

'And why would that be, Sarah?' Nina said, already knowing the answer. 'We have Bryn to look after us now.'

'The kids do seem to be getting on well with him.'

Sarah had been watching Bryn throughout their Sunday lunch the month before. Her friend's eyes had narrowed every time Liam, or especially Scarlett had spoken to him. And when Scarlett had disappeared and Bryn had fetched her back to the table, Sarah had made a fuss about Scarlett looking unsettled. The only reason she was unsettled was because Sarah had pulled the 'Are you OK?' routine on her too.

'Yes, they are. If anything, they're starting to take advantage of him. I'm sure Scarlett thinks he's her private chauffeur.'

'It's a shame he doesn't get on so well with his own daughter. Did you ever find out why she didn't show at the wedding?'

Nina had never met Bryn's daughter Caryn who lived in Wales with her mum. Bryn and his first wife had divorced when their daughter was in her early teens, around the same time his printing business had collapsed. Caryn was in her early twenties now and from what Bryn had told her, she hadn't had that much to do with him since his move to Sedgefield a few years ago. He had been hopeful that she would come to the wedding, but not surprised when she hadn't.

'I'm sure she had her reasons.'

'Doesn't that worry you?'

'Why should it, Sarah?' Nina said, too tired to control her frustration. 'If Adam were to remarry, I'm not sure either Scarlett or Liam would be rushing up to Scotland to wish him well. I'm not for a minute comparing Bryn to Adam, by the way, I'm only saying that family relations can get complicated.'

'OK, don't bite my head off,' Sarah said, her voice echoing because she had pulled the phone from her ear. 'I only say these things because I love you and I worry. And if I'm honest, I worry most of all about Scarlett.'

'You think I don't?'

'Of course you do, but you still see a little girl, whereas I can see a beautiful young woman emerging.' Sarah dropped her voice when she added, 'Is she on the pill yet?'

'No,' Nina said levelly. Through the windscreen, she peered towards her front door, which looked more inviting than ever.

'It's just that Miles and I were talking, and you know how impressionable young girls can be. They try to act all grown-up when they're still children – and by grown-up, I mean doing grown-up things.'

'I know what you mean,' Nina said. 'And you and Miles can put your minds at rest. We've had *that* talk.'

'Recently?'

'No, but nothing's changed,' Nina said, stopping short of saying that nothing had changed since the wedding, but she refused to play along with Sarah's game.

'Hmm,' Sarah said.

Nina had had enough. 'Look, Sarah, for the first time in years I feel like I have a fighting chance to be happy, and for my family to be happy. It might take time, but with patience things will settle into a new rhythm. Don't look for problems that aren't there. Please.'

'I only want what's best for you,' she said. 'As lovely as Bryn seems, I would have felt a whole lot better if you had drawn up a pre-nup, like I told you to.'

'Well, I didn't, and strangely enough I still manage to

sleep at night. If you really want what's best for me, Sarah, don't try to get me to worry about problems that don't exist. I'm sorry, but I have to go. There's a long, hot bath with my name on it and I'm looking forward to relaxing. Maybe you should give it a try.'

Nina let out a frustrated sigh as she ended the call, but the sigh transformed into a groan when the phone started ringing again the moment she went to open the car door. The call was from a mobile number she didn't recognize, and Nina was tempted to ignore it, but she went with her gut instinct which, despite Sarah's doubts, turned out to be as reliable as ever.

'Hello, Mrs Carrington?'

'Well, it's Mrs Thomas now.'

'Ah, yes, of course, sorry,' the man said. 'Mrs Thomas, this is Rob Swift. I'm Scarlett's form tutor.'

'Is everything all right?'

Nina had received many calls from school in her time, but it was usually during school hours when one of her children was ill. Neither Liam nor Scarlett had ever been a cause of concern, certainly not one that necessitated a call from a teacher out of hours. Not once.

'I hope so,' Rob said, but his tone didn't instil confidence. 'It might very well be nothing to worry about, but sometimes I think it's better to nip these things in the bud.'

After two difficult phone calls in quick succession, Nina dragged herself out of the car. The knot in her stomach twisted as she put her key in the front door. Inside the house, she imagined an idyllic scene where Bryn would be cooking dinner, humming to himself contentedly while

Scarlett and Liam were upstairs in their rooms. OK, maybe it wasn't idyllic, but at least her kids weren't hanging around on street corners causing trouble. Scarlett had a stable family life and more support than ever before. If she was in trouble at school, she had no one to blame but herself. Sarah would have that 'told-you-so' look on her face when she found out, but Nina refused to take responsibility for this one. She could feel her blood boiling and when she stepped into the house, she would have happily screamed out Scarlett's name but there was no way she would be heard above the commotion in the kitchen.

'But you hate my friends! You're only going so you can annoy me!' screeched Scarlett.

'It's working then.' Liam's tone was light with just a hint of smugness.

'I hate you!'

Silence.

'You do know it's fancy dress?' Scarlett said. 'What would you go as anyway? A zombie or something, because that's what you look like most of the time!'

'In that case I won't need fancy dress, will I?'

'I've got a pirate's outfit you could borrow.'

'He's not going, Bryn.'

'I am. And thanks, Bryn—'

Before Liam could finish, Scarlett said, 'I'll have it.'

From the hallway where she had remained, Nina heard Bryn laugh. 'It'll be too big on you. The jacket would be more like a dress.'

'Fine, that's how I'll wear it. Can I try it on now?'

'Erm, sure,' Bryn said.

Bryn appeared from the kitchen first while Scarlett hung back for one parting shot at her brother: 'Loser.'

'Hello, I didn't hear you come in,' Bryn said, startled to find his wife standing statue-still by the front door.

'I'm not surprised, given the racket those two were making.'

Scarlett squeezed between them and, ignoring her mother, said, 'Where is it, Bryn?'

Bryn kissed his wife briefly on the cheek. 'I won't be a minute,' he said, and followed Scarlett upstairs. Having temporarily lost her momentum, Nina went to check on Liam.

'What was that all about?'

'Eva's throwing a Halloween party for her birthday and I'm invited.'

'And are you going, or by some chance is this another way of winding up your sister?'

Liam shrugged. 'You keep saying I need to get out more.'

'So you are going?' Nina repeated. She wouldn't put it past Liam to keep up the pretence and therefore the tension between the warring siblings right up to the last minute. It didn't bear thinking about. 'I would have thought a room full of people, especially Scarlett's friends, would be torture for you.'

'I know you might not believe this, Mum, but I can actually function in the real world. I think I definitely will go now!'

With that, another of her children stormed off upstairs.

Nina dropped her handbag on the kitchen counter. These weren't big problems, she told herself; no doubt a similar scene was being repeated up and down the country. So why did the feeling of dread in the pit of her stomach persist as she slipped off her coat and headed upstairs?

Liam's door was firmly closed while the door to her bedroom had been left slightly ajar. One of the wardrobe doors was open and she could see reflections playing across the white gloss veneer.

'What do you think?' Scarlett was asking.

'It's a bit short.'

When Nina slipped into the room, she found Bryn standing close to the door while Scarlett was on the other side of the room in front of the bay window. The curtains had been drawn and the only light came from a bedside lamp, draping Scarlett's tall and slender body in shadow. Bryn's pirate jacket was swimming on her and its cavernous sleeves hung down over her hands. She was wearing opaque black tights, which was lucky because the jacket only just covered her bum.

'What do you think, Mum?' she asked.

When her daughter raised her arms and did a twirl, the jacket lifted up further. Nina was relieved to see that her school skirt had been hitched up rather than removed to give Scarlett at least a modicum of dignity.

'It is a bit revealing.'

'I was thinking of wearing it with a belt.'

'Which would make it ride up even further. If you're going to wear it, you'll need to wear leggings underneath. I'm not letting you out of the house if you don't,' Nina said, having momentarily forgotten about the call from Mr Swift. 'Actually, I might not let you out of the house anyway.'

Despite Nina's warning tone, Scarlett's body didn't sag

with a suggestion of guilt as once it might when she was younger. Instead, she squared up and simply asked, 'Why?'

'I've had a call from Mr Swift. I don't suppose I need to tell you what it was about.'

Her daughter's body froze. She was on the wrong side of the room to find an escape, but she looked for it anyway.

'What did he say?'

The question had come from Bryn.

'Scarlett's grades are slipping.'

'No they're not!' Scarlett cried. 'Not much, anyway. Mum, it's fine. I'm getting on with my work, honest.'

'Well, you can tell that to Mr Swift when we have our meeting.'

'He's called you in?'

'Yes,' Nina said. 'And I'm warning you now, Scarlett, if you've been messing about instead of studying then you're going to be spending the rest of the year locked away.'

'You can't, it's not fair! I haven't done anything.'

'Hopefully that's what Mr Swift will tell me on Friday.'

There was an awkward moment when no one knew what to do next. Scarlett was desperate to leave, but didn't want to run the gauntlet of her mum and Bryn. She dropped her head and slowly began to unbutton her jacket. Nina turned to Bryn. 'Can I smell something burning?'

'I hope not. I've made cottage pie but it's not in the oven yet,' he said, before realizing it was his cue to leave. He glanced back towards Scarlett who had taken off the jacket and was straightening her skirt. 'Maybe I should go and put it in.'

'Yes, that might be a good idea.'

When Bryn had left, Nina asked, 'What's going on, Scarlett?'

'Nothing,' her daughter mumbled as she stared at her feet.

'I don't believe you. There's something troubling you and I don't know why I didn't see it before. It's like I caught glimpses out of the corner of my eye, but every time I turned towards it, it was gone. But it is there, Scarlett, and the fact that your grades are slipping only proves it. You need to tell me.'

'Has Bryn said anything?'

Nina's insides twisted that bit more. 'Said what?'

When Scarlett didn't reply, Nina stepped further into the room to close the distance between them, but rather than take her daughter in a bear hug and squeeze the truth from her, Nina sat down on the bed and patted the space next to her. 'Sit,' she said.

Scarlett did as she was told, and Nina took hold of her hand. With mother and daughter staring forward, they both relaxed a little. 'What's going on?'

'Nothing,' Scarlett said quickly. 'I just moan about my friends to Bryn, that's all. They're so immature sometimes.'

'While you're growing up fast,' Nina said, but then paused to consider how slowly she should lead the conversation in the direction it needed to go. 'Are you having sex?'

'Mum!' Scarlett cried, glancing at her briefly before remembering herself and looking away.

'I'm not daft, Scarlett. I know it's going to happen eventually and you're showing all the classic signs of having man trouble.'

Scarlett laughed.

'So I am right?'

Her daughter had continued to laugh, but very quickly

she was gulping for air as she fought and failed to hold back the sobs. Terrified, Nina wrapped Scarlett in her arms and let her cry on her shoulder. She patted Scarlett's back to match the pace of her own heart thumping inside her chest. 'Oh, Scarlett. Please tell me what's going on.'

'I – don't – know – what – to – do.'

'About what? What's happened?'

'Nothing, nothing's happened and I don't know if it ever will.'

'But you want it to?'

Scarlett nodded. 'I think so.'

'You think? That doesn't sound so definite to me. You're fifteen years old, Scarlett. You might feel like you're all grown up, and I'm not saying you're not maturing faster than I'd like, but you're not there yet.'

'But I want to be, Mum. I want this bit to be over. I want to be middle-aged with a boring job and a family.'

It was Nina's turn to laugh. 'It's not all it's cracked up to be.'

'Neither is being fifteen.'

'I know. But I can't go back in time, and you can't fast forward. We are where we are.'

Scarlett hadn't finished crying, but she managed to control her sobs enough to lift her head from her mum's shoulder. 'I'm scared, Mum. I don't know what to do.'

'If this boy respects you, then he'll see you're unsure and he'll wait. Who are we talking about anyway? Is it Linus?'

Turning back to face the front, Scarlett put her hands over her face. 'It's OK,' she said. 'I can look after myself.'

'Do we need to make an appointment with the GP?' Nina asked.

Using the cuff of her jumper, Scarlett wiped away her tears. 'No, it's all right.'

'You're sure?'

'Yes.'

Nina hadn't realized she had been holding her breath until she released it. She should have felt relieved, but she didn't. Sorting out contraception was only ever going to be part of the solution. 'OK, I'm trusting you to do the right thing, Scarlett, but whatever happens, you can't let it affect your schoolwork. It's an important year.'

'Don't I know it.'

'No more going out with your friends until you've got your grades back up where they belong.'

'You can't do that! I'll turn into a weirdo like Liam if I never go out,' Scarlett said, not afraid to face her mum now. 'And what about the party?'

'Let's see how we get on with Mr Swift first, shall we?'

'Fine, as long as you know what you're doing,' Scarlett said with a hint of a warning. 'Don't blame me if I go crazy.'

In truth, Nina didn't know what she was doing. She was attempting to navigate through a perilous period of parenthood without a road map. She didn't know how to solve Scarlett's problems and help her towards the next stage of her life, all she could do was let her know she didn't have to do it on her own. She had a mum who loved her; a stepdad who would do anything for her; and a brother who would protect her if he knew what was good for him; not to mention Mr Swift, who would help her daughter get back on track, academically at least.

Scarlett

I was starting to feel weird around my friends. It was like I was out of sync with everyone. I tried to carry on as normal, but it was hard pretending not to have all these horrible feelings messing with my head.

Me and my friends spent most of our time hanging out in Eva's garage. We'd made it really nice in there with a couple of old sofas and big fleecy throws so it was all cosy. Sometimes it was just us girls, but mostly it was the boys too – and when I say boys, I mean boys. Everyone was getting excited about the Halloween party Eva was planning for her sixteenth, and I wanted to get excited about it too, but part of me didn't want to be around them any more. It was when I complained that the boys in our year were all lame that Eva came up with this stupid idea about inviting people from sixth form. If Liam was anything to go by, sixth formers weren't exactly mature either.

It had really got to me that he had called me a little girl. It was so annoying because I didn't want him to see me that way. That's why I went on the pill.

It was so horrible when Mum tried to talk to me about

it. Like I was going to tell her I'd already been to the doctor. And, oh my God, it was so disgusting when she just assumed I was thinking of going with Linus. As if! OK, we'd hung out together over the summer and we'd snogged a bit, but I never once said I was his girlfriend. It makes me cringe, thinking about all that fumbling around we did. I wanted something else. I wanted someone else and going on the pill was me being mature. I was getting prepared. I wanted to show him I wasn't a silly little girl.

I should say now, in my defence, that I still wasn't sure I'd actually do it, even if he wanted me to. Mum had said she trusted me and, for a split second, I honestly thought she did, but in the next breath she was having a rant about my schoolwork, which only proved she didn't really.

It was so unfair because I was keeping up at school. I'm not totally irresponsible. Maybe I could have focused more, but if Mum thought forcing me to stay at home and take on extra lessons was going to solve my problems, well, it turns out that was so the wrong thing to do. Everyone was trying to fix things and it was laughable. They didn't have a clue what was going on, none of them did, not Mum, not my friends and definitely not Mrs Anwar, who invited herself along to the meeting with Mr Swift.

'Do you know why we've asked your mum to come in, Scarlett?' Mrs Anwar said.

I was tempted to make some smart remark, but I bit my tongue and shrugged. She was sitting on one side of the table next to Mr Swift, while me and Mum sat on the other. It was a wonder my chair wasn't smaller than everyone else's so they could all look down on me. It was actually funny because I was taller than Mum and Mrs Anwar, and it was only Mr Swift who was on my level.

Mrs Anwar shuffled through a pile of papers in front of her and turned a couple around so Mum could read them. I didn't need to, the sheets were covered in my writing with comments from teachers in red ink.

I still didn't get what all the fuss was about and said, 'I got a B for that one.'

'And a C for the other one,' Mr Swift said. 'And for some of our students that would be a pretty decent result, but not for you, Scarlett.' He dug out another test paper further down in the pile. 'This is the kind of result you were getting last year.'

Mum leant forward to read the grade. 'An A-star.'

'And there are plenty more where that came from,' he said. 'Just not this year.'

'I've only been back five minutes,' I said. 'I don't understand why you're making such a big deal of it.'

'Don't you?' Mr Swift asked.

I held his gaze so he knew I wasn't a pushover, and then I bit my lip just to make him feel uncomfortable. It might have worked if he hadn't turned to look at Mum.

'We might only be halfway through the first term, Mrs Thomas, but soon there'll be no new learning as we switch focus to revision and mock exams, and after that it's the real thing. There's only a small window of opportunity to get Scarlett back on track.'

'What do we need to do?'

'We can draw up a revision plan together,' Mrs Anwar said. 'It will help Scarlett organize her time better, as well as giving you an idea of the amount of effort she should be putting in.' She turned to give me a smile. 'We're not suggesting you're in trouble, Scarlett – far from it. You're one of our best students and we want you to get the most out of the next few months so that you achieve the results we all agree you deserve.'

'Thank you,' Mum said, when I just sat there gritting my teeth.

'As well as the revision plan,' Mrs Anwar continued, 'Mr Swift has offered to give you extra support. That could simply be checking with you regularly to make sure you're keeping to the plan, but if you're stuck on a particular subject, he can arrange for you to get support from specific teachers. He's also kindly offered to give you extra revision sessions after class so you can continue to prepare for your exams in a school environment.'

'Does that sound OK to you, Scarlett?' Mr Swift asked. He was the only one to notice that I hadn't actually agreed to anything yet. 'If we can get started straight away, you'll have a schedule to work to over half-term.'

I was still playing it cool and shrugged.

'Great, that's exactly what I like to see,' Mr Swift said, rubbing his hands together, 'a student who's raring to go.'

'We can only make suggestions, Scarlett,' Mrs Anwar said. 'It's you who has to knuckle down and do the work.'

'So?' Mum asked me.

'Can I think about it?'

Mrs Anwar looked as if she were about to explode, but Mr Swift played me at my own game. 'Yes, of course you can, Scarlett,' he said. 'For all of fifteen seconds and then you're on your own.'

'And the longer it takes for you to get this sorted,' Mum

added, 'the longer you'll be grounded. It would be a shame if you missed Eva's birthday party.'

'OK, fine!' I said and glared at Mr Swift when I added, 'I'll do anything you want!'

There was a sigh from Mum. 'I hope you know what you're letting yourself in for,' she told him.

In a funny sort of way, I was up for the challenge. I'd started playing men at their own game. I'd had enough of feeling uncomfortable about the way they all looked at me. I hadn't realized that if I returned that look I could turn them into quivering wrecks. That way I could have them eating out of my hand. All of them.

7

The Accusations

When Freya came into their bedroom in the early hours of the morning, Vikki didn't complain for once. She didn't want to lie in bed pretending to be asleep while her husband lay next to her doing the same, but as she went to pull back the covers, Rob jumped up.

'It's all right,' he said, 'I'll see to her.'

Freya had climbed on to the bed and kissed Vikki's cheek. 'Me watch *Peppa Pig* with Daddy. You go sleep now, Mummy.'

Vikki closed her eyes, but the moment she heard Rob and Freya reach the bottom of the stairs, she let out a sob and had to press the back of her hand against her mouth. What had got into her? What was she so afraid of?

Ignoring her daughter's instructions, Vikki sat up and rubbed angrily at the tears she didn't want to fall. After everything they had been through recently, they were meant to be rebuilding their lives. Why couldn't she do that instead of looking for faultlines? She had the best family, the best husband she could hope for. Why did she suddenly doubt everything? Did she really think there was a problem between her and Rob, or was she imagining it? It had been tough on both of them when she had spent so much time with her mum, but that had only made them appreciate each other more. Hadn't it made them stronger? It had definitely made Vikki stronger.

Wrapping her arms around herself, Vikki attempted to pull her life into focus, but her eyes settled on Rob's mobile phone on the bedside cabinet. She reached for it without hesitation and quickly tapped out four digits before she had a chance to stop herself. She half expected Rob's old passcode to be rejected. It wasn't, and a second later the screen lit up.

Vikki had never checked Rob's phone before, or at least not without his knowledge. She had answered it often enough when he was driving, and occasionally had a sneaky peek at his messages, commenting on how often Mrs Anwar contacted him and suggesting the Head of School had a crush on him. But Rob deserved her complete faith and she hated herself for what she was doing. She hated herself more when she skimmed through a list of messages that revealed absolutely nothing to justify her doubts. Rob appeared to be more popular with PPI firms and mobile phone providers than he was with real people. A couple of teachers had been in touch and there were a handful of messages from pupils he had given his number to, kids who had needed extra support during the year, but none of these made her stomach lurch; none had been from Scarlett.

A creak on the stairs gave her a start and she almost dropped the phone as she closed it down and put it back where Rob had left it. By the time he came into the bedroom, she was curled up in bed with her eyes tightly closed.

She heard him pick up his phone before whispering, 'I'm making a cuppa if you want one?'

It was a gesture of kindness that Vikki didn't deserve and tears threatened again. Rather than look at him, she buried her head in her pillow to wipe her eyes. 'I'm going to grab a shower first,' she said, pulling herself up and managing to avoid eye contact.

Rob was more interested in his phone than his wife's odd behaviour and said, 'OK, see you in a bit.'

Vikki turned towards Rob and watched him disappear out of the room. There had been a time when she would have felt a physical ache whenever they were apart, and she knew Rob had felt the same. She didn't feel it now; in fact, she was looking forward to time on her own once Rob had set off for work. Was that just growing up and growing used to someone, or was this the problem she had been searching for? When was the last time Rob had ached for her, and what had he done when she hadn't been there to satisfy his needs?

8

Before

Sunday, 18 October 2015
Vikki linked arms with Rob as he pushed Freya's buggy along a winding country road. She liked the feeling of completeness it gave her. 'I've missed this,' she said, and was surprised to hear a catch in her voice. She had been staying at her mum's for the best part of a month and while she and Rob had tried to see each other every day, sometimes that hadn't been possible for one reason or another. Weekends were easier and she intended to keep Rob with her for as much of this Sunday as she could.

'It's not like we were ever in the habit of going for country walks,' Rob replied.

'You know what I mean. I've missed *this*,' she said, giving his arm a squeeze. 'I've missed doing stuff together. I've even missed having you looking over my shoulder to check what I'm buying when we go food shopping.'

'Is that all you've missed?'

She squeezed his arm again. 'Of course not.'

'No, I didn't think so,' Rob said and gave a soft chuckle.

'If only Mrs Anwar knew what we get up to when I sneak off for an early lunch.'

Rob had continued to refuse to stay over at her mum's, and their sex life might have suffered if it wasn't for their furtive meetings during the day while Freya was at nursery. 'It won't be for ever,' she said.

'I know and, if I'm honest, I quite like our little trysts. It reminds me of the old days.'

She smiled at the memories Rob was evoking. When they had first started dating, they had enjoyed a certain thrill in meeting up in secret. 'Shall we do it again? How about tomorrow?'

'It's a date,' he said.

They had strayed down one of the narrow lanes that criss-crossed the countryside around her mum's house, not giving much thought to which direction they were going, or so it seemed.

'We can't be too far from the old Ellison House,' she said.

Rob kissed the top of her head. 'Shall we see if we can find it?'

Vikki was too young to remember the last time the Ellison House had been open to the public. An entrepreneur had taken it over in the nineties with the intention of transforming it into an adventure playground, but he had run out of money before it had a chance to take off. Rob had fond memories of the place and had taken Vikki to show her the tree where he had fallen off a rope swing and broken his leg. The site had been cleared by that point and the house boarded up, and so they had come up with some adventures of their own making.

The bridle path Rob was convinced led to the house wasn't one in regular use and even if they weren't pushing a buggy, Vikki and Rob would have struggled to make their way through overgrown bracken and layers of crisp autumn leaves that hid a slimy rotten layer beneath.

'This is too hard and I'm getting blisters,' Vikki complained. 'Can we go back, please? I think Freya's about to drop off anyway.'

Freya had been walking with them at first, insisting she was a big girl now and didn't need her pushchair, but as Rob had predicted, her short legs had grown tired. She was sitting happily enough in the buggy and they hadn't heard a peep out of her for the last five minutes.

'I suppose,' Rob said, taking one last look to see if he could spy the memories he wasn't quite ready to release. He was about to turn the buggy around when he stopped and did a double take. 'Hold on, isn't that a chimney stack?'

They persevered down the path a while longer and found themselves on the outer edges of the long-abandoned park. There were signs of what had once been a clearing in front of the old house, although the tender saplings Vikki recalled from earlier visits had become more established.

'Fancy taking a closer look?' Rob asked as he glanced back to make sure she was following.

By the time they reached the dilapidated driveway of the old Victorian house, Freya was fast asleep. They left her buggy close to the wire-mesh fencing panels that guarded the perimeter of the abandoned house before squeezing between two sections so they could take a closer look. The metal shutters on the doors and windows were corroded but intact, and prevented unwelcome visitors from getting any further.

'It hasn't changed, has it?' Vikki said.

Rob slipped his arms around Vikki's waist. 'Ah, but have you?'

In the next moment, he had her pressed up against a nearby wall beneath a rambling wisteria. When they kissed, she felt herself falling back in time. 'Rob, we can't,' she whispered.

'That's not what you used to say,' Rob said and kissed her again.

'We didn't have Freya with us then. What if she wakes up and sees us?' she said when she could draw breath.

Rob's movements slowed as he began unzipping her padded coat. 'Does that mean you want me to stop?'

Vikki closed her eyes and groaned softly as Rob kissed her neck. She tried not to think of their little girl only feet away as Rob began undoing her jeans. She searched for a gap in his jacket so she could reach inside.

'This is what you've missed,' he said as he yanked down her jeans and knickers at the same time before pushing her against the wall. She cried out before she could stop herself as her bare bottom made contact with the ice-cold brick wall.

'Mummy!' cried a sleepy Freya.

Rob and Vikki let out matching sighs of frustration.

'Told you,' she said.

'God, I miss you,' he whispered softly. His hand was between her legs and he waited until she gasped before he stepped back.

'We can pick up where we left off tomorrow,' she

promised, but Rob had already turned away and slipped back through the fence. Fumbling with her clothes, Vikki was eager to follow, calling after him. 'Rob?'

He seemed not to hear as he rocked the buggy to soothe Freya back to sleep. When she reached his side, she whispered, 'I'll be home soon.'

'So you keep saying. I'm starting to think you don't want to come back, Victoria.'

'Of course I do!' she hissed. 'But I have to make sure Mum gets well enough to face the chemo. You want that too, don't you?'

Rob lowered his head when he said, 'Sorry, I'm being selfish, aren't I?'

'You really think I don't want to come home?'

Rob gave a vague shake of the head rather than answer as they walked away from the house.

'I suppose Mum is managing much better on her own now,' Vikki said when the silence became unbearable. 'And Lesley's insisting on dropping by most days, even though we haven't got any holiday bookings coming up.'

'It's your decision, Vikki. You know I'd never push you into doing something you didn't want to.'

They were walking down the country lane that would take them the long way back to her mum's. It was easier than tackling the bridle path again, but now it was the choice Rob was giving her that Vikki was struggling with. Her pulse raced as she prepared to tell him that she would come home, now, today, but the words wouldn't come. She kept thinking about her dad. Vikki had never had the chance to say goodbye to him, and he had been on his own when he collapsed. She couldn't leave her mum to the same fate.

They walked for a while without speaking, Rob waiting for her to decide, Vikki wishing she didn't have to. 'Are you OK?' she asked eventually, although what she had wanted to ask was, were they OK.

Rob sounded so dejected when he said, 'I thought it would be nice to have you home for half-term, that's all.'

'I want to be home by then too. I want us to take Freya trick-or-treating on Halloween. We can carve pumpkins and eat all her sweets for her own good,' she said, a bit too brightly. 'I've already got outfits for me and Freya. I made them myself. Mum's been nagging me for ages to learn how to sew and she's turning me into a proper little housewife, Not that there's anything proper about my outfit. I'm going to be a wicked witch. A very naughty wicked witch.'

Rob was smiling when he said, 'You drive me crazy, do you know that? As if I'm not missing you enough as it is. Still, don't worry about me, I'm sure I'll get used to being without you. Who knows? I might not want you back.'

Vikki refused to be taken in by Rob's brave words: he couldn't live without her. 'I love you, Rob, and I hate this as much as you do, but—'

'But what?' he asked sharply. In a lower voice, he added, 'I can't help thinking you're actually as desperate as I am to get back home. Is this your way of getting me to be the bad guy and tell your mum? I'm sorry, Vikki, but I can't do that. For what it's worth, I think it would be the right thing to do and I'll support you all the way, but you have to be the one to talk to her.'

As Rob picked up his pace, Vikki trailed behind and didn't catch up until they arrived back at her mum's house. They found Elaine in the living room, snoozing with a magazine on her lap. She held her body in an awkward position with the left side of her chest looking almost concave compared to her right breast. Vikki knelt down beside her and squeezed her hand.

When Elaine peeled open her eyes and realized she had not one but two onlookers, she immediately shifted up in her chair and pulled back her shoulders. 'Sorry, I must have dozed off. Do you want some tea?'

Tears were stinging Vikki's eyes. 'Mum, I've been thinking—'

'Vikki, maybe now's not the time,' Rob interjected; he had remained at the door. 'Let's leave it.'

Elaine looked at them both in turn. 'Leave what?'

Vikki had spent the last ten minutes walking in silence and rehearsing what she was going to say to her mum. She didn't know how to deal with this latest turn of events. 'I miss being at home, Mum. I miss being with Rob,' she blurted out in the hope that either her mum or her husband would reach the right conclusion for her.

'And I've had you to myself for far too long,' Elaine said, giving her daughter's hand a squeeze. 'I can manage on my own, of course I can, and the sooner you go, the sooner I can prove it to you all.'

'You don't have to do this, Elaine,' Rob said. 'I can manage perfectly well at home in my little bachelor pad.'

'Can you now? I'd say that's all the more reason for your wife to go back home.'

'Mum—'

Elaine didn't let her daughter finish. 'Go home, Victoria, and look after your family. You don't know how lucky you are to have a husband who loves and supports you. Don't take that for granted, not ever.'

Tears stung Vikki's eyes. Why did everything have to be so complicated? She didn't want to leave her mum to fend for herself. She was terrified of losing her, but now there was a new fear, one that she had never considered before. What if there was a risk of losing her husband too?

'Go home,' Elaine repeated.

Wednesday, 28 October 2015

When Rob lifted himself off her and collapsed on to the bed, Vikki turned on to her side and let her body meld into his, her spine curving against his chest so they were in perfect symmetry. It was moments like this that proved they were made for each other. Rob would look after her and love her for ever, like he promised he always would. When he slipped an arm around her waist, the warmth of his breath on the back of her neck sent a delicious shiver down her spine.

'God, Vikki, you're wearing me out,' he whispered in her ear. 'It's a good job I'm not in school this week.'

She smiled as she pushed her bottom against him in the safe knowledge that her husband was completely spent. 'When I suggested we should have an early night,' she said, 'I did actually mean so you could catch up on your sleep.'

'Yeah, sure you did.'

Since Vikki's return home, she and Rob had been behaving like honeymooners, but after ten days even Vikki's youthful athleticism was no match for her husband's needs. That evening she would have been more than happy to simply go to bed to sleep, and it was what she was desperate to do now, but Rob began nibbling her earlobe.

'I was thinking,' he said.

'Thinking what exactly?'

'Have you given any more thought to going back to work?'

Her eyes felt heavy, but the very mention of finding a job piqued her interest and staved off sleep. She had been idly surfing the net over the last few days, searching for vacancies even if she wasn't quite ready, or able, to commit to anything yet.

'I keep looking, but only out of curiosity. I wouldn't dream of applying for anything until Mum's finished all her treatment. But I will,' she added, and she was hopeful. Her mum had had her first round of chemo earlier that week and they were both surprised by how well she had dealt with the toxic chemicals that had been pumped into her system. The doctors had warned Elaine that it might take a week to recover from what would be three weekly cycles for the next three months. Everyone reacted differently apparently and there was likely to be a cumulative effect, but if this first round was anything to go by, then Vikki was hoping her mum would be one of the lucky ones.

Rob kissed her neck. 'But you do want more kids, don't you?'

'Eventually,' she whispered, although, if she were being honest, it was something she was happy to put off for as long as possible.

'Don't you think it might be better to do it now?'

'Now? As in while Mum's fighting for her life?' she asked, using the same argument as before for putting off the job search, only with a little more desperation.

'You know I didn't mean it like that. It's just that you're a natural when it comes to being a mum, and Freya's thrived because you've been able to stay at home and look after her. I know you, Vikki. You'd want to give our next baby the best start too, but if you were committed to a career, wouldn't you feel torn? Wouldn't it be better to complete our family first?'

'Is that what you think we should do?' she asked.

He nibbled her ear again. 'I want what you want, no more, no less. You're beautiful, and talented, and amazing. You can do anything you set your mind to.'

'But it's not my decision alone. It should be both of us.'

'And it is. We both agree we want more kids, it's all about the timing, that's all. I honestly don't mind either way, which means it's only right that you should choose the 'when' in our family plan.'

'But I don't know,' Vikki said, struck with sudden doubt. She had been counting down the days until Freya started pre-school and she had set her heart on finding a job that would get her out of the house, but so much had changed. Perhaps she should rethink her plans.

'Well, maybe it's something you need to at least start thinking about.'

'I will,' she said, and yawned deliberately. 'But now isn't exactly the best time to make plans, is it?'

She felt Rob's chest push against her back as he inhaled deeply and released a sigh. She was tempted to say something else, although what that something should be, she didn't know. Rob pulled his arm away and turned on to his back so that they were no longer touching. 'Sorry, you're right. I shouldn't have brought it up. I know your mum has to come first for now and, for the record, I think you're dealing with it all so well. I'm really proud of you, Vikki.'

'I'm proud of you too,' she said, turning to look at him.

With only the dull glow from the digital clock, she couldn't read his expression. 'I couldn't have coped without your support, you know that, don't you?'

Rob pulled the covers up over his chest. 'For what it's worth, you have it. Don't ever doubt that,' he said, and a moment later he was snoring softly. Vikki, on the other hand, held out little hope of finding sleep any time soon.

Friday, 30 October 2015

Vikki stood in her mum's bedroom, looking out across fields and thick woodland in the distance. The turning leaves of the ancient oaks and beeches lining the horizon had been aflame only yesterday, but in the grey light of a new day, they had turned brown and lifeless. Closer to home, the field that would normally be occupied by half a dozen horses was ominously empty.

It was almost Halloween, after which Vikki would begin counting down to Christmas, but what would the New Year bring? She imagined the field covered in layers of sand, stone and cement to make way for a development of sixteen detached homes, and everything else that entailed. Where once there were wildflowers and hedgerows, there would be Tarmac and block paving.

'I thought you'd gone.'

The ragged voice was frail and fearful, and had no right belonging to her mum.

'There's no rush,' Vikki said. 'Freya's having a nap and Rob's gone home.'

'Doesn't he mind you staying?'

'Rob was the one who suggested it,' Vikki assured her.

'He had another one of his extra-tuition classes this afternoon anyway.'

'As long as I'm not spoiling your plans. I'm sure I could manage on my own.'

Despite her claims, Elaine could barely manage the task of raising herself into a sitting position.

'So you keep saying,' Vikki said.

Before stepping away from the window, she took one last look at the picturesque setting that had made her parents fall in love with the house in the first place, and the reason her mum's paying guests came back time and again.

'Have the diggers moved in yet?' Elaine asked.

'You weren't asleep that long.'

'Maybe I should get up,' she suggested.

'No, Mum. You've spent the last few days pushing yourself too hard and look what's happened. The doctor said to stay in bed, so I'm here to make sure that's what you do.'

Elaine reluctantly allowed her daughter to support her as she pulled herself up. After four days of wondering what all the fuss was about, Elaine's body had provided an unwelcome reminder that this was a fight for life. When Vikki had arrived that morning for what was meant to be a quick visit with Rob and Freya, Elaine had still been in bed. She had caught a virus.

'And don't you worry about what might or might not be happening over the road,' Vikki continued. 'Even if the council does approve the planning application, I won't give up. I'll write to our MP, I'll start a petition. I'll do whatever it takes, even if it means lying down in front of the diggers if they dare to show up.'

Elaine patted the space on the bed next to her and when

her daughter sat down, she took hold of her hand. 'You're growing up fast.'

'I'm twenty-four, Mum. I know I don't always act it, but I am an adult.'

'Your dad would be proud of you.'

'Would he?' Vikki asked. 'Or would he be disappointed that five years after my *gap* year, I still don't have a degree or a career?'

'He might not have liked it when you announced you were taking a year out, but I think he was quietly pleased that you were strong-minded enough to go out and get what you wanted, so yes, he would be very proud of you. I know I am,' Elaine said with as much conviction as she could muster. 'You have a beautiful family, Vikki, and who's to say none of that other stuff won't happen in time?'

It was on the tip of Vikki's tongue to mention Rob's suggestion of another baby, but she couldn't yet trust herself to repeat the idea and make it her own. 'Maybe you're right.'

Hearing the uncertainty in her daughter's words, Elaine added, 'Don't give up on your dreams, that's what your dad would be saying to you.'

'I'm trying not to,' Vikki said, although she wasn't too sure any more what those dreams should be. 'But for now, I'm happy to take things one day at a time. Do you think you could stomach some food? Maybe some toast and a cup of tea?'

Elaine's features turned green at the suggestion. 'The only thing I need right now is my next dose of anti-emetics.'

Vikki was quiet for a moment as she wrestled with another decision she had been presented with. 'Lesley said she'd call in later, but it's not enough, is it? Truthfully, Mum, do you need me to stay with you for a few days?'

'Yes.'

Vikki felt a rush of panic. She had expected her mum to put up a fight and make some comment about Vikki's place being at home with her husband, but there really wasn't any fight left in her. Vikki's unease began to ramp up when she realized she would have to tell Rob what she had just done.

Under the guise of fetching Elaine's medication, Vikki went downstairs to make the call. She didn't think he would say no – he had told her she had his support – but even so, it had been such a struggle for them both last time. The knot in Vikki's stomach tightened as Rob's phone rang out and eventually went to voicemail. He would be at the library with his students so, rather than leave a message, she resigned herself to a nervous wait. Fortunately, he returned her call only a matter of minutes later.

'Am I disturbing you?' she asked.

'No, we were due a break anyway.'

'Right, the thing is, I'm still with Mum,' Vikki said slowly. 'She's no better. In fact, I think she's worse.'

'Ah.'

'I can't leave her, Rob,' she said, and bit her lip before adding, 'Would you mind if I stayed?'

'I think the point is, would your mum mind you staying after kicking you out less than a fortnight ago?'

'She wants me to stay, which only proves how sick she is.'

'Oh right, so it's all been arranged and it doesn't really matter what I think?'

'It wasn't like that. I thought she'd say no when I offered,' she said. 'If you don't want me to stay, Rob, then I won't. I just thought . . . '

'It's all right,' Rob said softly. 'Your mum's ill and I can hardly complain about coming second. I am going to miss my naughty witch, though.'

'You could still come over tomorrow so we can go trick-or-treating.'

'Erm, I think I might find some extra marking to do instead.'

'You're not angry with me, are you?' she asked.

'If I say yes,' he said, lowering his voice, 'does that mean you'll make it up to me when you do come home?'

'I'll do whatever you want.'

'That would be a first,' Rob said, and Vikki couldn't be sure if he was playing with her, or if he was genuinely hurt.

'No, I mean it. I love you,' she said. 'If you can put up with me being a terrible wife for a bit longer, I promise I will make it up to you.'

Scarlett

Do you want to hear about the first time we did it? I think I should tell you, just so you know it wasn't like people think. No way was he abusing me.

It happened on Halloween, which is quite funny when you think about it. I still wasn't sure how I was supposed to handle this secret power I had over men, and the next minute I was getting to use it. It wasn't planned or anything. I was too busy dreading Eva's party. I knew she'd be gloating about being sixteen, even if she wasn't going to be legal for another week. Not that she had anyone to get legal with at that point.

I know Eva's my best friend, and don't get me wrong, she is really pretty, but she has the most ridiculous laugh you can imagine. I think it was her laugh that put boys off, but that wasn't going to stop Eva trying, and I had this horrible feeling I know who she was after.

I'd been grounded all week and had only been allowed out to go to the library. I definitely wasn't allowed to see friends, which suited me fine because I much preferred adult company anyway. I was so over being a hysterical teenager and when Bryn dropped me and Liam off at the party, I didn't want to get out of the car.

'Call me when you're ready to come home.'

'Do we have to come home together?' I asked. There was no way I was going to waste my breath arguing with my drunken brother about what time to leave.

'I can walk home,' Liam said.

'I have a feeling you won't be walking in a straight line by midnight,' Bryn answered. And then to me he said, 'I'll pick you up together or separately, whatever you want, Scarlett.'

Seriously, that should have been within five minutes of stepping into the house, which was already full of schoolkids who were pissed before they arrived. I'd been invited for pre-drinks with Linus and a few of the others, but there was no way I'd say yes to him. I wanted Linus to know I wasn't interested in him, but he didn't do subtle.

'Here, you look like you need it,' he said as he handed me a pint glass full of gin and lemonade.

I must have downed it in a couple of minutes and I did start to relax after that, a bit too much, if I'm honest. A couple of hours later I ended up sitting on Linus's knee while a group of us talked about life-and-death decisions, like what was better, Burger King or McDonald's. Linus hadn't started trying to grope me yet, but it was like only a matter of time.

Anyway, I was messing about on my phone, which was much better than watching Eva and Liam sucking the faces off each other. I wrote out a message and dared myself to send it.

What are you doing?

The reply came maybe ten seconds later.

What are YOU doing?

I told you I'd hate this party and I do

Want to talk about it?

Yes

Want to meet?

Linus was stroking my leg and he kept slipping his hand under my pirate's jacket. I took one look around the room and asked myself what the hell I was waiting for, but I did hesitate, I swear. I didn't want to let Mum down, she trusted me. But then I reminded myself how she hadn't thought about me when she decided to bring Bryn into our lives. Maybe that didn't justify what I did, but I couldn't help myself. I sent the reply before I could change my mind.

Yes

Now?

Yes! Yes! Yes!!

Slipping out of the party was easy enough, I just said I was going to the loo and never went back. He was waiting at the top of the road where no one would see me getting into his car. We didn't really speak until he'd parked up on some quiet country lane that was miles away from anywhere. All I could hear was my heart thudding.

'I was waiting for your message. I knew you'd want to escape.'

'I suppose you think you know me so well now.'

He unbuckled his seat belt and turned towards me. 'I don't know. Do I?'

I didn't know what to say. I wasn't daft. I knew what might be about to happen and part of me wanted him to take control and tell me what to do, but he's not like that.

'What would you like to talk about, Scarlett?'

I told myself to stop panicking and use my superpowers. 'Tell me about you,' I said.

'What you see is what you get.'

I can't believe I had the nerve to say what I said next and it was a good job it was dark because I was blushing so much. 'Really?' I said. 'So what am I getting?'

He took hold of my hand and kissed it. I could feel the tip of his tongue licking my skin and you have no idea what it did to me.

'So what now?' I asked. I was desperate for the teasing to stop and to just get on and do it.

'I think you know.'

'Then say it. Are you too scared?'

'Are you?' he asked.

'I'm on the pill.'

He stretched his spine and groaned. He didn't look nervous one bit, while I was starting to shake like an idiot.

'Why don't we move to the back seat?' he said. 'There's more room there.'

When I got out of the car, I stumbled. It was the fresh

air making my head spin, but no way was I going to back out and make an idiot of myself again. We got into the back and sat next to each other like two strangers sitting on a bus. It was just too funny and I had to stop myself from giggling.

'You're a beautiful woman, Scarlett,' he said. 'Any man would be lucky to be in my position, but I need you to think very carefully about what might be about to happen. This is serious stuff and I'm trusting you. No one can know about this. You do realize how many lives we could destroy, and all because . . .'

'Because what?'

'Because it's Halloween and you've put me under your spell.' It was such a corny line that I really was about to laugh this time, but what he said next sobered me up straight away. 'I want you so badly, Scarlett. Do you want me?'

'Yes,' I said, and it was so weird because I suddenly wanted to cry. I don't know why. I wasn't frightened. I think I was just shocked that someone could want me so much that they would like, put their life in danger for me.

'I'm a virgin,' I blurted out.

He smiled. 'I know, and I'm not going to do anything you don't want to. You're the one in control, Scarlett.'

'But I don't know what to do.'

'Why don't you start by taking those off,' he said, patting my leg.

I took off my leggings.

'And your knickers.'

9

The Accusations

Nina loved her husband and that love ought to be absolute, with no doubts and no uncertainties. It didn't make sense that her skin should crawl as she looked at the man standing in the kitchen doorway. She had felt a similar sensation the day before when Bryn had tried to comfort her, reacting as if he were a stranger or, worse still, a threat. Her ears had strained each time he had gone upstairs. At one point she had thought she heard him go into Scarlett's room and she had crept to the bottom of the stairs to listen. When Bryn had come out of the bathroom and caught her, she had given him a spurious excuse about trying to work out if Liam had got up, but she wasn't sure he had believed her.

How had she failed as a parent so badly? She had assumed that, by giving her children more freedom, they could establish their independence, and if they made mistakes, they would learn from them. Now it would seem that the mistakes that had been made weren't all of her children's making, and there were some harsh lessons ahead for all of them.

Bryn was watching her intently as if he could read the

thoughts turning in her mind on an endless reel of regret and recrimination.

'Are you going to keep Scarlett off school too?'

Nina reached out for her cup of coffee in search of comfort, but it was stone cold. 'No, definitely not. I have a feeling she's going to miss enough school as it is.'

Bryn was about to ask a follow-up question, but decided against it. He picked up her mug. 'Do you want a fresh one?'

'You can go back to bed if you want, I'll see to the kids this morning.'

Her husband scratched his head and ruffled his hair. Even half-asleep in nothing but a crumpled T-shirt and boxer shorts, Bryn was an attractive man. 'I'm up now,' he said, 'and I don't think I could sleep if I tried.'

'I don't know how long I can go on without answers,' she said as he turned away to fill the kettle. 'It's eating me up inside, Bryn. You would tell me if you knew something, wouldn't you? You and Scarlett talk.'

Bryn stopped what he was doing and, for a second, he didn't move or say anything. His movements were precise as he placed the kettle down on the countertop without switching it on. His mouth was open as he turned towards her, but he was struggling to find the words. He knew. He knew what she was suggesting. She could see his chest rising and falling as his breathing became more rapid. 'Yes, we get on well,' he said.

Nina wished he hadn't taken away her coffee cup; her mouth was dry and her lips stuck to her teeth when she said, 'I'm struggling to understand how this happened.'

Bryn nodded. 'Me too.'

When Liam sailed into the kitchen, he didn't at first pick

up on the atmosphere. He dumped his backpack on the floor before heading to the fridge where he swigged orange juice straight from the carton. Wiping his mouth, he turned and that was when he noticed his mum sitting at the breakfast bar.

'What are you still doing here?'

'I'm not going into work today.'

'Oh, right,' he said.

Liam had so far remained on the outer edges of the family skirmish. He had looked genuinely shocked the day before when he had risen from his pit nursing a hangover and Nina had told him that his sister was pregnant. She had known before she questioned him that he could offer no further insight into Scarlett's secret life. They were hard pressed to share a bathroom, they would hardly share secrets. But Liam knew someone who would.

'Will you speak to Eva for me?' she asked.

Nina watched her son squirm. This was not a conversation he wanted to have. 'Mum, I already have. Sorry.'

'And you're sure you can't think of anything – *anything* that might hint at who Scarlett's been involved with?'

She had heard a muffled argument between Liam and Scarlett the night before. He had gone into her room and whatever passed between them was over in a matter of minutes, concluded by the slamming of bedroom doors.

'I'm meeting Eva before school. I'll try again,' he said.

'And Linus. She says it's not him, but it's possible that she's made up this story about a married man to protect him.'

'Whatever she's up to,' Liam said, 'I'm pretty sure it's not with Linus.'

'I'm not afraid to hear the truth, Liam. Do you understand?'

Liam gave a shrug as he grabbed a handful of biscuits and left the house. He hadn't understood what she was getting at and maybe that was a good thing. Bryn, however, knew exactly what she had been implying.

'Why haven't you gone to work, Nina?' he asked after they heard Liam closing the front door.

'Why do you think? I'm hardly going to be able to concentrate on anything else.'

'Is that all?' When Nina didn't answer, he reached the conclusion that Nina was loath to admit. 'You don't trust me to be at home alone with her, do you?'

Rather than look at Bryn, Nina stared at her hands, which were clasped in her lap. Each teardrop that fell on to the back of her hand felt like a miniature explosion ripping her life apart.

'You think it's me?' he asked in utter incredulity.

She wiped her eyes but still couldn't meet his gaze. 'I don't want to be one of those mothers who would rather stick their heads in the sand than see what's right in front of them. I would lay down my life for my children.'

'You think it's me,' Bryn said, no longer a question.

'No, Bryn, I don't!' she cried. 'In my heart, I don't think you're anything but the loving man I fell in love with. But the way she looks at you sometimes, it's like there's a secret between you. It's like you know her better than I do.'

10

Before

Wednesday, 11 November 2015
It was a cold November evening and Bryn was out working, which meant he wasn't responsible for the pungent smell of aftershave that assaulted Nina's senses. She had been in the dining room catching up on some paperwork, and if the smell alone hadn't been enough to give away her son's location, the whispered conversation coming from the kitchen did.

'But why not? You let Eva have it.'

'Yeah, and there's a good reason for that.'

'I doubt it. What's so interesting that you two would need it?'

'And what's so interesting about your boring life?'

'Please, Liam, don't be mean. If you let me have it then I promise to take down the baby pictures I've posted of you on Instagram, the naked ones.'

'You haven't!' hissed Liam.

'Not yet, but . . . '

'Seriously, Scarlett, don't think I couldn't hack into your account in two minutes and cause far more damage to you. Permanent damage.'

'Please,' Scarlett whined. 'I'll love you for ever.'

'Get off me, you freak,' he cried, presumably as Scarlett went in for a killer hug.

'Pleeeease, Liam.'

Her son released a long line of expletives before giving in. 'Give me your bloody phone before I change my mind.'

'And what exactly are you two up to?' Nina asked loud enough to make them both jump.

'Nothing,' one or both of them said.

'Can I see?' Nina asked, extending her hand towards Liam.

Using his height as an advantage, her son raised up Scarlett's phone so she couldn't see the screen and expertly finished whatever he was doing before handing it back to his sister.

'What is it you're sharing anyway?'

Liam was on the move, zipping up his jacket and pulling on a beanie hat. 'It's an app I've been working on.'

'What kind of app?'

'It collects all your metadata and feeds it into your chosen social media platform so you can make multiple status updates.'

Nina didn't have a clue what he was talking about and suspected she would be no further enlightened if she asked him to explain. 'I suppose I'll have to take your word for that,' she said.

Slipping past her, Liam ruffled his mum's hair. 'Don't you worry your little brain about it, Mum.'

She hit him. 'And where do you think you're going?'

'Out.'

'It's Wednesday.'

Liam opened his mouth but thought better of making another smart remark. 'I'll be back by midnight.'

'Eleven.'

Her son muttered something which she took as his agreement. Nina waited until he was at the front door before calling out, 'Give Eva my love.'

When they heard the front door close, Scarlett took it as a sign to make her move.

'Where are you going?'

'Upstairs.'

'Oh.'

The sound of disappointment in Nina's voice made Scarlett hesitate. 'Why?' she asked.

'I thought we might treat ourselves to a movie and a bowl of popcorn. We don't spend enough time together like we used to.'

'That's hardly my fault,' Scarlett said, and then her eyes lit up. 'Can we open a bottle of wine?'

Nina laughed. 'No, and not only because it's a school night.'

'I've got homework to do.'

'I can't believe I'm saying this, but you're spending way too much time locked away in your room lately. I swear the body snatchers have mixed up you and Liam,' she said.

'Yeah, well, you should be careful what you wish for.'

'Please, Scarlett, it'll be like old times,' Nina persisted. Unwilling to take no for an answer, she opened a cupboard and pulled out two large bags of popcorn. 'Sweet or salty?'

'You can choose the popcorn if I can choose the film,' Scarlett said, but before Nina could savour the victory, her daughter added, 'I just need to check my messages. I won't be long.'

Why Scarlett should feel the need to retreat to her room to message her friends, Nina could only imagine, but that was exactly what she had been doing ever since Halloween. If Nina didn't know better, she'd have said Scarlett was being furtive.

'Have you got much homework?' Nina asked when Scarlett joined her in the living room.

'Only a maths paper. Part of my revision schedule.'

Scarlett picked up the remote control and began browsing films. Nina was expecting her to pick some dystopian movie, but her daughter surprised her by suggesting *Of Mice and Men*.

'It's one of my set texts. I didn't want to watch it until I'd read the book and written up my notes, but I'm almost finished anyway.'

'Does this mean you're back to where you should be with schoolwork?'

'I think so.'

'Does Mr Swift think so?'

Scarlett scooped up a handful of popcorn and played with it as she considered her answer. 'I think it's going to take a bit longer before he's pleased. You know what teachers are like. He's said he wants nothing less than A-star grades in every subject.'

'And is that doable?'

'Hopefully. I don't want to let him down. I don't want to let you down either, any more than I already have,' she added quietly.

'You haven't let me down, Scarlett, and I'm not looking

for perfection. All I ask is that you try your best. I'm so proud of you, I've never seen you work so hard.' She bit her lip as she wondered if she should try to get Scarlett to open up. 'But at the same time, I'm worried.'

'About?'

Nina hesitated. 'You don't seem your usual self. You've changed.'

'Have I? How?'

Unsure how to explain something that was no more than a feeling in her gut, Nina said, 'You've been quiet lately and I know it's partly down to me that you're not going out as much but, even so, while you are here I feel like you've disconnected from everyone somehow.'

'I got told off for not studying hard enough, so that's what I've been doing,' Scarlett said.

Nina wasn't convinced. She had caught a look on Scarlett's face once or twice where she seemed to be wrestling with her thoughts, and it most certainly wasn't quadratic equations. 'I know you are – and I'm not complaining, believe me – but I'm worried there might be something else bothering you. Did something happen at Eva's party?'

'Yes, my best friend got off with my brother!'

Refusing to give in, Nina said, 'Which ought to have made you angry and stroppy with Liam, but you've been quiet, Scarlett. It's not the reaction I would have expected, which makes me think . . . '

Scarlett had her arms folded across her chest as she pretended to watch the movie that neither of them had been paying any attention to.

'Did something happen at the party?' Nina asked again.

'I'm thinking back to the conversation we had about you going on the pill and I'm wondering if maybe things have moved on.'

The Scarlett of old would have jumped up to accuse her neurotic mother of being obsessed with sex at this point, but she stayed put.

Taking a chance, Nina pushed a little harder. 'Maybe someone's been pressuring you into doing something you're not ready for. It's still my job to protect you, Scarlett, and I want to help.'

Scarlett held her breath and then released the tension from her body with a sigh. 'You don't have to worry, Mum. I've come to the conclusion that boys really aren't worth the effort.'

Nina only realized she had been tensing too when her chest became so tight she could hardly breathe. Unlike Scarlett, she wasn't ready to let it go so easily.

'You will be sensible, won't you? Don't rush into anything.'

'Honestly, Mum, if you want to worry about anyone sleeping around, worry about Liam.'

'I suppose I am guilty of double standards. I've not been too bothered about what Liam might be getting up to. Are they sleeping together?'

Rather than give a direct answer, Scarlett pulled a face.

'OK, stupid question,' replied Nina. 'Do you think they're having safe sex? Maybe I should buy Liam a job lot of condoms.'

'Oh, God, yes please. Can I be there when you give them to him?'

They were both smiling now and Nina rubbed a hand across her chest. Panic over, for the time being at least.

'I wonder if we should invite Eva over for Christmas,' Nina mused.

'Hmm,' Scarlett said. The idea of spending Christmas with her best friend would have been appealing once upon a time, but instead she pulled a face. 'I don't think her mum and dad would be too happy.'

'Maybe you're right,' Nina said. 'I just thought that, with it being our first proper Christmas together as the Thomas/Carrington family, we might do something special.'

'Why don't you invite Caryn?'

Nina was surprised Scarlett even remembered her stepsister's name. The subject of Bryn's daughter was a sensitive one that they had all been avoiding.

'I'm not sure that's such a good idea. Bryn was really hurt when she didn't come to the wedding. What does it say when your own daughter can't be bothered to even send a card?'

'That doesn't mean we should stop trying. What if I fell out with you? Would you hate me for ever?'

'That's different.'

'No it's not. If we had a horrible argument and one of us moved away, would you cut me out of your life?'

'I would forgive you anything, Scarlett, you're my daughter.'

'And Caryn is Bryn's daughter. He wants to invite her.'

'He's told you that?'

Scarlett looked uncomfortable and grabbed another handful of popcorn. She let the kernels drop slowly through her fingers, before she said, 'Sort of.'

'But you have talked about her?' When Scarlett shrugged, Nina added, 'So why hasn't he mentioned it to me?'

'He thinks you're angry at Caryn. And judging by that mini-strop, you so obviously are. He kind of only mentioned it to me because he wanted to know if I'd have a problem with her staying over. He didn't want to go through all the arguments with you only for me and Liam to make Caryn feel so awkward she would run back home.'

'She wouldn't come anyway,' Nina said, and then gave her daughter a curious look. 'What else did he tell you about her?'

'Not much.'

'You know she has anorexia?' Nina asked, and when Scarlett nodded, she added, 'It's an awful illness, I know, but it's so unfair that Bryn should be the one to shoulder the blame for what happened.'

Bryn had told Nina how his daughter had been dieting on and off since the age of twelve. After he and his ex-wife had split up, Bryn didn't appreciate how self-conscious Caryn was becoming, or that her mum was already concerned.

'He didn't realize that her being so thin was a symptom of something serious and, being a man, he thought he was being ironic when he called her fatty,' she added.

'He called her chubs,' corrected Scarlett.

'He really did talk to you about her, didn't he?' Nina asked. She wasn't sure if she should be pleased that Bryn and her daughter had reached a stage where they could talk openly, or if she should feel jealous.

Scarlett shovelled a handful of popcorn into her mouth and said, 'I'd made some comment about going on a diet and he had a right go at me. What he actually said was that there's no point trying to improve on perfection.' She had bits of corn stuck in her teeth when she smiled at her mum.

Nina smiled too. 'He's terrified of making the same mistake twice,' she said. After releasing a sigh, she added, 'Oh, I don't know, Scarlett. From what I've heard, Caryn's still going through a tough time. If she did come to see us, what if it only deepens the rift between them? I'm worried they'd hurt each other and wreck Christmas in the process. I need to speak to him, don't I?'

Scarlett said nothing; the answer was obvious.

Thursday, 12 November 2015

Nina and Bryn were in the kitchen eating the evening meal her husband had lovingly prepared, while Liam and Scarlett had grabbed their plates and disappeared upstairs. They had started married life with such good intentions of bringing everyone together at meal times, and Bryn had gone as far as redecorating the dining room, which had previously been part home office, part dumping ground. Unfortunately, Nina hadn't factored in the amount of nagging required to get them all around the table, and for once her children's cave-dweller mentality suited her.

'Why didn't you tell me you wanted to invite Caryn over for Christmas?'

Bryn didn't look fazed by the question. It was as if he had been expecting it. 'It was only an idea I'd been mulling over.'

'But you do want to invite her?'

'Would you mind?'

'I don't want to see you hurt, that's all.'

Bryn put down his fork and reached for his wife's hand to give it a squeeze. 'And chances are I will get hurt, but I'm not going to let her snub me again if that's what you're worried about. I'd like to go and visit her first so I can extend the invitation personally. I know I'll probably say the wrong thing, like I always do, and we'll be back to square one, but . . . '

'But you shouldn't stop trying,' Nina said, surprised that she should be repeating her daughter's sage advice. When had Scarlett become so mature?

'Does that mean you'd be OK with me asking her?'

'Asking her is the easy part, Bryn,' Nina said. 'If you mean will I be OK if it goes wrong, then no, I can't say I will, but you're not exactly going to find it easy either.'

Bryn had been chasing a piece of fish around his plate and it had almost disintegrated. 'It could be worse,' he said. '*Someone* could suggest we invite Eva, in which case we'd be spending Christmas playing referee between Scarlett and Liam.'

'I can see I'm going to have to watch you and Scarlett,' she said.

'Speak of the devil.'

Scarlett glided into the room in a flutter of pink and black satin. The dressing gown was wide enough to wrap around her twice and Nina supposed she ought to be glad that it was covering up her youthful body, even though the contours were enough to fill Nina with envy. 'I bet that doesn't look as good on me.'

'What?' Scarlett asked when she realized the comment had been directed at her. She had brought her dishes down and was leaning over to put them in the dishwasher.

'My dressing gown,' Nina said, 'with the emphasis on *my*.'

'Sorry, it's just that mine's really short and you moan about me parading around the house half-naked. I thought you'd be pleased.'

Scowling, Nina turned to Bryn, who was doing his best to ignore them both. 'I bought that to take away on our honeymoon, if we ever manage to have one.'

'And we will,' Bryn promised. 'You paid for the wedding, so it's only right that I cough up for the honeymoon. In fact, I'm planning on working extra hard in the run-up to Christmas so I can afford to whisk you away.'

'I don't think you'll be as productive as you were last year,' Nina said with a sheepish smile as she recalled their fateful meeting.

'Ah, yes, last year was quite exceptional.'

'Please,' muttered Scarlett under her breath.

'At the very least,' Bryn said loudly for his stepdaughter's benefit, 'I'll be able to stretch to a mini-break – one without the children, perhaps?'

'I'm *not* a child.'

Ignoring her daughter, Nina added, 'I could always ask Sarah if we could use her country lodge in the Lake District.'

There was a sharp intake of breath from Scarlett. 'You can't use something that's been bought with blood money.'

Nina looked from an equally puzzled Bryn to her daughter. 'Blood money?'

With her hand on her hip, Scarlett said, 'Do you have any idea what they're up to?'

'I'm afraid you'll have to give me a bit more information to work with.'

'Sarah and Miles are tearing up the countryside and killing old people as they go.'

All worries about her daughter growing up too soon were forgotten as Nina realized her little girl was still young enough to throw a tantrum. 'Nope, still as clear as mud.'

Scarlett huffed, then said, 'That new development they've been going on about. They're going to build houses on a field right next to this old lady who's dying of cancer. She'll end up spending her last days on earth watching them put up ugly houses.'

'Sarah's not mentioned anything to me about killing off old ladies.'

'Well she'd hardly go around shouting about it.'

'And how did you hear about it? Please don't say there's some campaign against them on Facebook.'

'No, but that might be an idea,' Scarlett said, and was temporarily confused when her mum waited for her to say more. 'Oh, right, yeah, it was mentioned at school.'

'I knew there had been planning objections, but nothing else. Sarah would be upset if she knew about this,' Nina said, and when Bryn raised an eyebrow, she added, 'She does have a heart, even if it is hidden beneath a thick skin.'

'Will you speak to her?' Scarlett asked. 'You have to stop them, Mum. Please.'

'I'll tell her, Scarlett, but I'm not sure what good it'll do. Sarah's invested a lot of money in that project and she wouldn't be able to pull out easily even if she wanted to. She might be able to make life easier for this woman, though. Do you know her name?'

'Erm, Mrs Swift, probably.'

'As in your Mr Swift?'

'Yes, except, thinking about it,' Scarlett said, pausing to bite her lip, 'her name wouldn't be Swift because it's his mother-in-law.'

'I could always ask your Mr Swift.'

'No, don't do that! I shouldn't have said anything really.'

Having abandoned his meal, Bryn was resting his chin on his hands as he followed the exchange. 'That would be your daughter interfering again,' he said, and gave Scarlett a wink.

'Yes, she's getting good at that,' replied Nina. 'All right, leave it with me, Scarlett, and I'll see what I can do.'

'Thanks, Mum.'

'If you really want to thank me, you can take off my dressing gown,' Nina said as Scarlett swept past her.

Scarlett stopped and pulled at the black satin belt that had been tied in a bow. Before the dressing gown could fall away, Nina said, 'Don't you dare, Scarlett Carrington. And when I say cover up, next time wear your onesie.'

Sunday, 13 December 2015

The moment the cobwebs from Halloween had been swept away, the florist shop had been immersed in glittering layers of artificial snow, but at home, Nina put off decking the halls with boughs of holly until mid-December. As she set to work, she thought how different it was going to be this year, especially if Bryn wasn't to be the only new addition.

He had set off for Wales the day before, and after an overnight stay with his brother, he was meeting his daughter for lunch. Hopefully, she would accept his invitation, but whatever the outcome, Nina was determined to transform the house and make his return home warm and welcoming.

'Are you sure you don't have somewhere else to be?' she asked Scarlett, who had more tinsel on her than the tree she was supposedly decorating. 'Like sleeping off a hangover?'

'I told you, I didn't drink last night. Me and Clara were practising for our French oral.'

Nina scrutinized Scarlett's face; if her daughter was lying, she was getting very good at it. Nina had only vaguely heard of this Clara person, who was presumably a replacement for Eva now that her best friend was otherwise engaged. And with Bryn away, Nina had gone against her better judgement and allowed Scarlett to stay over at her mystery friend's house. In theory, it had been so she wouldn't have to worry about Scarlett getting home, but she had worried anyway. It would seem that Scarlett was quickly making up for lost time as far as her social life was concerned, and it left Nina in two minds as to which version of her daughter she preferred, the studious hermit or the party girl. She wished there was a middle ground and her only comfort was that Mr Swift had phoned to say he was pleased with her current performance and didn't think further revision lessons were necessary. And if Mr Swift was happy then who was she to complain?

'I might as well help, because I've got nothing else to do,' Scarlett complained. She tried to pull a sad face but the effect was lost with the flickering fairy lights draped around her neck.

'Great,' Nina muttered.

'Can I have some of that?'

Nina had made herself a mulled wine to help along the Christmas spirit. 'Were you outside this morning, hanging up lights?'

'I would have helped if I'd been here.'

'Oh really? What's been your excuse every other year?' Nina asked, only to roll her eyes. 'Oh, for goodness' sake, take it. I'll make another.'

Scarlett took a sip of the proffered drink and pulled a face. 'Yuk, it tastes like medicine. Can I have something else?'

'Such as?'

'A gin and lemonade?'

'Erm, let me think about that,' Nina said. 'No.'

'Why?'

'Because you're fifteen years old.'

The child demanding to be treated like an adult flounced out of the living room and came back two minutes later with a strawberry milkshake. If she had added a dash of alcohol, Nina decided she was better off not knowing. She didn't want Bryn returning from what might be a fraught meeting with his daughter to be confronted by an equally tense atmosphere at home.

While Scarlett attacked the unfortunate spruce with tinsel and baubles, Nina set to work making a centrepiece. It was a complicated arrangement of pale green and silver foliage with bleached pine cones and bright red berry lights. Unfortunately, she had made the fatal error of not testing the lights until the arrangement was complete.

'Damn, are there any spare batteries left?' she asked her daughter, who had been tasked with firing up all the annoying singing snowmen and prancing reindeer.

Armed with new batteries, Nina pricked her fingers as she battled with lethal holly leaves, only to realize the problem was a loose wire rather than the power pack. She cursed herself for not checking before she had started. She would need to dismantle the arrangement in order to replace the entire light unit.

'When's lunch?'

Her son might not have been on a sleepover like his sister, but he had arrived home only a few hours before Scarlett, and this was his first appearance of the day.

'Lunch was an hour ago. I did shout and assumed your mumbled response meant you didn't want anything.'

'OK, I'll have some now.'

'All the soup's gone,' Scarlett said, turning her back on Liam before his scowl had fully formed.

'I could make you some cheese on toast while you take a look at this for me?'

'It's a holly bush,' Liam said, refusing to take the offending article from his mother.

'There's a loose wire. You're good with gadgets.'

When Nina offered it a second time, Liam had no choice but to take the display or risk being stabbed in the chest by dozens of prickly leaves.

'But I'm no good with wires and stuff.'

Nina ignored him and when she returned from the kitchen ten minutes later, the centrepiece was upside down on the coffee table with a miniature screwdriver sticking out of it.

'I can't do it,' he said. 'I've got blurred vision and my head's banging.'

'Serves you right for rolling in drunk at such a ridiculous

112

hour. You should have followed Scarlett's example. She can be out all night and still come home fresh as a daisy.'

Liam took a bite of toast, and with strings of cheese hanging from his mouth turned to Scarlett and asked, 'You were out? Who with?'

'One of my friends who you're not sleeping with,' Scarlett muttered.

'Clara,' Nina offered helpfully.

'Hmm, that's strange,' Liam said, assuming a well-practised tone that feigned innocence while knowing he would be getting his sister into trouble. 'Clara spent most of the night at Eva's until she threw up and her mum had to come and get her. I hope she was feeling better when she met up with you.'

Nina could feel the heat rising in her cheeks and it had nothing to do with the mulled wine. 'Care to explain?'

Scarlett spun around so fast that the tinsel she had been hanging almost pulled the tree down on top of her. 'What is this? Do I have to give you a list of everyone I see and everywhere I go now?'

'You said you were with Clara and you clearly weren't. Who were you with all night, Scarlett?'

'I didn't see Linus last night,' Liam said, sounding only half-interested in the conversation as he began pulling more strings of cheese from his toast.

'Fine, I was with Linus! And before you start on me, we were revising,' she said, making the last word stretch out to drive the point home. 'I only stayed because Bryn wasn't around to give me a lift; there's no other reason, Mum, so don't go trying to have *that* conversation with me again!'

Rather than launching into a debate, Nina was left dumb-struck and it was Bryn, appearing unnoticed behind her, who broke the tension. 'So what am I getting the blame for now?'

'Nothing,' Nina said, 'Scarlett will be taking full responsibility for her actions. I took it on trust that she was with who she said she was. Well, now I've learned my lesson. Don't even bother asking to stay over with a friend again, because the answer will be no.'

While mother and daughter glared at each other, Bryn shook his head. 'I've had a lovely time in Llangollen, thanks very much for asking. I can't say I'm getting on nearly as well with Caryn as you are with Scarlett but, you know, early days.'

Nina blinked as her mind switched between the thorny issue of her daughter's behaviour to the more prickly one of her husband's relationship with his only child. She went over and cupped his weary face in her hands. 'I'm so, so, sorry,' she whispered. 'I wanted everything to be perfect for when you came home. How was it?' When Bryn pulled a face that made him age a full decade, she added, 'That bad?'

'I got over the threshold,' he said. 'She even made me a cuppa, but it was still hot when I was asked to leave.'

'What happened?'

'I overthought things as usual,' he confessed. 'She looked really well, Nina, much better than I was expecting. I wanted to tell her how she suited having more meat on her bones, but I didn't,' he added quickly. 'I know I would have been accused of suggesting she was fat again, so all I said was that she looked good.'

'That doesn't sound too bad.'

Bryn shook his head. 'Caryn accused me of being obsessed with how she looked, and how I never thought about the person she was inside.'

'It sounds like there wasn't anything you could have done,' Nina said. 'She's still angry with you.'

Rubbing his eyes, which looked tired and sore, he said, 'I was really hoping for a breakthrough.'

'I'll get you a beer,' Scarlett said, putting her hand on Bryn's shoulder ever so briefly as she went past.

'Thanks, love.'

Bryn dropped down on to the sofa next to Liam and released a sigh that was part exhaustion, part defeat. It wasn't a sound Nina ever wanted to hear from him again. 'Do you want something to eat?' she asked.

'No, thanks. I grabbed a sandwich on my way back.' He leant forward to inspect the upturned centrepiece which Liam had all but trashed. 'What's wrong with this?'

'The wiring's knackered,' Liam said.

'Do you want me to have a go?'

'Could you?' Nina said, hoping that even a minor victory fixing lights might brighten her husband's mood.

Bryn unscrewed the back plate, disconnected a couple of wires and, using his teeth, exposed bright silver wire from beneath the green plastic coating. 'Technically,' he said to Liam, 'that's not the way to do it.'

'Do you know your way around electrics then?'

'Any idiot could rewire this,' Bryn said, and in a matter of moments the lights were on.

'I did a lot of the maintenance myself when I had the printing factory,' he told an impressed Liam.

'If you're that good, why don't you set yourself up as

an engineer or something? Must be better than spending half the night driving drunks home.'

'Because,' Bryn said, 'I don't have the proper qualifications. In fact, I don't really have any qualifications, except my driving licence. Me and my brother were too eager to set up our printing business to bother with school, you see.'

'But it could have worked out,' Liam said.

'And I suppose it did for a while, but, who knows, with more of an education behind us, we might have stood a better chance of keeping the business going. When we lost it, I had nothing to fall back on except an in-depth knowledge of obsolete printing equipment.'

Turning to his mum, who had been holding her breath, Liam said, 'You know I was only messing when I said I didn't want to go to uni?'

Nina gave a strangled cry, but Bryn silenced her with a warning glare. 'Quit while you're ahead, Nina.'

After taking a long, cleansing breath, she managed to say, 'Do you have a shortlist of universities and courses you want to apply for?'

'Sort of.'

'Right, priority number one; we get your application and personal statement and whatever else you need to do sorted by New Year.'

'I don't have to do anything until the end of January,' Liam was saying as Scarlett returned to the room.

She handed Bryn a tray with a bottle of beer, a glass and a bowl of his favourite olives. 'It looks like you and me have been shoved to the back of the queue again as far as Mum's attention goes,' she muttered to him.

'You,' Nina said, 'should be glad I've got other distractions.'

Scarlett

I remember Mum making this big announcement about having a boyfriend. She'd been acting weird for weeks, so I wasn't that surprised, not until she followed it up by saying they were getting married. I seriously thought she was having a mental breakdown and we would all be stuck with some psycho. No way could I understand how she got carried away like that and, if I'm honest, I was pissed off that she wanted to be with him all the time. Apparently I wasn't good enough company for her any more, which is why I spent most of the summer over at Eva's. I didn't realize back then what it was like to fall madly and deeply in love. I do now. I know exactly how she felt.

It was like an obsession, for both of us. From the moment he'd watched me putting on my lip gloss and said I would get him into trouble, we'd both known what was going to happen. There was nothing we could have done to stop it. OK, he was married, but he told me it had been a big mistake because me and him were soulmates. I could talk to him like no one else I'd ever known, and he told me things he couldn't tell her, especially his fantasies.

Whenever Eva droned on about my idiot brother being the love of her life, I'm sure she thought I'd be jealous. But what I had was so much more, and the problem was I wanted more. I was thinking about him every second of every day and I wanted us to take more chances, but he was way too careful – or maybe not, given how things turned out. Getting that phone app off Liam was so the right thing to do.

'Are you sure this will work?' he'd asked when I first told him about it.

'I've set it up on my phone and, yeah, it really does work.'

'Show me.'

'Send me a message,' I said with a mischievous smile and then watched him type it out.

What colour are your knickers?

When he pressed send, my phone beeped, but instead of the message he'd sent, it was one from some PPI firm telling me I could claim a gazillion pounds in compensation.

'So how do you see the proper message?'

I tapped in a pass code and there it was, but when I closed the message down again, it went back to showing the dodgy details. My brother really isn't as stupid as he looks.

'I'm impressed.'

After sending him the installation file Liam had used and setting it to encrypt all our messages, I sent him a reply. I watched while he read the message from Vodafone offering an upgrade and waited until my message got the reaction I'd wanted. He gasped and then laughed.

'This photo won't appear anywhere else on my phone, will it?'

118

'It won't let you copy it into your photo album and it won't let you forward it on to anyone else. It's perfect.'

'Not quite. Anyone checking phone records will see how often we contact each other.'

'Who'd bother checking?'

'I'm married, remember,' he said.

'OK, not a problem,' I said, because Liam wasn't the only one who was good with technology. 'It can piggyback off other apps too, you know, like Messenger, which only shows up as data usage.'

'I have to say, that brother of yours has thought of everything. He could make a fortune out of something like this, but he probably knows that already.'

To be honest, the comment annoyed me. This wasn't about bloody Liam. It was about the photo I'd sent him.

'What?' he asked, and that's when I knew he'd been teasing me. 'Oh, the photograph.'

I'm pretty good at taking selfies, but this wasn't one I was going to stick on Instagram, if you know what I mean. I was lying on my bed wearing Mum's dressing gown. The gown was open.

He let out a soft groan, and I leant over the table to kiss him. It looked like something was making it difficult for him to move towards me, not that he was going to anyway. He was too scared of someone barging in and catching us.

'You're getting too hard to resist, Scarlett Carrington,' he said. 'Oh, to hell with it. Come here.'

After we kissed, I was just as desperate as he was. 'I want us to spend the night together,' I whispered.

'No, we can't,' he told me. 'We have to be careful. If we were caught it would taint what we have and hurt the *people we love. Think of your mum, Scarlett. She wants so much for you, and so do I. You're capable of so much and I don't want to hold you back.'*

'You're not.'

'And that's how it has to stay, and not only until you're sixteen, but at least another couple of years after that. We have to wait until you're an adult in every sense of the word. Only then can we let the world know how we feel.'

'But that's like for ever, and I can't wait that long. All I'm asking for is one night. I love you.'

It was the first time I'd told him I loved him and I think I shocked myself as much as him. I'd known for a while, but I thought he'd think I was childish if I'd said it too soon.

I can't begin to explain what it felt like when he looked into my eyes and said, 'And I love you too.'

I'm not ashamed of what we did or how we feel, and I refuse to feel guilty. We couldn't help ourselves, and Mum of all people should know what that's like. She put herself first once and all I'm doing is following her example.

In the end, we only got to spend one night together because my stupid brother snitched on me, but I haven't given up, you know. I'll wait forever if I have to.

11

The Accusations

Vikki's legs felt wobbly as she got dressed and made her way downstairs. She could hear familiar piggy snorts coming from the TV along with Freya's giggles as she slipped past the living room and headed for the kitchen. She hadn't been expecting to find Rob in there, and at first he didn't hear her come in. He was leaning against the kitchen counter with his forehead resting against a cupboard door.

'Rob?'

He gave a start and ran his fingers through his hair as he turned towards her.

'Are you all right?'

'I've got a banging headache,' he said tightly, and there was certainly pain in his voice. There were dark circles beneath his puffy eyes that mirrored her own, although she had managed to conceal hers with makeup.

'Do you think you should stay off? You look awful,' she said.

Rob pinched the bridge of his nose. 'No, I need to be in school today. I'll go and have a shower to clear my head.'

'There's something wrong, isn't there?' she said, and felt

sickening dread twist her insides. 'You've been off all weekend.'

'It's nothing more than the usual problems of too much work, too many kids playing up and too much pressure on us all to perform. I'm starting to dread Mondays, but I'll be fine once I get myself moving.'

'How about I make breakfast?' she said, swallowing back the saliva filling her mouth as she fought a wave of nausea. 'What do you fancy?'

Rob's lips cut a thin line across his face, but gradually his features relaxed into a smile. 'Only you.'

Vikki's heart clenched, and it was a distinctly unpleasant feeling. She had always felt secure in the knowledge that theirs was a perfect partnership. She had never doubted her husband's devotion and his comment should have made her feel warm inside, but she felt oddly cold.

'I wonder if Scarlett will be in school today?' she asked.

Rob turned away. 'You shouldn't be worrying about her. She's not our problem.'

'But still, I can't help wondering what Nina's going through. She'll want to know who the father of the baby is. Did I tell you Scarlett says he's married?' she asked, knowing she hadn't. When Rob turned to look at her, she added, 'She thinks he's going to look after her, which means . . . ' Her words trailed off, because she didn't know what it meant.

Rob raised an eyebrow. 'What?' he demanded.

Vikki could feel her cheeks warming, convinced that Rob was about to realize what wicked suspicions had been keeping her awake all night. In panic, she said, 'There's a suggestion it's someone close to home, like maybe her stepdad.'

'Seriously, Vikki, since when did you start paying attention to malicious gossip? This isn't one of your soaps. Scarlett's bound to be covering up for some boy, and if her mum has any sense, she'll march her straight to the doctor's and get things sorted. Scarlett's a good student and as long as people don't build this up into something it's not, she could get through this relatively unscathed.'

'So you don't think it's Bryn?'

Rob was shaking his head as he stepped past her. 'I'd rather not think about it at all. And no, I don't want breakfast. I need to make an early start at school so I can help those students who haven't decided to throw away their lives.'

When Rob went upstairs, he left behind yet more questions that Vikki didn't have, or want the answers to.

12

Before

Monday, 14 December 2015

While Nina was busy getting everyone in the festive mood, Christmas was the furthest thing from Vikki's mind as she made up her mum's bed with fresh linen. She took a deep breath of air laced with fabric conditioner, a pleasant change from the nastier odours that had invaded her mum's room over the last few days. Elaine was fighting back after her third and most gruelling round of chemo so far, and Vikki was becoming adept at splitting her time between home and what was becoming a second home. She couldn't have done it without Rob's forbearance, and thankfully he had gradually accepted that once every three weeks she needed to stay with her mum.

Gathering up the dirty linen, Vikki opened the window just a crack to let in fresh air and refused to lift her gaze to the landscape that would be ravaged by developers in the New Year. She kept telling herself that there were worse things that could happen, but it was a thought that brought little comfort.

Returning downstairs, she found her mum sitting at the

kitchen table. It was the first time in three days Elaine had felt well enough to get up, and Vikki's next challenge was to stop her from overexerting herself. Usually, Elaine wasn't happy unless she was doing something. Rest, she said, was the reward earned after a hard day's toil, which only proved how desperately ill she must have felt to spend days in bed.

'How are you?' Vikki asked, hoping against hope that her mum didn't feel as awful as she looked.

Elaine had complained of being overweight in recent years but the weight she had lost since her diagnosis had the effect of making her appear much older than her years. Her features were gaunt and although she hadn't lost all her hair, the remaining wisps weren't enough to cover her scalp. She had acquired a wig which she wore for trips out, but preferred colourful scarves indoors. Today, however, she had put all her strength into the small matter of getting out of bed and had grabbed the first thing to hand. The grey beanie hat matched her complexion.

'I feel like I've been kicked by a horse,' Elaine said, 'but on the upside, I don't feel like I've been run over by a bulldozer like I did yesterday.'

The comment served as a reminder that it wasn't only Vikki who had been wondering about the view from her mum's bedroom window. The planning application for the new development had been approved, and Sarah Tavistock had wasted no time. Even though Elaine hadn't been well enough to get up and see what was going on outside, she had heard the gate opening and closing as one vehicle after another came to inspect the site. There had been a small digger at one point and Vikki had been horrified to think they could be starting work so soon.

'Do you think you'll be able to eat something?' she asked.

'Maybe later, when Freya's home from nursery.'

'All right. I'll go and put this washing on and then nip out to the cottages to open some windows. They could do with a good airing,' Vikki said, with a confidence she didn't feel. In assuming the role of carer, Vikki had taken to stealing her mum's lines, but it was only playacting.

'Do you want me to help?' Elaine asked, her shoulders tensing as if she were about to stand, but that act alone was enough to sap her strength and her body quickly sagged.

'It's OK,' Vikki said, her voice cracking. She wanted her mum back more than anything.

'I worry that you're taking on too much. If I'd known how useless I was going to be, I'd have taken the financial hit and cancelled the New Year bookings as well, but it's too late now, they'd never be able to make alternative arrangements,' she said before her daughter could challenge her. Her guests would arrive shortly after Elaine's next and final round of chemo, and neither were under any illusions that it was going to be easy. 'But at least they're regulars. I'm sure they'll understand if I let standards slip a little this year.'

'I'll do my best not to let you down.'

Elaine's eyes glistened. 'I know, and I wasn't suggesting otherwise, but you will tell me if you're struggling, won't you? I can always ask Lesley to come over more, or hire extra help.'

'We'll manage.'

Elaine slipped her fingers beneath the beanie hat and scratched her head. 'And you would tell me if there were any other problems, wouldn't you? It's just that I was surprised Rob didn't call in over the weekend. Is everything all right between you two?'

'Yes, of course it is. He's busy with school stuff, that's all.'

'Why don't you meet him for an early lunch and get some colour into those cheeks,' she said with a knowing smile.

Vikki pulled at the unkempt curls which had fallen loose from the elastic band she had quickly used to tie her hair back earlier that morning. 'Because I look a mess,' she said, 'and besides, now you're up and about, I'll be off home soon.'

Before Elaine could respond, Vikki hurried into the utility room. Trying not to think about how much she was missing Rob, she concentrated on loading the washing machine. With one job less, she slipped on her mum's parka and a pair of boots before heading out into the biting wind. She kept her head down as she followed the path to the front of the house and didn't immediately notice the Range Rover that had pulled on to the drive and was parking up outside one of the holiday cottages.

The driver, who was in her forties and immaculately dressed, was someone Vikki recognized even before she had rolled down the tinted window. She had imagined confronting Sarah Tavistock countless times, but for the moment she was lost for words. 'Oh,' she said.

'I wanted a word with Mrs Seymour. Is she in?'

'She's not well.'

Sarah shifted uncomfortably. 'Is there anyone else I could speak to?'

From her tone of voice, Sarah was in search of an adult

to speak to, and had clearly discounted Vikki. As well as not washing her hair, Vikki hadn't applied any makeup, having long since abandoned all hope of competing with the other mums at the school gates. There were far more important things to worry about. 'Can I help? I'm her daughter.'

'Oh,' Sarah said, taken aback. 'You wouldn't be Mrs Swift, would you?'

'Yes.'

'Gosh, I never expected you to be so young. Can we talk?'

More determined than ever to prove that she was not a child, Vikki led Sarah to the smaller of the two cottages. It was an open-plan design with split levels to accommodate a bedroom above the kitchen with a view over the living room. Ignoring the more comfortable seats, Vikki ushered Sarah to the small breakfast table. She didn't bother to put the heating on and kept her coat fastened. Her nemesis was twice her age, she was richer, more experienced and under present circumstances, had more power over Vikki's life than she should, but Vikki wasn't about to be intimidated – or at least, she wasn't going to let it show that she was. 'I don't want to leave Mum for long.'

'That's perfectly understandable,' Sarah said. She drew a deep breath before adding, 'I know you and your mum feel very strongly about the houses I'm building, and I should say at the outset that I'm not here to be persuaded to give up on those plans. I've invested too much in this project to abandon it now. Neither would I want to.'

'So what do you want?'

'To all intents and purposes, we're about to become neighbours, at least until the works are complete.'

'It's my mum who lives here, not me,' Vikki said. She had no interest in making friends with this woman. There would be no trips over the road with pots of tea and bacon butties to keep the builders happy.

'I know, and I can only imagine how difficult it must be for you both right now.'

Vikki was unimpressed. Sarah Tavistock was obviously well-informed, but her words of sympathy were worthless. If the woman had any decency, she would have withdrawn the planning application.

'I wanted to come over and at least talk to you about the development. I thought it might help allay some of your fears,' Sarah continued. 'As you'll know, we've been working with the planners to minimise the impact on the surrounding neighbourhood. We've agreed to move the main entrance road to the west side, which should be less disruptive. This has meant shifting a couple of the houses – I could show you a plan, if you'd like?'

'I've seen a copy, thanks.'

'Good,' Sarah said. She was doing her best to sound at ease, but her fidgeting fingers gave her away. 'I know your mum is used to seeing green fields from her doorstep, and that's going to be a loss, but we've agreed to plant trees along the perimeter of the estate to screen the new houses from view. The planners have specified the general type of tree, but we can choose the species and I thought that you—'

Vikki's heart raced as she felt a swell of anger. 'Is that how you think you can win us over, by letting us pick out trees? Look, I'm sure you mean well, but you're wasting your time offering olive branches, or any other species of tree you might choose. It's not going to make up for turning the field into a housing estate.'

Rather than take offence, Sarah simply raised an eyebrow as if she were bemused by this childish outburst. Vikki tried to imagine herself in the middle of a business meeting and pulled back her shoulders. 'Can I just ask, why did you need to build houses over there anyway when there are so many sites in town in desperate need of development?'

'Yes, I know, and the lists you provided in your objection letter were certainly thorough. You have a good eye for potential investments.'

Hating herself for feeling a swell of pride, Vikki said, 'I worked in an estate agents for a while, and my dad was an architect so I learnt a lot from him. I helped with the designs for this place.'

Sarah cast a critical eye over the cottage with its reclaimed oak beams and flagstone flooring. 'I'm impressed,' she said. 'And if you really want to know why I picked the site, it's because I was after something on a grander scale than my usual scatter-gun approach.'

'So you can be lady of the manor?'

Vikki blushed at her own rudeness, but Sarah smiled as if it had been compliment. 'I suspect you might be right. My father was a family butcher with the emphasis on the word family. I inherited the business, but carving up dead animals was never going to be my vocation in life. I much prefer breathing life into new projects, and I get the feeling that's something you might appreciate.'

'Not when it's right on my doorstep,' Vikki said, fighting against Sarah's charm offensive.

'Your mum's doorstep,' Sarah corrected. She was tapping her fingers gently against the surface of the table as she scrutinized Vikki's face. 'I'm sorry, I keep looking at you and thinking we've met before. Did you go to school with my daughter Charlotte, by any chance?'

'We were in gym club together,' Vikki said flatly.

'That's it! My goodness, you haven't changed a bit.'

Vikki felt her jaw clench. She would have been thirteen at most the last time Sarah had seen her.

'Charlotte was in awe of you,' Sarah continued. 'You could have gone far, but you gave it up, as I recall.'

'It took up too much of my time.'

'Yes, it was the same for Charlotte, although she never had anything like your ability. She's at university now,' Sarah added. 'Where did you go?'

'I left school after my A levels,' Vikki said, playing with the ring on her wedding finger.

Sarah shrugged. 'It's not for everyone, and I've managed perfectly well without some fancy qualification. Some things can't be taught; you either have an eye for property development or you don't – wouldn't you agree?'

Rising to the challenge, Vikki said, 'If you were looking for something bigger, did you never consider the old Ellison House?'

When Sarah looked none the wiser, Vikki added, 'It's a little bit further out of town, but no more than a five-minute drive from here. It used to be an adventure playground.'

'Of course; yes, I know the place. I never went there myself – it was known as a bit of death-trap. As I recall,

131

some poor boy broke his leg and they closed the place down.'

Vikki decided against confessing that the boy in question was Rob; their discussion was getting far too intimate for her liking and that wouldn't do at all. 'It's a beautiful house, or at least it could be.' She was about to offer ideas on how the property could be split into luxury apartments, but managed to stop herself.

'Do you still work for an estate agent? I'm surprised I haven't dealt with you before now.'

'No, I left to have my daughter, but it's something I might go back to now she's started nursery,' Vikki said as if it were a simple choice she could make on the spur of the moment.

'You should, you have a lot of untapped potential,' Sarah said. 'And unfortunately, so does the new site. Even if I were to consider mothballing the development, which I'm not, I'm sure I don't need to tell you that the land would be sold with planning permission. Someone would build on it eventually.' There was a sharp intake of breath. 'Sorry, I didn't think. I suppose a delay would be better than nothing, if it meant your mum wouldn't have to see new houses blight her view.' She gave Vikki a sympathetic look before adding, 'If it's not too intrusive a question, how long . . . ?'

She let her words trail off as if it were obvious what she was alluding to, but Vikki was momentarily confused, and then shocked. 'You mean, how long does she have left to live?'

Sarah nodded.

'She's not *dying*.'

Sarah's features paled. 'Oh, good Lord, I'm so sorry. I thought . . . I was told . . . '

132

'You were told what?' Vikki asked, while a frightened voice in her head wondered if this woman knew more about her mum's condition than she did. The Tavistocks had plenty of connections. Had they been able to access her mum's medical records to check how much trouble she might cause? Was this another secret her mum and Rob were protecting her from? Or, for that matter, were the doctors hiding the truth from her mum?

'I was obviously misinformed. I'm so, so sorry. I didn't mean to upset you. My friend's daughter goes to Sedgefield High, she must have picked up on the gossip and got it completely wrong. I should have remembered what a terrible rumour mill a school can be.'

'Mum is having cancer treatment, but she will beat it,' Vikki said firmly. She wished she could be angry with this woman, but Sarah looked mortified.

'I've made a complete mess of this. I came over with the intention of building bridges, but I've probably made things ten times worse.'

When they parted company, Vikki didn't know what to make of Sarah and was left feeling confused. It would have been so much easier if she hadn't visited at all. From a distance, Vikki could hate the cruel and callous property developer. In person, Sarah was something else entirely; she was someone Vikki reluctantly admired.

Friday, 25 December 2015
There had been moments over the last week when Vikki had caught Rob wincing as Freya raced around the house with boundless energy, and she wondered if he might be

missing his periods of solitude. She would be glad if he was; it would make leaving him again so much easier when her mum had her final round of chemo, scheduled between Christmas and New Year. It was something that Vikki certainly had mixed feelings about. The end of the year would mark the end of her mum's treatment plan, after which they would have an anxious wait to discover if it had worked – or not.

With so much uncertainty, Vikki refused to look to the future. She had lost her nerve, and if she had a plan at all, it was not to rush into any decisions. It was hard enough dealing with one day at a time; the idea of mapping out the rest of her life was beyond her, whether that was the life of a mother with a growing brood, or a motivated professional who would be an asset to any willing employer who would have her. Even Christmas, normally her favourite time of the year, was proving to be a challenge.

'Sorry for not helping more,' Rob whispered in her ear as they watched Freya unwrap her gifts on Christmas morning.

'I ordered most of it online, and had it delivered to Mum's,' she confessed.

'Including those?'

Rob tipped his head towards the pair of trainers she had given him. He hadn't been jogging for years, but running seemed to help relieve the stresses of school and family life and there was no doubt he had been under pressure of late.

'I could hardly ignore all those hints you were dropping, now could I?'

He kissed her neck. 'If only you'd made it so easy for me,' he said. 'I didn't have a clue what to get you.'

Vikki had been dropping hints about needing to get in shape and tone up her body. She had wanted a gym membership so she could join some of the other mums for a workout while Freya was in nursery, keeping fit and making friends at the same time. The hints had been far too subtle for Rob, however, and he had bought her silk lingerie that was a size larger than she wanted to be. She supposed she should be thankful he hadn't bought her some granny knickers.

'You did pretty well,' she said.

He traced a finger down the neckline of her pink silk robe and across her collarbone. 'I might be able to do better, though,' he said with a smile.

Before she could ask, he had pulled a small box from his pocket, and she squealed with excitement. Vikki shouldn't have been surprised that Rob would play a trick on her and hold back on the best present; he liked catching her off guard. And she wasn't fooled by the jewellery box: it was still big enough to conceal a gym membership card. When he opened the box to reveal a white gold pendant with a pretty cluster of sparkling diamonds, she felt a stab of disappointment which Rob didn't deserve.

'Oh, Rob, you shouldn't have, it's beautiful,' she said, recovering quickly.

Rob took the necklace from the box and fastened it around her neck before Vikki had time to look at it properly, so she had to rely on his description as he said, 'I know it's only small but, when I saw it, I knew it was perfect. Each diamond represents each of us. Me, you, Freya and even that last little one. A new baby that's still a twinkle in her mummy's eye.'

His words were choked with emotion and he had to look away. 'But not for ever,' she said, her guilt deepening. Was she denying Rob his deepest desire while she prevaricated?

When Rob turned back there was such an intensity in his eyes. 'You being away so much has only made me appreciate you more. I keep thinking of that first time we brought Freya home; it made our family complete and a new baby is going to make it so much stronger. I can't wait,' he said, but gave her the saddest look when he added, 'And that was not meant as a hint, by the way. I will wait, as long as you want.'

As if to prove the point, he left Vikki to her thoughts while he helped Freya unwrap another present. Vikki played nervously with the four small diamonds weighing heavily around her neck. 'Maybe we should think about it once Mum's got her results.'

Freya was perched on Rob's knee now as he turned back to her. 'I know, but can you imagine how happy Elaine would be if there was a new baby to look forward to? It would make her all the more determined to fight back, which is exactly what she needs. It worries me that lately she seems to have lost, dare I say it, her will to live.' When he realized Vikki was fighting back tears, he reached out and took her hand. More softly, he added, 'Your dad never got to see Freya, and I'd hate it for our kids not to know your mum properly either. I know we still have my parents, but how often do we go down to Plymouth to see them? Your mum means as much to me as she does to you. I'd do anything to help her get better. Wouldn't you?'

Vikki felt a sharp pain in her chest at the thought of her mum not being in their future. 'Yes, of course I would. I'd have ten babies if it got Mum through this.'

Rob's whole face lit up. 'So that's a yes?' Before Vikki could reply, Rob had lifted Freya up so she was facing him. 'Did you hear that, Freya? You're going to have a baby brother or sister.'

When Freya released an ear-piercing scream of delight, Rob winced and added, 'Although God knows why I'd want another one of these.'

'Yes, yes, yes!' screamed Freya, jumping up and down on her daddy's knee.

Rob had a wide grin on his face as he looked to Vikki. 'I know we shouldn't wish our lives away, but I can't wait until next Christmas now. We might have our new baby by then, if we're lucky. Can you imagine it?'

Rather than wait for an answer, he began tickling Freya until her face went bright red. 'Stop it, Daddy!' she screamed.

As Rob carried on tickling Freya, Vikki stood up to stretch her spine and felt a surge of nostalgia as she thought back to the later stages of her pregnancy when she had been carrying Freya. Was she ready to do it all again? Judging by Rob's reaction, she didn't really have a choice. And maybe he was right, maybe a new baby would give her mum a future to look forward to instead of one to dread.

Freeing himself from Freya, Rob got up and slipped his arms around a troubled-looking Vikki. 'Are you sure you want to do this?'

With her heart hammering in her chest, Vikki nodded. 'Yes.'

Rob lifted her off her feet as he kissed her and in that moment she knew she was doing the right thing. He nuzzled her neck and whispered, 'God, I love you.'

She groaned as she wriggled free. 'You're going to have to save all that loving, because I need to make a start on the dinner.'

He pulled at the ribbon around her silk robe. 'Wearing those?'

'I suppose I'd better get changed.'

Rob checked Freya, who had become half buried in an explosion of new toys. 'I'll help you undress,' he whispered, grabbing his wife's hand and leading her upstairs before their daughter could notice.

Less than ten minutes later, Vikki was back downstairs wearing jog pants and a T-shirt as she prepared to face the daunting task of preparing Christmas dinner on her own for the very first time. Elaine would be joining them later and had offered to come over a little early, but Vikki was determined not to accept any help. There would be no cheating, no ready mixes, no frozen Yorkshire puddings and, looking at the clock, not enough time to get everything done and nip back upstairs to shower and change properly without being distracted by Rob this time. She had planned out every stage of cooking and had even gone as far as putting it on a spreadsheet which she had tacked to the cupboard door.

Over the next hour, Vikki followed the instructions step by step while her mind pulled her back to the rash decision she had made that morning. She didn't feel quite the same level of excitement as Rob when she pictured next Christmas with Freya twice as excited because she had a little brother or sister's presents to open too. It would be exhausting, but if it meant her mum's place in their future was assured too, it would be worth it. Her stomach flipped every time she thought about it, and she wasn't sure if her nerves were caused by the current challenge of cooking dinner, the excitement of having another baby, or something else; fear, perhaps. She was yet to be convinced that another baby was something she really wanted, all she knew for certain was that this was something she really wanted to give Rob.

'I've had another thought,' Rob said.

Vikki hadn't noticed him coming into the kitchen wrapped in a bathrobe, his hair dripping wet. He gave her such a start that she dropped a jar of horseradish and it smashed on the floor.

'Shit!' she said, and felt a sudden, irrational urge to burst into tears. She quickly regained her composure and, noticing Rob's bare feet, added, 'You'd better leave me to it. I'll clear it up.'

'Sorry, I'll get out of your way,' he said.

It was only when he didn't move that she realized he hadn't told her whatever was on his mind. 'What?' she asked.

'Rather than have your mum drive over, I'll go and pick her up.'

'But what about getting home? There's no guarantee she'd be able to get a taxi, so unless we can convince her to stay over, one of us will have to stay sober and drive her home,' Vikki said, not wanting that person to be her. 'And Mum said she's not bothered about drinking.'

'I'll drive her there and back,' Rob said simply.

Vikki frowned as she tried to read Rob's expression. Despite his generous offer, there was something in his tone that made her question it. Or was it something else distracting him? Could he be having second thoughts about the baby? It had been a spur-of-the-moment decision for both of them, taken when they were feeling all warm and cosy as a family. They hadn't considered any of the practicalities.

'Are you sure?' she asked, and was about to follow it through with another question, but Rob's features softened.

'Look, I've taken the back seat over the last few months and today I'd like to look after you both. I don't like the idea of Elaine driving home in the dark. You said yourself how easily tired she gets, and on my way to fetch her, I could see if there's a corner shop open that sells horseradish.'

With the moment lost, Vikki returned her thoughts to the safety of the present and the dinner she was preparing. 'I'd say we could ask Mum if she had any, but that was hers.'

'Then it's sorted. I'll get dressed and nip out to pick her up.'

'What about Freya?'

'She's quiet enough watching *Frozen*,' Rob replied, and before Vikki could make a counter-argument he had slipped out of the kitchen and was hurrying upstairs.

When Vikki phoned her mum to let her know the change of plan, Elaine was as shocked as she had been. 'He really doesn't have to make a fuss. I'm fine.'

'It was his idea.'

'I know, but still,' Elaine said, sounding choked. 'You've both spoiled me so much this year. All the lovely gifts, the dinner, and now a door-to-door taxi service.'

'We're doing it because we love you,' Vikki said, thinking beyond Christmas to the plans they had made for the future.

'And the spa break too,' Elaine continued. 'I've only just spotted the envelope at the bottom of my gift bag. It's going to be a lovely treat for us both. I presume you're intending on being my plus one?'

'What spa break?'

There was a pause which gave them time to solve the mystery. They both laughed.

'It's Rob again,' Vikki said. With perfect timing, he reappeared in the kitchen with his coat on. 'Another surprise present.'

Rob smiled and came over to kiss her on the nose as she talked to her mum. 'Looks like I did pick up your hints after all,' he whispered.

Vikki would never have the heart to tell him he had got it wrong, but she supposed a gym membership would be of limited use to her anyway if she did get pregnant. A spa was the ideal gift to reenergize mother and daughter. Rob knew what he was doing.

'And by way of a thank you,' Elaine was saying, 'I've been speaking to Lesley and she's agreed to come and stay with me next week after my chemo. She'll be here for New Year's Eve, which means we can look after Freya while you and Rob go to the party.'

'What party?' Vikki asked, meeting Rob's gaze, but for once he wasn't in on one of her mum's secrets.

'I saw Sarah Tavistock yesterday,' Elaine said. Sarah had made a number of calls to the house since her initial visit, and had won over Elaine as easily as she had her daughter. Only last week she had dropped off a Christmas hamper for her mum, and a crate of Prosecco for Vikki. Vikki wasn't sure if Sarah's offer of friendship was genuine or if the gifts were simply bribes, but it was hard not to like her. 'She's invited us to a party at her house on New Year's Eve. I said you might go, but I didn't want to mention it until I was sure I could offer to babysit.'

'A New Year's Eve party at the Tavistocks, and we're invited,' Vikki repeated. She imagined it would be very extravagant, completely out of her league and her comfort zone, but it had been years since she and Rob had been out on New Year's Eve. She looked at her husband, not wanting to build up her hopes, and asked, 'Can we? Mum's offering to babysit.'

Rob's answer wasn't immediate, but after a moment's consideration, he smiled. 'Sounds like it could be interesting. Are you sure your mum doesn't mind?'

'Tell him it's the least I can do,' Elaine said, overhearing his comment.

'You can thank him yourself, Mum. He's leaving now, so shouldn't be too long.'

'Don't forget I have a little shopping expedition first,' he said, and was about to step away when Vikki grabbed his coat to stop him escaping.

She pressed the phone against her shoulder so that her mum couldn't hear her. 'I love you so bloody much.'

'And I love you,' he whispered.

When she pulled him closer for a kiss, Vikki wasn't sure if she imagined the tears in his eyes.

Scarlett

I think we got really good at pretending not to notice each other, but then, later on, he'd always tell me what he had been thinking. He did this thing of stepping close to me while he was talking to someone else. He'd only have to brush against me and I swear my insides would explode – I can't tell you how exciting it was. I'd message him sometimes and tell him I wasn't wearing any underwear because I knew it made him crazy for me. Stuff like that always made the time we did spend together SO exciting.

Except for that one time when it wasn't, when I drove him crazy and he didn't like it. I sort of don't blame him for getting mad at me, but it was Christmas and I didn't see why we couldn't spend some time alone together, even if it was only ten minutes. You can do a lot in ten minutes and, besides, I was his weakness and he couldn't resist me. That's why I sent him a message on Christmas morning, demanding he give me my Christmas present. I said if he couldn't give me what I wanted, I'd go elsewhere. I said I was sure Linus would be happy to oblige.

I knew I was behaving like a demanding brat, but I didn't

think he'd get that angry. He must have noticed how pleased I was when I got in the car because he didn't say a word as we drove out of Sedgefield. We sometimes parked up along one of the country roads but this time he took me to this old, creepy house that was all boarded up. He parked in front of a metal fence and just carried on staring straight ahead. I could see the muscles in his jaw twitching.

'Do I get my present now?' I asked.

Still not speaking, he got out of the car and waited for me. I thought we were going to get into the back, but he grabbed my hand and pulled me through a gap in the fence. For a minute, I thought he was going to make me go into the house, but he dragged me into a sort of alcove and turned to face me. It wasn't the first time he'd made my heart race, but this felt different. I couldn't read him, his eyes were completely blank and his mouth twisted into a snarl when he said, 'You're a little bitch, do you know that?'

'I needed to see you. I love you.'

'So now I'm here, and I want my Christmas present too.'

I wanted him to kiss me so badly and when he looked at my mouth and smiled, I thought he'd forgiven me. I stepped towards him, but he stopped me. He put his hands on both my shoulders and began pushing downwards. I didn't understand what he was doing at first, but then I did. I knelt down in front of him and gave him what he wanted.

13

The Accusations

Nina's heart was thumping so hard it reverberated through her body as she stood up. Bryn's eyes were wide and she suspected his pulse was racing too.

'If you think it's me, Nina, at least have the courage to say it. Ask me.'

Nina felt like a rabbit caught in the headlights and braced herself for impact when she said, 'Are you having an affair with Scarlett?'

'No.'

No was such a small and yet powerful word and one that Nina should have grabbed with both hands, but it left her feeling cold and alone. If Bryn were capable of sleeping with his underage stepdaughter, he was also capable of lying. And if he were a just and honourable man, she had accused her husband of an unthinkable crime, and he would never forgive her.

'This is where you're supposed to say thank God for that, Nina.'

Her lip trembled but the words wouldn't come.

'Wow,' he said. 'So that's it then.'

It was only when Bryn turned to leave that she forced herself out of a trance. 'Please, Bryn, wait.'

'For what?' he asked. 'Do you think I hadn't noticed how you couldn't even look at me yesterday? Even if by some miracle you did take me at my word, is that how it would always be between us? Maybe I do know Scarlett better than you do, but that isn't very hard, is it? You don't seem to understand anyone that well these days.'

'What are you going to do now?' Nina asked.

He shook his head. 'I think you know the answer to that one.'

'You're leaving me?'

'Apparently the man you married never existed. I'm a scheming conman, like Sarah suspected all along.' When he laughed it could so easily have been a sob. 'Oh, no, that's right, I'm far worse than that, aren't I?'

Bryn turned to go, but Scarlett was blocking his exit. 'What's going on?' she asked. From the look on her face, she had heard enough to hazard a guess.

'Ask your mum,' Bryn said, 'and when you've realized what you've put her through, tell her, Scarlett. Tell her everything.'

Scarlett's eyes widened. 'I can't.'

'Then there's nothing left for me here.'

'You're leaving?' Scarlett asked. She went to make a grab for Bryn, but held back at the last and he swept past her. 'You can't.'

'What did you expect?' he asked. 'Did you really think your actions wouldn't be without consequences?'

'I don't understand. Mum, what's happening?' Scarlett asked, raising her voice to be heard above the sound of Bryn stomping upstairs.

'I've just—' Nina began, and at that moment the weight of her accusation crashed into her. Her body convulsed as the first sob tore from her throat. Her ragged gasps weren't loud enough to drown out the two opposing voices in her head, one asking what had she done, and the other asking what had he done? She wasn't prepared to listen to either.

When she felt Scarlett's hand on her shoulder, she knocked it away. 'Don't! Don't you dare!'

'Why? What have you done, Mum?'

'What have I done?' Nina cried. 'What have you done, Scarlett? And I swear to God, if you say you can't tell me one more time, I'm not going to be responsible for my actions.' She took a step towards her daughter and Scarlett backed away, but Nina followed until she had her pressed up against the kitchen counter.

'Who is this married man of yours, Scarlett?' she asked. 'Is it Bryn?'

'No!' Tears were streaming down Scarlett's face. She had to gulp for air before adding, 'No, Mum. Why would you even say that?'

'Because,' Nina began, but she didn't have an answer. 'I don't know! I'm struggling to come to terms with the fact that it's *anyone*.'

'Is that why Bryn's leaving?'

'You can hardly expect him to hang around!' Nina screamed at her. 'Not after me accusing him of getting my selfish and irresponsible daughter pregnant!' It was then she saw the look on Scarlett's face and she put her hand to her mouth. 'Oh, no, please no. I'm wrong, aren't I?'

'Yes, Mum. You're so fucking wrong!'

14

Before

Thursday, 31 December 2015

When Bryn had driven Nina to Sarah's New Year's Eve party the year before, she hadn't even known his name, but she had found it surprisingly easy talking to the taxi driver – so much so that she had been bitterly disappointed when they arrived at her destination within fifteen minutes. Bryn told her later that he had seen how nervous she was and had been tempted to offer to be her escort for the evening, but he had done the next best thing by promising to pick her up later. And he had done, in every sense of the word.

There were no such anxieties this year as she waited for Bryn to pay the taxi driver. She shivered in the cold and her strapless shoes offered no protection from the inch of snow that had fallen during the day. Her black satin evening dress fluttered in the breeze, making the diamanté appliqué along its plunging neckline sparkle in the moonlight. Her outfit was a stark contrast to the demure, high-necked evening dress she had worn the year before, and Bryn was the perfect match for the elegant look she was aiming for. Her husband owned only one suit, the one she had bought him for their wedding, and to say he brushed up well was an understatement. She felt more complete than she had in years, and even though Christmas hadn't exactly gone to plan and she had spent more of it alone than she would have liked, she hadn't felt lonely.

She and Bryn had indulged in breakfast in bed on Christmas morning, but still managed to be up and dressed before either Liam or Scarlett had shown their faces. They had all opened their presents together – or, to be more precise, she and Bryn had watched the children open theirs. She had refused to be annoyed at them for not getting her a present; apparently, they had each been waiting for the other to sort something out, but she had been hurt that they had snubbed Bryn too.

Even so, Nina hadn't complained. Her family might not be perfect, but at least she got to spend the day with those she loved. Bryn had put on a brave face, but she could tell he was missing Caryn, and she wasn't surprised when he made an excuse to go out and pick up a few extra fares while she prepared dinner. She knew better than most how broken homes often revealed their jagged edges at Christmas. Adam had sent Liam and Scarlett their obligatory Christmas cards with a cheque inside, but because he had posted them late, they wouldn't arrive until a few days after Christmas. To add insult to injury, he hadn't bothered phoning his children until Boxing Day, and so they had both spent Christmas assuming he had forsaken them completely. Liam was too absorbed in his new love to expend energy on being annoyed, but Scarlett had sulked.

She had gone out briefly to meet Linus while Nina was up to her eyes peeling vegetables, and Nina had hoped she would come back in a better mood. She hadn't, and her sullenness showed every sign of persisting through to the next year.

Nina's obstreperous daughter had inexplicably fallen out with not only her father but everyone. She had turned down a New Year's Eve party invite from Eva because . . . well, Nina could only assume it had something to do with either Liam, Linus or both. Scarlett wasn't saying, and had been insisting on staying home alone, but Nina wouldn't hear of it. She could only imagine how uncomfortable it was going to be, having a moody teen in tow, but Nina would rather none of them went to Sarah's party than leave Scarlett alone to stew in her misery. Whatever had upset her daughter needed to be set to one side. She had an important year ahead and Nina was going to make sure it started off on the right footing.

'What are you doing waiting there?' Bryn asked when he noticed Nina still dithering at the roadside after he had waved off the cab.

He followed his wife's gaze to the lone figure standing in the middle of the road. Bryn held out his arm to guide Scarlett to safety, but she snubbed his gallantry and stomped past them both. Scarlett was wearing ankle boots and a pale blue lace dress which, in her mother's opinion, was too short for her long limbs, but as Nina had been told an hour earlier, her opinion didn't count. It was as much as Nina could do to get Scarlett dressed at all, and for once she hadn't made them late while she applied and reapplied her makeup. Scarlett could spend hours with her pots and brushes, perfecting her war paint, but this evening there had been minimal effort. She had pulled back her silky blonde hair into a ponytail and applied little more than mascara and lipstick. Scarlett thought she was making a point but, despite her best efforts, she looked stunning.

'I hope you're going to behave yourself,' Nina said.

'If you'd wanted that, you shouldn't have dragged me here.'

'In that case, if you have to drink, you had better pace yourself. Three is your limit, so make them last.'

'Three? What's the point in that?'

'The point is you remain in control of your actions. This is the first time in a long time I've been to one of Sarah's New Year parties without feeling like everyone's pitying me. Don't spoil things,' she said. 'Please, Scarlett.'

'I'll just go in the back room and play with the kids then, shall I?'

Nina chose wisely not to point out that Scarlett was behaving like a child. It wouldn't help the situation and she was holding out hope that Sarah's daughter Charlotte would be able to keep Scarlett occupied. The six-year age difference meant they had never been particularly close, but she had to be better company for Scarlett than Nina.

'Hello, lovelies,' Sarah said as she opened the black lacquered door to her opulent home. She looked the picture of sophistication, as always, although the flush to her cheeks wasn't her usual Elizabeth Arden shade and possibly had more to do with the bottle of Krug in her hand. 'Champagne, anyone?'

'Have you got any bigger glasses?' Scarlett asked, refusing the crystal flute being offered by the waiter shadowing his hostess. 'I'm only allowed three and apparently I need to make them last.'

'I'm sure I can dig out a pint glass,' Sarah said with a wink. 'Of course, the easiest thing to do would be to give the large glass to your mum so she forgets to keep track of how much you're drinking.' She turned to share a look with Nina. 'You're not driving, are you?'

'Not a chance.'

'And I hope you're off duty, Mr Thomas,' she said to Bryn. 'You're not going to get called away at a moment's notice?'

'After the hard time Nina gave me about Christmas Day, no, I won't *ever* be doing that again,' he said, to make a point to whoever would listen.

'I didn't say a word,' Nina said.

'You didn't need to, it was the look that did it.'

'I'd have given you more than a look,' Sarah said sternly as she led them through the cavernous hallway.

The click of Nina's heels against the black quartz tiles echoed off smooth white walls that reached the full height of the house above a wide spiral staircase. Sarah's ultra-modern home was perfectly presented with floor-to-ceiling windows and contemporary art illuminated at strategic intervals and providing the perfect mood lighting – assuming you felt at home living in an art gallery. Nina didn't. She couldn't imagine Sarah coming home after a long day and kicking off her shoes, slipping into her PJs and slouching on the sofa to watch endless box sets and eat takeaway pizza. Not that she herself did that very often, if at all, but at least she could if she chose. She had never seen Sarah look anything less than perfect in this house.

'I hope we're not the first to arrive,' Nina said. She could hear soft music coming from deep within the house but not the level of chatter she would normally expect from one of Sarah's parties.

'Apparently the snow's caused havoc on the motorways and some poor souls are still on their way, but no, you're not the first. Those that are here are a bit more civilized than what we're used to, that's all, but we'll soon put a stop to that.'

When they entered the main reception room the temperature dropped by a degree or two. The bi-fold windows running the length of one wall had been pulled back and an awning erected to extend the room out into the garden. There was a fully staffed bar and waiters milling around small groups of guests with trays of hors d'oeuvres. Nina linked arms with Bryn and raised her head high. This year, there would be no slinking around the edges of the room as if the wide-open floor were an ice rink.

'Wow, you look gorgeous,' Charlotte said. The young woman had disengaged herself from a small group to come over and welcome her mother's guests, and Scarlett especially. 'I haven't seen you in ages.'

'Please don't say I've grown,' moaned Scarlett.

Glancing over her shoulder at the group she had escaped from, Charlotte said, 'That's all I've been getting so far, but don't worry, the plan is to stay here only as long as we have to, and then I'm having my own private party upstairs. Some of my friends are on their way – but knowing them, they've been distracted by the snow.'

'Building snowmen?' Nina asked.

'More like writing in the snow with "yellow ink", if you know what I mean.'

'Is it warmer upstairs?' Scarlett asked.

'I thought you youngsters were impervious to the cold?' Sarah asked. 'You're always parading around half-naked.'

'Not me.'

'By that, Scarlett means she feels the cold,' Bryn said wryly.

Sarah wrapped a protective arm around each of the young girls. 'Don't worry, I'll look after you.'

At first Nina thought Scarlett was trying to wriggle free from Sarah's clutches, but rather than attempt to get away, her daughter hid behind her. Nina was about to ask what was wrong until she spied Miles coming into the room with two new guests.

'You invited Mr Swift?' she asked.

'It was more a case of inviting his wife and mother-in-law,' Sarah explained. Looking directly at Scarlett, she added, 'You know, the one who isn't dying – or at least her prognosis is far better than I was led to believe.'

'But she does have cancer,' Scarlett mumbled.

'It was lucky you didn't meet the mum first,' Bryn said, and for Scarlett's benefit added, 'It just goes to show how idle gossip can lead to all sorts of trouble.'

'Is that his wife with him?' Nina asked as she tried not to stare at the young woman with long curly hair in a tiny sequined dress.

'Yes. She's a sweet little thing, isn't she?'

'At first glance, I thought she was more Scarlett's age,' Nina said.

Clearly offended by the remark, Scarlett shot a look over Sarah's shoulder and said, 'She's way older than me.'

'I do remember her now, Mum,' Charlotte said, and for everyone else's benefit added, 'We went to the same gym club for a while. I never made the connection that she was the girl who married Mr Swift, and I can't believe she's got a kid already.'

'Saying that, I couldn't have been much older than her when I had you,' replied Sarah. 'Although I probably didn't look like I should still be in school uniform.'

Charlotte was scowling as she looked from the wife to the teacher. 'It's probably what he sees in her.'

'That girl's looks are deceptive, you mark my words,' Sarah said. 'All she needs is the right person to take her under their wing – and it just so happens I'm on the lookout for a protégée now that my daughter has turned her back on the family.'

'If that's meant to make me jealous, Mum, it's not working. I told you, I'm not buying and selling houses for a living, and I definitely don't want a career shifting slabs of dead animals.'

'Well, that's certainly good to know, Charlotte,' Sarah said with a sniff. 'And I presume that means you wouldn't want any of the financial rewards that come with my tedious business deals either.'

Nina shared a smile with Bryn. Sarah's brazen attempts to manipulate were entertaining when they were being directed at someone else.

'Whatever, Mother,' Charlotte said, and was smiling too when she added, 'Maybe I should go so you can talk business with your new apprentice. She's on her way over.'

'Can I come with you?' Scarlett asked. She had remained hiding behind Sarah as Miles approached with the two new guests.

'I'm so pleased you could make it,' Sarah said to Vikki

before turning her attention to her escort. 'Ah, the infamous Mr Swift. I can see why all the schoolgirls say they drool over you.'

'Not all of them,' muttered Charlotte. 'Vikki, hi, how are you? It's been so long since we've seen each other!' The two girls embraced with the slight awkwardness of schoolgirls meeting again as adults.

Rob was more interested in his current pupil who was staring intently at the floor, waiting for it to swallow her up. 'So what have you been telling them, Scarlett?'

Nina held her breath. Her daughter had arrived at the party under duress and it was only going to take one wrong word to upset her. Sarah and Mr Swift had already exceeded that particular quota, but to Nina's surprise, Scarlett stiffened and raised her head.

'Nothing about you, you're not that interesting,' she said coldly.

Vikki was the first to laugh. 'Nice one. The last thing you want is a teacher with an ego.'

Scarlett continued to scowl and Nina wished Charlotte would follow through with her threat to leave, taking her daughter and the awkward atmosphere with her.

'Shall I do the introductions?' Sarah said, showing no indication of being aware or concerned about Scarlett's discomfort – or Charlotte's, for that matter. 'Vikki, Rob, this is my dearest friend Nina and her husband, Bryn. Nina, of course you know Rob, but this is Vikki, who I hope will be my newest friend.' She beamed a smile at Charlotte as she emphasized the last word.

'Sarah was worried you wouldn't come,' Nina said. 'Aren't you supposed to be sworn enemies?'

156

'I am trying hard to hate her, but she won't let me,' Vikki said.

Charlotte was fidgeting. 'Shall we go and make some cocktails?' she asked Scarlett, and was about to take her away when she saw Vikki's eyes light up. 'Did you want to come too? Maybe if we get really drunk, we can do some back-flips on the dance floor.'

Scrunching her nose, Vikki said, 'I'm not sure I could do one of those any more.'

'You haven't tasted one of my cocktails yet. Anything is possible.'

Vikki's cheeks flushed with temptation. 'I'd better not.'

'Can we go now?' Scarlett asked, pulling Charlotte away from the group.

'And please, Charlotte,' Sarah said, 'remember Scarlett is still technically a child.'

'A man could get a complex,' Rob said after they had gone. 'Is my company that bad?'

'Would you want to spend time out of school with your teacher?' Miles asked, which made Nina smile. If one of her teachers had looked anything like Mr Swift, then yes, possibly.

'I don't suppose there's any chance they'll be making non-alcoholic cocktails,' Bryn said. 'I don't want to be carrying Scarlett home.'

Nina lifted her empty glass, which Sarah proceeded to fill. 'No chance at all,' she said, 'but I'm sure you can manage both of us.'

'Your daughter's very beautiful,' Vikki said to Bryn.

'She's my stepdaughter actually,' he said, 'so I'm afraid I can't take any credit for Scarlett's good looks.'

'No wonder she's giving you sleepless nights,' Miles added, not taking his eyes off the girls, who were giggling with the bartender.

'Is she?' Rob asked.

'No, not really,' Nina said. She wished she had never mentioned Scarlett's secret tryst with Linus to Sarah. 'You know what they're like at that age.'

All eyes remained on Nina as they waited for her to elaborate, but it was Bryn who read her mind. 'I'm sure Scarlett wouldn't want us talking about her private life with her teacher.'

'Spoilsport,' muttered Miles.

15

The Accusations

As Vikki watched Freya toddle off towards one of the nursery assistants, she felt her heart wrench. It wasn't that long ago that she had been looking forward to the prospect of her daughter starting school, and she hadn't given a thought to how difficult it would be, offering her up to someone else's care. She had to take on trust that these relative strangers would look after her little girl and that would be true for the entirety of her school life. Whether Vikki wanted them to or not, these people would play their role in moulding her child into a woman. How had she never realized before how frightening a proposition that was?

'Don't worry, she'll be fine,' the nursery assistant said when she noticed Vikki's hesitation.

But as Vikki left the nursery and walked across the small playground, she did worry. The future didn't just scare her, it terrified her. She wished she could go back to her teenage years and start again. Where would she be now if she had made different choices? And what decisions would Scarlett need to make in the coming weeks and months?

Vikki knew she ought to be worrying about her mum's hospital appointment that morning. It was an important one and Vikki had promised to go with her, but as she headed back to the car, she couldn't push Scarlett from her thoughts. Slipping behind the steering wheel, her anxiety began to build, bringing with it a wave of nausea that forced her to lean back out of the car and retch. How was she going to offer her mum any useful support when she was so desperately in need of it herself?

Wiping her mouth with one of Freya's wet wipes, Vikki took slow breaths. She could go home and try to eat some dry toast to settle her stomach, or she could use the time to settle her mind. She turned the key in the ignition and waited for a gap in the traffic. Driving away from the nursery, she didn't turn towards home, nor did she head south towards her mum's house. Vikki took a much shorter journey to Sedgefield High.

It had been six years since Vikki had been a student, but as she drove past the school, she had a good idea what was going through the minds of the groups of schoolkids milling around the gates. There was that desperate need to be accepted, a fear of not fitting in, and plenty of frustration about a world that didn't understand them; and this on top of the usual anxieties about exam results and the enormity of the future ahead of them.

Unable to find a parking space close to the main entrance, Vikki pulled up further down the road. She was still parallel with the school grounds, close to the staff car park on the other side of the railings where she thought she could spy Rob's Ford Focus. That wasn't why she was there, though. She hadn't doubted that Rob had gone straight to school, not really. The reason she had been drawn to the school came in the form of a young girl walking along the road in her direction.

Scarlett was on her own with her head down and the weight of the world on her shoulders. She didn't notice Vikki, even though she came within only a few feet of the car. She was oblivious to the fact she was being watched so intently, although she did scratch her head as if she knew someone was trying to drill down into her thoughts. When Scarlett had passed, Vikki released her grip on the steering wheel, leaving tiny fingernail indentations on the faux leather. Picking up her handbag, she got out of the car quickly before she lost sight of Scarlett – not that she had any idea what she was going to do next, if anything at all.

16

Before

Vikki wanted to pinch herself as she stood in the Tavistocks' home, sipping champagne. She couldn't claim to be completely at ease, but she was enjoying the occasion, even though most of the guests they spoke to preferred talking to Rob. Many of them had sons and daughters in Sedgefield High, or simply of school age, and were eager to seek his advice; and once they got talking, the conversations inevitably moved on to other subjects like sport or politics. It was all Vikki could do to concentrate long enough to nod at what she hoped were appropriate intervals.

While Rob was absorbed in a rather intense debate about school academies, Vikki looked around for a means of escape, her eyes lingering on Charlotte and her growing group of friends at the bar, whose laughter could be heard high above the drone of chatter. Vikki wasn't that much older, and wished she had had the courage to accept Charlotte's earlier invitation to join them, but where once she might have fitted in, now she had nothing in common with them.

It was perhaps a blessing in disguise: playing with the

children was hardly going to impress Sarah, and Vikki did want to impress her. Forgotten by the group she was with, including Rob, Vikki found herself gravitating towards the first couple she had met. Nina Thomas didn't have the airs and graces that Vikki found intimidating in the other guests and she knew she would be looked after.

'You got away then?' Nina said. 'I was wondering if I should go over and rescue you.'

'Oh, did I look that uncomfortable?'

'No more than I usually do at these things,' Nina admitted. 'You only have to ask Bryn. I wasn't even going to get out of the taxi last year. Do we need to rescue your husband?'

When Vikki looked over at Rob, a sixth sense told him he was being watched and he turned to give her a wink and a smile. 'No, I think he's quite happy where he is.'

Vikki was happy to leave him there too. She relied on Rob too much to take care of her. He always led the conversations when they were out at social gatherings, which she didn't particularly mind. He did his best to bring her into the discussion where he could, and if they were going to a school function, he would gently coach her so she would feel more confident in the role of a teacher's wife. His efforts, however, tended to reinforce the feeling that she was still a student. She supposed she was something in between: too old to get away with back-flips on the dance floor, and too young to convince anyone she had a view on the latest immigration policy, or whatever adults were meant to talk about.

'Would you ladies like more drinks?' Bryn asked, looking at their empty glasses. 'More champagne? Or how about one of Charlotte's cocktails?'

Despite feeling a little woozy, Vikki would happily have kept going, but she didn't want to appear too gauche and embarrass herself in front of Sarah, or let Rob down. 'Maybe I'll have a soft drink instead.'

Nina saw through the act. 'She wants a cocktail, and so do I.'

'What's this?' Sarah asked when she spotted the two alone and without drinks. 'Have you drunk the bar dry so soon, Nina?'

'Bryn's getting us cocktails.'

'Oh good Lord,' Sarah said to Vikki, 'she'll be queen of the dance floor after a couple of those.'

Nina laughed. 'I'll have you know I have some serious moves.'

'So there really is a dance floor? I thought Charlotte was joking,' Vikki said.

'It's in the next room. We don't fire it up until the food has been cleared away. We can't have guests slipping on escapee blinis.'

'I haven't been dancing since Freya was born.'

'You must have had her very young,' Nina said.

'Yes, I suppose I was. I remember being heavily pregnant at my twenty-first party,' Vikki said as she recalled what had been a sober and distinctly sombre event. She hadn't been able to compete with some of the wild parties her peers were having and was so out of touch with them all that she doubted anyone would come if she had invited them. So instead she had gone out for a meal with her mum and her husband, and tried to ignore the empty chair her dad should have occupied.

'So how did you meet Rob?' Nina asked.

164

From the way Nina averted her eyes, Vikki guessed at the follow-up question she was too polite to ask. Had they met at school? It wouldn't be the first time the suggestion had been made and she could reel off the answer without even thinking. 'I was in sixth form when Rob started at Sedgefield High, but it was only after I'd left that we got to know each other. I worked in an estate agents and he was looking for a house. The rest is history.'

'It must have been weird to begin with, though,' Sarah said. 'Dating your teacher.'

'Not really,' Vikki said. 'Sedgefield was his first teaching position and he wasn't that far off being a student himself.'

'Not that you were dating him back then anyway,' Nina reminded her.

'But it does happen, doesn't it?' Sarah said. She was looking over at the crowd of youngsters at the bar. Charlotte and her friends were being circled by an older group of men who were more interested in watching the girls than trying to catch the bartender's attention. 'They're like bees to a honeypot.'

'That's no excuse,' Nina said, surprisingly soberly. 'However sweet the honey, they're still children.'

'Exactly,' Sarah said.

Bryn arrived a moment later with their cocktails: exotic concoctions laden with fruit and glowing in the dim light.

'How's Scarlett doing?' Nina asked.

'I might have suggested she try a mocktail next.'

'I thought I saw her give you a funny look,' Sarah said.

Bryn gave an apologetic shrug to his wife. 'I did try.'

After their cocktails, Sarah announced that the dance floor was open. Vikki tried and failed to persuade Rob to join her, but she was more than happy when Nina took pity on her and offered to be her dancing partner. It came as a shock when the lights were turned up as midnight approached and guests were instructed to go out into the garden to count down to the end of one year and the beginning of the next.

The dancing had sobered Vikki up and she separated from Nina as they each went in search of their partners before the firework display started. Sarah had thought of everything and there were piles of blankets and fleeces for those guests who might need protection from the deep frost that had made the snow crunch underfoot. Vikki grabbed a thick woollen wrap at the same time that Bryn was reaching for the pile.

'Your wife's looking for you,' she said.

'If you see her, tell her I'm over with Scarlett by the water fountain.'

Vikki watched him push through the crowd to a spot where she glanced the top of the young girl's head. Vikki had never heard Rob mention her, but she was someone you would most certainly notice. Her violet eyes were startling and Vikki had felt almost intimidated by her beauty. She had been surprised when Nina had told her she was only fifteen. She had an air about her that seemed much older, or at least she had at the beginning of the evening. The crowds had parted and Vikki could see that Scarlett was decidedly worse for wear. Bryn draped a blanket around her and Scarlett buried her head into his shoulder.

'Those two worry me.'

Vikki turned to see the anxiety etched on Sarah's face. 'Sorry?'

The shadow passed. 'Oh, nothing. Come on, do you want to help set off the fireworks?'

'I'd better find Rob first.'

'We'll be on a raised platform. He'll see you before you see him.'

And so it was that Vikki found herself at the epicentre of the New Year's Eve party hosted by the woman whose name she had been loath to speak in recent months. As they counted down from ten, Vikki was preparing to see in the New Year without her husband, but suddenly he was there, slipping an arm around her waist. The crowd shouted down to one and she held out a safety lighter to set off her section of fireworks. Shivering, her hand shook so badly that she couldn't keep the glowing ember on the fuse until Rob put his hand on hers and stilled her body with the warmth of his own. As the night sky was set alight she turned and kissed him.

'This is going to be such an amazing year, Vikki,' he said.

Scarlett

In case you haven't worked it out yet, I'm good at keeping secrets. You should also know I'm good at telling lies. I suppose that's why Mum's gone a bit crazy. She was convinced she had everything under control. Liam was being normal for a change and she thought I was still young enough to be ordered around. OK, so she saw how drunk I was at the New Year's Eve party, but it's not like she wasn't expecting it. That's what teenagers do, isn't it? The thing is, she didn't have a clue what else I was up to, even though it happened right under her nose. I just wish things could have carried on like that, so no one got hurt.

I suppose now you want to know what I did get up to at the party, don't you? Well, Charlotte had been in charge of ordering the cocktails and the barman was one of her old school friends. She'd come up with a new recipe which she called the Tavistock Molotov cocktail. Yes, it's hard to say, but that was the point. You could only have one if you were capable of asking for it.

Eventually, we couldn't, so Charlotte invited us all up to her room. I was glad to get away. I was still a bit in shock

*after what happened on Christmas Day. I wasn't sure
whether I should be angry, sad, or ashamed. Mostly, I just
wanted to cry. I hated him, and not because of what he got
me to do, it was the way he made me feel. It wasn't like
he forced me or anything. I didn't say no. I did exactly
what he told me to, and afterwards I was so confused. He'd
always been really gentle before. He showed me how to do
things, stuff that we both liked, and that's what I'd wanted
from him. It was Christmas, for fuck's sake! Why was it so
bad for me to want to spend some time alone with him?
Why did he have to be such a prick? Like, I was ready to
give myself to him, but I ended up feeling used. How does
that work?*

*I didn't understand and I had no one to talk to. I wouldn't
speak to him. I didn't even want to look at him. I felt sick,
knowing he was downstairs at the party, pretending to be
in love with someone else – and he didn't love her, he told
me. Charlotte and her friends were starting to get on my
nerves too, talking about which of the men there they would
and wouldn't do it with. They talked about him and tried
to embarrass me, so I got up and left. I didn't exactly go
looking for him, but he found me anyway.*

*I'd gone outside to the summerhouse I used to play in
when I was little. Sarah had a new, posh one built, so the
old one had been moved to an unused part of the garden,
and it was a bit tricky getting there because it was so icy
and I was drunk. I left a pretty good trail for him to follow,
though.*

*The wooden hut smelled of musty garden furniture and
I collapsed on to a chair. I was absolutely freezing, but that
wasn't the only reason I was trembling.*

He appeared at the door, stepping inside just enough so no one would see him and said, 'You're not speaking to me.'

I glared at him and sniffed the air as if there was a bad smell under my nose. I didn't say anything though. I was keeping my mouth closed this time.

'You're angry.'

I carried on scowling.

'Scarlett, answer me.'

'What do you expect?'

'What I expect is for you to be more mature about it, if I'm honest.'

I could feel tears stinging my eyes, but I wasn't going to cry. 'You used me.'

'And you use me, Scarlett, all the time.' He let out a long sigh. 'I'll admit I was angry. I didn't appreciate being blackmailed.'

'I didn't blackmail you!'

'You wanted to get me jealous and it worked. I didn't want you going off with some boy. I thought I could trust you.'

'Meanwhile, I have to put up with you sleeping with you-know-who every night.'

'I know, I know,' he whispered. He moved closer and knelt down in front of me, like he was begging for forgiveness. 'Would it help if I said we don't have sex that much these days? I want to save myself for you, but we don't always get what we want and maybe that's how it's meant to be for us. We have our own lives, Scarlett, and a responsibility to keep other people happy. They've done nothing wrong.'

'But neither have we.'

'I know,' he said. 'Look, we were meant to be, and there was nothing either of us could do to stop this from happening, but that's not how other people will see it. We have to keep this completely separate from the other parts of our lives. It's the only way.'

As apologies went, this wasn't exactly what I wanted to hear. 'Forever?' I asked.

'Can't we simply make the most of what we have? Take it one day at a time?'

As he talked, he placed his hands on my knees, which I'd pressed tightly together. I wasn't going to make this easy for him. 'But I hardly get to see you.'

'You see me all the time.'

'Not properly.'

'Doesn't that excite you, though, Scarlett?'

He trailed a warm finger across my thigh and then slipped his hand beneath the hem of my lace dress, but only just. He wasn't making demands. He knew he wouldn't get away with it a second time.

'It's not enough,' I said.

His hand had stopped moving and that's when I began to panic. I thought I'd pushed him too far and I was so scared he was about to say we should end it. I didn't want to finish with him, not then, not ever. It would break my heart.

'Are you still angry with me, Scarlett?'

I knew I had to think fast, but even though the cold had shocked some sense into me, I wasn't exactly sober. I really wanted to teach him a lesson but I was terrified that if I pushed him away, it would be forever. Why does love have to be so frightening all the time? It's not supposed to be like that, is it?

'Scarlett,' he said. 'Tell me you forgive me.'

His hand was still resting on my thigh, but he wasn't touching me, not the way I wanted.

'Of course I do. I love you,' I said.

'Will you let me make it up to you?'

'How?'

'Last time we met, all the pleasure was mine, and now it's your turn,' he said with a smile as he began to relax. It took both his hands to pull my thighs apart. 'We might not be able to spend as much time on our own as we'd like, but we're going to make every moment count. This is going to be the best year ever.'

17

The Accusations

After Scarlett had stormed out, Nina was left paralysed by an intense fear that not only affected her movement, but her ability to think, or at least her ability to think rationally. She didn't know what to believe or who to trust. Scarlett's words were worthless, given how many lies she had told over the last . . . the last what? Six months? A year? Whoever had been coaching her had trained her well.

Fifteen minutes after Scarlett had gone to school, Bryn returned downstairs carrying a holdall. She should have told him to stay. No, she should have *begged* him to stay, but instead she waited for Bryn to speak first. She searched her husband's face as if it were a route map that would lead her through the lies to the truth, but she was already lost.

Bryn shook his head. 'I was ready to step up, Nina. I would have done anything to help you and Scarlett through this, but you're on your own now. Good luck.'

Nina didn't stop him. She didn't say a word and when he left, she was utterly and completely alone.

Staring at the phone, she considered calling the police.

Scarlett was underage and she had been sleeping with a man who was married and therefore old enough to know that what he was doing was wrong, even if her daughter didn't. But she hadn't named her mystery man and Nina doubted that the police would fare any better dragging the truth from her. Even after witnessing her family being torn apart, Scarlett had been determined to protect the bastard. How could she do that? Why?

For one person in particular, the answer was obvious.

'Oh, Sarah, what have I done?'

Sarah's sigh down the phone line told Nina that she wasn't that surprised by the news Nina had just imparted. 'You've done the right thing,' she said.

'But Scarlett . . . she says it isn't Bryn. What if I've made a terrible mistake?'

'Wouldn't you rather that than risk him staying under your roof so he can continue the abuse? Yes, it's going to be awful if it turns out not to be Bryn, but while there's a chance you're right,' Sarah said, 'your conscience is clear.'

'How can my conscience be clear if it's me who let this happen? I'll never forgive myself.'

'It wasn't only Scarlett he was grooming, though, was it? These men are expert manipulators, and they start with the mothers.'

'I shouldn't have let things move so fast,' Nina said, her voice wavering. 'I should have waited until I knew Bryn well enough to be absolutely sure I could trust him with my children.'

'You were blinded by love,' Sarah said kindly, 'and I didn't exactly figure out what Bryn was planning either. I was convinced he was looking for a meal ticket – a man with a track record of losing money meets a divorcée with her own business, her own house. She showers him with gifts while all he can manage is a bunch of flowers from the local garage. She pays for the wedding, buys him a new wardrobe, and suddenly he's doing pretty well for himself.'

'It wasn't like that.'

'It wasn't far off,' Sarah said, having long forgotten any promise to give Bryn the benefit of the doubt. 'And, with hindsight, did it really make sense for a man who has fallen out with his own daughter to get along so well with Scarlett? What if he had been doing the same thing to her? I should have spoken up sooner.'

'I wouldn't have listened.'

'It's not your fault, Nina. Let's just concentrate on making this right. Have you decided what to do next? Do you need me to come over?'

'No, it's OK. I'm going to freshen up and head over to the school. I'd like their advice before going to the police.'

'I did ask Vikki to speak to Rob, see if he's had any hints from Scarlett, but she hasn't got back to me yet.'

Nina didn't hesitate in voicing her next suspicion. She was getting used to it. 'Has it crossed your mind that it might be him? He's Scarlett's form tutor; he's given her extra lessons outside school; and he's nearer Scarlett's age than Bryn.'

'Since when did age stop men of a certain disposition from being interested in young girls?' Sarah sighed, then added, 'I know you'd rather believe it was anyone except Bryn, but you're clutching at straws. What we really need is for Scarlett to put you out of your misery and name him. That girl of yours has a lot to answer for. I swear you have more patience than I do, Nina. I would have throttled the answer out of her by now.'

'It might still come to that,' Nina said, realizing there was more truth to that statement than she would have liked.

After ending the call, Nina went straight to Scarlett's room.

The blinds were drawn, the bed unmade, and Nina spent a full minute staring as if it were a window into her daughter's life. All she needed was that one *key* that would unlock Scarlett's secrets. What that key might look like, she didn't know, but she set about finding it.

At first, she was respectful of her daughter's possessions, but as she searched, she replayed the morning's events in her mind. Scarlett had seen Bryn as he prepared to walk out of her life and one of two things had been going through her mind. She could have been looking to her lover to confess all and face the consequences, before silently acquiescing to his decision to let Nina's torment continue. Alternatively, Scarlett might have been watching an innocent man being accused and her mother's marriage disintegrating before her eyes, and then done nothing to stop it. The second scenario might be the lesser of two evils, but it was no less palatable. Scarlett was a victim, Nina knew that, but it wasn't enough to dampen her anger at how far her daughter was willing to go to protect her abuser.

Within minutes the bedroom was a mess. The bedclothes had been pulled off the bed and the mattress turned over. Drawers had been pulled open and their contents scattered across the floor. A jewellery box had been emptied, along with a couple of makeup bags. School books had been rifled

176

through as she searched in vain for doodles of Scarlett's initials entwined with those of the man who had got her pregnant. What she did find was her daughter's stash of contraceptive pills, which Nina took into the bathroom and flushed away.

Once she was dressed, Nina dragged herself downstairs and slipped on her winter jacket, which seemed so much heavier than it should. She wasn't sure she should be driving and almost wished she had taken up Sarah's offer to come over, but she had been right to refuse. Sarah hadn't come out and said, 'I told you so,' but it would be written all over her face. The person Nina needed more than anyone else right now was the man she loved, but the person she married had been erased from her life. Guilty or not, Bryn was lost to her.

Nina was determined not to cry again, and her jaw was set so firm that it ached. When her mobile rang and Charlotte Tavistock's name appeared, she didn't know if she should answer the call. She wasn't sure she could physically speak.

'Nina, it's Charlotte.'

It was obvious that Sarah's daughter had heard the news. She spoke in a hushed tone as if she were talking to someone recently bereaved, which was perhaps appropriate since Nina felt a perverse form of grief.

'I'm sorry, Charlotte, I was just on my way out.'

'I won't keep you,' she said, but continued anyway. 'Mum told me about Scarlett, and I know this is a bad time, but I had to phone. I take it you still don't know who it is?'

Nina was standing in the hall. She had managed to get

as far as the front door but hadn't opened it. She rested her head on a cold window pane. 'No,' she said.

'Well, I'm not saying I have the answers, but there's something I need to tell you. Something I've never told anyone, not even Mum.'

18

Before

Sunday, 24 January 2016

After the trials and tribulations of Christmas and New Year, Nina was happy to take January at a more leisurely pace. It was Sunday morning, and both her children had been out the night before, enjoying the brief respite between the end of their mock exams and the start of the real thing. Liam had gone out with Eva, and Scarlett with the enigmatic Linus, whom her daughter still contested was not her boyfriend and therefore not worthy of introductions to the family.

They had returned home in the early hours and Bryn had come home even later, but unlike his stepchildren, he had risen in time for a late breakfast with his wife. He was stretched out on the sofa, apparently reading the paper but with his eyes closed. Nina had settled at her desk tucked away in a corner of the dining room, even though work couldn't have been further from her thoughts.

There was no doubt she felt more happy and contented than she had in a long while, but the fiery passion that had drawn her and Bryn together in the first place had cooled somewhat. It was time to do something about their overdue honeymoon, and once she had surfed the net to work out all the details, she went in search of the two people who hadn't been factored into those plans.

She knocked on Liam's door first, leaving only a short pause before barging in. There was no doorstop blocking her access and, to her surprise, the curtains had been drawn back. The unmade bed was empty, though the musty smell in the air suggested the room had only recently been vacated by a slovenly teen.

The bathroom was unoccupied and Nina was certain she hadn't heard Liam leave the house, which left only one other place he might be, though it was the last place she would have expected to find him. It was a rare occurrence to find both her children in the same room at the same time, and of their own accord.

'What's this?' she asked when she walked into Scarlett's room. 'Don't tell me you two like each other all of a sudden.'

'OK, we won't,' Scarlett said.

She was sitting on the floor with her back against the wall facing her brother. Liam had his back to Nina and was perched on Scarlett's bed with his head in his hands. He didn't turn around.

Chewing her lip, Nina asked the question she should have asked first. 'What's going on?'

Scarlett's anxious expression reformed into a more familiar pout. 'Why does something have to be going on?'

Nina waited for one or both of them to provide an explanation, but whatever they were up to, it was obvious that neither had any intention of offering information willingly. Determined not to be sidetracked from her original mission, she said, 'Look, you know me and Bryn have been trying to get away?'

Again she left a pause, refusing to continue until she was sure she had their full attention. Liam huffed and turned to look at her. 'And?'

'I've been looking online and I've come across a city break to Rome during half-term. The thing is, even if we went after Valentine's Day, it's still not cheap. I'd have to pay for cover at the shop and Bryn would lose his earnings while he's away. We simply can't afford it, not if we *all* go.'

Picking up on his mum's not-so-subtle hint, Liam said, 'I wouldn't want to go anyway.'

Nina looked to Scarlett. 'It's only for three days and I know I've never left you home alone before, but you're both old enough to look after yourselves.'

'You've never said that before,' Scarlett said.

'Well, I'm saying it now. You'll be sixteen in a few of months and Liam's practically an adult.'

'That's debatable.'

Scarlett still hadn't agreed, but Nina could see the cogs turning in her mind.

'Please, Scarlett. I'll never get a honeymoon if I have to wait for Bryn to save up.'

'And Bryn's OK with you paying?'

'He will be – I won't give him a choice. I thought it best to make sure you're OK with the idea first. So, are you?'

There was a loud sigh, followed by a tut. 'Fine, whatever,' Scarlett said.

Nina should have been satisfied with their first answers, but she had expected them to jump at the chance of having the house to themselves and their lack of enthusiasm was unsettling. She had thought half-term week ideal because she wouldn't have to worry about them sleeping in or skipping school all together. She could freeze plenty of meals and ask Sarah to keep an eye on them, but what would they get up to with all that free time in an empty house? How easy would it be to abandon their revision plans and fill the place with friends? Would people stay over and, more importantly, where would they sleep?

'Are you sure?' she asked.

'Yes!' Scarlett and Liam cried.

They were waiting for Nina to leave and she almost did but turned back. 'Is there something I should know about?'

Liam had his back to her again and refused to answer, so it was left to Scarlett to respond for both of them.

'No, Mum, there's absolutely nothing you should know about.'

Sunday, 14 February 2016
Being a parent had its rewards, but it also had its challenges and Nina had had her fair share. There had been all the usual new mother problems which, with hindsight, were nothing compared to what was to come. No sooner had her children started school and freed up some of her time than she had become a single parent and had spent the best part of a decade being pulled in at least two opposing directions, often more. At the point when she had married Bryn, Liam and Scarlett had both been learning to be independent, and Nina had mistakenly thought that her time would gradually become her own, to devote to her own needs and those of her new husband. So far, that hadn't

happened. While she wasn't suggesting Liam and Scarlett should be expected to fend for themselves, she was beginning to wonder if it was no coincidence that they had required more maternal intervention and not less since her marriage.

Her children had changed. Liam had transformed from cave dweller to social butterfly, while Scarlett had become more introverted. Sarah had told her it was natural for them to be affected by Bryn's arrival, but Nina refused to accept full responsibility for the changes in their personalities, which weren't necessarily problems anyway. Liam had needed to get out more, while Scarlett had let her studies slip. They were teenagers, they were making it up as they went along, and if ever there was a clash in the family, it was more often with each other than the usurper her mum had invited into their home. Liam had stolen Scarlett's best friend, and Scarlett had distanced herself from both of them.

It was sometimes hard to keep up with her children's complicated lives, but it didn't take long for Nina to notice when their respective positions changed again, or figure out the reason why.

'Have Liam and Eva split up?' she asked Scarlett, who had surprised her by being up and dressed when Nina returned home from a morning at the shop. She suspected Valentine's Day had something to do with it, which was also what prompted her question. Scarlett's brother hadn't ventured out of the house since coming home from school on Friday afternoon.

Scarlett was lounging on the sofa and didn't take her eyes from the TV. 'Looks that way.'

'What happened?'

Scarlett shrugged. 'Stuff,' she said helpfully.

'Will he be all right?'

From the blank expression on Scarlett's face, Nina could only presume his sister didn't know or care. 'And what about Eva? She must have told you how she feels. Is that why you're spending so much time with her again?'

'It's Valentine's Day, Mum, of course she's upset.'

'You don't think they'll make it up?'

'Doubt it,' Scarlett said. 'Can I have some breakfast?'

'Help yourself,' she said, but rather than let Scarlett off the hook so easily, she followed her into the kitchen. 'Did you get a Valentine's card, by any chance?'

'Why, would you like to see it?'

'I was only asking,' Nina said. 'Is it wrong to take an interest in my daughter's affairs?'

Rather than answer, Scarlett began making toast.

'He's a lovely boy,' Nina said, with a little more authority than she had previously possessed. Linus had called over the day before while they were all having dinner. As Nina might have predicted, the moping teenager had been overshadowed and overpowered by her daughter, who had been furious with him for turning up unannounced. 'Are things getting serious between you two?'

Another shrug.

Nina gritted her teeth as she prepared for another serious talk. She and Bryn would be flying off to Rome on Thursday. They would be away for three days, and more importantly, two nights. She trusted Liam to behave responsibly, with or without a girlfriend, but Scarlett worried her. It was natural for a parent to feel more anxious about their daughters, but Nina's opinion was also founded on their respective personalities. Liam was the more considered of the two, while Scarlett was impulsive. If it had been Scarlett who had split up with her boyfriend, the whole house would have been expected to suffer too. Her son kept his troubles to himself.

Leaning against the kitchen counter, Nina watched her daughter. She was amazed how quickly Scarlett was transforming into a young woman – every day Nina was losing a little more of her baby girl.

'Will he be coming over while we're away?'

'I don't think I could stop him.'

'I hope you can,' Nina said. 'I hope you're confident enough to tell him when he's going too far.'

The jar of Nutella in Scarlett's hand slipped momentarily in her eagerness to finish making breakfast and escape the conversation.

'I don't want him staying over,' Nina continued. 'I'm not saying it's never going to happen, but not yet, and not by a long mark. And most definitely not while we're away. I've told Sarah to drop by at any time and without notice. You might think you're in control, Scarlett, but sometimes things can move at a much faster pace than you're expecting. I don't want you being caught out if that happens.'

'Mum,' groaned Scarlett.

'No, you've wriggled out of this conversation for long enough. We need to talk about it and we need to talk about it *now*.'

'If you're *that* worried, why are you going away? Stay at home if you don't trust me.'

Nina was very much aware that she was the one putting Scarlett in a potentially vulnerable situation, which made her all the more determined to protect her daughter – from herself as much as anything else. 'I do trust you. Tell me this isn't an issue. Tell me I don't need to run out and buy you some condoms. I know I can't stop you having sex for ever, but I want to know that, when it happens, you're prepared.'

'Oh for God's sake, Mum!' Scarlett yelled.

To Nina's surprise, her daughter didn't continue with the rant. She simply held her mother's gaze and waited for her to work out what she wasn't saying. It took a long, uncomfortable moment, but eventually Nina had no choice but to listen to the unspoken confession.

'You have done it? When? How? What happened – God, no, please don't answer that.'

Nina was mortified. She wanted to know everything while at the same time she wasn't prepared to hear any of it.

'Can I go now?'

Nina nodded.

'And if your next suggestion is for me to go on the pill, then save your breath. I already am.'

Nina stood in the same spot long after Scarlett had left, staring into space and wondering what she was supposed to do next. She had known this day would come and had hoped it wouldn't be for some time yet. Scarlett was almost sixteen, she had a steady boyfriend and she had enough common sense to arrange to go on the pill all by herself. She was pretty sure that Liam and Eva had had a sexual relationship. How could she object to her daughter sleeping with her boyfriend when she had silently condoned her son sleeping with someone else's daughter who was only just sixteen? Technically, Scarlett wasn't old enough, but was that such a big issue these days?

If there was a problem, surely it had to do with Nina's relationship with Scarlett and the fact that, despite their previous conversations and her daughter's assurances, she hadn't turned to her mother for advice or support. Scarlett hadn't wanted Nina there when she had explained to the doctor that she was about to have adult relations. Was that a reflection of their relationship, or was it simply that Scarlett was growing up?

A kiss on the cheek gave her a start.

'Penny for your thoughts?' Bryn said.

'Oh, you don't want to know,' she replied, although she desperately wanted to tell him. She would have closed the kitchen door and shared every last detail, but looking at her husband, she suspected he didn't have time. She had left him sleeping after a late night on the taxis and hadn't expected him to get up until mid-afternoon, but he was already showered and dressed. 'Are you going out?'

'I couldn't sleep so I thought I'd start my shift early. With any luck I might earn enough to treat us to the odd ice cream or two while we're away,' he said, still smarting from Nina's insistence that she pay for the holiday.

'Oh, OK.'

'You don't mind, do you? I know it's Valentine's Day, but we said we'd save the romance for Rome.'

Glancing over at the champagne and chocolates Bryn had left out for her that morning, she said, 'Yes, I've had my fill of romance for one day.'

'Is something wrong?'

Nina took a deep breath and exhaled slowly. 'No, everything's fine,' she said. 'Different, but fine.'

Scarlett

I think I became quite good at leading a double life. Most of the time I was walking around as if I were still the same boring old me, with the same friends, same idiot brother, same nagging mum and a dad who forgot I existed most of the time. But once in a while I got to be someone else, someone who was like this sex goddess who had men falling at her feet. It was a-maz-ing.

But as well as the fun bits, there were times when he was proper annoying. We'd arrange to be together and then something would happen so he couldn't make it and I'd be left feeling really, really frustrated. I should have been glad that time I got him back – when it was me standing him up for a change – but it was even worse!

I'd been complaining that we wouldn't be spending Valentine's Day together properly, so to make up for it, he'd promised to spend the evening before with me, and not just a snatched hour either. It should have been easy because Liam and Eva had split up and there was no one to check or double-check my story, and the story was I was going out with Linus. I felt a little bit mean about using Linus.

He used to follow me around like a puppy dog and didn't mind that everyone thought we were going out when I wouldn't even let him kiss me any more. But to be honest, I felt even meaner on Eva. I should have gone over to see her really. We were back being best friends and she needed me, but Eva wasn't the only one with problems. Things had been a bit weird after New Year, it was like he expected me to be happy about keeping things the way they were, as if that was how it was going to be for ever. He could have me pretty much when he wanted and the rest of the time he played at being this oh-so-loving husband at home. It wasn't fair. I didn't want things to stay the same. I just didn't realize how much things would change.

So anyway, we had everything planned for my pre-Valentine's Day treat, but before I could go out, Mum made us all have dinner together. We never used to bother sitting down at the table before she married Bryn and it sort of annoyed me. It was like she couldn't be bothered doing the stuff she used to do with me, like going out on our shopping sprees, and she thought forcing us all together once a week would make up for it. I only went along with it because sometimes it was better to give a little so she wouldn't pick up on the big things – like how awkward I felt sitting there, pretending everything was normal.

So we were all there, only when Mum was dishing up some weird fish pie she started making these huffing and puffing noises.

'There, I've switched off my phone,' Bryn said.

When he winked at me, I turned mine off too and gave Mum a big smile. Liam shoved his in his pocket.

'This looks lovely, Mum,' I told her.

Mum looked stunned, although, in fairness, she was shocked most times I said something nice. I suppose I can't blame her, I had been such a narky cow over Christmas, but my plan was to start the new year with a new me – God, I made a mess of that, didn't I? One thing I did change was my makeup, because he'd told me how much nicer I looked wearing less. Not that I wouldn't wear any, but I experimented a bit and found a new look that saved me a fortune on eyeliner.

'I wanted to do something special,' Mum said. 'It's a new recipe with lobster in it.'

'Very decadent,' I told her.

Liam laughed at me. 'You can tell you've been swotting all week. Or is it those extra lessons Mr Swift gave you?'

'Shut your face, Liam,' I said.

'Ignore him, love,' Bryn said. 'Use frilly words all you like, it might rub off on the rest of us luddites.'

Liam gave me a look. 'How does Scarlett always manage to get people to take her side?'

'I don't take sides,' Bryn said. 'I'm equally happy letting both of you run rings around me. I presume you'll be wanting a lift to Eva's later?'

'No!' Liam said, like it had been a stupid question.

Mum's ears pricked, but before she could say something, Bryn turned to me. 'Oh, right. How about you, Scarlett? Would you like to book my services?'

'I'm going to see Linus, if you don't mind dropping me off? I won't stay out too late.'

'And you'll be wanting me to pick you up again?'

I nodded politely like a good girl.

Everything was going to plan, but the minute Bryn started

clearing away the dishes there was a knock at the door. No one was expecting anyone, so Mum was nominated to chase off the salesman. She's used to it at the shop and for a minute I thought she must have slammed the door on him, because she came back really quickly, only she had this weird look on her face.

'We have a visitor,' she said, looking directly at me. She was dying to see my expression when Linus walked in.

'What are you doing here?'

'I tried phoning,' he mumbled.

My cheeks were burning and Mum must have thought I was mortified, but I was so bloody angry. 'And?'

Linus struggled to get the words out. He was such an embarrassment. 'I dunno,' he said. 'I was just around.'

'Aren't you going to introduce us, Scarlett?'

It was Bryn asking and I just glared at him.

'We've heard such a lot about you,' Mum said. 'It's lovely to meet you at last, Linus. This is my husband, Bryn, and of course you know Liam.'

'All right, mate,' Liam said with a bemused smile.

Mum made Linus sit down, and straight away Liam and Bryn stood up.

'I think I'll have a quick shower before I go to work,' Bryn said.

Liam didn't make any excuses, he just followed Bryn out of the room with a stupid grin on his face.

'You should have asked me first,' I hissed.

'But you were complaining about it being too cold to come out. I thought you'd be pleased.'

Oh, great, I thought. Now you've buggered up any plans I had for getting rid of you.

191

'Well, *this is nice,*' Mum said, and for a minute I thought she was going to sit back down at the table. 'If you two want to stay in, you can go into the living room, if you'd like. I'll stay in here and get on with my monthly accounts. You'll hardly know I'm here.'

I knew what Mum was doing; she didn't want me taking Linus upstairs to my bedroom in case we went too far. God, if only she knew that was the last thing on my mind. In fact, if I hadn't been so annoyed that Linus had messed everything up, I might have laughed. It was too late to worry about taking precautions as far as Grandma Nina was concerned.

19

The Accusations

As Scarlett continued on her journey to school, Vikki remained by her car, her impulse to confront the schoolgirl ebbing away as she struggled to think of an opening line. 'Hello, Scarlett, I hear you're pregnant,' was hardly a great start, but then neither was asking her directly who the father was. And even if she had been brazen enough to ask, she could hardly expect an answer. Not that a reply would be necessary to uncover the truth; all Vikki would need was to see Scarlett's reaction to the question and the person asking. But her courage had failed her and as she heard the distant shrill of the school bell, she knew she had missed her opportunity.

The road began clearing of parents' cars and the raucous chatter from the kids was eventually contained inside the school buildings. The silence only served to intensify the thudding of Vikki's heart, bringing waves of fear that made her feel slightly seasick. She needed to act. She needed to do something. If she were going to keep her promise to her mum, she had to leave now so they could go together to the hospital, but when she did move, it was to walk away from the car.

She kept her head down and pulled her bag close to her chest as she walked through the school gates. It was easy to imagine being back at school on one of those rare occasions when she had been late for class, and she was halfway to the entrance before she reminded herself that she wasn't on her way to lessons. She needed to turn around and leave because she didn't belong here. What if Rob saw her? What would she tell him? What could she say to anyone when she couldn't even admit to herself why she was so afraid?

It would all blow over, she told herself. Scarlett might think that her mystery man would stand by her and her baby, but how could he? He would know that the moment he stepped forward he would be arrested. And if Scarlett went ahead and had the baby without him, a DNA test could still be used to prove his guilt. Vikki didn't know Scarlett, and she didn't know what it was like to be in love at fifteen, but she knew what it was like to be in love so deeply that you would be willing to sacrifice anything and everything. Scarlett would protect him. She would do the right thing and have an abortion so that her lover would never be revealed. The suspicions would be forgotten and life would get back to normal. Who wouldn't want that?

Veering away from the school buildings, Vikki headed towards the staff car park with no plan other than to avoid going back out through the school gates and giving up. When she reached Rob's car she was shivering, and the touch of steel was so cold it made the tip of her finger burn as she trailed it along the length of the bodywork. She could see slithers of paper on the front passenger seat and recognized them as the remnants of a tube of indigestion tablets.

Rob hadn't eaten that morning, but his stomach had been churning, perhaps in sympathy with hers. Perhaps not. On the back seat there was one of Freya's books, but it wasn't images of a little girl that her mind summoned, or at least not that little girl.

I want my mum, Vikki thought, and the need for comfort was at last strong enough to send her off in the right direction, but as she approached the gates, a car turned into the school and sped past her. The driver screeched to a halt and Vikki wondered if she could slip out of the school without being noticed, but Nina was looking directly at her when she got out of her car. When Scarlett's mum began walking towards her, Vikki felt a new surge of nausea.

'She's pregnant.'

'I know, Nina. I'm sorry . . . '

'She won't say who did this.'

'Sarah said.'

'Did she tell you he's married?' Nina asked. She was talking fast. She hadn't come to the school expecting to see Vikki, who was now wishing she had had the good sense to stay away. Nina had somewhere else to go, something else to do.

'She did.'

'I accused Bryn,' Nina said, and gasped as she too swallowed back tears. 'Do you know what it's like to look at the man you thought you would love forever and think him capable of something like that?'

Shaking her head, Vikki's jaw clenched along with her stomach as she tried to stop herself from throwing up, bursting into tears, or both.

'I wouldn't wish it on anyone,' Nina said, and for a split

second, she looked as if she were about to give Vikki a hug. She didn't. She simply said, 'I'm sorry, Vikki, I really am. I have to go.'

Before Nina could leave, Vikki had to ask the question she was pretty sure she didn't want to know the answer to. 'What are you going to do, Nina?'

Nina closed her eyes and inhaled deeply, held it, then let it go. 'I think I accused the wrong man. I need to speak to Rob. I need to know if all those extra lessons he gave my daughter were strictly on the curriculum. I'm sorry,' she said again, and when she turned away this time, there was no hesitation.

Vikki turned away too, heading once more for the exit, but after only a couple of steps she had to stop and throw up. After searching in her bag for more wet wipes, she pulled out her phone. Should she warn Rob? Probably, but first she needed to let her mum know that she wouldn't be able to make her hospital appointment.

20

Before

Monday, 15 February 2016

The old Ellison House had an air of mystery that had captivated Vikki from the moment she had first seen it. Her dad had taught her how to deconstruct old buildings in her mind's eye, stripping away the decay in search of foundations on which to build. Even during those visits when her mind had been on other things, she had wondered what potential lay undisturbed behind the large oak doors trapped behind crude metal shutters. But as she and Sarah walked up the steep limestone steps, Vikki couldn't summon up the initial excitement she had felt when Sarah had taken her by surprise by inviting her along to view the property.

It had taken Sarah weeks to track down the landowner, but she was making up for lost time and had already visited with a property agent. She was back, she said, for a second opinion and a business matter she wanted to discuss with Vikki. What that might be, Vikki could only imagine, and she was trying not to. She wasn't sure she could deal with what would be a tantalizing glimpse of the life of a professional, not now, when her life was taking her down another route.

'You're very quiet. Are you all right?' Sarah asked.

'Just tired.'

Sarah smiled. 'Ah, young love. Was Valentine's Day exhausting?'

'Actually, it was pretty quiet. Mum and I were at a spa on Saturday and stayed over, so yesterday I was having breakfast with Mum. I thought those things were supposed to reenergize you, but I got into my onesie as soon as I got home and spent the rest of the day snoozing on the sofa. Rob was exhausted too because Freya had been playing up for him while I was away. I think he was expecting to have her in bed by seven so he could watch non-stop sport and have a few beers – which is what he did on Sunday afternoon instead.'

'I can't say I'm sorry to hear someone else's day was as mundane as mine,' Sarah said as she unlocked the padlock on the metal shutters. 'Miles does his best, bless him, but even diamonds can't add much of a sparkle when you've been married as long as we have. Not that I'm complaining. I wouldn't want to be a newlywed again, far too tiring. Nina, on the other hand . . . she's off to Rome on a mini-break this week for a belated honeymoon. It must be nice, being so easily pleased.'

'She seems such a lovely person, and Bryn too.'

'Like I said, easily pleased,' Sarah said, almost to herself as she opened the metal shutter. She searched out the last key to open the oak doors, and when she twisted the door-knob, it turned with surprising ease. 'Shall we?'

Although the day was clear and bright, the house was

trapped in complete darkness and the meagre light that crept over the threshold surrendered itself to the inky blackness after only a few steps. With all the windows boarded up and no electrics, Sarah had come prepared with two spotlights which they used to sweep across the rooms, bringing brief life to the ornate cornices and high ceilings. It was possibly a blessing that there wasn't enough light to pick up the full extent of the dilapidation, not to mention the décor, which was more in keeping with the eighties than the period features it clashed with. Whoever had been responsible for the later interior design had been more interested in covering over cracks with Artex than reviving the house to its former glory.

After a very quick sweep of the ground floor and the two principal upper floors, the women stopped to catch their breath. There were additional rooms in the attic space and, if they were feeling adventurous, a basement too, but for today, Sarah had only wanted to get a feel for the place.

'OK,' Vikki said. 'Are you ready to tell me why I'm here, Sarah?'

Rather than answer, Sarah asked, 'What do you think?'

'You'd have to get a proper structural survey, but it does feel solid enough.'

'If I were after a surveyor's opinion, I'd have brought one,' Sarah said softly. 'What do *you* think?'

Pressure began to build at the back of Vikki's nose as tears threatened, making her feel not only silly and childish, but unworthy of Sarah's belief that her opinion might count. 'I love it,' she said. 'I want to pull down the shutters so we can get some light and life back into the place. I want to start peeling away all that ugly woodchip, strip away the layers of flaking paint and pull down the plasterboard you know will be hiding some amazing original features.'

'But what would you do with the house? Create one grand estate or split it up into apartments?'

'Oh, definitely apartments. From outside, you can see the natural divisions that would give you a penthouse with a roof terrace and two apartments on each of the other floors, maybe even a sixth in the basement.'

Sarah nodded. 'That's exactly what I expected you to say. And now I have a proposition for you. I've all but given up hope of Charlotte returning to take up her position in the family business, and I need help. I'm not looking for an expert – I have a team of builders, architects, technicians and project planners – I simply want someone to help with the paperwork and act as my sounding board. I know you're looking for work, and I'm not suggesting I could offer you either a full-time or permanent position, but assuming this project gets off the ground, then the job is yours.'

'I can't.'

'Of course you can,' Sarah said, never having considered the possibility of Vikki refusing. 'It's not only the Ellison House I see potential in, Vikki. You would be an asset too.'

'Oh, Sarah,' Vikki said as the sob she was holding back caught in her throat. 'Six months ago this would have been a dream come true, but things have changed. My family has to come first.'

'Nonsense, a girl like you can do both. I know you have other commitments, but I can be flexible. I wouldn't need much help immediately, it'll take months to get the project off the ground – you never know who's going to object when we go for planning permission,' she reminded her.

Vikki felt like an imposter. She had somehow tricked Sarah Tavistock into thinking she was something she very clearly wasn't. 'I'm sorry, Sarah. I'm shocked that you'd put so much faith in me, but I can't accept. I'm . . . ' Vikki had to take a deep breath as if she were about to impart terrible news. 'I'm pregnant.'

They were standing beside a large picture window that would provide the perfect vantage point to take in the full beauty of the surrounding Cheshire countryside, but it was impossible for Vikki to see through the dark.

'Are you happy about it?' Sarah asked eventually.

'It was planned,' she said, although it had come as a shock to both her and Rob that her body should respond so quickly to the decision they had taken on Christmas morning.

Even in the dim light, Vikki could sense the curious look Sarah was giving her. 'My goodness, I don't know what to say. I suppose I should admire you. I could barely cope with one, let alone two babies at your age.'

'It makes sense to have another one before I start concentrating on my career, and it gives Mum more time to enjoy her grandchildren.'

'But I thought her treatment had finished. She was doing so well.'

'And she still is,' Vikki said quickly. 'Mum has a meeting with her consultant next week and hopefully he'll tell her she doesn't need any more treatment.'

'Oh, I see,' Sarah said, in a tone that suggested she blatantly didn't.

'I'd rather you didn't tell anyone else I'm pregnant. It's still early days and we haven't even told Mum yet.'

'I won't say a thing,' Sarah said. 'Wow, you have taken me by surprise. I had you down as a career girl.'

'But I am,' Vikki said, shocked by her own admission. She had been telling herself for so long that she didn't really know what she wanted, but when she had stepped into the Ellison House and let her imagination run free, she had known exactly what she wanted to do with her life. 'I want a career more than anything.'

'Except another baby,' Sarah reminded her.

And that was the point: Vikki did need reminding.

Friday, 19 February 2016

Vikki could remember quite clearly her first trip to the midwife when she was pregnant with Freya. She had felt out of place amongst the other expectant mums, who seemed much older and far more experienced than she. Second time around, she had earned her place amongst the other mothers, and as she looked around the waiting room in search of familiar faces, she was pleased to spy an old school friend.

'Hi, I haven't seen you for ages,' she said as she took a seat opposite the girl whose name escaped her for the moment. 'What have you been up to?'

Rubbing the swell of her belly, the mother-to-be said, 'I would have thought that was obvious.' She smiled and added, 'Bloody hell, it must be five years since we saw each other. And if you really want to know what I've been up to, well, I went to uni, obviously, got my degree, came home, got a job, and then, oops, got pregnant. My boyfriend is still in shock. We were saving up for a house, but it looks like that'll have to wait until I go back after maternity leave.'

Vikki was still racking her brain, trying to recall the girl's name. She had lost touch with so many of her friends – which hadn't been difficult, given how their lives had gone in different directions. Every one of her mates in sixth form had either got apprenticeships or gone off to university. In less time than it took to get a degree, Vikki had left school, married Rob and become a mother. This girl, whose name was . . . Amy, had lived another dream.

'I can't believe our paths haven't crossed before now,' Amy said. 'I go out with some of the others every once in a while. Ah, but you never were one to go to gigs, or out clubbing, were you?'

'No, I suppose not,' Vikki said, thinking of all those times she had turned down invites until her school friends had stopped asking.

'Are you still with Mr Swift?'

It was Vikki's turn to smile. 'Except it's been a while since I called him Mr Swift. Yes, we got married and we have a little girl. Rob's looking after Freya now – it's half-term.'

'Is he still gorgeous?'

Blushing, Vikki said, 'Yes.'

'I know I shouldn't say this, but I had the most ridiculous crush on him at school and I was so jealous of you. You were one of the cleverest in the year and it drove me mad that you were the one being offered extra lessons. Should have been obvious, I suppose!'

Vikki looked over at the reception desk, where a midwife had appeared. She waited in the hope that she might be next on the list, but another name was called. It was going to be a long wait. 'I didn't start dating Rob until I'd left school.'

'Yeah, yeah,' Amy said. 'That's the official line and you're sticking to it.' She shrugged and added, 'But it's no one else's business.'

Vikki could continue to argue her innocence, but Amy was right, it was none of her business. 'You said you have a job, what is it you do?'

When Amy explained that she worked for a major manufacturing company, Vikki felt a pang of jealousy, even though it was a company she had never heard of. That wasn't the point. The point was she was doing something she clearly loved and, while the baby wasn't planned, she was determined that it wouldn't set back her career goals.

'I'm only taking four months off. I'm under no pressure to go back, but as much as I love the idea of being a mum, I think I'd be demented if I had to stay at home. What was it like when you had your little girl? How long did you take off?'

Vikki watched a heavily pregnant woman struggling to stand as her name was called. 'I didn't go back.'

Amy frowned as if the idea were an alien one. 'Do you like being a full-time mum?'

'Freya most definitely does. She started nursery last September, but she still sobs every time I leave her.'

'Doesn't it get boring, though, without any adult conversation?'

Vikki laughed and immediately wished she hadn't. It sounded as false as it felt. 'It's not like I'm in solitary confinement. I get to meet other mums and I help my own mum out quite a bit. She rents out holiday cottages and she's not been well lately so I've practically been running the place.'

'Sorry, Vikki, that must have sounded really rude of me. I'm sure I'll find out soon enough that being a mum is a job in its own right. It's the ones who want to stay at home but can't that we should feel sorry for,' Amy said, trying too hard to make up for being so dismissive of Vikki's chosen role in life. 'I just can't see me being one of them. It's not that I don't want this baby, it's simply that I love my job too. Is it so bad to want both?'

After turning down Sarah's job offer only days earlier, Vikki knew exactly what Amy meant. 'You're not the only one,' she said. 'I was offered a job—'

'Sorry, that's me,' Amy said when a midwife called her name. 'It would be nice if we could meet up again, Vik. If I don't bump into you here, then once I'm on maternity leave, I'll track you down.'

'Yes, that would be nice,' Vikki said, and meant it. 'I want to hear how you get on, juggling a career and mother-hood. It might give me the nerve to do the same.'

'It's a deal.'

Vikki was about to suggest they quickly swap phone numbers but Amy was one step ahead and handed her a business card. Of course she would have a business card, thought Vikki. 'I'll message you so you have my details too,' she said.

Twenty minutes later, Vikki's name was called. The first meeting with the midwife was perfunctory and uneventful. The more noteworthy events, such as hearing her baby's heartbeat for the first time and her first scan, were still some time away, so Vikki came out feeling no different than when she went in. She loved being a mum and she would love this baby as much as she loved Freya, but she couldn't feel the excitement she knew ought to be there. She had wanted this baby, she kept telling herself while she played with the business card in her pocket.

On her way out of the clinic, Vikki had her head down and only looked up as she approached the exit. Movement on the other side of the door caught her eye and she glimpsed the swish of ponytails as two girls turned and ran – and they had been girls, even though one was a couple of inches taller than Vikki. When she stepped through the door, Vikki glanced quickly down the corridor and spied the two running away as fast as they could. They turned a corner, but before they disappeared, the taller girl glanced over her shoulder. Her violet blue eyes fixed on Vikki for the briefest moment and widened in fear. Vikki had seen the girl at Sarah's New Year's Eve party. It was Nina's daughter, Scarlett.

After her visit to the midwife, Vikki didn't return home immediately but paid a quick visit to see her mum. Rob had suggested that they shouldn't tell Elaine until they had reached the critical three-month mark, but Vikki was over-ruling him, something she rarely did but she hoped he would understand. She needed someone to remind her how excited she was supposed to be and, as expected, her mum was overjoyed. A new grandchild was going to be the perfect remedy to a year that would otherwise be focused on her own health. Elaine could look forward to baby scans instead of dreading MRIs and follow-up appointments.

Her mum's enthusiasm gave Vikki's spirits a temporary lift, but only until she reached the Ellison House, which was her second detour. She pulled up outside the entrance and noted the tyre tracks on the drive that stopped short of the metal fence skirting the perimeter of the property. It had been less than a week since she had turned down the job offer, but Sarah wasn't the type to let a minor setback like Victoria Swift thwart her plans. She would have been back on site with a variety of builders and architects – all those people who would be part of her project team. Everyone except Vikki.

By the time Vikki reached home it was getting late and she suspected Rob and Freya would be starving. She didn't relish the idea of making dinner, which would reinforce the role she had assumed as opposed to the lost opportunity she might never get back, and was about to suggest they get a takeaway, but Rob had other plans.

'You're going out?' she asked when he met her in the hallway. He was wearing his running gear and holding a water bottle in one hand and his car keys in the other.

'I thought you'd be home ages ago. I've been waiting, Vikki.'

'I texted to say I was going to see Mum.'

He kissed her cheek. 'I know, I'm not complaining, but I've been cooped up for hours and I need to get out.'

'You should try doing it full time,' she muttered.

Shrugging out of her coat, Vikki could barely lift her head, let alone the corners of her mouth to return the smile her daughter gave her. She had toddled out of the living room with her arms open wide for Vikki to scoop her up.

'Mummy home!'

'Hello, pumpkin. Have you been driving Daddy crazy?'

'Yes,' Freya said proudly.

Vikki glared at Rob, who was now at the front door. 'Good,' she said.

'I'll drive over to the park, do a few circuits and be back before you know it,' he said. After a moment's thought he added, 'But if you and Freya want to eat now, I'll grab something later. There's bound to be a microwave meal at the back of the freezer somewhere.'

Vikki didn't reply.

'Right, see you later,' Rob said. He had opened the door and managed to ignore his wife's glare until she stopped him in his tracks.

'Everything was fine, by the way,' she said. 'In case you were wondering how I got on at the clinic.'

There was a flash of irritation. 'Yes, I know. You said in your text,' he said. He looked about to leave but, with a sigh, he let his shoulders sink so he would appear suitably admonished. 'Look, I won't be long. You can tell me all about it later.'

Vikki turned without saying another word and it was Freya who waved goodbye to her daddy. In the living room, she was dismayed to find the floor covered in toys and crumbs. Rob had obviously let Freya do whatever she wanted to keep her quiet.

'Are you hungry?' she asked.

Freya pointed at the mess on the floor. 'More bikkies, please!'

'I don't think so. How about you help me tidy up this mess and then we can have some fish fingers?'

'And beans?'

'Yes, and beans.'

'Yay!' Freya said, clapping her hands. 'Me love beans, and chips, and ice cream, and Mr Tumble, and Daddy, and Peppa Pig, and Anna, and Elsa, and Olaf, and you!'

Vikki knelt down on the floor and began gathering up toys as Freya continued with a list of all the loves of her life. It was only when Vikki dared to put Olaf into the toy box that Freya stopped to take him back out.

'No, me love Olaf best. Mummy give him a big kiss.'

Freya held out the toy and when Vikki looked up, the little girl's smile wavered. Dropping the toy, she stepped closer and placed her sticky palm on her mother's cheek. 'No cry, Mummy,' she told her.

Vikki wanted to say it was all right, that Mummy was happy and then give her daughter the biggest smile she could manage, but she dropped her head instead.

'Would you like some help?'

Vikki didn't know if it was guilt or kindness that had brought Rob back, nor did she care, she simply wanted him by her side. Not trusting herself to speak, she waited for him to kneel down beside her, and they cleared away the mess in silence.

'Better now,' Freya said. She still had a frown on her face.

'All better,' Rob agreed, and in a forced tone that was meant to be light, he said, 'How about we put some music on and you can show Mummy the new dance we made up today?'

With their daughter preoccupied, Rob sat down on the sofa and pulled Vikki on to his knee. She rested her head on his shoulder.

'Let's try this again,' Rob said. 'How did you get on at the clinic today?'

'I'm fine. We're both fine.'

Rob wiped the tears from her cheek before trailing his

fingers down her arm and across her thigh. He gently placed the palm of his hand against her abdomen. 'Have you got a proper due date?'

'Twenty-seventh September.'

'Wow,' he whispered.

'Wow,' she said, although she wasn't quite sure why. Neither of them had sounded surprised or excited.

'We said we would let things happen, and they have,' he said. He hooked a finger under her chin and lifted her face towards him. 'It's what you wanted, Vikki.'

'I know.'

'And I don't mean to sound harsh, but you have to stop sulking over the Tavistock job. It wasn't meant to be, not yet,' he said as kindly as he could. 'If anything, doesn't your reaction now prove you weren't ready to take on something like that. Imagine how a burly builder would react if you started blubbing every time you didn't get your way.'

'But I wouldn't,' she said. 'It's just . . . It's just my hormones.'

'I know it is. And I'm not suggesting for a minute you can't manage, of course you can, you're about to be a mum of two.' He drew her gaze to Freya, who was grinding crumbs into the carpet as she jumped and twirled. 'And a far better parent than I am.'

She wished she had Rob's certainty and wondered how life had become so confusing. It wasn't always the case. Her dad had helped her map out her life from an early age, from the subjects she chose, the after-school clubs she should – and shouldn't – attend, and what university course she should be aiming towards. It had taken Rob to make her see that she had been following someone else's dream, and

210

should make her own choices in life, and she had. Or had she? Was this really where she wanted to be?

'It feels different this time,' she said. 'With Freya, it was all new and exciting, but now I know exactly what I'm taking on, what we're taking on. Playing happy families is harder when you know it's not a game.'

'Tell me about it,' he said. 'Freya's been driving me to distraction, asking why you were out so long. She was inconsolable, and that's why I was so desperate to go for a run. But I'll stay if you want me to. I'll even make tea, if you don't mind beans on toast.'

Safe in Rob's arms, Vikki's anxieties began to ease. 'I'm afraid I've promised Freya fish fingers,' she said, 'and before you claim not to know how to cook them, you showed me, remember?'

'I suppose I could jog on the spot while they're in the oven.'

'Oh for goodness' sake, go on your run.'

Rob shifted along to the edge of his seat, sliding her off his knee in the process. 'Only if you're sure,' he said.

Standing up, Vikki held out her hand and helped him to his feet. 'Go, that's an order. And when you get back, I'll tell you who else I saw at the clinic.'

'OK,' he said, not in the least bit interested in anything except getting out of the living room before Freya noticed.

'She was someone you'd recognize from Sedgefield High,' Vikki said, casually offering another clue.

'A student? Doesn't surprise me,' Rob said, having reached the door. 'We should have a staffroom sweep for which students will be waddling down the corridors by the end of the year. You can spot them a mile off.'

Vikki waited until Rob had stepped out into the hall. 'Would you expect Scarlett Carrington to be one of them?' she called after him.

Rob poked his head around the door, his eyes wide. 'Are you sure it was her?'

'She looked right at me,' she said. 'But she was with another girl and they might not have even been there for an appointment. They could have been there for some other reason, but . . . '

'But?'

Vikki bit her lip. 'They did turn and run when they saw me, as if they had something to hide.'

'Oh, shit.'

'Do you think I should say something to Sarah? I thought maybe she could have a quiet word with Scarlett's mum, but I don't want to be a snitch.'

Rob leant against the door, his hand gripping the handle. 'What if she's going to have an abortion anyway? It's not our secret to tell.'

'She was at an antenatal clinic, Rob. Whichever one of them is pregnant, they were planning on keeping it.'

'Then fine, tell Sarah. Someone needs to talk some sense into them.'

'I know, but they're what, sixteen? It's their choice. Isn't that what you've always told me? I wasn't much older when I had to make some serious life choices. Would you have been happy if my mum and dad had said I was too young to get married?'

'And would you be happy if it was Freya who got pregnant when she was still at school? Well, would you?' Rob said, raising his voice in disbelief.

At the mention of her name, Freya made a beeline for her father, but Rob was too quick and retreated back out into the hall. 'We'll talk later, I have to go,' he called out. The front door slammed, and he was gone.

Vikki didn't give Scarlett another thought as she went into the kitchen to prepare dinner. Taking out a box of frozen fish fingers, she wondered if she was that good a mum. Didn't real housewives go out and buy fresh fish, cut them into goujons and cover them in homemade breadcrumbs? Would that give her more self-satisfaction in her chosen career? She wished it were that simple.

The sound of a phone ringing pulled Vikki from her musings and it felt strangely portentous that it should be Sarah calling.

'Hi, Vikki, I hope I'm not disturbing you,' she said and, presuming the answer was no, quickly added, 'I wanted to let you know that we've had our offer on the Ellison House accepted.'

'An offer? I didn't even know you'd put one in.'

Vikki had been in the middle of sliding the grill pan under the heat, but it was catching on the runners and she pushed harder than she intended. The pan slipped and fish fingers rained down on to the bottom of the oven. She held back the curse which had as much to do with the news as it did the mess she had made. The Ellison project would be done and dusted before Vikki had a chance to recover from the birth of her baby.

'I know it's quick work, but once I get an idea in my head, there's no stopping me. Look, you sound busy so I won't keep you. Maybe we can meet up for coffee and have a little brainstorming session? I've tried talking to Miles about it, but he's still sulking that I've jumped to another project when I haven't even completed the last. I'll admit it's a bit of stretch but most of the houses on the other development have been sold off plan. I think I could stretch to paying you in Danish pastries for your time, if you'll help.'

'Oh, OK. I'd like that,' Vikki said, and she would. But it would also hurt like hell.

'Great, we'll speak soon.'

Vikki's mind raced as she wondered if she should mention Scarlett. Rob had a point about how she would feel if it were Freya. 'Before you go,' she said, 'have you seen Nina lately?'

'She's enjoying herself in Rome as we speak.'

'She didn't take Scarlett with her, did she?' Vikki asked, wondering if today had been a case of mistaken identity.

'No, she and Liam can manage fine on their own. Miles was over there today, checking up on them, and apparently they haven't trashed the house yet,' Sarah said before asking a question of her own. 'Why do you ask?'

'I think there's something I need to tell you.'

Scarlett

I know it doesn't always seem like it, but I do love Mum. It's just not as simple as it used to be when I was little and all she had to do was give me a hug and everything would be all right. And that's all I was after I suppose, but when I told her I was pregnant, she went mad and started pointing the finger at everyone. Couldn't she see how scared I was? I really would have told her everything, and I mean everything, but it wasn't just my secret to share, was it?

He wasn't exactly happy about it when he found out either, and even though he kept saying it was my choice, it was so obvious he wanted me to get rid of it. 'Oh, it's your body, Scarlett,' he'd said and then, in the next breath, 'It would be such a shame if you never got to live your dreams first.'

I'd told him I needed time to think about it. I didn't want him getting the idea he could manipulate me and, if I'm honest, I wanted him to squirm for a bit, but, bloody hell, I didn't realize how far Mum would go. It was horrible when she accused Bryn and I was so glad to get out of the

215

house. I thought I'd be safe at school, but apparently not. I was in double English when she turned up.

Mr Swift was making us all sit in silence to read our revision notes, but we got restless and Linus started up some banter, except Mr Swift wasn't in the mood and sent him straight to the Cooler, and Mr Swift never sends anyone to the Cooler. So we all stayed quiet after that and the tension was unbearable. And I thought things were tense at home! I so jumped when someone prodded me in the back, and when I looked over my shoulder, Eva used her eyes to get me to look out of the window. We had a good view of the car park and I spotted Mum's car straight away because she hadn't parked in a space and was blocking everyone in – not a good sign.

It was like a slow-motion film as I turned back to the front and just stared at Mr Swift, who was flicking through essay papers. There was the rustle of paper and the odd sigh, and this tapping noise from a pen nib being struck against the hard surface of a desk, muffled slightly by the piece of paper caught in between. The pen left tiny black-ink wounds on my revision sheet.

Mr Swift looked up. 'Scarlett, be quiet,' he hissed.

I was prepared to hold his gaze but he was already picking up his phone. I watched him frown and then his face went grey and I mean, literally grey. I don't know why, maybe I've got some psychic ability or something, but I felt sick with dread. I carried on watching him, but he never looked back up again, not until Mrs Marshall, the school secretary, marched straight into the room without knocking. She had twenty-four faces to choose from, twenty-five including Mr Swift, but it was me she looked at first. Shit, I thought.

Mr Swift stood up and she whispered something in his ear. She kept her mouth covered, so we couldn't work out what she was saying, but I had a sinking feeling I didn't need to. Mr Swift's grey face turned bright pink in like the space of a few seconds. Everyone was whispering by now and I felt another prod in my back, but I ignored Eva this time and kept my eyes to the front.

Mrs Marshall finished whatever she had come to say and Mr Swift took a couple of steps towards the door, but he sort of stumbled to a stop. He turned back to look at his briefcase, which was next to his desk. Mrs Marshall picked it up and handed it to him and when he took it, his hand was trembling. It was just awful and I was getting so, so scared.

The school secretary put a hand on his arm and this time I could read her lips. 'We'll get this sorted,' she said. When she realised that Mr Swift wasn't going to say anything to the class, she turned to us and added, 'Mr Swift has been called away, but Mr Caldwell will be here in two minutes and we expect you to sit quietly in the meantime.'

Rob didn't look up as he stepped towards the door again. Other than me, and maybe Eva, no one was interested in what was going on any more – it doesn't take long for a group of Year 11s to get bored. When he did turn to the class, he ignored everyone else and stared straight at me. I knew what was happening, I just didn't want to believe it. Mum wasn't going to stop accusing people until one of them confessed.

I wanted to rush over and tell Mr Swift I was sorry, but he gave me such a look it turned my blood cold. I knew what he was thinking, even though he didn't say a word.

This is all your fault, Scarlett.

I suppose he had a point.

21

The Accusations

When Nina arrived in the main office, Mrs Marshall was sitting behind her desk keeping guard over two closed doors facing opposite each other; one was the Head of School's office, the other her deputy's.

'Is Mrs Anwar in?' Nina asked.

'Well, yes, but she's in a meeting. Did you want to make an appointment, Mrs—'

'Thomas. I'm Scarlett Carrington's mum.'

'Ah yes, of course. She is rather busy today, perhaps I could put something in the diary for later this week?'

Nina took a step nearer the office on the left where only a few months earlier she had thanked Scarlett's English teacher for taking extra-special care of her daughter. 'No, I need to see her now,' she said, not knowing when her courage would fail.

She had almost lost her nerve when she saw Vikki in the car park and she didn't know how she had managed to look her in the eye, knowing she could be about to destroy her husband's reputation and Vikki's life along with it. When Mrs Marshall pulled a face as she looked at her computer screen, Nina surmised there was a polite refusal on its way. She reached Mrs Anwar's door before the secretary had a chance to react.

'Please, you can't just—' Mrs Marshall began, but Nina was already stepping inside.

The room was bright and airy, despite the piles of books and papers crammed into every available space. The furniture was modern with a desk close to the window and a generously sized conference table that took up half the office and was currently occupied by half a dozen members of staff. All faces turned to the uninvited guest, but it was the woman with almond eyes and a warm glow to her complexion that invited Nina's attention. If the head were annoyed or offended by the interruption, she wasn't letting it show.

'I need to speak to you about Scarlett.'

'I see, perhaps—'

'She's pregnant.'

'Oh, I'm sorry to hear that,' Mrs Anwar said, shaking her head, 'and surprised too, if I'm honest.'

Mrs Anwar looked about to say something else, but Nina ploughed on, ignoring the curious looks being cast around the table. 'That's not why I'm here,' she said, as if her first piece of news hadn't been earth-shattering in itself. 'Scarlett's refusing to say who the father is and I think your Mr Swift might be able to fill in some of the gaps.'

Everyone sat up in their seats with the exception of Mrs Anwar, who rose to her feet. 'As you can see, I'm busy now, but if you like, I can speak to Mr Swift afterwards.'

'No, I'd rather talk to him myself.'

'All right, if you think it will help,' she agreed. 'I'll send a message for him to come over during morning break and we can sit down together. In the meantime, I'll finish my meeting as quickly as I can. If you wouldn't mind waiting outside, I think I can wrap things up here in fifteen minutes.' She looked to her colleagues and received nods of agreement.

'I don't think you appreciate how serious this is,' Nina insisted. 'My daughter is fifteen years old and if the school isn't willing to cooperate then I'm going straight to the police.'

Mrs Anwar's body stiffened..

'Please, I need answers.'

The young woman who had been sitting next to Mrs Anwar picked up the papers in front of her. 'If I might suggest, we only have a couple of items left on the agenda and I think we can manage without you, Nadia. We'll decamp to the staff room.'

'Thank you, Jane, that's good of you.'

'Shall I fetch Mr Swift?'

Nina turned to find the school secretary standing behind her. She had been there for some time.

'Yes, please, Pam.'

When the room had emptied, Mrs Anwar motioned Nina to a chair opposite and poured her a glass of water, which Nina took gratefully with shaking hands.

'Perhaps while we wait for Mr Swift, you could tell me how you think the school might be able to help.'

'Not the school. Mr Swift,' Nina said, but stopped herself from saying more. She had been too quick with her accusations so far, she needed to take her time. At the very least, she wanted Rob Swift in the room before she made another accusation. 'All I know is that Scarlett is pregnant to a married, and therefore much older man. There are only a limited number of men she has contact with who fall into that category, and I think she has confided in her form teacher.'

Mrs Anwar remained outwardly calm but her left eye twitched. 'Mrs Thomas, we have a very strict policy about safeguarding our pupils and there are procedures to follow which protect not only the student but, to some extent, our teachers too. If Mr Swift had been aware of any issues, he would have had a duty to act on them.'

'He knows something, and I won't leave without answers.'

'Perhaps the solution to this is rather obvious. We need Scarlett to explain herself.'

Nina shook her head. 'You really don't know my daughter, do you? She won't say who it is – and believe me, I've tried. She'll protect him at the cost of everything and everyone else. She wouldn't even name him when . . . When . . . '

Mrs Anwar stood briefly to fetch a box of tissues from her desk and waited for Nina to compose herself. 'This is obviously a testing time for you, Mrs Thomas, but I promise you the school will do all it can. We have specially trained staff and, of course, I'll do my best to support you and Scarlett.'

'And I suppose Mr Swift will be happy to help too,' Nina added.

There was a twitch of the eye again as Mrs Anwar said, 'What exactly do you think Mr Swift will be able to tell you?'

Nina's breath caught at the back of her throat. From the other side of the door, she could hear movement. She was about to come face to face with the man who had ripped the heart out of her family. 'That he's been sleeping with my daughter.'

The door opened and Mr Swift came into the room, closely followed by Mrs Marshall, who asked, 'Shall I organize some tea?'

Nina and Mrs Anwar were both too stunned to speak and simply shook their heads.

'None for me, thanks,' Mr Swift said with a confident smile. He approached the table and put his hand on the back of a chair. 'Shall I take a seat?'

'Actually, I'm not sure you should,' Mrs Anwar said, pausing until Mrs Marshall had left the room and closed the door behind her. 'Mrs Thomas has made a serious allegation and I don't think we can carry on with this meeting, or at least not all together, not until I know the facts.'

Mr Swift straightened up, but didn't look immediately concerned. 'What kind of allegation?'

'Did you know Scarlett is pregnant?' Mrs Anwar asked.

Rob pursed his lips and bowed his head as if the news were a burden he shared with the family. 'Yes, Vikki told me she'd spotted her at an antenatal clinic, and it was confirmed later by Sarah Tavistock, who is a mutual friend. It's such a shame. She had— she *has* so much potential.'

Nina scrutinized her daughter's teacher with new eyes as she tried to hold on to the courage of her convictions. He carried a calm and compassionate presence, or was he simply cool and calculating? It had been a joke to think how many of his students had a crush on him, but what if those feelings had been reciprocated? Bryn, by contrast, was not the obvious candidate for a schoolgirl's infatuation. Not only was he that bit older, but he didn't have Rob Swift's natural ease or sophistication. Bryn was genuine and honest, how else could he have persuaded her children to love and trust him, almost as quickly as he had persuaded her?

She wished she could be sure which of the two men she had accused this morning had stolen her daughter's heart and her innocence – or was it someone else entirely? Charlotte Tavistock didn't think so, and despite Mr Swift's sympathetic expression, neither did she.

'Mrs Thomas is understandably upset, not least because Scarlett won't say who the father is,' Mrs Anwar continued carefully.

Rob looked surprised and pulled a face. 'Does Scarlett need to name him? It's no secret that she's been dating Linus Vincent.'

When Nina spoke there was iron in her voice. She wasn't going to be taken in by his charm like some teenage girl. 'She says she's never slept with him.'

Rob gave her a look as if to say, And you actually believe that? Nina wanted to slap him.

'What Scarlett has said is that the man is married and he's promising to look after her,' Nina continued. She held his gaze and neither of them blinked when she added, 'And I think that man is you.'

'And this is where the meeting ends,' Mrs Anwar said, looking directly at Nina. 'I'll speak to our Safeguarding Officer and instigate a formal investigation. We'll need to take statements from everyone before deciding what to do next.'

'No, let's do this now,' Rob said.

Nina tore her eyes away from the head to watch as Rob took a seat. He rested his elbows on the table as he leant towards Mrs Anwar and said, 'You and I both know, Nadia, that an investigation will take for ever. Mrs Thomas wants answers now and I'm more than happy to cooperate as much as I can, if it will put her mind at rest.'

With her eye still twitching, Mrs Anwar said, 'If you're sure, Rob, but I warn you both: if we can't resolve this with an informal chat, I'm going to have to step things up.'

Nina, having no desire for chat, demanded, 'Did you sleep with my daughter?'

'No, Mrs Thomas,' Rob said. 'I get on well with Scarlett, as I do with many of my students, but, apart from anything else, I'm a happily married man with a beautiful wife who's expecting our second child.'

Nina's thoughts turned again to Vikki standing in the car park. What was this going to do to her? She was little more than a child and the last thing Nina wanted was to put her through the kind of ordeal she herself had experienced that morning. Unfortunately, Vikki's innocence didn't absolve Rob of his misdeeds. She had come this far. 'Charlotte Tavistock saw the way you kept looking at each other at the New Year's Eve party,' she began, 'and she remembers what it was like to be one of your students. I'm sure you remember that too.'

Rob stared at Nina without answering and it was Mrs Anwar who broke the tension building between the two adversaries. 'I think it best if I lead the questions from here, Mrs Thomas,' she said. 'Now, Rob, I'd like to say from the outset that I have the deepest respect for you as a teacher, but sometimes even the best of us make errors of judgement. You're an honourable man and I hope you would admit to any indiscretions and face the consequences rather than put innocent people like Mrs Thomas through further anguish. Is there, or has there ever been a relationship between you and Scarlett Carrington?'

'No.'

'And nothing that might have been misconstrued?'

'She's pregnant, for God's sake,' Nina cried. 'It's not like he might have accidentally impregnated her.'

'No to that as well,' Rob said.

Nina caught the beginnings of a smile on Rob's face. He had remained relaxed throughout. The bastard thought he was going to get away with it. She wished Sarah had been there to at least even out the numbers, but with a heavy heart Nina couldn't be sure which side of the table her friend would be on. She wondered if Charlotte had spoken to her mum yet.

'What about the extra lessons?' she asked, feeding Mrs Anwar the questions she wasn't supposed to be asking herself. 'She was determined to prove to him how well she could do.'

'That in itself doesn't constitute an inappropriate relationship, simply a positive one,' Mrs Anwar said. 'And if it gives you any reassurance, my staff work within specific parameters when it comes to building relationships with students, which, as I said, are there to protect them as much as the student.'

'I can't imagine anyone who would abuse a fifteen-year-old child being interested in working within specific parameters, do you?' Nina asked. When Mrs Anwar didn't answer quickly enough, Nina turned to the man who had barely taken part in his so-called interrogation. 'You have a history of being too friendly with your students, don't you? It's an open secret that you became involved with Vikki while she was still at school.'

'Malicious gossip does not equate to fact,' he said. 'And I can assure you, as I've assured Mrs Anwar in the past, my involvement with my *wife* did not begin until after she had left school.'

Turning to Mrs Anwar, Nina asked, 'And you simply took his word for it? Did you not consider he might be a potential danger to other young girls?'

Mrs Anwar's features gave no indication of unease or doubt in her fellow teacher. 'I can assure you I would never put any of my students in danger. And if you don't mind me saying so, Mrs Thomas, there really is very little evidence you're presenting that would make me doubt one of my most valued members of staff. Mr Swift is an excellent teacher and yes, I do trust his word. He knows the rules and he abides by them.'

Rob licked his upper lip where beads of sweat had appeared. 'Actually, I may as well say now, I might have worked around the rules a bit,' he said, 'but Scarlett was failing and I wanted to help, and I did help. My interventions got her back on track, didn't they?'

'What exactly do you mean, "work around them"?' Mrs Anwar asked sharply.

Rob did his best to look suitably embarrassed, as if he were about to confess a good deed. 'Scarlett was eager to catch up and wanted to continue the extra lessons over the autumn break. We met a couple of times at the library, that's all.'

'You weren't supposed to?' Nina asked, momentarily confused. The library trips had been around the time she had grounded Scarlett, and Nina had thought of it as adding to her punishment. What a fool she had been.

'We generally provide extra support within school premises,' Mrs Anwar explained. 'I only allow teachers and students off-site under special circumstances – school trips and suchlike.'

'So he's admitting to seeing her in secret?' Nina asked, ignoring the fact that she herself knew. She wanted a reaction from Mrs Anwar, and when it came it wasn't what she wanted.

'And there's nothing else, Rob?'

'I swear, no,' Rob said.

The faint creases on Mrs Anwar's brow deepened as her eyes narrowed. 'Do you have anything else that you want to add? Anything you might know that could shed some light on the situation?'

Rob shook his head. 'I appreciate how upset you are, Mrs Thomas, and it's understandable that you would want to believe it's anyone except Scarlett's stepfather, but it's not me. I swear, it's not me.' When Rob saw the look of confusion on Mrs Anwar, he feigned surprise. 'Did Mrs Thomas not tell you she's accused her husband of the same crime?'

'And I was wrong!' Nina cried.

'And you're wrong now,' Rob answered. When he leant back in his chair, Mrs Anwar did the same. The questioning was over.

Nina's jaw dropped. 'Is that it? You're going to leave it there?'

'Not quite,' Mrs Anwar said. 'I suggest the next line of questioning is directed at Scarlett.'

Nina felt tears sting her eyes but she refused to cry. If

this was Mrs Anwar's version of interrogation, they would get no closer to the truth. Scarlett would eat her up and spit her out. Nina needed to tell her what had happened to Charlotte, but Mrs Anwar was already on her feet.

22

Before

Friday, 19 February 2016
There was so much to see in Rome that Nina regretted limiting their break to only two nights. They had arrived at midday on Thursday and, after dropping off their luggage at a boutique hotel, they had set off to explore as many piazzas, fountains and basilicas as they could find. Only when they were ready to drop did they stop at a little taverna, where they remained long past midnight before returning to the hotel utterly exhausted.

The second day was turning out to be even more hectic, beginning with an early morning tour of the Vatican. Though they weren't particularly religious, the sheer grandeur of the architecture had been breathtaking, and viewing works of art by old masters such as Raphael, Bellini and Da Vinci had been overwhelming at times. The tour had almost ended prematurely when Bryn was caught attempting to take a photo in the Sistine Chapel, which was strictly forbidden. Nina hadn't appreciated how much Bryn loved art and she was stunned by his depth of knowledge on the subject. He knew all about the Roman Empire too, and as they walked around the Colosseum and then up the Palatine Hill after lunch, his running commentary rivalled that of any tour guide.

The one thing Nina did outdo him in was her stamina. Unlike Bryn, she was used to spending all day on her feet, and he didn't argue when later that afternoon she sent him back to the hotel while she scoured the shops for gifts for Liam and Scarlett, which she knew wouldn't be appreciated, but there would be sulks if she chose not to bother. Laden with tacky tourist souvenirs, the odd bag of speciality pasta and a Roman art book that she thought Bryn would like, Nina eventually dragged herself back to the hotel. It was after six and she would need to get changed quickly if they were to go out and enjoy their last night in Rome at a more leisurely, and hopefully more romantic pace.

Slipping quietly into the hotel room, she had expected to find Bryn snoozing but he was gazing out of the window with his mobile pressed to his ear. He hadn't heard her come in.

'You can't do that,' he said softly. He raked his fingers through his hair as he listened to the answer. 'I know, my love, but it's only one more night. We'll be home tomorrow.'

As Bryn listened to the next response he turned and was so shocked to find Nina eavesdropping that he took a step back and thumped his arm against the windowsill.

Nina's blood ran cold as all of Sarah's earlier warnings came back to haunt her. Her friend had told her not to rush into marriage. She had told her to take more time getting to know her prospective husband and yet, here she was, in the middle of a foreign city with a man who had hidden depths, the latest of which was only now being exposed. His voice had been so soft and soothing as he spoke to this other woman, and there was no doubt it was another woman on the other end of the line.

'Scarlett, your mum's here now,' he said.

It was Nina's turn to be stunned. She had been on the verge of demanding to know who Bryn was talking to, had imagined herself breaking down when he told her what a terrible mistake they had made and how he was in love with someone else. In that split second before Bryn had revealed he was talking to her daughter, Nina had even gone so far as to imagine how the divorce might go. Could the marriage be annulled? Would Bryn take her for every penny she had, exactly as Sarah had predicted? She waited for the relief to wash over her, but felt no more than the merest trickle.

'What's wrong?' she asked.

Bryn handed her the phone. 'She said she's been trying to call you.'

Nina would have to trawl the bottom of her bag to find her mobile. If it had rung, she wouldn't have heard it.

'Scarlett?'

There was a loud snuffling noise. 'Why didn't you answer your phone?'

'I didn't hear it. What's wrong? Are you upset?'

'I want you to come home.'

Turning away from Bryn, Nina sat down on the corner of the bed so she could give Scarlett her undivided attention. 'Why? Tell me what's happened.'

'Nothing. I just want you to come home.'

'It doesn't sound like nothing.'

'I miss you, that's all. Is that so hard to believe?'

Nina felt a little more reassured that Scarlett wasn't so upset that she couldn't be her usual snarky self. 'Have you been crying? You sound all bunged up.'

'I'm getting a cold.'

Nina wished that were true, that it was nothing more than a case of her daughter feeling ill and wanting her mum home to look after her, but her gut instinct told her that wasn't even close to the truth. 'Where's Liam?'

'In his room, probably.'

'Have you seen him today?'

'I've been out most of the time.'

'Out where? With Eva? Linus?' she asked, taking a more circuitous route to seek out the truth of the matter.

'What is this? Am I supposed to keep a diary of all my movements while you're away?'

Realizing Scarlett was far more adept at running rings around her than the other way around, Nina lost patience. 'Scarlett, I'm simply trying to understand what's happening so I have a better idea of why you're so upset that you want me to jump on the next flight home.'

'Does that mean you're not going to?'

'Honey, we'll be home by teatime tomorrow anyway. Tell me what's so desperate that you need me to come home now.'

There was silence on the other end of the phone and Nina felt frustration rising up her body like a red tide. She had always done her best to be the perfect mother; when her children were younger, whether she was scolding or cajoling them, she could usually find a way to make them see the error of their ways. She had never raised a hand to them, but right now she wanted nothing more than to reach down the line and shake some sense into her daughter. She wanted to scream at her until Scarlett told her what was wrong. She needed to know if she should be as worried as she felt, or if Scarlett was simply attention-seeking.

With her last scrap of self-control, she said, 'Tell me what's wrong. Please, Scarlett.'

'Nothing,' Scarlett said, stretching the word out as if her mother were being dim.

A wave of frustration crashed into Nina, obliterating her goodwill. 'Fine, don't tell me! Where's Liam? I want to speak to him.'

'He's out.'

'So he's not in his room?' Nina said, which was only marginally better than coming right out and calling her daughter a liar.

'He's with Eva.'

'They're back together?'

There was another sullen silence.

'So is that it? You're upset because Liam and Eva have made up and you've lost your best friend again?' Before Scarlett could answer, Nina added, 'I despair of you sometimes, Scarlett. The moment you're feeling left out, you think everyone else has to run around after you. Couldn't you think of other people's feelings for once? And by "other people", I mean me! Thanks for wrecking my first holiday with Bryn, not that—'

Nina didn't get any further because, halfway through her rant, Scarlett put down the phone.

'Can you believe she's hung up?' she said to Bryn, her mouth agog.

'What did she say?' he asked.

'Liam and Eva are back together and she wants us to

233

come home. She's lonely, by the sounds of it. What did she say to you?'

'Same sort of thing, although I didn't know about Liam. You can't blame her for feeling left out.'

Nina's anger had quickly dissipated and the cold fear from earlier trickled back into her veins. 'Do you think I was too hard?' She looked at the phone still clenched in her hand. 'I should phone her back.'

'You really think she'll answer?'

'I'll text her.'

'I'll text her too,' he said. 'And once she knows we love and support her, can we please resume our holiday?'

Nina was already composing her text. 'I suppose we can try,' she said, knowing there was little chance of relaxing now. The mood had changed and any idea of romance had been overpowered by a growing sense of anxiety. After years of putting her children first, Nina had thought she had earned the right to indulge her own needs for a change. Scarlett and Liam were almost adults and life was supposed to get easier from now on, but something didn't feel right and she wished she knew why.

As homecomings went, Nina and Bryn's was a muted one. The house was devoid of life.

'At least there doesn't seem to be any evidence of mad parties,' Bryn said.

'I'll see if either of them has left a note in the kitchen.'

After the desperate call from Scarlett the day before, Nina had eventually tracked down Liam. She hadn't expected him to offer any further insight into his sister's welfare, and he hadn't let her down. He had said she was fine, as far as he knew, and promised to keep an eye on her and let Nina know if there was anything to worry about. This was cold comfort from a seventeen-year-old boy who had been known to deny even knowing Scarlett in public.

While Bryn took their bags upstairs, Nina did a quick inventory of all the downstairs rooms on her way to the kitchen. Other than the odd pair of shoes and an empty cereal bowl, the place was surprisingly neat and tidy. The kitchen was another matter entirely; while there had been plenty of activity, it hadn't involved water, washing-up liquid or the dishwasher. Amongst the piles of plates and crumbs, there were no notes. Whatever was going on in Scarlett's life, she was no longer desperate to see her mum.

'Any clues?' Bryn asked.

Nina stood staring at the detritus that obscured the sparkling kitchen she had left three days earlier. 'I'll feel better when I've seen them both,' she said.

'You've been saying that for the last twenty-four hours, Nina,' Bryn said.

She wasn't surprised by the irritation in her husband's voice. Her mood had been awful since Scarlett's phone call. She had never felt so tense, or so afraid of *nothing*. It was as if she were expecting a bolt of lightning to strike her down at any moment, and she couldn't work out which direction it would come from. Her temperament hadn't been conducive to romance and she had tensed whenever Bryn had touched her. It wasn't his fault, but neither was it hers. She needed to speak to Scarlett.

'I'll try phoning them again,' she said, as Bryn began loading the dishwasher.

Neither of her children answered their phones, so she sent a message to each letting them know she was home and demanding that they call her.

Liam was the first to reply, but only by text. He was at Eva's house and Scarlett was there too. Neither would be home until later.

Scarlett didn't deign to respond, but at least Nina knew where she was.

'Why don't I run you a bath, and afterwards we can have another go at a romantic meal for two?' Bryn said. 'If we turn the lights down really low, we can pretend we're still in Rome.'

Nina exhaled slowly, forcing the tension from her body whether it was ready to leave her or not. 'It's worth a try,' she said. 'And I am so sorry for being such a cow. I promise I'll do better.'

Bryn switched on the dishwasher and took her hand. 'Come on,' he said, 'I'll scrub your back.'

As the bath began to fill with warm soapy suds, Bryn turned his attention to his wife and slowly began to undress her. It wasn't often that they had the house to themselves, but this wouldn't be the first time that Bryn had run a bath for her only to join her in the tub. If he initiated sex, she wouldn't object, but it wasn't what she wanted or needed right now and with an ache in her heart, she realized Bryn knew her well enough to know this too. He kissed her gently on the lips just once, and then taking her hand, helped her step into the bath.

'I'll bring you a glass of wine – assuming the kids haven't drunk it all.'

Nina slipped into the chamomile-scented suds and closed

her eyes. She wanted to cry and might have given in to the temptation if her phone, which had been within constant reach since the previous evening, hadn't started to ring. Sadly, Liam and Scarlett were continuing with their radio silence.

'Hello, Sarah, how are things?' she said.

'Where are you?'

Nina splashed warm water over her body. 'I'm in the bath.'

'At home?'

'Yes, we've not long got back.'

'How was it?' Sarah asked.

Deleting from her mind the disastrous ending to their trip, Nina said, 'It was beautiful. You were right about how much there is to see, but we gave it a good go.'

'That's good,' Sarah said, as if Nina had been describing a trip to the supermarket. 'Are the kids home?'

'No. So much for missing me.'

Sarah's tone lowered to such a degree that Nina struggled to hear. 'Is Bryn with you?'

'No, he's downstairs clearing up the mess. What is it, Sarah? You sound odd.'

Sarah must have been pursing her lips because, when she exhaled, her breath was released with a slow hiss. 'I don't want to worry you,' she began. 'It might be nothing.'

With one breath, the tension returned and Nina sat up straight in the bath, preparing herself for the lightning bolt. 'Too late. Tell me anyway.'

'It's about Scarlett. The information is pretty scant, so it could be something and nothing.'

'Please, Sarah, if you draw this out slowly, it's going to be torture. Just tell me!'

'She was seen at an antenatal clinic yesterday. She was with another girl, and there might be a perfectly reasonable explanation.'

Nina jumped out of the bath. 'No there isn't,' she said. 'Sorry, Sarah, I have to go.'

She dressed quickly and her T-shirt stuck to her damp body as she raced downstairs to find Bryn pouring the glass of wine she had been promised.

'I have to go out,' she said. It was an odd thing to say, nowhere near the explanation she ought to have given Bryn, but it was the best she could do with so many thoughts scrambling her brain.

The neck of the wine bottle chinked noisily against the glass. 'Where? Why?'

'Where are the car keys?'

Bryn put down the bottle. 'Nina, you're scaring me. What's wrong?'

She made a first stab at telling him but her body began to shake and the tears, when they came, were hot and angry. Gasping, she managed to say, 'She's pregnant.'

Her knees were buckling and she had to lean against the kitchen counter. 'I *knew* something was wrong,' she sobbed. 'That's what Scarlett wanted to tell me, that's why she wanted me to come home. I should have bloody listened to my gut. I should have got on the first plane home!'

Nina took several gulps of air as the shock gave way to cold determination. There was an element of relief in knowing what she was up against. She knew what the problem was and she needed to start making things right. 'OK,' she said, wiping away the tears and managing to stand up straight. 'I'm going to get Scarlett and we're going to sort this out.'

Bryn hadn't said a word or moved towards his wife, in fact, he hadn't moved at all. Nina looked at him. 'Did she tell you? Did you know?' she demanded.

The accusation shocked Bryn out of his paralysis. 'No! Of course not. What did Scarlett say?'

'I haven't spoken to her yet, but I'm going to.'

'So how do you—'

'I'll explain later. First I need to see her.'

Nina's hand trembled as she reached for the car keys that Bryn had dug out of his pocket, but before she could take them, he withdrew his hand. 'No, Nina, you can't drive in your state. Maybe you should wait until you've calmed down. I hate to suggest it, but it might even be better if you slept on it. If you drag her home now, how much of a reasonable discussion do you think you'll be able to have before it turns into a screaming match?'

'I doubt we'd make it to the car, but I need to know what's happening.' Nina rubbed the back of her neck, wiping away cold bath suds. 'I can't leave it until tomorrow, Bryn.'

'Then let me pick her up,' Bryn suggested. Instead of the keys, he handed Nina her glass of wine. 'Give yourself some time to get your thoughts in order. Whatever happens, you have to let Scarlett know that she doesn't have to deal with this on her own, and neither do you. We're in this together, Nina.'

Bryn kissed her forehead and went into the hall to put on his jacket. As she waited for him to leave, she put down the glass of wine. She was going to need a clear head for what had to be the most difficult conversation a mother could have with a teenage daughter, an underage teenage daughter at that. She heard Bryn open the front door and waited for the house to fall into silence, but to her surprise she heard returning footsteps along the hallway.

The kitchen door opened slowly and when Scarlett appeared she had her eyes cast down. Bryn followed close behind.

'I'm sorry, Mum,' Scarlett whispered.

Nina's heart had been racing and the sound of her daughter's childlike apology threatened to tear it apart. She was still a child. She shouldn't be dealing with this, not at her age. Where had Nina gone wrong? Had their talks about contraception unwittingly encouraged Scarlett to have sex before she was ready? Had she given her daughter too much freedom? The answer to that particular question was obvious.

'Oh, Scarlett, what's been going on?'

Scarlett simply shook her head.

'I wish you'd come to me sooner. Am I that unapproachable? Don't you know you can tell me anything? *Anything*, Scarlett.'

When Scarlett looked up there were tears in her eyes and so much uncertainty. 'I can't,' she said.

'You have to,' Nina insisted. She longed to pull Scarlett into her arms and tell her it was going to be all right, but she held back. Before forgiveness and understanding, she needed her daughter to acknowledge the problem. 'You're pregnant, aren't you?'

Scarlett snapped her head towards Bryn and then back to her mum. 'I thought this was about me phoning you while you were away?' In a fraction of a second the little girl had vanished and the petulant teenager returned. 'Oh, my God, how paranoid are you? I'm not pregnant, Mum! I was upset, probably because I'm due on,' she said, to make the point. 'I missed you, that's all, and God knows why now. You're so suspicious! It's like you keep waiting for me to mess up, like you actually want me to!'

'Of course I don't!' Nina said, raising her voice to match Scarlett's. 'And this isn't paranoia, Scarlett. You were seen. If you're not pregnant, what were you doing at an antenatal clinic?'

'How did you find out about that?'

'Never mind how. Why were you there, Scarlett? Please, tell me I'm being paranoid, because I'd rather that than have to deal with the consequences of you being pregnant! You're fifteen years old, for God's sake!'

In the midst of her outburst, Nina had taken a step closer to her daughter. Scarlett had taken a step back, almost knocking into Bryn. She placed her hands on her hips. 'No,' she hissed. 'I'm not telling you a thing. You couldn't handle the truth, Mum. Seriously, you couldn't.'

'What does that even mean? Stop speaking in riddles, Scarlett, and talk to me!'

When Scarlett gave a snort of derision, Nina knew she had lost the chance to get any more from her voluntarily. 'Fine,' she said. 'If you're not saying, I'll go and speak to Linus's parents. If you are pregnant, they'll need to know.'

The threat wasn't received with the horror Nina had expected. 'Why would you do that? This has nothing to do with Linus.'

'Oh really?'

'Really, Mum,' Scarlett said. 'I've never slept with Linus.'

This one fact ought to have given Nina some comfort. It didn't, but she clung to a strand of hope. 'So you're *not* pregnant?'

'That's not what I said.'

'So are you now admitting that you are pregnant?'

Scarlett glanced behind her again. Nina wasn't sure if she was looking at Bryn or the exit.

'Scarlett, answer me.'

When her daughter turned back she had a look of fear in her eyes. She nodded.

'How pregnant?' Nina said as she gave her daughter the once-over. There were no obvious signs, so hopefully there was still time to consider all options.

'Eight weeks.'

'And the father *isn't* Linus?'

There was an imperceptible shake of the head.

'So it's someone else?' Nina asked with a sinking heart. 'Who, Scarlett? Why would you sleep with someone else when you've been going out with Linus? I don't understand.'

Tears welled in Scarlett's eyes as she whispered, 'I can't tell you.'

'You can, and you will.'

Scarlett stood her ground. 'No, I won't.'

'You both got into this mess and you're both going to deal with the consequences.'

'We will,' she said, choosing her words carefully. 'He's going to look after me, Mum. I know he will.'

'Who is?'

'I – Can't – Say!'

Nina knew the conversation was turning in dizzying circles but she wouldn't give in. 'At least tell me why not.'

Scarlett took a deep breath that caught in her throat. 'Because he has to tell his wife first.'

Nina felt suddenly faint. She was scared to look down because she had a feeling the ground was opening up beneath her, so she turned instead to her husband. Bryn had turned deathly pale.

Scarlett

I *can't tell you how bad it was,* sitting in class and not knowing what was going to happen next. It took Mr Caldwell ten minutes to get everyone back in their seats and under control, not that I was interested in what was going on around me. I was too busy checking my phone to see if there were any new messages, but the last one had been not long after Mum had started kicking off that morning. He'd told me to delete every last trace of us from my phone.

I didn't see why at the time because even if Mum did check my phone, I was using Liam's app, so what was the problem? The problem was Mum was now in the school and things would get so much worse, but as I started deleting stuff, that stupid Mr Caldwell decided to pick on me. He was all red in the face because the lads were giving him lip, and when he saw me with my phone, he confiscated it!

Sitting and waiting for something to happen was just torture after that. I needed to speak to him. I needed to know what I was supposed to do. When he'd found out I was pregnant, he'd said he would look after me, but this *was not looking after me. This was deleting me from his life and pretending I didn't exist.*

It was kind of a relief when Mrs Marshall came back into class. I didn't have to guess why she was there, even though this time she didn't look at me when she came in. The ever-so-helpful Mr Caldwell gave her my phone before he called me to the front. I grabbed my things and as I left my desk, Eva pulled at my arm.

'Are you going to tell them?' she whispered.

'Never,' I said.

Mrs Marshall marched me over to the office without saying a word and made me wait while she called Mrs Anwar out of her office. I kept my head dipped so I looked all timid. It was obvious Mum had told her I was pregnant by that point, so I couldn't act completely innocent but I was going to give it a good try.

'Your mum's here,' Mrs Anwar said, 'but I'd like to speak to you on your own first.'

That was fine by me, I don't know what I would have done if Mum and Mr Swift had been there, listening to me deny everything except that I was pregnant. Mrs Anwar on her own was so much easier. She took me into Mr Whittle's office and she spoke really softly when she told me what Mum was saying.

'You won't be surprised to hear that your mum has told me about the pregnancy. You've been to see a midwife?'

'Yes, miss.'

Mrs Anwar nodded. 'You'll need to have a sit-down with your mum and discuss what you do next, and we'll offer whatever support we can, but that's not why you've been called here, Scarlett.'

'Oh?' I asked, looking surprised, even though I kind of knew what was coming.

'I understand you've refused to tell anyone who the father is?'

I nodded.

'Am I right in saying that he's married?'

Again I nodded.

'And you're fifteen years old.'

I so nearly rolled my eyes but remembered I was supposed to be acting, like, all meek. I played nervously with my fingers instead.

'This must be an extremely stressful time at home,' Mrs Anwar continued. She leant forward a little in her chair when she added, 'But then there has been a fair amount of change in the last year for you all. It must have been quite a difficult adjustment when your mum got married.'

'It was all right,' I said.

'And you get on well with your stepfather?'

Here we go again, I thought. 'Up until Mum threw him out this morning, yes.'

'Because she thought that he might have something to do with your pregnancy?'

I'm sorry, but I almost laughed. What was that supposed to mean? If she wanted to ask me if he had got me pregnant, she should have had the guts to come out and ask.

'Please, Scarlett,' Mrs Anwar continued. 'We all want what's best for you. Your mum has a certain responsibility for your welfare and so do I. If there are things that you can't say to your mum, please know that you can tell other people, people who can act as a go-between if you like. You can talk to me.'

She left a pause which I know I was supposed to fill, but as if. The only sound was Mrs Anwar sighing, and then she said, 'What would you say if I told you that your mum has also accused Mr Swift?'

'I never said anything about Mr Swift.'

'Even so, an allegation has been made.' Mrs Anwar's tone had hardened. She was letting me know this was serious stuff – as if I needed reminding. 'Which means we have to investigate fully. I should warn you now, Scarlett, that unless you start explaining yourself, there's a good chance the police will be involved.'

My stomach did this horrible flip and I wanted to be sick. I'd seen CSI; the police could do all kinds of tests and stuff. They would find out our secret and he'd be arrested and. . . I couldn't even think about it. My lip started to tremble as I tried to remember what he'd said to do if something like this happened. As long as I denied everything, then it would all be OK. I just had to keep my nerve. Well, actually, it was more like finding my nerve – and quick, because it wasn't only my lip that was trembling, I was shaking so bad.

'A lot of people are going to get hurt,' Mrs Anwar continued. 'Did you know Mrs Swift is pregnant too? I can't imagine what this will do to her if her husband is accused of child abuse.'

'Oh, God,' I whispered.

'Now, I'm not trying to frighten you deliberately,' Mrs Anwar explained. 'I simply want to make it very clear what the implications are if this accusation is taken further.'

'But I never accused him. He didn't do anything, miss. Honest!'

'Nevertheless, your mum is desperate for answers. Answers that you hold, Scarlett.'

When the bell rang, I was ready to get out of there, but there wasn't going to be any escape for me, not until I gave Mrs Anwar some kind of answer. She was leaning with her elbows on the desk and had her hands clasped in front of her while she gave me some thinking time. And that was when I worked out what I had to do. I could give her an answer, even if it wasn't the one she was expecting.

23

The Accusations

Vikki had made it as far as the main gates, but she hadn't been able to cross the threshold and turn her back on the school and whatever was going on inside. She was scared that if she tried stepping back into her old life, she might find that it didn't exist any more; if it ever had. Nina could be confronting Rob at that very moment and while she could imagine that he would deny everything, this didn't give her any comfort at all.

As she pondered her future, a Range Rover sped through the gates and past her before coming to a sudden stop nearby. When Vikki had called for backup, her options had been limited. Standing in the school playground, she had been acutely aware of the friendships she had lost. At Scarlett's age, she would have had half a dozen of her peers to call upon, but all she had now was a business card from Amy, who had become a relative stranger. Vikki needed someone who would have more faith in her than she had in herself and, more importantly, in her husband too. Sarah Tavistock had been the first to suspect Scarlett's stepfather, and would dismiss Nina's latest theory as utter nonsense, but when Vikki had phoned to let her know what was happening, Sarah's only response was to cut the call short, and now she was here.

'You should go home, Vikki,' Sarah said as she got out of her car.

Feeling like a child who was being sent out of the room while the adults talked, Vikki said, 'But I want to know what's happening. I want to hear what Rob says.'

With a tilt of her head, Sarah asked, 'Does that mean you're not sure? Do you doubt him too?'

'No – of course not. Why would I?'

There was a heart-stopping moment when Sarah might have asked more, but she simply said, 'In that case, maybe you should be there. Let's go.'

Sarah didn't explain what she intended to do, and Vikki was too afraid to ask, as was the receptionist who took one look at Vikki's pale complexion and Sarah's glowering features before sending them up to the main office.

Mrs Marshall was sitting behind her desk when they arrived. She looked no different than when Vikki had been a student, except perhaps her grey hair was a shade lighter. She gave Vikki that same look as if she had just been sent out from class, and Vikki did feel like a schoolgirl again. She was only grateful that they would be dealing with Mrs Anwar and not her predecessor. Mr Taggart had terrified students and teachers alike.

'Where's Mrs Anwar?' Sarah demanded as she looked towards the office door, which had been left ajar.

'And you are?'

'Your worst nightmare, if you don't find her right now,'

Sarah said, and before Mrs Marshall had the chance to respond, she headed for the open door.

Not wanting to be left behind, Vikki followed and was shocked to find Nina and Rob sitting silently at the conference table. Nina wouldn't look at her, but focused only on her friend.

'Did you speak to Charlotte?' Nina demanded.

Sarah gave a brief nod. 'I can't believe she never told me,' she said, the words paining her but seemingly having no effect on Nina, who looked away as her friend took a seat without being invited. Sarah folded her arms and glared at Rob.

Vikki was the only one left standing. The exchange between the two friends unnerved her and she felt faint. She also felt very alone.

'What are you doing here, Vikki?' Rob asked.

'She wants answers, as do we all,' Sarah answered for her.

Rob returned Sarah's glare. 'Perhaps more to the point, what are you doing here, Mrs Tavistock?'

'Let's just say I have a vested interest, too,' Sarah told him, and without even looking at her, added, 'Sit down, Vikki.'

There were several seats to choose from and Vikki didn't know which to take until Rob pulled out the chair next to him. 'This is ridiculous,' he said under his breath.

'Mrs Anwar is talking to Scarlett,' Nina said to Sarah. 'She asked that we don't discuss anything until she gets back.' She glanced towards the door, which had been wedged open on purpose, presumably so Mrs Marshall could raise the alarm if they broke the rules.

'I take it you've denied everything?' Sarah asked Rob.

'And I imagine Scarlett is confirming everything I've said.'

'Would that be because you've trained her so well?'

'No, it would be because it's the truth,' Rob said, directing his comment to his wife. He grasped her hand. 'I'm sorry, Vikki, you shouldn't be listening to this. If I'd known it was going to turn into a witch hunt I would have let Nadia do this formally, and to hell with the damage to my reputation. There's nothing to tell, and nothing to hide.'

'Don't be so sure about that,' Sarah said. 'I had an interesting chat with my daughter this morning. She told me what happened between you two.' She glanced briefly at Vikki, before adding, 'She told me about the kiss.'

Rob took a sharp intake of breath. 'That was a complete misunderstanding,' he said, letting go of Vikki's hand and leaning forward. '*She* kissed me.'

'She was an impressionable seventeen-year-old, and it was not a misunderstanding,' Sarah replied in a low growl. 'It was grooming, Mr Swift. My daughter was so embarrassed that she's spent the last four years pretending it never happened. But it did happen, didn't it?'

'Did you hear me deny it?' Rob demanded. 'But you can't build this up into something it's not.' He ground his teeth as he composed himself. 'I'd kept her back after class this one time to go through a piece of coursework she was struggling with. I leant towards her to explain something and she thought I was moving in for a kiss, and that was what she did. It was over in a split second, and it was right that she should forget about it.'

'Did you report it to the school?'

'Of course not. It was a schoolgirl infatuation, and I was hardly going to add to her humiliation.'

Rob turned to Vikki for support, but she was too busy trying to work out when this might have happened. Could it have been around the time her dad had died, when she had been staying with her mum? Was there a pattern, or simply a jumbled mess that could be twisted and turned to make the picture fit the crime?

Vikki wished she'd had the courage to speak to Scarlett earlier. It felt as if her life and her marriage were hanging by a thread, and as the school bell began to ring, she imagined a knife slicing it clean through. 'Will they be long?' Vikki asked faintly.

For the first time since entering the office, Nina looked directly at Vikki. 'I'll wait as long as it takes to get answers,' she warned, her eyes filling with tears. 'I won't let him get away with this.'

Vikki thought she might burst into tears too, and concentrated on holding them back and nothing else as the minutes ticked by. The silence was eventually broken by the sound of voices outside the office. One was a male voice and the other was Mrs Marshall. The school secretary's tone was harsh as she told the young man to go back to class, but a moment later he was stepping through the door, closely followed by the red-faced secretary and a schoolgirl who Vikki thought looked vaguely familiar.

'Liam, what are you doing here?' Nina demanded.

'Is it true?' he asked. 'Have you kicked Bryn out?'

Before Nina could respond, Mrs Marshall spoke up. 'I'm sorry, I couldn't stop him,' she said as she gave the intruder a withering look. 'Liam, this does not concern you. You have to leave this minute.'

'Seriously?' he asked. 'You honestly think this isn't my business?'

Vikki had never met Nina's son before, but she had heard a little about him from Sarah. The tall young man squaring up to the ferocious school secretary was nothing like the image Sarah had painted of the gangly teen who spoke in monosyllabic sentences.

'It's all right, Pam,' Rob said, assuming control. 'I can handle this. Liam, come in. Take a seat.'

Liam stood his ground and put his hands in his jeans pockets. 'I'm fine standing, thanks,' he said curtly, turning to glare at the grey-haired woman until she got the message.

'I'll leave you to it then,' Mrs Marshall said with a sniff, but she made a point of testing that the door wedge was firmly in place before she left.

'Well?' Liam said to his mum.

'Yes, Bryn has gone.'

'Because you think he and Scarlett were up to something?'

The schoolgirl who had remained at his side slipped her hand into his pocket so she could hold his hand. 'Scarlett told me what happened this morning,' she said to Nina.

'Did she also tell you who got her pregnant?' Nina asked.

Eva's head dropped and she fell silent.

'For goodness' sake, I can't take any more of this,' Sarah said. 'Someone needs to start talking!'

'I suppose it had better be me,' Liam said, 'and I think you need to prepare yourself for another shock, Mum.'

24

Before

Complaining that time was running out before school resumed on Monday, Rob had locked himself away in his study all weekend to finish marking mock exam papers. On the rare occasions that he did emerge, it was only to go out for a run, and he would return home exhausted.

The stress Rob was under made Vikki have second thoughts about ever starting a career, and especially one in property development. Her dad would often work long hours whenever projects fell behind plan, and although the job Sarah had in mind was mostly admin, she would have high expectations. Given the limited help Rob could offer, Vikki needed to be realistic. She would be better off staying at home caring for her family, she kept telling herself, and if Sunday evening were anything to go by, she was doing a pretty decent job. Freya was in bed and there was a slow roast in the oven ready for whenever Rob came downstairs looking for food, except when he did appear, he was in his running gear.

'Again?' she asked. 'You were out running this morning, Rob. I've hardly seen you.'

'I'll only stay out long enough to clear my head,' he promised.

'Liar,' she said as he leant over and kissed her cheek. She had a laptop balanced on her knee with a web page open on a site that gave nutritional advice for expectant mums. When she heard Rob close the front door, she opened up the page she had minimized when she had heard Rob coming downstairs. She read through the email twice before she was ready to pick up the phone.

'Hi, Sarah, I'm not disturbing you, am I?'

'No, it's fine, I could do with the distraction,' she said. 'I suppose this is about my proposal.'

Sarah had sent her details of an online project management course that would be ideal for the person she was looking for. Vikki took one last look at the message on screen before closing the laptop lid. 'The thing is, Sarah, it's a lovely offer, but I just can't accept. I'd be wasting your time, and your money.'

'Nonsense,' Sarah said in her usual brusque way. 'And I should warn you now, Vikki that I'm in no mood for an argument. I've already had more than my fair share of those today. If you must know, I sent the course details through to Charlotte first, to give her one last chance to pay me back for everything I've invested in her so far. I suppose I should admire her for knowing what she wants and setting out to get it, but I'm not happy she's turned me down and I'll be damned if I'll let you do the same.'

'But I'm not Charlotte,' Vikki began. 'What if you pay for this course and I can't do it? I don't want to mess you around.'

'Do you think I'd be making this offer if I didn't think

you were capable? You can do the course while Freya's at nursery and have it finished easily before baby number two comes along.'

'But—'

'Let's be positive and say Elaine makes a full recovery. She can help look after the baby while you start your apprenticeship with me. The timing and the hours can be agreed later on, and we can negotiate on pay to take account of what I'm paying out for you now with this course.'

'But—'

'Look, I'm probably only doing this because I want to get back at my ungrateful daughter, helped along by a couple of generous glasses of Chablis. I warn you now, this is strictly a time-limited offer. So?'

When Sarah stopped to draw breath, Vikki's ears were ringing. She needed to tell Sarah that she wouldn't be forced into doing something she had phoned to refuse. The problem was, that *something* was giving her the most beautiful butterflies in the pit of her stomach. She wanted this. 'Do you really think I could do it?'

'Have you not been listening to a word I've said?' Sarah asked.

'Yes, every syllable, and I can't believe I'm saying this but, yes, I'll do it,' Vikki said, pushing to the back of her mind the small matter of clearing it with Rob. 'Thank you. Thank you so much, Sarah.'

'At last, something I've done right,' Sarah said, her voice losing its strength at the last.

'Are you OK?'

'If you must know, I've put my foot in it with Nina,' she said. 'I'm so worried about her, Vikki.'

'Is this about Scarlett? Is she pregnant?'

Sarah exhaled so loudly it was a wonder she had breath left to speak. 'It's so much worse than that. Apparently, she had it out with Scarlett the moment she came home last night. Yes, she's pregnant, but rather than launch straight into the discussion of whether she should keep it or not, Scarlett's thrown a spanner in the works.'

'How?'

'According to Scarlett, the father isn't her boyfriend.'

'How does that work?'

'She hasn't slept with him.'

'Oh,' Vikki said, not sure what else to say.

'But she's had sex with someone,' Sarah continued, her words slowing as she considered how much more information to share. 'Up until this year, Scarlett was the model daughter, and by that I'm talking about her behaviour and not her looks, although she has those too.'

'She is stunning.'

'Yes she is, and it's not very difficult to imagine the kind of effect she has on the opposite sex, and not just the boys, but men too.'

Vikki knew how attractive schoolgirls could be and the effect they could have. She was nowhere near as beautiful as Scarlett, but she could remember thinking she held a certain power. 'You think she's been seeing an older man?' she asked uneasily.

'Someone old enough to have a family, yes. She told Nina she's involved with a married man and she's waiting for him to tell his wife. I'll be honest with you, Vikki, that scares me.'

It scared Vikki too, but she said nothing and let Sarah continue.

'When something like this happens, you question everything, and that's what I've spent most of today doing, as has Nina, although we haven't necessarily reached the same conclusions. Did you know Nina had only known Bryn for six months when they announced they were engaged?' Sarah paused long enough to take a gulp of whatever she was drinking. Vikki suspected it was the remainder of the Chablis. 'I told her in no uncertain terms that she was taking a huge risk and begged her not to go through with the marriage. Now, I know I shouldn't be telling you all this, but Charlotte won't listen, Nina won't listen and I have to tell someone . . . '

'Tell someone what?'

'That I was right to be worried. What if Bryn *was* out for whatever he could get from Nina? And what if that included getting his hands on her daughter?'

To her shame, Vikki felt a rush of relief as if she had just dodged a bullet. 'You think he's the one who got Scarlett pregnant? But he seemed so nice.'

'And I suppose I can understand why Nina was attracted to him,' Sarah said. 'He's not my type, but he can be quite charming in the right company. I really did hope his intentions were honourable, but it all happened too quickly for my liking.'

'Does Nina think it's Bryn?'

'Oh, I think there's doubt, I could hear it in her voice when we spoke earlier. We went through who Scarlett has contact with and what opportunity she would have to be with him. Bryn lives under the same roof, for goodness' sake! And he gives her lifts quite regularly, which means if she was up to something with someone else, he would surely have worked it out. If you ask me, he's part of the secret and I can tell you now, Bryn has his secrets. His daughter didn't go to their wedding and Nina has never met her. Apparently, he invited her for Christmas too, but she refused. What if Bryn has a past he doesn't want to share?' Sarah coughed nervously to clear her throat of all the secrets she had so easily divulged. 'That's the gist of what I said to Nina, which is why she's none too pleased with me.'

'I can't believe this is happening.'

'Neither can she,' Sarah said, 'which is what worries me most. What if I'm right and she refuses to face up to it? I honestly don't know what to do for the best, but I have to do something. I'll go to the authorities myself if I have to.'

'But don't you want to give Nina and Scarlett a chance to work it out themselves first?'

'He's there with them now, Vikki, under the same roof. It gives me goosebumps just thinking about it.'

'But what if you're wrong, Sarah?'

'It would be the end of my friendship with Nina, which is why I'm not going to do anything yet. Yes, I might be wrong, and I hope I am. But who else could it be?'

Refusing to answer, Vikki let the laptop slip off her knee. She was no longer interested in looking to the future. It scared her too much.

'What about Rob?' Sarah asked, making Vikki's heart leap into her throat. 'Could he help? Maybe the school could intervene?'

Vikki took a moment to catch her breath. 'I could ask him, Sarah, but maybe you should sleep on it first,' she said, thinking she would do the same before speaking to Rob. The last thing she wanted was for Rob to become embroiled in the affair. He was stressed enough as it was, she told herself as if that were the only reason.

'You mean wait until I've sobered up?' Sarah said, and with a sigh, added, 'You're right, of course you are. Hopefully we'll all see things more clearly in the cold light of day.'

The call left Vikki with an uneasy feeling that only kept building as she imagined what it must be like to be in Scarlett's shoes right now. It wasn't as difficult as it should be.

Scarlett

There was this tiny, tiny moment when I thought it was all going to go away. I told Mrs Anwar all she needed to know, and when I'd finished I was expecting her to drag me by the hair back in to see Mum. She didn't, obviously, but I could tell she wanted to.

Anyway, I never got the chance to make my dramatic entrance because Liam had beaten me to it. The minute I stepped out of Mr Whittle's office, I could hear his voice. Well, actually, it was Sarah's voice I heard first.

'If you know something then tell us! Can't you see what this is doing to your mum?' she was saying.

'Tell them, Liam,' someone said quietly and it took a moment to work out it was Eva. I hadn't realized how big an audience we had, especially if you included Mrs Marshall who, just by chance, had some filing to do right next to Mrs Anwar's door.

We all must have been holding our breath, because there wasn't a sound.

'OK,' Liam started, 'would it help if I told you that Scarlett isn't pregnant?'

There was this weird strangled noise and then Mum said, 'What?'

'I went with Scarlett to the antenatal clinic,' Eva said. 'Except, it was my appointment, not hers.'

'She was lying to cover up for us, Mum,' Liam added.

'Eva's pregnant?' Mum asked. 'But why would Scarlett—'

'To give us more time. We wanted to keep it a secret until it was too late for anyone to stop us.'

Sarah actually laughed. 'You're planning on keeping it?'

'Keep out of this, Sarah, this has nothing to do with you,' Mum said. 'In fact, it has nothing to do with anyone in this room. Liam, we can talk about it later.'

Her voice sounded weird, like it wasn't really her talking. I suppose she was in shock and, yes I know, I couldn't exactly blame her. And I'd like to say right now that I didn't do it on purpose. I never wanted anyone to think I was pregnant, but Mum pushed me into a corner and after that I had to keep up with the lies.

We still hadn't gone into the office to face everyone at this point, but Mrs Anwar gave me a prod and she had to push really hard to get me moving. Mrs Marshall was looking down her nose at me as I went past, and I so wanted to poke my tongue out at her.

As I stepped through the door, Mr Swift was repeating what Liam had told them, as if he couldn't believe his ears. 'So Scarlett's not pregnant?'

'That's right,' Mrs Anwar said. She put her arm around me, which might have looked like she was being supportive, but it was only to stop me running away. 'She's just told me.'

The look on Mum's face was horrible and it matched

263

her weird-sounding voice. 'So you made the whole thing up?' she asked. 'There is no married man? There is no abuse?'

'No.'

'You little bitch,' Sarah said under her breath, but loud enough for everyone to hear.

What they all seemed to forget was that I'd actually been protecting my brother and my best friend. I had to cover for them. Once Eva's mum and dad found out, they would make her have an abortion. She so wanted the baby and I said I'd help. So even though I was technically lying, it was a good thing I was doing. It seriously was not my fault that Mum went ballistic and started accusing everyone. I felt really bad about what was happening, but I'm not sorry for trying to save a baby's life. I was not a bitch, not completely anyway. I was lying for a good reason.

And now I bet you're wondering exactly how good a liar I am, and if I've been making all the other stuff up too.

25

The Aftermath

Nina could feel her ears about to pop. She was sitting at the conference table, but it might as well have been the eye of a storm. For a moment, and it was all too brief, she felt a wonderful sense of calm. She couldn't quite believe how well she was taking the news that it was Eva rather than Scarlett who was pregnant. A few days earlier she would have been devastated to discover that her seventeen-year-old son had got his girlfriend pregnant, but in the course of one morning, she had seen her family torn apart piece by piece and she had reached saturation point. She didn't dare think how this would affect Liam's future, but she would use the last of her strength to defend her children, or one of them at least. She wasn't so sure about Scarlett. How could her daughter have remained silent while her lies destroyed not only her own family but threatened the Swifts' marriage too? Why had she let things go so far? It didn't make sense.

'Look,' Mrs Anwar said, 'if you think it would be helpful, Mrs Thomas, I'm happy to continue talking around the table with you and your family. It might be better having a third party involved in the discussion.'

Nina agreed, if only because she wasn't sure her legs were strong enough to carry her out of the office. She had been holding her body so tense that every muscle cried out with pain.

'I don't think Mr Swift need stay,' Mrs Anwar continued. 'After all the upset, you might want to take your wife home. Take the rest of the day off and we can talk things through tomorrow.'

'Wait,' Vikki said. She had been so quiet that Nina had forgotten she was there. Her voice carried a sense of urgency. 'Is that it?'

'Yes, Vikki,' Rob said. He stood up and with his hand under her elbow, encouraged his wife to her feet. 'It's time to go.'

'But I want to hear what Scarlett has to say,' Vikki insisted.

'She's right,' Sarah said. 'At the very least they deserve an apology.'

'From me?' Scarlett asked, looking shocked when all eyes turned to her. 'I never said it was Rob in the first place!'

It just happened that Nina's eyes were on Rob at that moment and she caught the look he gave her daughter. A message had passed between them that Nina couldn't hear and wasn't supposed to see. With a shudder, she realized it had been a warning and, as she replayed Scarlett's words, she saw the mistake. There was a rushing sound in her ears as the storm began to build again.

Mrs Anwar was more concerned by the tone her student was using. 'Scarlett, whether you made direct accusations or not, you have to accept some responsibility for the pain you've caused today.'

Slowly and deliberately, Nina placed her palms down flat

on the table. Only as it began to shake did she realize her whole body was trembling. 'It wasn't all lies, was it?' she said. 'Oh, Scarlett, what have you done?'

'Mrs Thomas, are you feeling all right?'

'Of course she isn't,' Sarah said. She reached across to take hold of her hand. 'Nina, it's going to be all right. Take a deep breath.'

Sarah's voice seemed to come from a distance because Nina was too busy dealing with the stampede of thoughts trampling through her brain. The horror of it all was almost too much to bear, but Nina pressed her toes into the blue carpet tiles and steadied herself. Pulling her hand from Sarah's grasp, she grabbed hold of a thought, and went with it.

'Just because you're not pregnant doesn't mean you're not involved with someone, does it, Scarlett?' she began. 'Why make up a story about a married man? Why not say you had been sleeping with Linus, unless of course you hadn't?'

Horrified that Nina was openly discussing her sex life, Scarlett cried, 'Mum!'

Nina continued unabashed. 'You couldn't say it was Linus because I would have gone around to his parents and confronted him, only to discover that he wasn't prepared to stand by you – and rightly so. Which makes me wonder, Scarlett. If you weren't sleeping with Linus, who were you sleeping with?'

Rob Swift had been edging towards the door, pulling his wife along with him. 'I really think we should leave you to it.'

'No,' Nina said quickly. 'I want you to stay. I want you

to hear this.' Nina wasn't looking at Rob but Vikki. 'Scarlett told me she was sexually active.'

'But I'm not, Mum!'

'Don't you dare!' Nina said, her voice rising. 'Don't you dare tell me any more lies, Scarlett! You're on the pill, I found them this morning. You have been sleeping with someone and of all the lies you've told lately, I don't think the story about the married man was one of them. I've been sitting here wondering where I went wrong and how I could have missed what had been going on under my nose. I took everything at face value because I wanted to believe we were one big happy family, but you've made me doubt everything, Scarlett, and everyone.'

She stopped only to glance at Sarah. 'And you didn't help. You've been waiting for me to fail. Was it so awful to see me happy? Did it make your marriage look so dull and lifeless, Sarah? Perhaps if you'd spent more time examining your own life instead of judging others, you might have been there when Charlotte needed someone to turn to. She was being groomed by her teacher, and if she hadn't convinced you to pay for private tuition when a certain someone suggested extra lessons, who knows what could have happened.'

'You're still going along with this crazy idea that I'm involved with your daughter?' Rob interrupted.

'Yes!' Nina cried out. 'My head's been spinning all weekend and it's still spinning now, but at last it feels like I'm getting nearer the truth.'

Nina cast her gaze around the room. Liam and Eva had their mouths open while Scarlett had hers pursed tightly shut. Vikki's eyes were widening with horror, while Mrs

Anwar appeared as confused as ever, but it was Rob who Nina settled her gaze upon.

'It didn't help that I had no idea what I was looking for, but I think I saw it a moment ago, in this room, *Rob*,' she said, emphasizing the name Scarlett had used so casually, so intimately.

'Look, Mrs Thomas,' Rob said, 'you're in shock and I can appreciate how confused you must be. Like you said, your head's spinning, but blaming someone else is not going to make your husband feel any better about you accusing him.'

'Which makes me wonder how you knew,' Nina said. The adrenalin had kicked in and her befuddled thoughts had cleared just enough to make the connections she had missed earlier. 'You knew about Bryn walking out before I'd even mentioned it. How did you know?' She turned to Vikki. 'Did you tell him?'

When Vikki shook her head, a tear slipped down her cheek. 'I only texted him to say you were on your way to accuse him.'

Vikki was torn between wanting to return to the table to continue the debate, and running straight out of the door. She could do neither because Rob was holding her arm. His grip was firm and as the accusations began to fly, he was no longer holding but clinging to her.

When Nina had said they should stay, Vikki had been relieved, but not in a nice way; she had a morbid curiosity that had to be satisfied. It reminded her of the time she had been caught up in a traffic jam following a horrific accident. When she had driven past the scene she had craned her neck for a better look. What she had seen had given her night-mares for months and she wondered how long this latest one would last. She could turn away now and hope never to know the gory details, but she wasn't going to do that.

'Mrs Thomas . . . ' Rob began.

'How – did – you – know?'

'Scarlett told me,' he said. 'I won't deny that we have a good student–teacher relationship. When she came in this morning she was understandably upset and naturally I asked her what was wrong.' He turned to Mrs Anwar. 'It's our job to pick up on changes in behaviour.'

Nina turned to face her daughter. 'OK, Scarlett, this is your last chance to redeem yourself. You want to be an adult? Well, start acting like one. If you've done something wrong, at least have the courage to stand up and admit it.'

Vikki's heartbeat drummed against her ears and she couldn't hear Scarlett's mumbled response, although it clearly wasn't the confession her mother was praying for. Nina stared in disbelief until Scarlett broke eye contact and looked away.

'Don't look at him!' screamed Nina.

'Mum.'

It was Liam this time. He had taken the seat next to her and put a hand on her trembling shoulder. 'Are you sure about this?'

Nina attempted a smile and cupped Liam's face in her hand. 'No, son, I'm not. I'm not sure of anything any more.'

'Do you want to find out?'

Everyone in the room tensed as one. Liam wasn't asking his question out of curiosity. It was an offer.

'Yes, I do.'

'Me too,' Vikki said, before she could stop herself. Feeling the need to explain, she turned to Rob. 'Isn't it better that we find a way to prove to Nina that it isn't you?'

She didn't add that she was just as desperate for that proof, that his word alone wasn't enough, but from the look on Rob's face, she hadn't needed to. He let go of her and folded his arms across his chest in disgust. They all watched Liam rise to his feet.

The young, self-assured man turned to his sister and held out his hand. 'Give me your phone.'

With a look of pure horror on her face, Scarlett said, 'No, Liam.'

'She has an app on her phone that I created. It encrypts messages,' he explained to anyone who would listen, which was everyone except Scarlett, and possibly Rob.

'This is outrageous,' he said. 'I was happy to work outside of protocol to sort this out, but enough is enough.' He looked to Mrs Anwar for support but she was as enthralled as the others.

'Give me your phone,' Liam repeated.

'No.'

'I have it,' Mrs Anwar said, taking a silver phone with a diamanté-encrusted cover from her pocket. 'It was confiscated this morning in class.'

'You can't, I have rights,' Scarlett told her.

'Yes, you do,' Mrs Anwar said, 'but I think yours are secondary to your mother's at this present moment.'

As the head handed over the phone to Liam, Scarlett launched herself at him. 'No, Liam! That's mine! You can't do this!'

Rob moved forward too, but took no more than half a step

before changing his mind. It was Sarah who found her chance to act and she was there in a flash, manoeuvring herself between the feuding siblings so Liam could check the phone.

Scarlett began wailing, but no one in the room paid her any interest. Vikki had spent a restless night worrying about the schoolgirl, but her present behaviour wasn't generating the level of sympathy Vikki had imagined. If anything, she wanted to slap her.

'The app hides messages and anything else sent to or from specific contacts, and you need a passcode to access them,' Liam said, sounding quietly confident and unmoved by his sister's histrionics. His only response was to raise his voice as he provided a running commentary on what he was doing.

'The thing is,' he continued, 'the best programmers always leave a backdoor so they can get back in if someone messes around with their software, which means I have the magic key.' He had a smile on his face when he tapped in the override code.

'What's in there?' Nina asked when Liam went quiet.

'She's set up encryptions for a few contacts, Eva for one, but I'm guessing no one's interested in those conversations,' he said, glancing briefly at his girlfriend before turning to Nina. 'I think one of them is Bryn's number too.'

'See!' Rob said. 'Can we go now?'

His question went unanswered as they waited for Liam to reveal more. 'Sorry, Mum, but I can't see any messages. She must have deleted them, and if that's the case, then the software makes sure they're gone for good. Unless . . . '

As he tapped away, everyone grew impatient. 'Unless what?' asked Sarah.

'There are a few messages still in the cache memory. Yeah, one that must be to Bryn saying 'Can you come now?' and one to someone else, that says, 'What do you think?' Oh, wait, there's a photo attachment. I might just be able to—'

'Please, Liam, stop,' cried Scarlett.

'Scarlett's right,' Rob said. 'We have safeguarding procedures, including respecting a student's privacy. I can tell you now, Mrs Thomas, that what you're doing will have a significant impact on your relationship with your daughter going forward.'

'I'm willing to take that chance, Mr Swift.'

'I'm inclined to agree,' Mrs Anwar added.

Vikki wasn't paying much attention to the exchange. She was watching Liam, waiting for his reaction, and then she saw it. His face went pale and the tall, handsome man shrunk back, leaving an insecure teen who didn't want to be the centre of attention any more.

'What have you found?' Vikki asked.

Liam turned to his sister. 'Really?'

Scarlett buried her head in Sarah's shoulder. 'I want to go home.'

'Show me, Liam,' Nina said.

Liam was struggling for words and, although his face remained pale, his cheeks had turned blood red. It was Eva, who had been looking over his shoulder, who said, 'It's a bit, erm, explicit.'

'Who did you send it to, Scarlett?' Nina asked. She didn't wait for an answer but turned back to Liam.

'The number's embedded in the data.'

'I'm sure the police could trace it,' Mrs Anwar said. 'And, sadly, I think that's where all of this is heading.'

Liam took a deep breath and exhaled loudly. 'Or I could just ring it.'

'Do it,' Nina said.

Sarah unravelled Scarlett from her arms and took a step away as Liam made the call. She looked from Nina to Vikki, unsure who she would need to comfort first.

Vikki noticed Rob's body tense as they all strained their ears. Her husband's ringtone was 'Another Brick in the Wall' by Pink Floyd. He had thought it ironic and perhaps it was the perfect song to herald the end of his teaching career and his marriage. Except it didn't play.

Rob let out a sigh, 'Can we go now?'

As he took his first step towards the door, Vikki heard a jangling noise coming from his pocket. She knew immediately that it couldn't be loose change alone: Rob's phone was vibrating.

Scarlett

So everyone turned to Rob as if he were a child snatcher. I felt so sorry for him and I started crying again, only this time no one came to put their arms around me. Mum stayed where she was at the table while Sarah went to stand next to Vikki, who had moved away from Rob, and Liam was fussing around Eva, who was in tears too.

'For God's sake, Scarlett, stop crying and tell them what happened!' Rob yelled.

That only made me worse.

He turned to Mrs Anwar and said, 'It was a schoolgirl crush that got a little out of hand, that's all. When I was giving Scarlett extra lessons, we got on really well, but she got the wrong signals and that was when she sent me the photo. I deleted it straight away and then we had a chat and moved on. If I'd known how incriminating it would look, I would have thought twice about covering up for her mistake. She's a silly girl in too much of a rush to grow up, that's all.'

And there it was, someone else turning against me, and I was sort of glad when no one believed him. I was in so much pain and maybe I should have been thinking about all the people who had been hurt, but, if I'm honest, in that moment, I didn't care if Mum and Bryn never got back together, or that Eva's parents would force her to have an abortion. I didn't care that Rob's marriage was over and that Vikki would be left with two snotty kids to bring up on her own. My life was over.

Mrs Marshall must have had the police number on speed dial because they were there minutes later. Everyone was split up and I was taken to a room with Mum. I was about to be interviewed by the police and I was so scared, but Mum hadn't so much as put a hand on my shoulder. Eventually I was so exhausted that I stopped crying and we sat in silence right up to the moment we heard a policewoman on her radio just outside the door.

'You tell them everything, Scarlett,' Mum told me. 'You tell them everything or I'll never forgive you.'

What the hell was I supposed to do? I'd told her over and over there was nothing between me and Rob, or me and Bryn for that matter, but I swear, no one wants to listen because it's not what they want to hear. I'm sorry, but what kind of person wants to hear all about the sex life of a schoolgirl anyway? If you ask me, it says more about them than the man they were hunting down.

The more I thought about it, the angrier I got. I was almost tempted to give up and tell the police what they wanted to hear, or at least what Mum wanted to hear. I could so easily have told them I was having mad passionate sex with Rob, and the photo I'd sent was nothing he hadn't already seen in the flesh.

Or maybe I could have told them a different story, one

where I was being abused by my wicked stepfather who had taught me how I shouldn't be ashamed of my body. Maybe I'd only sent the photo to Mr Swift because I thought it was what all men liked to see? Maybe I only did it to shock him.

Then again, I might have given the police a story that none of them had thought of yet. What if it was someone else entirely, someone so clever that he had set up everyone else as suspects? Now that would be a man worth knowing, don't you think?

What I actually told the nice policewoman was that I was still a virgin and I only went on the pill because I had bad period pains. She asked me if I was sure and I said it was the honest truth. The thing is though, truth and lies are all just stories we tell each other, and when I told mine, I begged the policewoman to believe me. I don't think she did, and neither did Mum, which I suppose means she's never going to forgive me.

26

The house was cold and dark when Nina returned home, darker still when she realized she would never again step into the house to find Bryn cooking up a storm in the kitchen. She hadn't tried to get in touch with him yet, there hadn't been time between her arrival at the school and the interviews with the police, and even if there had been, she was at a loss as to what to say. If she knew her husband, and apparently she didn't know him that well at all, Bryn would be reading her silence as reinforcement that she still suspected him. She had thrown away her marriage and lost the only person who could have helped her through this crisis. What had she done?

'Do you want me to make us something to eat?' Liam asked.

Nina had got no further than the hallway. If she'd had the strength she would have crawled upstairs to bed and never come down again. She was out of her depth, so much so that she felt as if she were drowning, weighed down by so many problems, each one devastating in its own right, but when added together – she was going under and she was struggling to breathe.

'Mum?' Liam asked again. 'What should we do?'

Nina fought for her next breath and won. The answer was simple. What she needed to do next was act. It didn't matter what she did, as long as she kept moving.

'Right,' she said, 'first things first. Scarlett, I want you to go upstairs, wash your face and get changed. We have to be prepared that the papers might get wind of this and I do not want anyone taking pictures of you in your uniform. Just because the press aren't allowed to publish details, it doesn't mean journalists won't be sniffing around.' There had been a suggestion that they should have a police officer close by, but Nina had refused, for now at least. Their family had been intruded upon enough.

'Liam, you can make us all some pasta,' she said, returning to his earlier offer.

'I'll help him,' Eva said.

Looking carefully at the two of them, Nina added, 'And in the meantime, I'm going to make some calls. One of them is going to have to be to your parents, Eva.'

'Please don't,' she said, but without much hope.

'I'm sorry, but I have to.'

'Eva has a right to privacy,' Liam said. 'We made sure of that before she saw the doctor.'

'A doctor might be bound by the Hippocratic oath, but I'm a florist. They need to be told,' she said. Seeing tears threaten when too many had been spent that day, she added, 'Let's have something to eat first, and later you can tell me exactly how you both thought you could manage with a baby. And *then* I'll call your parents. Unless you want to do it yourself?'

Eva shook her head.

After Liam and his pregnant girlfriend disappeared into the kitchen, Scarlett remained.

'Go,' Nina said without looking at her, and would have liked nothing better than to turn away, but Scarlett had no intention of making Nina's life any easier.

'I know you don't want to hear this, but I'm never going to change my story,' Scarlett said.

'So it is a story?'

'What does it matter? Why is everyone so fucking obsessed with me anyway? Why can't people just leave me alone to get on with my life?'

Nina closed her eyes briefly. Not only was she drowning, her own daughter had a hand on her head and was pushing her beneath the surface. 'To be honest, Scarlett, I don't care one bit what you want,' she said quietly. 'I only care about how you behave, and right now I don't care too much for that either. Go upstairs and do as you're told because I'm in no mood for reasoning with you, or cajoling you into telling the truth. Right now, I'm finding it difficult to even speak to you.'

Scarlett looked as if she were about to say something else, but instead she gulped back a sob and stomped upstairs. There was a brief cry of rage as she realized her mum had trashed her room earlier, and then a door slammed shut. Nina felt a surge of anger too, which she would have liked to direct towards her heartless, home-wrecking daughter, but she needed to focus on actions that would be far more productive.

She went into the dining room and sat down at her desk. Taking a sheet of blank paper, she wrote down all the people she needed to speak to and the things she had to do. She chose one of the easier tasks to start with and picked up the phone.

'Hi, Janet, it's Nina. How was today in the shop?'

Janet reeled off the main highlights, including the drama of getting to the flower market so late. She had struggled to find the rainbow of gerberas, chrysanthemums and lilies they had planned for a funeral wreath, but she had found alternatives and by the sound of it had done a good job. It had been a challenging day, she told Nina.

'The thing is,' Nina continued, 'I'm afraid it's not going to get any better. I need to take the rest of the week off, and I wouldn't lay bets on me being in the week after either. Something's happened.' She hadn't practised this part and wasn't sure where to begin, so she evaded the subject completely. 'I was thinking that you might be able to get your cousin to help out, if she's available. I know that still leaves you doing all the hard work, but I haven't got time to find another qualified florist. The only other option would be to close up shop, and I don't want to sound like I'm trying to pressurize you, but if I can't find a way to keep things going, Janet, it's possible that I might have to shelve the business for the time being. I said it would be a week or two but, honestly, I don't know when I'll be back. I'm so sorry about this.'

Nina felt her words begin to choke her. This wasn't good enough. She had to be strong if she were to pick up the fragments of her life and start piecing it back together. There really was no choice.

To her credit, Janet sounded less concerned about her future job prospects than she did the welfare of her friend and boss.

As Nina struggled to say thank you for what was

much-needed support, she looked at her handwritten list. If this was how she handled the easiest task, how would she cope with the rest? She rubbed her gritty eyes and was glad she hadn't made the same mistake as Scarlett by wearing lots of makeup. Not that Nina had cried, or at least not since she had left the house that morning. She had been at first too shocked and now she simply didn't have the energy.

There was the creak of a door behind her, and Nina's body tensed. She thought it might be Scarlett, at long last ready to seek forgiveness, but it was a young man's hands that rested on her shoulders. Liam leant over and planted a kiss on the top of her head. He had arrived just in time, because on the other end of the phone, Janet had asked the question that still needed an answer: what had happened?

'One of Scarlett's teachers has been arrested,' Nina said, and it wasn't for Rob's benefit that she didn't name him. She simply wasn't ready to hear it spoken in her house. 'He's being questioned as we speak over an alleged relationship. We've been with the police all afternoon and we'll no doubt be back there tomorrow.'

She hadn't come right out and said that the alleged relationship was with Scarlett, but Janet got the message. She asked if she should worry about journalists and Nina did her best to reassure her that the student was underage and couldn't be named, and neither could the teacher until he was charged. If Janet did come across anyone acting suspiciously, then as long as they bought something in the shop, they should be treated like any other customer.

'That's one problem down, nine hundred and ninety-nine to go,' Nina said as she twisted around in her chair.

Liam glanced down at the piece of paper trembling in her hand. 'You're going to tell Dad?'

'I have to,' she said, and her empty stomach lurched. 'Even out on the rigs, he'd get to hear about it eventually, and I'd rather do the explaining myself than let him hear it second-hand.'

'Do you want me to tell him?'

Liam's kindness weakened her resolve not to cry, but she held it together as she stood up to face her son. She even managed a smile. 'It should come from me.'

'Maybe, but it'll be one less thing on your list. I'll do it.'

Nina didn't argue a second time and was about to ask when he had grown up, but reminded herself that Scarlett wasn't the only crisis she had to manage. 'Why didn't you come to me about Eva?'

'Because,' he said slowly, 'if we're old enough to get into this mess then we have to be mature enough to deal with it.'

'By deciding to keep the baby? You think that's a mature decision?'

'I told her I thought she should have a termination,' he said as he stepped away from his mum.

Liam wanted to say more, but he couldn't do it while looking at her. He walked over to the bookshelves and ran a finger over the spines of Nina's treasured collection of Brontë novels as if his story could be lifted from their pages. She wasn't sure if he was setting himself up as the hero or the villain.

'That was why we split up. She said she couldn't go through with one, so I told her she was on her own. I thought it would make her see sense, but she went ahead and sorted out all the medical stuff by herself. Scarlett went with her to the clinic, which is when everything around here started going crazy.' He had the saddest smile on his face when he added, 'The way Eva took control made me realize she was being far more mature about it than I was.'

'I might beg to differ.'

'I know it sounds totally mad, but we've worked it all out, Mum. Eva's still working on getting her GCSEs, she'll have the baby in the summer and, if she can get support with childcare, there's an apprenticeship programme she's been looking at. Meanwhile, Manchester has offered me a place so I'm going to put it as my first choice, which means I can stay at home and help Eva.'

'Home? Whose home would that be?'

'We want to support ourselves, but I know we'll need help from you and Eva's parents for a while. We have a plan, though. Won't you at least hear us out?'

Nina rubbed her temples. 'OK,' she said, 'but maybe not right this second.'

'I promise we won't add to your troubles,' Liam said.

'If only your sister were being so considerate.'

Nina had sat through the police interviews with Scarlett, as well as giving her own version of events, initially at the school but then later at the police station, for all the good it had done. Nina could only speculate on what had happened, or why, for that matter, while Scarlett had ignored her mother's threat about never forgiving her and had denied everything except the words that Rob Swift had so expertly put in her mouth during the confrontation in Mrs Anwar's office.

Scarlett had told the police that she had had a crush on

Mr Swift and that was why she had sent him the photo, which Nina had the unenviable task of looking at. Her daughter had been naked except for a satin dressing gown, Nina's dressing gown, which she would be burning just as soon as she could.

From what Nina could gather, the fact that Rob had received the photo wasn't enough to incriminate him, unless they could find evidence that he had done something with it. If he hadn't, then he might be in serious trouble with the school for not reporting the incident, but not with the police. Nina wasn't interested in what the school might do: she wanted Rob Swift locked up, but as far as she was aware, he still hadn't been charged. Before leaving the station, the police officer in charge, a DS Alice Cunliffe, had told Nina that they would continue to question Rob and take more statements. They would gather as much evidence as they could, most notably from Rob and Scarlett's mobiles and laptops, although, according to Liam, his clever little app made sure any deleted data on their phones was overwritten and it was unlikely that Forensics would find what they were after.

Charlotte Tavistock had been contacted and would be arriving the next day to give a statement too, but according to Alice, their best hope of securing a conviction was from Scarlett's testimony. Nina was expected to talk some sense into her daughter before they returned to the station the next morning, but she was struggling to talk to her at all.

'I don't know what's got into Scarlett,' she said.

'I think you do, that's the problem,' Liam muttered under his breath.

If they hadn't been talking about Nina's fifteen-year-old daughter, the comment might have been funny, but Liam's innuendo turned Nina's stomach. 'Don't, I can't bear to think about what that man might have been doing to her. But do you know something, Liam? It's not so much the physical aspect of what he's done that bothers me most, it's the way he's managed to take complete control over her. She had a choice today, to tell the truth and start making things right, or put that man before her own family – and she chose him. She chose to lie for the man who's been abusing and manipulating her while he was playing happy families at home with his poor wife. Scarlett didn't even flinch through it all, and do you know what's worse? I haven't once heard her say sorry.'

'Of course I'm sorry,' came a voice from behind her.

Nina spun around to find Scarlett standing by the door. Her face was freshly washed and, without the rivers of mascara, her cheeks glowed baby pink. Her eyes, however, held no childlike innocence. Despite being red and puffy, the violet in them sparkled with defiance.

'No, you're not,' said Nina.

'I'm sorry I got Rob into trouble.'

'If that's an apology, I'd rather you kept it to yourself.'

'What do you want me to say, Mum? That I'm sorry I've disappointed you?' she asked. 'I'm in love, that's all. People do it all the time, unless you've forgotten. I don't remember you thinking about me and Liam when you married Bryn. All I'm doing is following in your footsteps.'

'I won't take the blame for this,' Nina said quietly, even though there was a grain of truth in her daughter's cruel words. 'Did you sleep with him, Scarlett?'

Scarlett gave her mother the same sneer she had given the police. 'With who?'

'The man who abused you.'

286

'The only people abusing me right now are you and the police.'

'Did you have sex with *that* man?' Nina asked.

'Who says I haven't been sleeping around with loads of men? What if Rob wasn't the only one I sent the photo to?'

Ignoring her, Nina asked, 'Did you sleep with Rob Swift?'

'You're not listening to me!'

'Because you haven't said anything worth listening to!' Nina yelled back before continuing with her single line of enquiry. 'Did he fuck you, Scarlett?'

Scarlett put her hands over her ears. 'Stop it! Just stop it!'

'Not until you tell the truth, not ever, so you'd better get used to it!' Nina shouted, but her daughter had backed out of the room before she had finished the sentence. Nina went to follow her, but Liam put a hand on her shoulder.

'Don't,' he said.

'Did you hear what she said?'

Liam cleared his throat. 'Every word, and that was not the kind of conversation I ever want to hear between my mum and my sister again.'

'Sorry, but I can't promise that,' growled Nina. It was only her anger keeping her going and she couldn't let go of it, even though Scarlett had stormed back upstairs and slammed her bedroom door, again. 'I won't stop asking, Liam. I already know the answer, but I won't stop asking.'

'You really think they . . . you know . . . ' Liam asked, struggling to find a description that Nina hadn't yet used about the alleged affair.

'Don't you? What does Eva think?'

Liam's cheeks gently simmered as he was forced to consider his sister's sex life. 'Seeing that photo, there was obviously something weird going, but . . . ' He shook his head. 'I know it's an awful thing to say, but while I can believe it of Scarlett, I thought better of Mr Swift. He's a good teacher, Mum. The girls flirt with him like it's a sport, which made me think all the gossip over the years was just bitchiness. He ignored them and it drove them crazy.'

'I think Charlotte Tavistock might not share your view.'

'But she's not saying they actually got together, is she?'

Nina could hear the doubt in her son's voice. With so many different and opposing views, it was impossible to piece together a single cohesive picture of what might have happened and who was to blame. Even as she spoke, she was trying to make sense of it. 'I know he's a popular teacher, but what if that's his way in? What if he's been fooling everyone – you, Mrs Anwar, Vikki, and even me. You said he ignored all the girls' innuendos and flirtations. What if he was deliberately driving them into a frenzy? Like an expert predator, he was encouraging them and they didn't even realize it. All he had to do was pick out the one that would take the bait, separate her from her friends and pounce when the time was right.'

'Do you think maybe Scarlett didn't need those extra lessons, that it was all a trap?'

'Oh God, I hadn't even thought of that,' she said, holding her head in her hands, but only briefly. There was a long way to go before they would get answers. 'Go and help Eva with the food and I'll mark one more thing off my list before I join you.'

'You're going to speak to Bryn, aren't you?'

'I'm going to try. That's as much as I can do for now.'

Nina didn't think for a minute that Bryn would pick up the phone, but if he didn't, she would leave a message. She would tell him about Rob Swift and let him know what was happening, if only so he wasn't surprised when the police contacted him. What she needed to say most of all was how ashamed of herself she was. Sorry didn't cover it, but it would be a start, something Scarlett could learn from. She would tell Bryn that she wasn't looking for forgiveness, because what she had done was unforgivable, but she was determined to make amends. She would tell him she was ready to fight for their marriage, but before she could do any of that, she needed to stop shaking.

When Vikki arrived with Freya at her mum's house, the toddler rushed straight through to the kitchen.

'Hello, my little sunshine,' she heard her mum saying, followed by giggles as Freya was presumably caught in a bear hug.

From the tone of her voice, Elaine had had a good meeting with her oncologist, unless of course it was all an act and she was hoping to put off bad news too. Vikki slipped off her coat and rubbed her face. Her cheeks were cold and her skin felt rough where salty tears had dried. She could feel the corners of her mouth being pulled down and, while a smile was beyond her, she did her best to organize her features into a neutral expression. She would have to tell her mum what had happened, but first she wanted to savour that sense of normality that her mum and her daughter could offer before she gave up holding up the sky and let it fall.

If Vikki was hurting, if her heart had been shattered and

289

her body torn apart by the shrapnel, then she couldn't feel it any more. The numbing sensation had taken over at some point between going into the school with Sarah and that horrible moment when they had all heard Rob's phone rattling in his pocket. When the police had arrived, she had started to cry, but if she were honest, it was because she felt that was what she ought to be doing if only she could feel something.

She had left the school on her own, insisting that she had to pick up Freya from nursery and refusing Sarah's offer to collect her instead. Her daughter couldn't be protected forever, but for now it would be as if none of this was happening.

'Have you eaten?' her mum asked when Vikki walked into the kitchen.

'Freya's had a sausage roll.'

'Ah, that explains the flakes of pastry all over your coat,' Elaine told the innocent child in her arms. Freya squeezed her nan's cheeks with greasy fingers before giving her a kiss.

'Me get down now, please, Nanna.'

'All right, but sit at the table. We have chocolate cake.'

Freya clapped her hands and toddled over to a dining chair which would keep her preoccupied for a good minute as she set about climbing up by herself.

'Are they for me?' Elaine asked, taking the bunch of bright orange and yellow tulips Vikki was proffering.

'They're only from the supermarket,' she admitted. 'I didn't fancy going into the florist's.'

'Oh, they're lovely. You must have known I had good news.'

Elaine could barely look at her daughter, but her grin was nearly splitting her cheeks. 'The consultant is really pleased with me. The results of the latest scan were as good as can be and my bloods are better than expected, too. He said he's quietly confident – and the best news is, he doesn't think radiotherapy is necessary. The only further treatment we actually talked about was reconstructive surgery. It won't be for another couple of months, but the thing is, I feel like I'm on the road to recovery now.'

When Elaine had finished her speech, she had fire in her eyes and she cast them directly at Vikki. In a flash, the light was gone. She rushed over to her daughter and cupped her face in her hands as if she were holding a butterfly. 'Vikki, what's wrong?'

'Oh, Mum,' she said through trembling lips. 'It's horrible, it's so horrible.'

Elaine tried to draw more information from her daughter, but Vikki couldn't speak. Eventually, her mum asked, 'On a scale of one to ten, how bad are we talking?'

'Ten,' Vikki said as her whole body began to shake. 'Twenty, a hundred . . . '

When Vikki's legs started to buckle, Elaine wrapped her in her arms and rocked her while her daughter buried her face in her neck. For fear of upsetting Freya, Vikki managed to swallow back her sobs while Elaine whispered soothing words which, for the most part, simply involved telling her daughter to breathe. Only when she was sure Vikki had mastered this art did she fetch a glass of water.

'Cake, Nana!' Freya shouted when she saw Elaine walking straight past the counter where the chocolate gateau was sitting proudly on one of her best china platters, brought out only for special occasions.

Elaine handed Vikki a glass and whispered, 'Sip it slowly.'

Returning to the cake, her determined mother placed three slices on individual plates before giving one to her granddaughter, along with a beaker of milk. 'Don't make a mess,' she said. Thinking better of it, added, 'Oh, to heck with it, make as much mess as you like.'

While half of Freya's hand disappeared into the middle of the cake, Elaine returned to Vikki, who was biting her lower lip so hard it had turned white. 'Let's sit down, shall we?'

At the table, Vikki gave Freya a sideways glance and found it impossible to begin. She was too young to understand what her mum was about to say, but even so, Vikki didn't want her to hear the pain in her voice. Reading her mind, Elaine said, 'Why don't we all watch *Frozen*?' she said. 'You can never see it too many times.'

Elaine somehow managed to maintain a smile as she switched on the film, and Vikki wished it were genuine. Her mum had been ready to celebrate after her visit to the hospital and deserved to enjoy this major victory in her fight back to health.

Taking Vikki's hands in hers, Elaine looked a vision of calm. 'OK,' she said, 'I'm being as patient as I can, but you have to do your best to explain what's going on before my heart implodes.'

Vikki's throat hurt as she swallowed back the lump in her throat. The sensation, as unpleasant as it was, was nothing compared to the emotional pain her mind continued to block out. Speaking in a rush, she said, 'Rob's been arrested. They think he's been involved with an underage girl, one of his students.'

Elaine's grip on her daughter's hands tightened briefly as if the shock had sent a jolt through her body, but then she relaxed again. Her eyes never left Vikki's face. 'That's ridiculous.'

'He's denying it.'

'I should think so too.'

'And so is Scarlett.'

Elaine's poker face twitched. 'Scarlett? The one who's pregnant?'

Finally, a smile broke free, but it twisted Vikki's features. 'It turns out she's not pregnant after all. Every cloud . . . '

Before she could swallow back the next sob, it escaped and they both turned to check Freya's reaction. Enthralled by her favourite snow-covered kingdom, the little girl wasn't even paying attention to the handful of chocolate cake she shoved into her mouth.

'She was covering up for a friend who's pregnant by Scarlett's brother.'

'What a family,' Elaine said under her breath, before concentrating on her own. 'But I don't understand. What does any of this have to do with poor Rob? You need to tell me everything.'

So Vikki did tell her everything, or at least everything from that morning. 'I'm scared, Mum,' she said. 'What's going to happen if they charge him? What will we do?'

Elaine shook her head. 'It won't come to that,' she said firmly. 'I haven't spent the last six months fighting for life only to have some schoolgirl come along and destroy my family. Rob is innocent, you have to hold on to that.'

Vikki's shoulders shook as she fought to compose herself enough to speak. 'But what if he's not? He's admitted kissing Charlotte Tavistock, Mum, and I was thinking, that would have been around the time that we lost Dad, when I was staying here with you, remember? And this thing with Scarlett would have happened – if it happened – around the time that I was here looking after you.' She gasped before quickly adding, 'Not that I'm blaming any of this on you being ill!'

Elaine's expression was surprisingly calming. 'I know you're not,' she said softly. 'And if by some chance Rob is guilty then he alone is responsible for his actions, not me, and not you either. But that's a very big *if*, Vikki. Don't fall into the same trap as Scarlett's mum and let this mudslinging destroy your marriage. You know Rob better than anyone. He's devoted to you. He wouldn't do something like this.'

And that was the problem, Vikki did know Rob better than anyone. So why couldn't she share her mum's staunch faith? 'But what if the police find something else? What if there's more than just this photo of Scarlett? They asked me to go back to the house with them so they could get Rob's computer. I told them to help themselves. I don't want to go back there, Mum. Is it all right if we stay here?'

'But what happens when Rob's released?' Elaine said, still certain that he would be. 'He'll expect you to be at home, surely?'

Vikki's lip trembled so much that at first she couldn't reply. 'I can't – I can't go back. Please, don't make me. Not until all this is over.'

Elaine stood up only to lean over Vikki and hug her tightly. 'Oh, sweetheart, I won't make you do anything you don't want to.'

'The police want me to go to the station tomorrow to give a proper statement. Will you come with me?'

'Of course I will. I'll do anything to help you through this.'

Elaine rested her head on top of Vikki's as she gently rocked her. They were both looking towards Freya, whose eyes remained glued to the TV screen. She was absent-mindedly rubbing chocolate butter icing in her hair.

'Oh, what a mess,' Elaine said.

When Nina awoke the next morning, her first surprise was that she had slept at all. She had retreated to her bed sometime in the early hours still clutching her mobile and hoping that Bryn would stop ignoring her messages, of which there had been many. As if to compensate for her husband's silence, there had been plenty of other people who had been more than happy to speak to her.

DS Cunliffe had phoned to let her know that Rob would remain in custody overnight, but they would have to either charge or release him the next day. She explained that it was highly likely that he would be released because, as things stood, she didn't have enough evidence to persuade the Crown Prosecution Service that they had a case.

There had also been a call from a cheerful-sounding lady from social services who had informed her that they would be working with the police to support Scarlett and assess her family's needs. She had stressed that their involvement was purely supportive and, as if to press home the point, had offered to make arrangements for Scarlett to see a counsellor. When the woman had reassured Nina that she wasn't to blame, Nina had been tempted to ask her to put it in writing so she could show it to not only her daughter but her ex-husband too. Liam had spoken to his dad and tried to explain what was happening, but Adam had insisted on speaking to Nina.

Oblivious to his own failings, Adam was apoplectic that Nina could let both her children run wild and, worse still, 'allow' some pervert to molest his little girl. Nina had been too exhausted to care what Adam thought of her and she let the one-sided argument rage on, waiting until he had run out of breath before she suggested he take a leave of absence. She told him she would be more than happy for him to come to Sedgefield and talk some sense into Scarlett so that the pervert in question didn't escape justice. Adam had gone quiet after that and she didn't expect to see him on her doorstep anytime soon.

Sarah had been in touch too, telephoning while they were all having dinner together. Scarlett had been forced to join them at the dinner table, but had sat through the entire meal with her arms folded and her mouth shut. Liam and Eva had attempted to make small talk, but it had been interspersed with long silences which should have made Sarah's call a blessing, except it had been equally awkward.

They had last spoken in the school car park as Nina was leaving to go to the police station. So much pain had been inflicted in such a short space of time that she had held back from telling her so-called friend exactly what she thought of her. When Sarah had made the mistake of phoning only a matter of hours later, however, Nina was more inclined to be direct. She had had enough of letting things happen to her and was on the attack, as Scarlett had discovered earlier.

'How is everyone?' Sarah had asked.

'You mean out of the family I have left?' Nina asked as she stabbed at the pasta congealing on her plate.

'I know, and I can't begin to tell you how sorry I am about Bryn.'

Clearly, Sarah had thought she could and had taken a deep breath to make a start, but Nina got there first. 'Then don't,' she said. 'Don't apologize for spending the last year demonizing my husband. Don't apologize for making me doubt the sweetest, kindest man I had the brief pleasure of knowing.'

'But I—'

'But nothing, Sarah,' Nina said. 'You were supposed to be my friend. I don't think even my worst enemy could have done a better job of destroying my marriage. I can't forgive you, Sarah. And I won't.'

When Nina had ended the call abruptly, she had glanced around the table at three bowed heads. No one had dared offer a comment, and they had continued their meal in silence until Liam had the good sense to clear away their untouched food.

Nina didn't regret her harsh words, even though she blamed herself as much, if not more than Sarah, and would forgive her oldest friend eventually. For one thing, she would need Sarah's cooperation if they were going to put Rob Swift in prison for abusing both their daughters, but in the meantime, it would do no harm to make Sarah suffer. There were lessons she had to learn before Nina would ever consider resuming their friendship.

Other calls that night had been from well-meaning acquaintances and distant relatives who had picked up the rumours and were more interested in hearing the juicy details than offering any real support. Nina had put together an edited version of events that she could reel off in under a minute before cutting the call short in case Bryn was trying to get through.

But he hadn't got in touch until the wee hours of the

morning, and that was Nina's second surprise when she awoke. She was annoyed that she had slept through a message alert, but the real shock was that the text was from Bryn. She didn't care what he said, knowing that the connection between them was still open gave her some hope. He had thought about her and he had wanted to get in touch.

Raising herself up, Nina crawled from beneath the bedclothes and sat on the edge of the bed. She didn't dare look at her reflection in the dressing-table mirror, but stared at her husband's name on the screen while she did a quick reality check. Of course she cared what the message said, which was why the phone was trembling in her hand. It wasn't going to be a nice message, she was prepared for that. The question was, how bad could it be?

Leave me alone.

Nina cried out, muffling her pain with her fist. She was tempted to hurl the phone at the mirror, but instead she clutched it to her chest. Her pulse raced and she took deep breaths as she prepared to sink beneath the waves of misery. She wanted to burst into tears, but she was holding to her resolve not to break down. She wasn't going to let Rob Swift destroy her family any more than he already had. She was fighting to get her family back, and it started with a brief and succinct reply to Bryn.

No, I won't leave you alone. Hate me all you like, I deserve it, but I won't give up.

She had more to say, but she would need time to compose

a message that would be strong enough to break through the barrier of her own construction. Pulling back her shoulders, she braved a look in the mirror to find her reflection surprisingly familiar. The world around her was changing by the hour, but she was the same person she had always been, the one who had brought up two children on her own and kept the family business going.

Only a week ago, she had been living in blissful ignorance. She had thought she was doing a good job as a wife and mother: a stable marriage, her oldest child almost off to university and the other aiming for top grades in her GCSEs. Nina would spend the rest of her life wondering where it all went wrong, but if she were going to judge herself, it should be on what she did next.

She considered going into Liam's room so they could start the conversation they had managed to avoid the night before. Eva had gone home after dinner with a vague promise of telling her parents that she was almost nine weeks' pregnant, and extending Nina's offer, which was to gather the two families together so they could talk through the options, even though Liam and Eva were insisting the most crucial decision had already been made. Nina would have admired their determination to keep the baby if she wasn't absolutely convinced it would be a terrible mistake.

Standing up, Nina went to grab the dressing gown hanging from the back of the door, but quickly recoiled. It was the one she had taken to Rome, which had failed to add spice to the trip because Nina had been too worried about what had upset Scarlett. It was also the one that had featured in the photograph sent to Rob, and Nina shuddered in revulsion as she lifted the gown off the hook. Falling short of creating a bonfire in her bedroom, Nina scrunched it into a ball and shoved it into a drawer where it would remain out of sight until she could dispose of it permanently.

It was Bryn's towelling dressing gown she wrapped around herself as she went into Scarlett's room. She had been prepared to drag her daughter out of bed, but Scarlett was up and dressed.

'I'm going to the police station,' Scarlett said.

'I know you are. I'll get ready and then we can head straight over.'

'I'm going on my own.'

Nina opened her mouth to say more, but thought better of it. She could engage in an argument or she could keep to her original plan. Scarlett's opinion didn't matter, not unless she had had an epiphany overnight and was eager to provide the evidence the police needed to lock up Rob Swift and throw away the key. There was a simple way of testing that particular theory.

'Did you have sex with Rob Swift?' she asked.

'No, I made it all up.'

Nina turned and left without another word. She went downstairs and made sure all the exits were deadlocked. Next, she collected all the house keys, including the one from Scarlett's school bag that had been discarded in the hall. Satisfied that her daughter had no means of escape, Nina locked herself in the bathroom. She took a long, hot bath, luxuriating in the false sense of calm it gave her while ignoring the commotion outside when Scarlett realized she had been trapped.

'You'd better get used to it,' Nina whispered softly. 'This is only the beginning.'

Scarlett

I don't know if I want to say any more. What else is there anyway? I could start again from the beginning and promise to tell the truth, the whole truth and nothing but the truth, but that's not going to happen, not ever. No one is getting any more information out of me.

'Did you have sex with him?' 'Did he touch you?' 'Did he force you to do anything you didn't want to do?' I was asked over and over and over again by practically every single person I was allowed to come into contact with while Mum had me under house arrest. If I was supposed to be the victim, then why were they treating me like a criminal, especially Mum? She didn't even try to hide how much she hated me, and it was like I didn't have a mum any more. I thought it was bad enough when she got together with Bryn and we stopped doing the stuff we used to do, just the two of us, but this was ten times worse. It was horrible and so was she, which I suppose was a good thing in a weird sort of way because it stopped me feeling sorry for her. Mum had turned into this heartless cow who had kicked her husband out and locked up her daughter,

and not once did I see her cry. The only time she softened up was around Liam. She was nicer to Eva than she was to me.

But no matter how much Mum controlled what was going on around me, she couldn't get inside my head. I suppose that's what the counselling is supposed to be about, but I'll tell you now, I won't be threatened, or bribed, or hypnotized into changing my statement. I think that police-woman, Alice, realized that when I went back to see her the day after Rob was arrested.

She didn't badger me like you see on TV and it was kind of good when she kept telling Mum off for trying to answer for me. I was surprised how quickly Alice gave up, but after we left the interview room, I had to hang around while she took Mum to one side. She kept putting her hand on Mum's arm and squeezing it, like Mum was the one who needed all the sympathy.

I overheard her telling Mum that they only had a few hours left before they would have to charge Rob or let him go and it was looking like they would let him go. I couldn't help smiling, but then Alice clocked me listening in. I think she wanted me to overhear, it was probably some trick, but no one was going to trick me into anything.

'You care a lot about him, don't you, Scarlett?' she asked.

'He's a good teacher.'

'Not any longer. Whatever happens, I doubt he'll be teaching again.'

We were standing in a corridor with dirty cream walls covered in scuff marks. There were lots of doors and Rob could have been behind any one of them.

I thought he might be close enough to hear me so I raised

my voice when I said, 'That's not fair, he hasn't done anything wrong.'

'Not with you, perhaps, but you're not the first, are you? I doubt you're even the second. We only need one girl to be brave enough to come forward and testify.'

I didn't answer. The interview had officially ended and I wasn't going to let her trip me up.

'How will that make you feel, Scarlett?' Alice asked, 'To find out that you're not so special to him after all? Will you wait for him if he does get convicted? And then what? Do you think he'll be interested in you when you've grown out of your uniform? Men like Rob Swift aren't interested in women who have a mind and a will of their own. He prefers silly little girls who don't even realize he's pulling their strings.'

'Not even the amazing Mr Swift could get me to do anything I don't want to,' I said. 'I'm a stubborn cow, aren't I, Mum?'

Mum didn't answer. At this point, she only talked to me when she was giving an order, like, 'Put your coat on, Scarlett,' or, 'Answer the question.'

'So why did you lie about being pregnant?' Alice asked. 'It wasn't only to protect your friend, was it? You wanted to get back at him after finding out his wife was pregnant, didn't you? If you thought you were so in control of the situation, why did you need more leverage?'

It was a good theory, but I said nothing. I was shit-scared, if I'm honest. Scared about what might happen if she did manage to find evidence somehow that would send the man I loved to prison, but I didn't let it show, I wouldn't give her the satisfaction. I just glared at her, not even blinking once. 'If you want to ask more questions, shouldn't we go back into the room so you can record it? Is this questioning even legal?'

Alice took a couple of steps towards me until I could smell her coffee breath. 'Now you listen to me. My job is to protect young girls like you from predators like Rob Swift, and if that means breaking the odd rule, fine, I'll take that chance. I'm sorely tempted to throw you in a cell and charge you with obstruction. I don't think your mum would have any objection.'

'Only if you released her before she's eighteen,' Mum muttered.

'So you are panicking,' I said.

Further down the corridor, a policeman appeared. He was the miserable-looking desk sergeant who had let us in earlier, only now he was smiling. 'We have a couple of new arrivals for you, Alice.'

'They're here?'

'I'll put them in Room 4.'

Alice had this smug grin on her face when she turned back to me. Whoever had arrived, she thought what they had to say was going to be a game changer.

27

When Elaine parked up in front of the Swift family home, Vikki had no intention of getting out of the car. It had been as much as she could do to drag herself out of bed that morning and it was her mum who had got Freya ready. When Vikki had failed to make an appearance after breakfast, Elaine had returned upstairs and repeated the process of washing and dressing her grown daughter.

They had gone together to drop Freya off at nursery, but rather than return home, Elaine had driven to the house where Vikki had lived for the last five years. It looked like the perfect family home, but it would seem that looks could be deceptive.

'You need to pack a bag,' Elaine said. 'I have precisely two sets of clothes and one set of pyjamas for Freya and it's not going to be enough. And as lovely as you look in my dress, it's swimming on you.'

Staring at the front door, Vikki could remember feeling anxious the day before as she locked it behind her. She had been worrying about her mum's impending hospital appointment and something else, something that she hadn't been able to name. If only she had kept her promise to go to the hospital with her mum, if only she had been allowed to share in her mum's relief, if only Rob hadn't . . .

'I can't,' she said, tearing her gaze from the front door to plead with her mum. 'You said I didn't have to go back if I didn't want to.'

'But what are you so afraid of?' Elaine asked softly.

Vikki frowned. 'I don't know,' she said, and for a fleeting moment wished that Rob was there to tell her she could do this, but she could no longer trust his judgement, or her own for that matter. She didn't know how deep Rob's guilt ran, but she had this sick feeling he was guilty of something. Doubting every promise he had ever made, she said, 'Maybe I'm scared that nothing I had before was real.'

'Of course it was real, it still is,' Elaine said, her soothing voice replaced by one that hinted at her frustration. 'You have to think of Freya, Vikki and the new baby too.'

'I am,' Vikki said solemnly as her uncertainty about having another baby came back with a vengeance. 'I'm trapped, aren't I?'

'You shouldn't make any rash decisions. You're in shock, and I know Rob has questions to answer, but once everything settles down . . . ' Elaine inhaled deeply to compose herself. 'Well, you'll see things differently. This accusation about Scarlett is probably nothing more than childish fantasy, and as for what went on with Sarah's daughter, it could have happened exactly as Rob said: she was a schoolgirl who misread the signals, that's all. It's not like anyone has suggested it was more than one kiss.'

'But the police aren't going to take Rob's word for it.

306

They'll be looking for other girls to come forward. What if they start asking me about how we met? What happens when they find out the school nearly sacked him when they found out about us?'

Elaine's body jerked. 'What? When was this?'

Vikki squirmed under her mother's gaze. 'It was shortly before Mr Taggart retired as head. He found out Rob was dating an ex-student and wanted to launch an investigation. I think it was Mrs Anwar who talked him out of it when Rob explained we were getting engaged.'

Releasing the breath she had been holding, Elaine said, 'And rightly so. Mr Taggart always was a cantankerous old goat and I doubt he liked seeing anyone happy. You and Rob didn't start seeing each other until after you had left sixth form, so it had nothing to do with the school, and that's how the police will see it too.'

'But—'

'But nothing,' Elaine said abruptly. 'Now is not the time to rake up the past.'

Silenced by her mother, Vikki stared out the window and watched as her neighbours came out of their house. The middle-aged couple had moved in only a few months earlier and their exchanges so far had been limited to polite hellos. The woman, who had a son at Sedgefield High, spotted Vikki sitting in the car but quickly glanced away as if she hadn't seen her.

'Do you think everyone knows?' she asked as the couple got in their car and drove away.

'It's a small town, so I don't suppose it would take long for the rumours to spread. Which makes it all the more important that you think carefully about how you respond to all of this, and more importantly how you're seen to respond.'

When Vikki dropped her head, the first teardrop trickled down her nose and plopped on to her hand. 'You think I should stand by him?'

'Oh, Vikki, I don't have all the answers, sweetheart, I wish I did,' she said, taking hold of her daughter's hand and giving it a tight squeeze. 'But I can't help worrying that, if Rob is charged, the punishment won't be his alone. It's not going to be just the police looking to the past. The press will have a field day raking through his private life and, I hate to say it, but they'll be judging you as much as him. Of course, if he has done something terrible then he must be punished, and we'll have to deal with the aftermath, but I find that so hard to believe. I understand that you're angry with him for flirting with these girls, but you can't let that cloud your judgement. Above all, you can't let the police see that you doubt him. Let *them* find the evidence, if it exists – that's all I'm asking.'

Vikki released a sob. 'I'm scared, Mum.'

'I know, and I'm sorry,' Elaine soothed, 'but it had to be said. You have to be strong, Vikki, and I promise we'll get through this together.' And with that, Elaine let go of Vikki's hand. 'Now, get out of the car, Victoria, and pack some bags. When you've done that, we're going to the police station.'

Vikki followed her mum's instructions to the letter because that was what she was used to doing; letting someone else tell her what to do, what to think. But there was a part of Vikki that was resisting this learned response, the part of her that had come to the fore while she was caring for her mum and making decisions on her own. She had liked that person, the one who had impressed Sarah Tavistock so much, the one who wanted a career and not another baby. If Vikki could only get to know that version of herself a little better, she might be able to think her own way out of this mess. She just needed more time.

Nina couldn't wait to leave the police station. It had been a long morning and she was desperate for some fresh air. After Scarlett's interview with DS Cunliffe, they had been cornered by social services and the counsellor who had been assigned to them. For the first time that day, someone had offered kind words to her daughter; not that this tactic had any more effect than the threats. Scarlett told the counsellor in no uncertain terms that she wasn't interested in talking to her, so it was Nina who accepted the offer on her daughter's behalf. They needed all the help they could get.

Heading for the exit, Nina presumed Scarlett was following but she didn't care enough to turn around and check. In time, she would remember how much she loved her daughter, but right now she couldn't stand to be near her, and she suspected the feeling was mutual. Nina hadn't completely lost all maternal feeling; she was intent on bringing Rob to justice and protecting Scarlett from further physical or emotional harm, but what she had lost was any concern for Scarlett's feelings. She had to keep reminding herself that her daughter was a victim, but it was a tall ask when Scarlett refused to recognize herself as one.

Tucking her chin into her chest, Nina stepped outside and marched towards her car. Alice had warned her that the press had started sniffing around, but it wasn't a journalist who had been waiting for her.

'Nina, slow down.'

Turning to face Sarah, Nina asked, 'What do you want?'

'To put things right.'

Nina was already turning back to the car when she said, 'Good luck with that.'

'Wait, please. Can we talk? I have news.'

Scarlett had been following at a distance but the mention of news drew her closer. Nina pointed the keys at the car to unlock it.

'Get in and wait for me.'

'I'm happy staying here.'

'Scarlett, in case you haven't worked it out yet, your happiness is not on my list of priorities. Get in the car and wait.'

When Scarlett was safely out of earshot, Sarah said, 'Charlotte's giving her statement now.'

'For what good it'll do. I'm not sure a kiss will be enough to convince the police they have a case.'

'It convinced you, didn't it?'

'And has it convinced you? Are you ready to accept that Bryn is – was good for me?'

Sarah ground the toe of her pointed boot into the Tarmac as if she were crushing a bug. 'For fear of repeating myself, I am truly sorry, and I'll do anything I can to put things right between us. Rob Swift won't get away with this.'

It didn't escape Nina's notice that Sarah had avoided giving Bryn her blessing, but there were more important battles to fight. 'I don't see how we can stop him if Scarlett doesn't come to her senses soon.'

'She's still not saying anything?'

Nina glanced over to the car where Scarlett was watching

them intently. 'Not a word. Nothing incriminating, at any rate.'

'Don't worry,' Sarah said, surprisingly confidently, 'Scarlett isn't the only schoolgirl he's interfered with. I've had a long talk with Charlotte, and we both agree that she's had a lucky escape. I can't imagine what might have happened if I'd accepted his offer for extra lessons rather than getting her some private tuition.'

'I think I can.'

'Well, we've gone through exactly what did happen and, more importantly, what she needs to tell the police. There's no question that Rob was grooming her. She's pretty sure now that he was the one who initiated the kiss and wanted to take it further. Like I said, he won't get away with it.'

'You've been coaching her?'

'Don't look at me like that,' Sarah said. 'OK, I know my interfering has caused enough trouble, but this is what we all want, isn't it? She's not exactly going to lie to the police, Nina, she's simply seeing the situation from a different perspective.'

'If only I could get Scarlett to do that. Look, I have to go. Thanks for letting me know.'

'Nina,' Sarah called after her. 'I'm trying to make amends.'

'In that case you're going to have to try a bit harder,' Nina said, and wished it wasn't true. She had gone through some tough times in her life and Sarah had always been there as her last refuge. She needed a good friend now more than ever and, sadly, she couldn't be sure that friend was Sarah.

Vikki's visit to the police station hadn't been entirely worthless and she had left with more information than she had been able to offer. Elaine didn't argue when Vikki insisted they cut short Freya's morning session at nursery and, with a growing sense of urgency, they had all squeezed into a car already crammed with their belongings, leaving barely enough space for the passengers.

Unloading and unpacking took quite some time, and only Freya seemed excited at the prospect of sharing a room with her mummy. Unlike their temporary stays, this had a feeling of permanence as they began filling cupboards in the guest room with all of Freya's favourite toys and clothes, which the little girl promptly took out again.

'Maybe I should take Freya downstairs and start lunch,' Elaine suggested.

'Good idea.'

'Will you be all right?' Elaine asked.

They both looked at Vikki's mobile phone on the window-sill.

Vikki nodded. 'I'll be fine.'

She had managed to empty a large suitcase and two holdalls when the call she had been dreading came. Rather than pick it up, Vikki remained at a safe distance and contemplated shouting for her mum. She had to remind herself that she was no longer a child, that she was in control of her own destiny, even if her family's fate lay ultimately in the hands of one schoolgirl.

She took her time drawing closer and by the time she reached the window, the call had diverted to voicemail. There was no time to feel relief because a second later, it rang again and the caller display glowed with one single word that felt like a kick in the stomach.

Rob was using the house phone and if she didn't answer, he would keep ringing or, worse still, show up at her mum's.

'Well, you picked up. I suppose that's something,' Rob said when the call was answered. Vikki had yet to speak so he added, 'That is you, isn't it?'

'Yes.'

'Vikki,' he whispered as if her name alone were sweet balm. 'I've missed you so much. The last twenty-four hours have been hell, and all I could think about was getting home to you and Freya. And now I am home, the only welcome I've had is a hand-delivered letter from Mrs Anwar informing me that I'm suspended. I need you, Vikki. It feels wrong, being here without you.'

'You've managed on your own before.'

She could hear his breath catching in his throat as he inhaled deeply. 'I know you're angry with me, and even though I was awake all night trying to work out what to say to you, I know there's nothing I can say to make this better.'

It was his opening shot, but Vikki knew her husband better than that. He would have a plan, he simply wasn't letting Vikki see it from the start. 'Why don't you try,' she said.

'Do we have to do this over the phone? I want to see you, Vikki. Come home.'

From downstairs, Vikki could hear Freya singing. Their daughter would be excited to know her daddy was on the phone. Rob was a good father and husband; that was what her mum kept saying and it was what Vikki wanted to believe. It would be so much easier to ignore the doubt.

'I can't,' she said. 'Not until all this is over.'

'The police have released me without charge, Vikki.'

'But you're suspended from school and the police are still investigating you,' she reminded him. Her pulse was racing but her voice remained surprisingly firm. 'And what if you are charged? Who knows what's going to happen when the press get hold of the story. It's safer for me and Freya if we stay with Mum.'

'But I've done nothing wrong.'

'Haven't you? What about Charlotte? And why would Scarlett send you that photo, unless she thought you wanted to see it? Whatever the police decide, you have done something wrong, Rob. You've destroyed our family and wrecked your career. And for what? Was she that good? Was she worth it?'

'I need to explain,' he said. 'I didn't touch her, Vikki, I swear.'

'How can I believe anything you say, Rob?'

'If you won't come home then at least agree to meet me,' he insisted. 'Give me a chance to explain. Please, I love you. I know this nightmare isn't over yet, but it will be soon, I promise. I need you, Vikki. You can't imagine how cold and lonely it feels here without you.'

Listening to his persuasive voice, there was a part of Vikki that wanted the same things he did: for all of this to go away and for life to return to normal. 'Don't do this,' she said, as much to herself as to him.

'Why? Don't you want to see me? I haven't changed, have I? I'm still the man you married. Come to the house later, after Freya's in bed. I won't pressurize you to stay. All I'm asking for is an hour of your time. After five years of marriage, don't I deserve that?'

It wouldn't be the first time Vikki had sneaked off to be with him while she was living with her parents, but when she tried to recall one of their secret meetings, it was an image of Scarlett in her uniform that sprung to mind.

'No!' she said. 'I can't.'

'But you want to. I know you, Vikki, you still love me. There's no one else, I swear. There never was and never could be. You have to believe that.'

Freya's voice grew louder as she stomped up the stairs singing about rainbows. 'I have to go,' she said. 'I need some space, Rob, and if you do love me, then you can at least give me that.'

Rob started to say something else but Vikki cut off the call.

When Nina stepped into the house, her ears were trained for the slightest sound coming from upstairs.

'Wow, that went well,' Liam said. He had followed her into the house and now rested his back against the front door in an attempt to keep out the demons that were constantly on the family's tail.

'Scarlett! Are you home?'

When no answer came, Nina yelled again, only louder.

A door opened upstairs. 'Where else would I be!'

The door slammed. Nina relaxed.

It was the first time she had left Scarlett on her own, but taking her out with them hadn't been an option. She had relied on the ongoing police investigation to be enough of a deterrent to keep Scarlett from contacting Rob and risking exposure. Even so, Nina had been a tiny bit relieved when Eva's parents had kicked them out of the house so quickly.

'I need a drink,' she said, and went straight to the kitchen

315

to retrieve a bottle of wine that had been cooling in the fridge for her return. Turning to Liam, she added, 'Fancy joining me?'

'I'd better not. I was thinking of going back to school tomorrow. I've already missed a week and I don't want to fall too far behind.'

'Of course not. What was I thinking? And what would the McEldrys say? Not only am I a terrible mother with two delinquent children, now I'm plying them with drink!'

'They were angry, Mum, and it's natural for them to be upset. Up until today, I think they really respected you, looking after a family and a business pretty much on your own. Even with everything that's gone on with Scarlett, they never once blamed you.'

'At least Eva's told them. One less secret to contend with.'

Eva had waited until the weekend to tell her parents, and her mum had been in tears when she had phoned Nina to arrange a family conference on Sunday evening at the McEldry house.

It was clear from the moment they arrived that Eva's parents had assumed that Nina would be opposed to Eva having the baby as much as they were, and up until that point, she had. Eva had been instructed to stay in her bedroom and wasn't even afforded the opportunity to take part in the discussion. When Liam had the effrontery to complain, he was shouted down by Eva's dad. The only item on the McEldrys' agenda was agreement to withdraw all support from Eva and Liam should they persist with their family plan; and by support, they had meant everything, including a roof over their heads. They were intent on limiting Eva's options to just one: a termination.

'I don't want you to think I agree with what you're doing, Liam,' Nina said, while pouring a large glass of wine. She took a gulp before adding, 'I think you're both too young and, with the best will in the world, this baby is going to limit your prospects for the future. It might be that the two of you can build a happy life together, but having a baby now will make that less likely, not more.'

'So you agree with Eva's parents? But you said—'

'I disagree completely and utterly with the way they're going about it. This is Eva's choice. It's her body and no one should be manipulating her into doing something she doesn't want to,' Nina said. She could hear her voice rising and her emotions along with them.

'Is this still about Eva?' Liam asked.

He was leaning against the kitchen counter with his hands in his pockets. He had surprised her time and again over the last week by how quickly he had matured. Her unwashed and ungainly son who never left his room had transformed into a young man who had the insight to see into her soul.

'She's still a child, Liam, but that doesn't mean she's not old enough to understand the consequences of her actions. There's a choice to be made, and while I won't change my mind on what I think that choice should be, I accept that she's the one to make it.'

'Talking about me again?'

Scarlett had appeared in the doorway. Her time in the house alone had not been wasted and she had whiled away the last hour primping and preening herself. After almost a week without makeup, Scarlett had spent time on a look that was subtle and understated, apart from the red lipstick, which made her pale skin look ghoulish.

'This may come as a surprise to you, Scarlett, but you're not always the centre of attention.'

'Oh no, what am I going to do now? Maybe I'll have to make up some more lies.' She adopted a sarcastic 'shock-horror' face, which made Liam turn away in disgust.

'So what are you saying?' Nina asked. 'That this whole mess has been nothing more than your way of getting attention?'

'I could do without your kind of attention, thanks.'

Nina held on tightly to the glass of wine in her hand and resisted the urge to knock it back. She had been making a conscious effort to be civil to Scarlett, but any conversation they had always reverted to Rob Swift, and until Scarlett told the truth and guaranteed that man was locked away for good, Nina couldn't let go of her anger.

'Oh, that's right,' Nina said, 'you don't need me interested in you when you have so many other people lined up to hear what you've been up to.'

'Or *not* been up to.'

Nina had raised her glass to her mouth, but paused long enough to say, 'Let's get one thing straight, Scarlett. You can say what you like to the police and social services, or anyone who cares to listen, but when you're talking to me, I'd rather you kept your mouth shut than tell me more lies.'

Scarlett pursed her lips but a second later, the words were spilling out of her mouth. 'Why won't you listen? I made it up, Mum! You think I like admitting that? Do you have any idea how embarrassing it is to admit I had a crush on my teacher and for people to see *that* photo? He didn't do anything!'

Nina slammed her glass down on to the granite counter

so hard that the edges of the base splintered. 'Fact one, you sent him a provocative photo and he kept it to himself! Fact two, he has a history of interfering with his pupils. Fact three, the school are convinced enough to suspend him. Fact four, you didn't tell me you were in a fantasy relationship, Scarlett, you told me you were having sex with someone! Fact five, you told me you weren't sleeping with Linus. Fact six, Linus has made a statement supporting that assertion. Do I really need to go on?'

Her daughter's violet eyes were cold and piercing, but it was her next words that cut deep into Nina's heart. 'Maybe there was someone, Mum. Maybe I got sick of being ignored by you and turned to someone who was more than happy to give me some attention. And maybe I didn't have to leave the house to find *that* someone.'

Nina didn't realize she was launching herself at Scarlett until Liam caught hold of her. She fought against him, but he had grabbed both her arms and she couldn't get close enough to Scarlett to cause any damage.

'Scarlett, go to your room,' he said.

'Seriously?' Scarlett asked, although she was already backing away. 'I'm supposed to take orders from you now?'

'If you don't get out now, I'll let her go.'

Nina continued to struggle free. 'Get out, Scarlett! Get out now!'

Only when Nina was sure Scarlett was out of sight and out of hearing did she stop fighting. Liam let her go and as she wrapped her arms around herself, she could feel the back of her throat burning with bile and unspent tears. 'Why does she hate me so much?'

'She doesn't hate you.'

Suddenly overcome with self-doubt, Nina asked, 'But she doesn't seem to care how much she hurts me. How can she do that to me? To our family?'

'Honestly, Mum? I think the sooner you realize that Scarlett's a selfish little bitch, the sooner you'll be able to deal with all this.'

'You're supposed to think that of her, you're her brother,' Nina said, trying and failing to make light of the situation.

'It's still true.'

'Liam, I'm not missing something, am I? What if I am as incompetent a mother as Eva's parents think I am? What if I still can't see what's happening right in front of me?' She shook her head before he could answer, and said, 'Don't answer that.'

'I wish Bryn were here,' Liam said. 'I think if you could only talk to him it would stop Scarlett messing with your head. And she is messing with your head, Mum.'

'And doing a very good job of it,' Nina said. 'Maybe it's not only Scarlett who should be seeing a counsellor.'

'Maybe. But we'll get through this together.'

Except they weren't together, and Nina didn't know how to begin to put them back. Bryn might have been a late addition to the family but he was an essential part and she missed him for more reasons than she could count. But the longer he stayed away, the longer she had to doubt that love. She hadn't needed much prompting to think the worst of him, and he had walked away without a fight. She had told him she wouldn't give up on him, but maybe this latest fight with Scarlett proved that she should. If she could still doubt him – and for a split second she had – then Bryn deserved better.

Scarlett

It was nice having the house to myself and for the first time in ages I felt calm. I was still in this horrible situation and the house was still a prison, but at least I didn't have Mum breathing down my neck. And before you ask, no, I didn't go out. I could have done, but I didn't. It just shows I can be trusted after all.

I had a bath with one of the Lush bombs I liked to use when I knew I was going to be with him. The smell reminded me of all the things we'd done, and I lay in the warm water thinking of him. God, Mum would have a nervous breakdown if she could read my thoughts some times.

Afterwards, I blow-dried my hair until it was nice and shiny, and I even put on some makeup, promising myself I wouldn't start crying again and mess it up, which is what always seems to happen these days. I didn't go over the top, I know he doesn't like it when I wear too much and I was really pleased with the result. I wished I could take a selfie so I could send it to him, but the police still had my phone. I was desperate to hear from him. I'd promised to take our secret to the grave, but it wasn't that simple, was it? The police weren't giving up the search for my mystery man and he needed to tell me what to do next because, seriously, I didn't have a clue.

I was hungry for the first time in ages and I was about to go downstairs and make something to eat when I heard Mum and Liam come back. I thought they would have been gone for hours and I was angry even before Mum screamed up the stairs to check I hadn't gone out. I told you she didn't trust me. She didn't want me seeing anyone ever again. Not that I had anyone to see other than him. Eva had her own problems, obviously, and as for my other friends, some had passed on nice messages through Eva, but not everyone, not even close.

I so needed to see what was being said about me on Facebook, but the police had my laptop too, and I couldn't use Mum's because Liam had shown her how to lock it with a password. It was probably a good thing I couldn't get online because I don't suppose the comments would have been nice. Liam said there'd been a petition at school to get Mr Swift back and expel me for wrecking his life. I think Liam was only winding me up, but I don't know. I think if it had been another girl and not me, I would have signed it.

With everyone back home I'd lost my appetite, but I went downstairs anyway. I wanted to know what was happening with Eva. Mum was going to stand up for Liam no matter what, even if she did think they shouldn't keep the baby. It's typical, isn't it? She's ranting on about someone abusing me, but she's not said a thing about Liam sleeping with Eva when she was underage. They first did it the day before *her sixteenth – I know, Eva told me. I don't see anyone arresting him.*

As I crept downstairs I could hear Liam and Mum chatting in the kitchen. They were talking about me and it wasn't so much what they were saying that got to me, but how they were acting together. Mum talked to Liam like he was her best friend all of a sudden. She speaks to me like I'm something left at the back of the fridge that's gone off; she actually makes a face like there's a bad smell when she's talking to me.

I used to think Mum was clever, but she didn't seem to get it. The sooner everyone would give up trying to get me to talk, the sooner it would all be over. Maybe things wouldn't get back to normal, but we could pretend nothing had happened and get on with our lives. Who wouldn't want that?

But Mum just kept pushing and pushing. OK, I'll admit it, I did lose it and I shouldn't have said what I said. Not because it upset her, but because it gave her more ammunition to keep going. When she flipped, I swear I thought she was going to strangle me. She hates me, but that's fine because I hate her too. I know you think I'm just saying that, but it's true.

28

Vikki's first trip out following Rob's release was an unscheduled visit to see her midwife. It was a miserable day and on her way back to her mum's, the roads were wet and slick. The rain had stopped for now, but the dark clouds were holding their position above her head, making it difficult to spot if she were being followed.

Rob had initially acceded to her wishes and stayed away, but after more than a week of separation, he was losing patience. He had phoned while she was waiting for her name to be called at the clinic, but she had ignored it. Whatever they might have to say to each other, it couldn't be said in public and, besides, she didn't want him to know she had left the house. After several failed attempts, Rob had left a voicemail message.

Pulling on to her mum's drive, Vikki took a moment to look around. The wind had picked up, turning every low-lying branch into a shadow that could be her husband, and her heart was hammering as she took a chance and jumped out of the car to race into the house.

'How did you get on?' Elaine asked, looking anxiously

at her daughter who was still catching her breath when she appeared in the kitchen.

'Everything's fine,' she said as her mum motioned for her to sit down at the kitchen table. 'The midwife said the cramps are normal and my blood pressure was surprisingly good, considering the stress I've been under. I didn't have to explain what was going on with Rob, everyone seems to know. Remember Amy? She was there again and she knew.'

'What did she say?'

'She was really nice about it actually. It made me wonder why I stopped being friends with her in the first place.'

'Yes, I've wondered that too. Wasn't she the one you were always going off to gigs with when you were younger?'

'Probably,' Vikki said as she struggled to recall the lie rather than an actual memory. 'I suppose we just stopped liking the same things.'

Elaine caught a hint of deception and seemed about to ask something, but chose to waft the question away with her hand. So many of their conversations were cautious lately, as if they were afraid of inadvertently turning over a rock to find something they would rather not see. 'Freya's in the living room playing at being in school and I've made a start on lunch. The baked potatoes will need another half hour, so how about a hot drink first to warm you up?'

Vikki watched her mum as she set to work. She was still wearing headscarves, and even though her scalp was showing early signs of regrowth, it would be some time before it was long enough to style. In every other respect, however, Elaine had gone from strength to strength. It was almost as if the most recent trauma to beset the family had given her a renewed vigour and purpose. Vikki supposed she should be thankful that Rob's misbehaviour had been good for something.

'Rob wants to see Freya,' she said.

Her mum took a moment as she set out the cups. 'And what did you say?'

'Nothing yet, it was only a voicemail. I'll have to phone him back.'

'How do you feel about seeing him again?'

'It's Freya he'd be spending time with, not me,' Vikki corrected, and before her mum had a chance to push her on the matter, she added, 'Not yet, Mum.'

As if on cue, Freya toddled in from the living room. She had a sticker book in her hand, although it would appear that most of the stickers had been used to cover her jumper. Vikki had bought a whole range of activity books online to make up for the fact that Freya wasn't going to nursery. For the moment, Vikki didn't want anyone else looking after her other than her mum.

'Mummy, look what I did,' Freya said.

Vikki pulled her daughter on to her lap and tried not to think about handing Freya over to Rob. She didn't think he was the type to use their daughter as a bargaining tool, but nothing would surprise her any more.

'If Rob does get charged,' she began, 'he'd be classed as a sex offender, wouldn't he? They wouldn't let him see Freya, even if he did stay out of prison.'

'Not without supervision, I should think,' Elaine said slowly as the frown forming on her brow began scrunching up her headscarf. 'But we're a long way from that, Vikki. You do trust him with Freya, don't you?'

Burying her face in Freya's golden curls, Vikki said, 'I don't know what to think. The police talk about him as if he's a monster, and they've made me question everything about him. What if he does like young girls, Mum?'

'If you seriously believe that, then we need to have another talk right now. I don't want to see you or Freya put in harm's way. I won't allow it.'

Vikki held her breath and for a moment her body and her thoughts stilled. 'No, I don't believe that. I just don't want to see him, that's all,' she said in a small voice that sounded like Freya's.

'Would it help if I was the one who took Freya to see him?'

When Vikki nodded, a single tear trickled down her cheek. She wiped it away before Freya noticed. 'Would you?'

Freya had lifted her head at the sound of her name. 'Where we going, Nanna?'

'On a little trip,' Elaine said, knowing better than to mention it was to see her father. Freya had been asking after Rob incessantly, and she would give them no peace if she knew a visit was on the cards. 'But not yet, young lady. First you need to finish your sticker book.'

Freya wriggled free of Vikki's grasp and disappeared back into the living room, unaware of the trouble her daddy was causing. 'Don't pour my tea yet,' Vikki said. She was feeling too warm all of a sudden and needed some fresh air. 'I'll go and air the cottages now it's stopped raining.'

'There's no rush, we've still got another week before guests arrive,' Elaine said as Vikki rose to her feet, but then realized her daughter's ulterior motive. 'Tell Rob that Monday would suit me best.'

Vikki went into the utility room and swapped her shoes for a pair of wellington boots before leaving the house by the back door. The ground was sodden as she trekked the short distance around the side of the house towards the guest cottages. It would soon be spring, but it was hard to imagine that the dead earth underfoot had any chance of bringing life back into the world. She tried not to think about the new life growing inside her. Like everything else, it was something that had happened to her and she was dealing with it as best she could, that was as much as she could do.

Trudging across the grass towards the first cottage, Vikki's ears pricked at the sound of an approaching car. She held her breath as the roar of the engine grew louder. When the hedgerow glowed with a car's sidelights and the noise reduced to a purr, Vikki rushed towards her Corsa before the unknown visitor turned into the drive. She didn't have the keys, but she could at least hide behind it.

She tried to analyse the sound of the growling engine; she didn't think it matched the whine and wheeze of Rob's old Ford Focus, but she couldn't be sure. The engine cut off and a car door opened, then closed again. From the lightness of foot, Vikki guessed it was a woman, but again she couldn't be sure. The footsteps drew closer and a familiar figure loomed over her.

Sarah clasped her chest. 'Good lord! I thought I'd spotted a fox or something, I wasn't expecting you!'

Feeling silly, Vikki rose to her feet. 'Sorry.'

'Who were you hiding from?'

Vikki sighed. 'Do you want a list?'

Unaware that she was on that list, Sarah gave Vikki a

hug. 'Oh, my dear, how are you? I've been thinking about you constantly. I'm sorry I haven't called sooner, but I didn't know if you were up to visitors.'

'We're not, but that hasn't stopped people coming to see us. I was hoping to hide away until all this is over,' she added, if only to test Sarah's reaction. They would each have different views on how the investigation should be concluded, and Sarah wasn't the type to be overly concerned about collateral damage if it meant bringing Rob to justice.

Sarah visibly tensed. 'And it can't come too soon,' she said. 'Can we talk?'

'I was on my way to open some windows in the cottages,' Vikki said, which Sarah presumed to be an invitation.

The first cottage was where they had had that very first meeting, back when Sarah had been the enemy. Vikki was afraid that, despite Sarah's kind words, her old adversary had returned.

'How's business?' Sarah asked, making the opening question an easy one.

'It's always quiet at this time of year, but we have guests arriving at the end of next week, and after that we're pretty much booked up from Easter right through until the end of summer.'

'That's good,' Sarah said, but then added, 'or is it? Is your mum up to the task?'

Vikki was wandering through the cottage, opening windows. She inhaled a deep breath of damp air. 'She's doing really well.'

'It must help to have you here again. Dare I ask how long you're planning to stay?'

'I don't know,' she said with a shrug.

Sarah was silent for a moment. 'And what does Rob think about your decision?'

Vikki could almost smile at the idea of it being a decision. If anything, she was avoiding one. 'We haven't spoken, not really.'

'I understand perfectly. It can't be easy for you,' Sarah said. 'If he had any decency, he'd own up to what he's done and not put his family or Nina's through this nightmare of not knowing.'

Vikki turned quickly and demanded, 'Is that why you're here? To get me to persuade Rob to confess?'

Sarah took a seat at the bistro table, unaffected by Vikki's outburst. 'Actually, I came to let you know that we need to start excavations on the land opposite. I wanted to hear how you and your mum felt about it, and to say that, if it's going to add to your woes, I can put everything on hold. It might only be for a matter of weeks, but I'll do what I can.'

The brief flare of anger had caught Vikki by surprise and when it dissipated, it left her drained. She sank down on to the chair opposite. 'Sorry, Sarah. For some strange reason I'm suspicious of everyone these days.'

'Oh, don't worry about it. It's good to see you've still got some fight in your belly.'

'Amongst other things,' Vikki said under her breath as she leant forward and lowered her head into her hands. 'Most days, it's all I can do to get out of bed. I expect Nina's feeling the same.'

'I wouldn't really know. Charlotte's probably spoken to her more than I have.'

'I heard she came home,' Vikki said diplomatically.

'How do you feel about that?' Sarah asked. 'About what Charlotte's told the police?'

'Pretty much as you'd expect. Embarrassed, humiliated, sickened,' Vikki said. 'Have I missed anything off the list?'

'How about angry?'

'For that it takes energy.'

'At risk of upsetting you for the second time, can I ask you something?' Sarah said, and proceeded to ask anyway. 'Do *you* think he did it?'

Vikki had been expecting the question and, if anything, she found Sarah's directness refreshing. She was more used to people framing the question as no more than a comment about how shocked she must be, or how devious he would have to be for her not to know; comments that alluded to her guilt as much as his.

Vikki couldn't reciprocate Sarah's openness, she had too much to lose. 'He's admitted he made errors of judgement,' she said, quoting her husband, 'but that doesn't make him a monster.'

'Are you sure?'

No, Vikki wasn't sure. One minute she was convinced of Rob's innocence, and the next . . . She could quite easily imagine how charming Rob might be around impressionable schoolgirls, and how he might persuade them to cover for him. If Scarlett had secrets, she would keep them until her dying day.

When Vikki refused to answer, Sarah pushed that bit harder. 'Why were you hiding behind the car?'

'I thought you might be a journalist, that's all,' Vikki replied. She stood up and added, 'Sorry, I've still got the other cottage to see to. Thanks for letting me know about

331

the excavations. I'll check with Mum but, to be honest, it's the least of our problems.'

Ignoring Vikki's retreat, Sarah remained seated. 'There is one other thing I've been wondering about. Why were you at the school that morning? You never said.'

'What? Why does that matter?' Vikki replied, stumbling over her words while avoiding giving an answer.

'Did you already suspect he was up to something? Did you look at Scarlett and think history was repeating itself?' Sarah asked, and this time she didn't expect or wait for an answer. 'And before you say it, I don't think anyone's convinced by the story that you two weren't involved while you were at school. From what I can gather, Rob was facing an internal investigation.'

'But I'd left school long before that,' Vikki insisted.

'Oh, who are you trying to kid, Vikki?' Sarah said, losing her composure. 'It's obvious the only reason you and Rob rushed into marriage was to get him out of trouble. Are you honestly saying you didn't have other plans, other aspirations? Of course you did!'

'I married Rob because I loved him.'

Sarah got to her feet. 'Have it your way,' she said, 'but think long and hard about what you're doing, and what you'll be returning to if Rob is allowed to get away with this. Do you really think you'll carry on playing happy families?'

When Vikki opened the door, Sarah marched straight out and for a moment it looked as if she would leave without another word, but her pace slowed to a halt. She turned and, although her features remained hard, her voice softened. 'I want to help, Vikki, and I will, just as long as you do the right thing. You're a lot like Scarlett in many respects, you don't see that you need protecting.'

Vikki couldn't hold her gaze and busied herself locking the cottage door and closing her ears.

'We'll be putting security on the site once work starts,' Sarah added. 'If you're worried about who might show up here, I could ask them to extend their patrol? Assuming your mum has no objection to the work starting, they could be here in a day or two.'

'You don't have to do that.'

'No, but I'd like to.'

Vikki thanked Sarah and with regret on both sides they parted with a nod rather than hugs. Vikki didn't have a good track record of keeping friends, it would seem. She had been forced to take sides, and she would always put her family first.

As she made her way to the second cottage, Vikki took out her mobile. Rob had been a constant in her life, the first person she wanted to see in the morning and the last person she thought of at night. He was her protector, not some security firm. Could it be that the reason she was feeling so insecure was simply because he wasn't there to look after her? Would it be such a bad thing to go back? Wasn't it inevitable?

When the doorbell rang, Nina didn't move from the sofa. Gone were the days when the worst she might face was a persistent sales rep who had dared to interrupt her Saturday evening. Her only response to the unexpected caller was to mute the TV programme she hadn't been watching anyway.

Pulling herself up slowly, Nina crept across the room. The hallway was in darkness and the glass panes in the front door revealed movement but not much else. As she took a couple of steps closer, the doorbell rang a second time, making her heart leap into her mouth. Whoever it was, he was persistent.

Nina had been waiting for Rob to make his presence known. An innocent man would know to stay away, but Rob's claim of innocence rested on Scarlett's continued silence, and her daughter wasn't known for her patience. If he couldn't find a way to reassure her that she was telling the right story, she might make a mistake. It was what they were all waiting and hoping for because, even with Charlotte's statement, it wasn't going to be enough.

She had taken another step when a door opened upstairs. From the heavy footfalls she knew it was Liam before he appeared out of the shadows. 'Eva's getting soaked out there,' he said, rushing to the door.

When Eva came into the house she was wearing only a light jacket and her hair was dripping wet. She was shivering and looked utterly miserable. 'You poor thing,' Nina said, 'I didn't know you were coming over.'

Eva's face crumpled and she began sobbing. 'I didn't know either,' she said, 'but I couldn't take it any more. Just because I've said I'll do what they want, it doesn't make it right. What if I'm making a horrible mistake? I won't be able to live with myself.'

Before Nina could reach her, Liam had Eva in his arms. 'It's all right.'

'No, it's not, Liam. It's all arranged. Mum and Dad are going to make me get rid of it next week.'

'It doesn't matter what they want,' Liam persisted. 'They can't make you do anything against your will. There are always choices, aren't there, Mum?'

Her son was looking over Eva's head towards her, waiting for her to repeat his words of comfort. 'I'll get a towel,' Nina said, 'and Scarlett will have some clothes you can borrow.'

When Nina came back downstairs, Liam had taken Eva into the living room. They were sitting on the sofa holding on to each other while the TV screen flicked silently through comic scenes of celebrities covered in flour. In another universe, life was simple and the worst that could happen was burning a cake.

'Here, you can wear these,' Scarlett said. She had followed Nina into the room, the latest drama having created a temporary truce in another ongoing battle.

The pyjamas Scarlett gave Eva were brand new and had tiny images of Tinkerbelle printed on them. They had been a Christmas present, back when Nina had still thought of her little girl as just that.

'Do your mum and dad know where you are?' Nina asked as Eva dried her hair with the towel.

Eva nodded. 'We had another argument, which was basically a rerun of all the old ones. Dad said if I didn't keep the appointment next week, I'd better find somewhere else to live.' She stopped to bite her lip, but it wasn't enough to stem the flow of tears. 'They didn't stop me when I said I was coming here.'

'I'll make you a hot drink while you get out of those wet things,' Nina said, 'and then we can have a talk about it.'

It was Liam who stood up first and pulled Eva to her feet. 'Come on, we'll go to my room. I'll come down for the drinks in a minute.'

Watching them leave, Nina said to Scarlett, 'I get the feeling I'm a bit surplus to requirements.'

'Now you know how I feel,' Scarlett said.

Not wanting the truce to fail, Nina asked, 'Would you like a drink? I was thinking hot chocolate with loads of marshmallows.'

She hoped that the arrival of Scarlett's friend would give them something to talk about, something that didn't have to end in an argument. They could pretend, if only for a short while, that they didn't hate each other. Not that Nina did hate her daughter, not really, not ever, but their exchanges were too often simply reactions, or overreactions, and she was out of practice when it came to showing her daughter the unquestionable love and devotion she felt for her.

When Scarlett shrugged, Nina was preparing for the refusal, but her daughter surprised her by saying, 'OK.'

Nina warmed the milk while Scarlett pulled a large bag of mini marshmallows from the back of a cupboard. For a while they worked in silence, until Scarlett asked, 'Are you speaking to Sarah yet?'

'Not unless I have to.'

'How about Bryn?' said Scarlett, as if that hadn't been the first question she had wanted to ask.

'I've been bombarding the taxi firm with calls, but so far I've not been able to get through to him. One of the lads, Mike, let slip that he was staying with him. I suppose I should be glad he hasn't gone back to Wales.'

'I like Mike. He lives near the school and Bryn stopped to talk to him sometimes when he was giving me a lift.'

'Bryn's sleeping on his sofa, apparently, so I assume it's only a temporary arrangement until he does his back in,' she said, speaking from experience. Nina had taken to sleeping downstairs more often than not. She didn't like getting into an empty bed and preferred to be closer to the front door, should anyone try to sneak out in the middle of the night.

'He will come back,' Scarlett said.

'I wish I had your certainty,' Nina whispered. 'I miss him, Scarlett.'

Scarlett was staring at the bag in her hand. She might have been thinking about the damage she had inflicted on the family, but she could so as easily have been working out how many calories were in each marshmallow.

'Do you fancy watching a movie or something?' Nina asked. 'I doubt Liam and Eva will come down for a while, and I could do with a bit of escapism.'

'What's going to happen, Mum?'

Nina felt an unfamiliar flicker of hope, and not simply because Scarlett had ignored the opportunity to divert the conversation. Her daughter, who in that moment sounded achingly like the sweet girl she used to be, was reaching out to her, and all Nina had to do was take her in her arms and tell her it was going to be all right, as she done many times in the past. But Nina had lost faith in her ability to put things right, or read her daughter. She had also learned to be cautious. 'About Eva and Liam, or other stuff?' she asked tentatively.

The bag twisted in Scarlett's hand. 'Both.'

'What happens to Eva depends on the difficult decision she has to make,' Nina said. 'And what happens with the other stuff depends on the difficult decision you have to make. You can choose to talk about what happened, or you can let this problem fester for what could be a very long time.'

'I am talking about it,' Scarlett replied. For once her tone was neither defensive nor offensive, merely stating a fact. 'I've been telling the counsellor all about what happened.'

'Everything?' Nina asked.

'Sort of.'

Nina had remained in the waiting area during Scarlett's sessions with the counsellor, and her daughter had so far refused to say what they discussed. The counsellor had set the ground rules from the start: Scarlett's sessions would be in private and they would be confidential. There were a few caveats – for example, if the counsellor thought Scarlett was a danger to herself or others – but for the most part, she could tell this woman every lurid detail in the strictest confidence. Nina had been told that she might be invited in if there were issues Scarlett wanted to discuss with her but, so far, that hadn't arisen. The only information Scarlett had been prepared to share was that the sessions had gone 'OK'. Could they really be making progress?

Scarlett tore open the bag of marshmallows with her teeth and before Nina could think of a follow-up question, she said, 'It would be nice to have a baby in the house, don't you think?'

Nina lined up four mugs and poured warm chocolatey milk into each. Don't push her, she told herself. Let Scarlett take it at her own speed. And while Nina would prefer Rob off the streets now, she would play the long game if she had to. 'It's easy to say that when you'd only be dipping in and out of being Auntie Scarlett. Imagine what it would be like to be trapped in the house with a screaming baby.'

'I already know what it's like to be trapped,' Scarlett said, but again without the surliness Nina had become accustomed to. 'Actually, I was thinking . . . '

Nina had a sinking feeling her daughter's sudden transformation had nothing to do with her counselling and everything to do with whatever Scarlett was about to ask next. 'Go on.'

'Liam's gone back to school now, so why can't I? I know it's going to be horrible and people will give me funny looks, but I have my exams coming up and it's really hard trying to do everything at home with no one to talk to and no one to ask.'

Nina's first reaction was to say no, but there would come a point sooner or later when she would have to let Scarlett out of her sight. That it should be so soon was uncomfortable, but it wasn't as if Rob would be allowed near the school, and if Nina could be released from sentry duties, then she could return to work too. 'It is just returning to school we're talking about, isn't it?' she said, framing it as a question to give Scarlett some semblance of control over her own fate, even if it were superficial.

'Yes, Mum. You can drop me off and pick me up, if it makes you feel better.'

Nina chose not to point out that she wouldn't consider agreeing to it otherwise. 'I'll have to check with Mrs Anwar first to make sure proper arrangements are in place, but OK, I'll speak to her on Monday.'

Scarlett took a generous handful of marshmallows and dropped them into one of the mugs before picking it up. 'I'll pass on the film, if you don't mind. I'm kind of tired.'

'OK,' Nina said and found herself smiling at her daughter for the first time in a long time. 'Good night, sweetheart.'

Nina was awoken in the early hours by the creak of a step as someone made their way downstairs. She had been asleep on the sofa and opened her eyes to check the soft glowing hands of the clock on the mantelpiece. It was ten past three.

Rubbing her forehead, she tried to remember if she had accidentally left the house keys on the radiator shelf in the hallway. She kept them in her handbag during the night, but Eva's arrival had upset her usual routine of locking up, and locking in Scarlett. She couldn't remember so she sat up and concentrated on the approaching footsteps. When the door opened a fraction, she held her breath. If it was Scarlett and she was fully dressed, Nina wasn't sure she had the energy or the inclination to resume warfare. As her vision adjusted to the gloom, Nina locked eyes with Eva.

'Sorry, Nina, were you asleep?'

Nina's eyes felt heavy and gritty, but she smiled. What else would she be doing at three o'clock in the morning? 'Don't worry about it. What's wrong?'

Eva edged further into the room. 'Me and Liam have been talking,' she said as she took a seat opposite Nina. She played nervously with her fingers, but seemed unsure what to say next.

'Have you reached any conclusions?'

Eva nodded. 'We could still make it work, even if Mum and Dad did disown me,' she said, with more resignation than defiance.

'I know they're angry with you now,' Nina said, 'but

whatever's been said, they still love you.' What Nina couldn't say with certainty was that they would forgive her anything and stand by her no matter what. Emotions had a funny way of getting in the way of doing the right thing.

'And I love them too, I suppose,' Eva said. 'I just wish they'd stop treating me like a child.'

'Which you're not,' Nina said, 'but neither are you quite an adult. I was twenty-five and married when I had Liam, and I still got it wrong. I was blinded by love when Adam and I met, but when I could see the faults in our relationship . . . well, I couldn't see anything else. I'm sure we had our strengths too, but it wasn't enough. The strain of looking after children can do that to a relationship.'

'You don't think I should have the baby?'

As Nina considered her answer, she thought she heard another creak on the stairs. Before her son interrupted their private chat, Nina asked, 'What does Liam think? The only thing he's said to me is that he wants what you want.'

'He says the same to me.'

'Very helpful.'

'He takes after you. You still haven't said what you think.'

'Fair point,' Nina conceded. 'OK, if you want my opinion, I agree with pretty much everything your mum and dad have said – except perhaps the bit about me being an incompetent mother. But then again, maybe that too.'

'You think I should keep the appointment?'

Nina thought for a moment. 'It's an abortion, Eva. If you do decide to go ahead with it, I'm afraid you have to think of it in those terms. The baby isn't going to magically disappear, and I know that sounds harsh, but you're going to have to live with this decision for the rest of your life, so get it clear in your head what you're doing.'

'That's the hard bit.'

'I know it is,' Nina said, 'but for what it's worth, and to make myself perfectly clear, I think it would be the right decision for you.'

'I do too,' Eva said.

From the doorway, Liam added, 'We both do.'

Scarlett

Have I told you everything? Probably not. I definitely haven't told you that I've seen him again.

Oh – My – God, that was so exciting I can't tell you. No one had a clue what I was up to but I so nearly got caught. It was the middle of the night and Mum was on guard downstairs as usual, but everyone had been in a flap with Eva turning up so Mum forgot to hide her keys. I spotted them on the shelf when I was going upstairs and I knew I had to grab my chance. I waited as long as I could, and I was about to make a run for it when I heard Eva get up and go down. Perfect, I thought. She could distract Mum.

I got to the front door and I was literally about to open it when I heard Liam coming out of his room. I nearly died! I only just managed to slip out before he caught me, either that or he did see me and wasn't bothered. He's got other things on his mind, I suppose. Not that he tells me, no one comes to me with their problems any more. I can't believe Eva would go and talk to Mum instead of me.

It had stopped raining, thank God, because I had to walk

for miles. He didn't know I was coming and when I turned up at the door he was furious. Luckily, he was on his own, but he might not have been. I hadn't thought of that.

'No one knows I'm here,' I said and with that he grabbed my arm and pulled me inside.

'Do you have any idea what risks you're taking? Scarlett, you can't do this. We can't do this,' he said. He had me pinned up against the wall and his face was only inches from mine. His breath smelled really foul, like he'd been drinking, and his voice was all gravelly.

'Did I wake you up?'

He didn't answer. He was still angry.

When I put my cold hand on his face it made him flinch, but I wouldn't take it away. I traced my fingers down his neck and across his chest before slipping my hand inside his dressing gown. I couldn't believe what I was doing, but he's always said I'm insatiable. I'm not sure I'd been convinced, not until then. God, I wanted him so badly. I'd spent two long weeks thinking I would never see him again, and I still didn't know if this was going to be our last time, so I had to make every second count. My fingers were still cold when I slipped them inside his boxer shorts, but he didn't flinch this time.

He kept his expression fixed as my hand warmed up and so did he. 'You'll put me in jail,' he said.

'I'm here to keep you out of jail,' I told him. 'Tell me what to do, and I'll do it.'

His cheek twitched and I knew he was about to smile but the next thing I knew he was kissing me and it was so hard and desperate that it made me want to cry. His hands were all over me and he was pulling at my clothes. As soon as I could draw breath, I said, 'You do still love me, don't you?'

'Yes,' he answered. His head was buried in my neck as he lifted me off my feet and I wrapped my legs around him. 'God, Scarlett, yes I do.'

I stayed long enough for us to make love twice, but the longer I stayed, the more chance there was of Mum finding out I'd escaped. There was still time to make our plans, though. I bet you want to know about them, don't you? Well, I don't think I should tell. All I'll say is that he set me a challenge and, if I do say so myself, I think I did a good job.

29

Nina wasn't surprised when there was another knock at the door that weekend, but as she invited her guests into the house, she couldn't summon up a warm, welcoming smile, not even when she was handed a bottle-shaped gift bag.

'What's this?' she asked.

'It's a peace offering,' replied Sarah.

Nina took out the expensive bottle of red wine. 'I'm tempted to open it now.'

'Am I allowed to join you?'

Nina had lost count of the times the two friends had sat down with a bottle of wine and shared their troubles, but she hesitated before saying, 'I suppose.'

Sarah turned to Charlotte, who was carrying gifts of her own, and added, 'You can drive us back home, can't you?'

'I'll stick to overdosing on chocolate with Scarlett then, shall I?'

'Ooh, did I hear someone mention chocolate?' Scarlett asked as she came downstairs to give their guests a far more cordial reception than her mother.

'Why don't you young ladies retire to Scarlett's room while I have a chat with Nina,' Sarah said, before following her friend into the kitchen.

'Do you think it'll work?' Sarah asked after closing the door.

'I honestly don't know,' Nina said as she filled two wine-glasses. She handed one to Sarah, but rather than head to the living room, or take a seat at the breakfast bar, she stayed where she was, resting her back against a kitchen counter as Sarah did the same. She took a sip before adding, 'But the signs are good. It was Scarlett's idea to invite you over, which makes me think that she might be feeling guilty at last, if only the tiniest bit.'

'And of course you're taking advantage of the situation.'

'Wouldn't you?' Nina challenged. 'And it's not like Scarlett hasn't been curious about how Charlotte was getting on.'

Sarah smiled. 'You won't get an argument from me. Charlotte knows she's here to press all the right buttons and get a reaction from Scarlett, whatever that might be.'

'All I want is for Scarlett to see that she's nothing special to him, that he's not worth any of this.'

'And Charlotte will explain all of that in no uncertain terms,' Sarah said confidently, but then she sighed. 'I have to admit though, I wish this hadn't been the only reason you invited me over, Nina. I so want us to be friends again. Proper friends.'

Nina dipped her head. She wasn't looking for an argument, but if they were ever to move on, there were things that needed saying. When she was ready, she looked Sarah straight in the eye. 'Proper friends don't set out to destroy

347

someone's marriage based on . . . Well, based on what, Sarah? Why did you never give Bryn a chance?'

It was Sarah's turn to look down. 'You suggested the other week that it was because your love life made my marriage look dull and boring.' There was a sad smile on Sarah's face when she straightened up. 'I think you were closer to the truth than I'd like, and it didn't help that I've dealt with more than my fair share of sharks in my time; the type who see a middle-aged woman and think a bit of flattery is all it will take to get me to pay over the odds for work. I misjudged Bryn, and I misjudged you too.'

'Does that mean you don't think I was having a midlife crisis?'

'You appear to have a better grip on reality than I do,' Sarah conceded.

'And you're willing to accept that Bryn is one of the good guys?'

'Nina, I'm more than ready to accept anything you ask if it means we can get back to where we were, or at least make a start at repairing the damage. Can we?'

Taking a sip of wine, Nina considered her friend's words. Sarah was more or less admitting she would say whatever Nina wanted to hear. It wasn't exactly the reassurance Nina had been hoping for, but unless Bryn was willing to give them both a second chance, Sarah's opinion of him didn't matter anyway.

'If you can find a way of getting Bryn to talk to me again, I might be willing to consider it.'

It wasn't a genuine suggestion. She had simply wanted to see Sarah's reaction and was surprised to see her friend considering the proposal.

Swirling the wine in her glass, Sarah said, 'Personally, I would never go for the direct approach.'

'Meaning?'

'Bryn's world has been smashed to smithereens and, as far as he's concerned, you're the one caught holding the sledgehammer. You need to show him that you're just as capable when it comes to construction as you are demolition.'

'And how do you propose I do that?'

'The daughter.'

Nina's jaw dropped. 'Scarlett?'

'No, the other one. Bryn's daughter,' Sarah replied.

'Caryn?'

Sarah's mouth twisted as she tried to formulate a plan. 'I'm not saying it'll work, but if you can get this Caryn on your side, maybe she can be your advocate. From what you've said, Bryn would love to rebuild his relationship with her. If you can do that, then even if he still refuses to speak to you, your conscience will be eased knowing you've done something positive. It would certainly ease mine.'

Nina had spent sleepless nights replaying the moment she had accused Bryn and wondering how it must feel to be on the receiving end. It wasn't the first time he had been labelled a monster; Caryn had hurt him too, and if Nina could make things right between them . . . maybe Sarah had a point. 'But how do I go about convincing Caryn?'

'Be honest with her. Tell her what's happened and . . . I don't know,' Sarah said. 'If you can make her feel sorry for him – or you, for that matter – she might be persuaded to let him back into her life.'

'I don't know, Sarah. I could end up doing even more

349

damage, you know, with that sledgehammer in my hand.' The wine had warmed her up and so had Sarah. Despite her doubts, the idea was growing on her. 'Would you come with me?'

'I was about to suggest the same thing.'

The two friends sealed the deal by refilling their glasses while speculating on how their daughters were getting on. They didn't have to wait long. When the two girls appeared in the kitchen after being together for less than an hour, it quickly became apparent that one of them had had a major change of heart. Unfortunately for Nina, it wasn't Scarlett who wanted to change her police statement. It was Charlotte.

Vikki had two options: she could keep herself busy, or she could obsess about what might be happening a few miles away in Victoria Park. She chose the first and set to work cleaning the oven. There was something therapeutic about scraping away the grease and grime, but once she had sprayed a layer of toxic foam on the inside of the oven, she had time to kill. She leant against the sink with her arms folded and stared out of the window.

She hadn't told Freya that her daddy was taking her to the park, and wondered how she would have reacted to seeing him again. Would she be too excited to show any interest in the swings and roundabouts? Or would she pick up on the tension as Rob forced himself to play their usual silly games, knowing all the while that passers-by would be giving him curious looks. There had always been plenty of people in the park who recognized Rob during their regular visits with Freya, and given his recent notoriety, his latest appearance would attract attention.

When a knock at the door roused her from her thoughts, Vikki went to one of the front windows and checked the drive. She felt only limited relief when she spied Sarah's four-wheel drive.

'Is this a bad time?' Sarah asked as she took in the grease-smeared apron and the Marigolds.

'I was in the middle of cleaning the oven,' Vikki said. She was in no rush to invite Sarah inside if it meant a rerun of their last conversation.

'I thought I'd pop by to let you know that the excavations will be starting tomorrow. I didn't hear back from you, so I presume your mum didn't have any objection?'

'No, it's fine.'

'Good,' Sarah said, shifting from one foot to another. 'You might see an increase in traffic while they get all the plant and machinery on site.'

'OK, I'll mention it to Mum.'

Sarah glanced to her side and the spot on the drive where Elaine's car would normally be. 'Is she in?'

'She was dropping Freya off with Rob and then going to see a friend for a few hours.'

At the mention of Rob's name, Sarah raised an eyebrow but knew better than to comment. 'Actually,' she said as if it were an afterthought, 'I'm glad I caught you on your own. Can I come in?'

To avoid the fumes from the oven cleaner, Vikki left her apron and Marigolds in the kitchen and took Sarah into the living room. Sitting down on the sofa, Vikki expected Sarah to take the chair opposite, but she sat down next to her.

With a flutter of panic, Vikki asked, 'Why are you really here, Sarah?'

'For one thing, I'd like to say I'm sorry if I overstepped the mark the other day. I put you in an impossible position and you have every right to be annoyed at me.'

From Sarah's behaviour, Vikki had been expecting bad news and was taken aback by her kindness. She bit the inside of her mouth to keep her emotions in check and didn't dare speak.

'I think, subconsciously, I saw you as my replacement Charlotte,' Sarah continued. 'You were interested in the kind of things I'd spent years attempting to get my daughter involved in, and I suppose, somewhere along the way, I decided I could interfere in your life the way I have in hers. Unfortunately, it turns out you both have minds of your own.'

'It was nice having your support,' Vikki said.

Taking her hand, Sarah said, 'You still have it, Vikki. I know I have to leave you to make your own decisions, but I'd still like to help where I can. At the very least, I want to make sure you make an informed decision.'

'So you haven't only come here to say sorry?' Vikki said, pulling her hand from Sarah's clutches.

'I wish that was all, but yes, there is something else.' She stopped to take a deep breath. 'I thought you should know that Charlotte is with the police as we speak. She's going to amend her original statement.'

Vikki's heart missed a beat. This was the moment she had been dreading, to be told that Charlotte had been more intimately involved with Rob than she had first suggested. Vikki hadn't been Rob's one true love, his soulmate, she had simply been the first in a series of affairs.

'When it came to that kiss,' Sarah continued. 'Charlotte

352

wants to make it clear in her statement that she was the one who initiated it and he didn't kiss her back.'

'But that's what Rob's been saying all along.'

'Yes, I know.'

'I don't understand,' Vikki said. 'Does this mean she doesn't think he tried to groom her now?'

Sarah winced. 'She's going to keep to the facts, and leave it to the police to interpret what Rob's motives may or may not have been.'

'But she has changed her story, which means she was lying when she said he kissed her. Did you know?'

Sarah pulled back her shoulders. 'She and Scarlett had a bit of a talk yesterday. I was hoping Charlotte might convince her that they both needed to speak up against Rob so that no other girls got hurt,' she said. 'But it was Scarlett who did the convincing. Charlotte's worried that she might have got it wrong, especially as she's on her own in coming forward, and she doesn't want to take the chance that her testimony could be destroying an innocent man's life.'

'Are you saying this was all a mistake?' Vikki cried. 'That I've been doubting Rob for no better reason than he'd attracted the attention of these girls and they'd got the wrong message?'

In her mind, Vikki was working out how long it would take to get across town to Victoria Park. She needed to see Rob. This was her chance to get back the husband she had thought she had lost forever. He wasn't a predator; if anything, he was a victim. Rob loved her, and *only* her.

'No, Vikki, I'm not saying that at all,' Sarah said, rubbing her forehead as she gathered her thoughts. 'None of this changes the fact that Rob had an inappropriate interest in Charlotte. She might have stretched the truth in her statement, but, if you want my opinion, he *was* grooming her, I'm sure of it.'

'So you did know she was lying?'

Sarah wouldn't be admonished. 'He mocked her, Vikki. He teased her and called her a little girl, and he was daring her to prove him wrong. That was why she kissed him.'

Vikki's hand flew to her mouth, but it was her ears she wanted to cover.

Sarah pushed on. 'I wouldn't be surprised if that's how things started with Scarlett, and who knows how many others. But one thing's clear: not one of them sees him for what he really is, and I don't expect you do either.'

'No,' Vikki whispered, shaking her head, and then again, louder, 'No.'

She didn't want to end up on her own, divorced with two kids. She was only twenty-four. It wasn't fair. 'Why can't it be Bryn?' she asked. 'You were sure it was him not that long ago. You said he'd been interfering with his daughter too.'

'I was wrong,' Sarah said gently. 'I'm going with Nina tomorrow to meet Bryn's daughter, but there's no doubt in my mind that Bryn has been an innocent bystander. I'm sorry, Vikki.'

'Sorry?' Vikki repeated. 'You've ruined Nina's marriage, and now you want to ruin mine?'

Sarah's jaw had clenched, but her words were surprisingly soft when she asked, 'If I'm so wrong, why aren't you with him?'

'Because I needed to be sure,' she said.

'And now you know what happened with Charlotte, are you?'

Vikki wished so much that she could say yes, but there was an image in her mind that wouldn't let her speak. She could see a young, inexperienced schoolgirl sitting next to Rob. He was leaning forward, telling her she was a little girl, and daring him to prove her wrong. Unable to supress the memory, Vikki burst into tears, and offered no resistance when Sarah wrapped her in her arms.

'The case against Rob is about to fall apart and we may never get to the truth,' Sarah told her in gentle tones. 'That means Nina will never find peace and, from the look of it, neither will you. I accept that I've been wrong before, and there's a part of me that wishes for your sake that I'm wrong again. The only sure way of bringing this man – whoever he is – to justice is for one of his victims to have the courage to speak out. You must see that.'

'This isn't fair,' complained Scarlett. She was sitting behind Nina in Sarah's car while the two friends ignored her. Releasing a dramatic sigh, she added, 'And you said I could go back to school.'

'As I recall,' Nina said through gritted teeth, 'I only promised to speak to Mrs Anwar about it, and that's what I've done.'

Nina hated herself for snapping at her daughter but her frustrations had been getting the better of her ever since Charlotte had announced she was changing her statement. In contrast, Scarlett had been in an annoyingly good mood.

'But I don't see why you had to drag me along. Since I'm *not* at school, I should be home studying like mad. I'm already stressed out like crazy, and this is only making it worse.'

'Speaking of which,' Sarah said as she tried to divert the argument. 'How are the sessions with the counsellor going?'

'She's got another one on Thursday.'

'And I'll definitely need counselling after today,' Scarlett muttered.

Sarah checked her rear-view mirror so she was looking at Scarlett when she said, 'But don't you see how important this trip is?' she asked. 'Don't you want Bryn home again?'

'Except we're not going to see Bryn, are we? I seriously do not see the point of this.'

Refusing to explain herself to her daughter, Nina left Scarlett's comment hanging as the road began to rise towards the Welsh hills.

'How's Liam doing?' Sarah asked, to fill the silence that followed.

'He's working hard and ignoring all the gossip, as far as I can tell. I'm praying he'll do enough to get the grades he needs for uni.'

'I don't see why not,' Scarlett said. 'He passed the fertility test with flying colours.'

Before Nina could let loose the ever-present fury building inside her chest, her mobile began to ring.

'Lucky escape,' Sarah said to Scarlett under her breath.

The call was from DS Cunliffe. She wanted to arrange another interview with Scarlett and Nina.

'Is there something new?' Nina asked. She was choosing her words carefully in front of her daughter.

'No, not exactly,' Alice said, and from her tone of voice, she didn't sound like someone in hot pursuit. She sounded more like someone watching their prey disappear over the horizon. 'We've had to review the case in light of Charlotte Tavistock's revised statement, and I'd like one more go at getting something from your daughter.'

'And if you don't?'

Rather than answer, Alice could be heard shuffling papers. 'We're still gathering whatever information we can.'

'Mrs Anwar mentioned they were still working with you, but she wouldn't give any details. Have you found anything?' After the debacle at the school, Mrs Anwar was being a stickler for procedures. It had been Alice who had told Nina about the school's historic concerns about Rob and Vikki's relationship, and Nina was hoping there was more to tell.

'One thing came to light when they were re-marking some of your daughter's papers,' Alice said. 'It turns out Scarlett wasn't doing as badly as you were led to believe. It looks like Mr Swift was overly harsh with her English papers, which suggests he was deliberately downgrading them to engineer the extra lessons.'

'Bastard.'

'I couldn't agree more, but another view could be that he was nothing worse than a poor teacher. CPS are breathing down my neck to find proof positive that he and your daughter had a physical relationship. Thanks to your son's technical prowess, we have nothing other than the photo on Scarlett's phone, which doesn't come close to making a case. Rob's phone was clean as a whistle and we couldn't prove he ever had the app your son created. I'm sorry, but while the school might have a good case for dismissing him, it's nowhere near enough for us to charge him.'

Not ready to give in, Nina said, 'How soon do you want us to come in?'

'Today?'

'We're in Wales at the moment, could it wait until tomorrow?'

'I'm wrapped up in a court case tomorrow. Thursday?' Alice asked.

'Scarlett has a counselling session in the morning,' Nina said. She rubbed the back of her neck as she felt her daughter's eyes boring into her.

'In the afternoon is fine. I'm not exactly in a hurry if it means we have to close the investigation. I'm sorry to sound so pessimistic, but as I've said from the start, what we really need is Scarlett's testimony. Perhaps you can use the next couple of days to talk her round.'

Like I haven't been trying already, Nina thought, but she said, 'I'll do my best.'

'Who was that?' Scarlett asked the moment Nina ended the call.

'The police want to interview us again. I've said we'll go in on Thursday afternoon.'

'Why?'

Nina and Sarah exchanged a look. 'It's standard practice,' Nina said, adding, 'They wait a while and then bring you back in so they can crosscheck your previous answers against whatever stories you might want to come up with this time.'

She had wanted to unsettle her daughter, but Scarlett sounded smug when she said, 'You mean like they did with Charlotte? They know they were wrong now, don't they? Does that mean it'll all be over soon?'

'No, Scarlett, it does not,' Nina said. 'Even if the police

do decide to drop the investigation, don't think for one minute I'll let it rest, not ever.'

For once, Scarlett didn't have a smart response and the journey continued in silence. Nina stared out of the window and tried to concentrate on the matter in hand. She had made all the arrangements with Caryn's mum, who had given no hint as to how her daughter felt about meeting her, and so it was left to Nina to imagine what kind of reception she might receive.

Sarah must have seen the anxious look on Nina's face as the satnav prompted her to make the last turn. 'Are you ready?'

Nina was about to respond but her words caught in her throat as she spotted Bryn's car parked outside the house. 'Drive past!' she cried.

'How the hell did he know—' Sarah began, but then glanced over her shoulder. 'Did you tell him?'

'Don't look at me!' cried Scarlett.

Still reeling from the first shock, Nina received another. 'Oh my God, you still think it might be him,' she said to Sarah. 'Is that why you got me down here? To check out his past and accuse him all over again?'

Sarah's jaw dropped. 'No, absolutely not! I swear, I'm here to help you and Bryn get back together. I didn't mean to suggest . . . OK, maybe for one second I thought . . . I simply didn't expect him to be here.'

Not listening, Nina spied a coffee shop. 'Pull over, now!'

For once, Sarah did as she was told. The moment she pulled to the kerb, Nina got out of the car. Her mind raced and she fought through a red mist of thoughts, none of them pleasant. When Sarah reached her side, Nina was ready for her.

'You never could stand being in the wrong, could you? You wrecked my marriage and there's still a part of you hoping you'll be vindicated. Why do you have to be so bloody manipulative? Why can't you *just* be a friend, Sarah? Why does your happiness have to be relative to everyone else's? Why do you have to push me down so you can feel tall?'

'That's not true. You're my best friend, Nina. I only want what's best for you.'

'Would I still be your best friend if I was happier than you, more successful than you? Or would you go off and find someone else you could pity?'

Sarah held up both her hands. 'Please, Nina, I know you're angry, I get that, and I probably deserve everything you're throwing at me, but right now you have better things to do. Setting aside my first reaction, I'm guessing Bryn's ex-wife told him you were on your way, which means there's a chance he's come down here because he's looking for a reconciliation too, but you won't know that unless you're part of the conversation he and Caryn are having right now.'

Nina was ready to explode. She had attacked her friend and Sarah had simply rolled with the punches. She was unbelievably infuriating, not least because on this occasion she was right. 'Fine, but I'm going alone. You can wait in the coffee shop.'

She was turning to walk away when another voice piped up, 'Erm, what about me, Mum?'

'You stay with Sarah,' Nina said, without looking back. She didn't want Scarlett with her when she faced Bryn, and she didn't dare try to explain why that might be. She wasn't ready to admit that her reaction on seeing her husband's car hadn't been so different from Sarah's.

Nina didn't know what to expect when she got to Caryn's. She was prepared for anything, except perhaps the anti-climax she felt when Bryn sped past in his car as she reached the end of Caryn's street. She watched her husband recede into the distance before continuing her journey, and when she knocked on Caryn's door, it was with a sinking heart.

The young woman who answered was waiflike and pale, but it was her eyes that Nina noticed first. They were slate-grey like her father's and they were brimming with tears.

'I tried . . . I tried to get Dad to stay, but he wouldn't,' Caryn sobbed. 'Why does he always end up leaving me?'

After meeting Sarah, Vikki was more confused than ever. She had wanted some time away from Rob to collect her thoughts and reach conclusions of her own, but it would seem she wasn't capable. Had she been one of Rob's victims? Was the man she had fallen for someone who abused his authority and took advantage of impressionable young girls, or was his only crime that he had been adored by his pupils? Vikki knew which of the two versions of her husband she preferred, and she wished she could silence the doubt and take that leap of faith which would bring her family back together again.

Parking her car close to the gated entrance of the Ellison House, Vikki was relieved to see she was the first to arrive. As she slipped through the gap in the fence, the rust from the metal barriers left an ochre smudge on her hands that brought on a sudden wave of nostalgia. This had been their secret meeting place back when Rob had been sharing a house with a group of teachers and Vikki had yet to tell her parents about her new boyfriend. She had lost count of the number of times Rob had gently wiped her hands with the corner of the blanket he had always thought to bring with him whenever they had met.

Walking around to the side of the house, Vikki dipped below the trailing wisteria which had given them shelter in all but the bitterest months. She let the shadows cast by its twisted stems play across her upturned palm until she heard the sound of an approaching car, followed by footsteps searching her out in the undergrowth.

'I wish we could go back in time,' Rob said when he reached her side. 'Back to when you still believed in me, before I let you down.'

He had left a safe gap between them and Vikki was relieved that he hadn't reached out to touch her. She couldn't be sure if her instinct would be to recoil from a monster, or fall into the arms of the man she loved.

'How are things?' she asked politely.

'Awful, if I'm honest,' he said. 'All I can do is sit and wait for this ridiculous investigation to be dropped. I hate what it must be doing to you. Are you all right? The baby?'

'We're fine,' she said.

'You have no idea how much I miss you and Freya. It was heartbreaking, seeing her the other day and then having to say goodbye. I think Elaine felt it too.'

Her mum had been upset when she had returned home the day before with a sobbing Freya, and it was obvious she hoped Vikki's meeting with Rob today would bring an end to their separation. Vikki wondered if her mum would think differently if she knew why Vikki had chosen to meet Rob at the Ellison House, but Elaine had become adept at not asking questions she didn't want to know the answer to. 'Mum hates seeing Freya so confused. She's desperate for us all to get back to some sort of normal,' she said.

'And you?' he asked. When he didn't receive an answer, he added, 'It doesn't matter what anyone else wants you to do, Vikki, it's what you want that counts. I dread to think what rubbish people have been filling your head with, but you're a smart girl, I know you'll reach the right conclusions. I have to believe that, because the alternative is unthinkable.'

Vikki couldn't draw her eyes away from the patch of earth where Rob had laid her down so many times. He was looking at the same spot too when he said, 'I know I've been stupid, Vikki, but I've done nothing wrong, you have to believe that. I might be passionate about my students, but not like the police are suggesting. I'll admit I was flattered whenever one of them had a crush on me, I'm only human, but if anything I used it to their advantage, not mine. I got them to try that bit harder, and if it went too far, like it did with Charlotte Tavistock, I'd set new boundaries and we'd move on. You do know she's changed her statement, don't you?'

Vikki nodded and turned her back on their abandoned love nest. 'But what about Scarlett? What boundaries did you set with her?' she asked.

'I know I should have taken a step back and informed the school when her infatuation got out of hand, but I thought I could handle it. And I was lonely,' he added, so quietly that she almost didn't catch what he had said at first.

'You're blaming me? This is all my fault because I was too busy caring for Mum to give you the attention you needed?'

'I'm blaming no one but myself,' he said, and when Vikki walked away, he caught up with her. 'I was helping Scarlett with her grades, that was my only motive in giving her the extra lessons. And when she sent that photo, I told her she was out of order.'

'Was that before or after you installed an encryption app on your phone?'

'I don't know anything about this app Liam created, Vikki. The police checked my phone and found nothing, and that's because there's nothing to find.'

When Rob stopped suddenly, Vikki carried on a few steps before turning to face him. There were tears in his eyes.

'I didn't do what they've accused me of, Vikki. What everyone seems to forget is that Scarlett isn't suggesting I did either.'

'But she would protect you at all costs, wouldn't she, Rob? She thinks it's her fault. You knew it was wrong, but you couldn't say no, not to her. Isn't that how it goes?' Vikki asked, her eyes focusing somewhere in the dim and distant past until Rob's stricken features came back into view.

'Please, Vikki, don't. You want to punish me for showing an interest in these girls, even a professional one, I understand that. But don't let your jealousy jeopardize what we have together. You are, and always will be the love of my life, and I only want what's best for you.' He reached out to her but let his hand drop when she didn't move. 'But maybe what's best for you is that I walk away now. Tell me to go, Vikki, and I'll go,' he said, pausing long enough to take a breath, but not for Vikki to answer. 'Or am I right in thinking there's a reason you asked to meet here? Did you want to remind yourself that what we have is worth fighting for?'

'You always could read my mind,' she said, not sure if that was a good thing any more. 'Especially while we were over there on the blanket.'

As Rob followed her gaze to the shade of the wisteria, he said, 'God, I remember lying with you in my arms, and it feeling so right. You used to tell me how all you wanted was for us to spend the rest of our lives together. Remember?'

Like the tangle of shadows beneath the wisteria, Vikki's memories had become twisted. She could recall saying something like that, but was that really all she had wanted? Sarah had been right, she had had other aspirations beyond marriage. Why did everything seem so different, looking back?

'I remember you telling me not to live my dad's dreams for him, that I should do what I wanted to do, but who's to say going to uni wasn't what I wanted too?' she asked. 'Yes, I wanted you, but why did I have to give up everything else?'

'You make it sound like I forced you.'

'No, I know you didn't,' she said, 'but sometimes, you told me what I wanted before I'd worked it out for myself, like I had a secret I was too afraid to share.' She laughed but it caught in her throat. 'Remember how I got a thrill from kneeling down in front of you and giving you a blow job? It was what I wanted and you were only following orders. That was what you told me I was thinking, and I didn't say it wasn't.'

Her thoughts, spoken out loud, shocked Vikki as much as Rob. She had wanted to hurt him, she supposed. She needed him to question their relationship as much as she had been doing, and from the look on his face, it had worked. 'If I made you do things you didn't want to—' He stopped speaking to shake his head. 'I'm so sorry. I thought it was good that we knew how to please each other. I thought what we had was special. Are you saying none of that was real?'

He swept his hand over his eyes, as if she hadn't seen his tears. 'No, it was real,' she said softly. Perhaps Rob was right, she had returned to Ellison House to remind herself that what they had.

'But you wanted other things, too, like a career,' he said. 'I realize that now, but I swear, I never knew at the time how strongly you felt about it. You didn't tell me, how was I supposed to know?' He took a step closer, bringing him within touching distance. 'If you can find it in your heart to give me a second chance, I will make things right, I promise. I'm almost certainly about to lose my job, but maybe that could be a good thing? I could look after the kids and you could be the breadwinner, if that's what you want.' He shook his head and tears slipped down his cheeks. 'You might have to be. Who would want me now?'

Vikki was trying not to let Rob's raw emotions get to her, but there was a warmth in her chest that had started to melt her frozen heart. He was crying openly as he dropped to his knees and rested his hands on her hips.

'I don't blame you for doubting me,' he said, 'but I swear I never have and never will love anyone the way I love you. We belong together. Freya needs us, and the new baby needs us too. I'm the one on my knees now, and I'm begging you, Vikki. Please come home.'

With Rob looking up at her, Vikki felt as if she were towering over him. He had told her so many times that she was the one in charge, but this was the first time she had actually felt as if she were in control of her own destiny, and his too. 'Tell me you didn't touch her,' she said. 'Look at me and swear you never had sex with Scarlett.'

Rob took deep breaths as he struggled to compose himself. He used his shoulder to wipe away tears while his hands moved from her hips to her abdomen. He placed a protective palm gently over their unborn child. 'I swear to you, Vikki, I never slept with her.'

When he kissed her stomach, Vikki closed her eyes and let her body find the answer to the question that had been consuming her for weeks. She didn't recoil from the touch of a monster, she felt a connection that had been there all along, one that linked her life to Rob's and always would.

Rob stood up and when he wrapped her in his arms, it felt so right, exactly as she remembered from those early days. This was what she wanted more than anything, to have her old life back, and Rob's kiss was the sweetest and most satisfying feeling she had ever experienced.

Her hands moved lower and she held on to his hips to pull him closer. Her need for her husband was so intense that she was tempted to lead Rob back to their favourite spot, but something began vibrating in his back pocket. She managed to grab hold of the phone before Rob had time to react.

'Give it to me,' he said.

It wasn't so much the words but the panic in his voice that forced Vikki back towards the shadows she thought she had escaped only seconds earlier. The phone in her hand was one she didn't recognize, a cheap plastic thing that Rob must have bought as a temporary replacement. When he tried to take it from her, Vikki twisted away from his grasp. The caller's number was withheld and as she lifted it to her ear, her heart filled with dread.

Rob tried one last time. 'Please,' he said.

Scarlett

I'd been feeling pretty pleased with myself after convincing Charlotte to tell the truth. He'd said if I could do that, the investigation would be over and there would be no chance of the police ever linking me to him. But then it all went so wrong and now I wish I was dead. I swear I can't do this any more. I don't know what I'm going to do. It's a complete mess.

None of this would have happened if Mum hadn't dragged me to Wales. It was horrible when I got stuck on my own with Sarah. She was all wound up because of the way Mum had spoken to her, which she so deserved. It was about time someone told her what a manipulative bitch she can be. I hate people like that.

While Mum was trying to find out why Bryn had turned up, we waited in a coffee shop. Sarah didn't want to talk to me and spent most of the time on her phone. She phoned Miles and went on about all the trouble I'd caused. She thought she was making me feel guilty, as if I cared!

Actually, I did care, but no way was I going to let Sarah know. It was the same with Mum. I know I've been angry with her like forever, but it's only because I miss how it was before everything changed, when it was just me and her – and, OK, Liam too, but you know what I mean. Before things got so complicated.

So I was sitting there, ignoring Sarah, when I saw Bryn's car drive straight past. Sarah didn't notice, she was too busy making one call after another because she's so bloody important. I waited until she was in deep conversation with some solicitor when I told her I was going to the toilet. The minute her back was turned, I headed straight out the door and went to a phone box I'd seen further up the road.

I'd memorized his number, but until that point I'd been too scared to phone him. I didn't have my mobile and I couldn't use the house phone in case the police were listening in, you never know. This was my first chance and I knew I'd have to talk fast, but I should have been more careful. I should have made doubly sure it was safe for him to talk, but when I heard him speak, he sounded so desperate. 'Please,' he'd whispered and I wanted to reach down the line and hold him and never let go.

'Oh God, I miss you so much,' I told him, and I didn't care how frustrated he sounded, I was going to make him need me even more. I was going to make sure he would see me again, and soon. 'I keep thinking about the other night. I want you to fuck me against the wall again.'

'Please, no,' he said again.

I was about to smile. I had him. And that's when I heard her voice and everything stopped. I wanted to throw up. I wanted to slam down the phone and just start running, but my legs had turned to jelly.

'So it's true,' the voice said. It was Vikki, and that's when

I realized Rob hadn't been begging me, he'd been talking to her. She was the one holding the phone and now she was talking to me. 'I think we need to talk, Scarlett.'

I dropped the phone, but when I turned, Mum was there in my face, while Sarah was racing up the road towards us.

'Who were you talking to?'

Do you know? At that point I really was going to tell her everything, honestly I was. It wasn't like I could keep it a secret any more, but Mum didn't give me a chance.

'Oh, don't bother. I doubt you could tell the truth even if you tried.'

'Sorry, Nina,' Sarah said after she had caught up with us. 'She was there one minute and gone the next.' She gave me this snarly look – as if that was going to scare me. I had enough to worry about, thank you very much.

Mum wasn't as worried about my mystery phone call as she should have been. She was all hot and bothered after speaking to Caryn and from the beaming smile on her face, I could tell it had gone well. I was glad for her, and I honestly and truly do mean that. It wasn't so great for me though. It looked like I might have to face Bryn now, on top of everything else.

30

Vikki's jacket fluttered behind her as she ran, the sleeve torn where she had snagged it on the fence in her haste to get away from Ellison House and Rob. When she realized his car had been blocking hers in, she had run straight past and continued down the road. If Rob was chasing her, her heart was thumping too loudly to hear his footfalls. He hadn't called after her, she was sure of that.

'It's over,' she had said when she had thrown the mobile back at him, but she doubted Rob would understand the enormity of that statement. The time had come for Vikki to stop letting other people think for her and to take control of her life.

She ran until her lungs were ready to explode, and then she just kept going. She almost missed the bridle path that would take her through the woods and across farmers' fields towards her mum's house. She was retracing the route she and Rob had taken with Freya only a few months earlier, but her mind was taking her further back in time; *much* further back.

Vikki had never been one of the popular girls at school,

but by the time she reached sixth form she had an established group of friends, which had included Amy. Her social life hit the right balance between studying hard for the grades that would get her into university, and letting off steam when the pressure became too much. She was never a wild child, never allowed the partying to get out of control, and she had made her dad proud.

It had come as a surprise when her grades had started slipping. English had been her strongest subject and Mr Swift had been a fantastic teacher, even though he was pretty new to the job, but she suspected he was still the problem. She had had such a ridiculous crush on him, and when he offered to give her extra lessons, she was almost grateful that she had been failing the subject.

The thing she liked about Rob, particularly when they were on their own, was the way he talked to her as his peer. He listened to her opinion and sometimes changed his after she gave a stirring argument about Hamlet's motivation for revenge, Steinbeck's use of narrative or the best cheese to put on toast. He had treated her like an adult at a time when it was still a novelty and her crush had turned into something far more potent.

She would spend every moment she could with him, pretending to pore over the latest set text when all she could think about was how close he was sitting next to her. She couldn't quite recall the moment she realized he felt the attraction too. It started with little compliments, quickly followed by apologies for speaking out of turn, mixed messages that told her he was as confused as she. Then one day she had been leaning in close enough to feel his breath on her face and she had dared herself not to move away.

'You want to kiss me, don't you?' he had said, just like that.

And she almost had, but pulled away at the last minute.

Rob had given her such a sad smile. 'Maybe you're right, Victoria, you usually are. I'm your teacher and you shouldn't be having this effect on me. Mr Taggart certainly wouldn't approve. You're seventeen and still a girl.'

'No, I'm not,' she had answered angrily.

'Really?' he had asked before leaning over to whisper the challenge that was to be her undoing. 'Prove it.'

And that was how it had begun, with Rob telling her what she wanted. It was how he had controlled her, it was how he had controlled them all. She had seen the similarities – Scarlett's extra lessons, that kiss with Charlotte – but she had been as blind as they were. She hadn't wanted to admit that all the time he had been telling her how clever she was, she had been such a fool. But she saw it all too clearly now.

Rob had been the one to form her ideas, and for the most part she hadn't even noticed that they weren't her own. There had been times when she had done things that she hadn't wanted to do, but she hadn't corrected him because Rob had said she was his downfall. He was risking his career for her schoolgirl smile, and she had wanted to prove herself worthy.

She had given up her friends, using them as an alibi so she could be with Rob, and eventually they had stopped asking her along on nights out. She had rejected the life her dad had thought was all mapped out, and all because Rob had called her a rebel. Not that taking a gap year to work in an estate agent's had been particularly rebellious.

With hindsight, Vikki realized she had simply traded one authority figure for another, and one far more controlling.

When she had completely shelved the plan to go to university so she could marry Rob, it hadn't seemed such a big sacrifice, not if it meant protecting his reputation. She might have disappointed her dad, but her mum had been relieved to see her so happy and settled. And Vikki had been happy because she was convinced she had the one thing she really wanted; the love of the man who had been prepared to risk everything for that first kiss and all the ones that followed.

When Vikki reached home, Elaine's car wasn't on the drive, which meant there was no one ready to catch her. She burst into the house and let out a howl that had risen through her body on a tide of anger. How could she have been so stupid, so gullible? Hitting her fists against the door she had slammed behind her, Vikki drew breath and cried out again, and again, and again, only thankful that Freya wasn't there to hear her sobs.

She hated the person she had become. Expertly moulded by Rob, she was nothing more than a product of his imagination. Even when she tried to think about the baby she was carrying, it made her feel no more than a vessel for Rob's use. She pulled off her trainers and the jacket that had been pressed up against Rob's chest, dropping them on the utility room floor. Not stopping there, Vikki pulled off her jumper and her jeans and her socks, until all she had on were her knickers and bra. She scooped them all up and shoved them in the washing machine with some detergent, but before switching it on, she added her underwear too.

No longer in a hurry, Vikki walked with slow, deliberate

steps through the house. She didn't care that her naked body was on show as she walked past open windows. No one could see her. She wasn't there. She felt nothing, even though she was shaking uncontrollably. It was possibly a reaction from the heat of her recent exertion, or even from the cold. She didn't know. She couldn't feel a thing.

Heading upstairs, she switched on the shower and turned the setting to scalding hot. Not flinching as she stepped beneath it, Vikki scrubbed and scrubbed her body, but no matter how hard she tried she couldn't get clean. A shower wasn't going to wash away the disgust and loathing she felt for herself. At seventeen, she had been clever, clear-headed and determined. Her dad might have had plans for her, but they had been based on *her* dreams and she had been grateful for his help because she had been overwhelmed by all the possibilities he made her believe were hers for the taking. It had been scary and exciting all at the same time, but these emotions were nowhere near as compelling or addictive as her feelings for Rob.

Vikki wondered at what point she had stopped being what Rob wanted. At what point had he felt the need to search out a new student to mould to his needs? Was it when she had become a mother? When she had lost her dad? Or was it when her mum had been ill and Vikki had her first real taste of independence? And if she had outgrown him, where was this new woman she had become, the one who had impressed Sarah Tavistock? Vikki had to believe she was still in there somewhere. She wasn't defined as Rob's wife and she wouldn't be defined as his victim either. Overwhelmed by a new surge of anger, Vikki screamed out again, but it caught in her throat as she looked down and saw the blood. So much blood.

Nina had slept in her own bed for the first time in a long time, and what was more, she had slept soundly. For once she hadn't lain awake worrying about Scarlett and the failing investigation, or wondered how Liam and Eva would get through the next few days. She hadn't wrestled with the constant guilt of leaving Janet to run the shop on her own and, most surprising of all, she hadn't spent the night wondering if Bryn could ever trust her with his love again. She had closed her eyes and she had fallen into a deep sleep, not waking until sunrise.

There was a reason for this unusual sense of calm and it was simple: she had made progress. No matter how many steps back she might be forced to take, yesterday she had taken a step forward, and she had liked how it felt.

When she had been greeted by a distraught Caryn at the house, Nina had refused to let insidious doubts invade her heart. Instead she had felt it clench as she held close the love she felt for her husband. She had taken Caryn into her arms as if she were her own and told her it was going to be all right, promising they would work out what to do together. She had briefly wished she could do the same with Scarlett.

'Mum told me what happened, and it's my fault,' Caryn had told her. 'I was so angry with Dad for moving away and giving up on me. When he married you, I thought I'd lost him for good. I'm sorry I didn't come to the wedding. I was angry, I suppose. But I never wanted any of this to happen.'

'It's not your fault, Caryn,' Nina had told her.

'But if you'd met me, if you'd known how good a person Dad is, you'd never have thought he would do, you know, the things you thought he had, and you'd still be together.'

'I should have known he was a good man, anyway. I should have loved him enough to never doubt him,' Nina had said, and then it was Caryn consoling her.

Caryn explained how she had been trying to make things right by inviting Bryn over. She hadn't told him that Nina was on her way too until he was in the house, thinking it would be relatively easy to bring them together, but she hadn't factored in how much her dad was hurting. It would have taken all his courage to face Caryn, fearing he would be hurt again, and dealing with Nina had been too much for him. He had panicked, and he had run away.

The two women had sat down with cups of hot tea and slices of bara brith while Caryn shared small glimpses of her life; the past and the present. The rich fruit loaf featured in Caryn's daily rituals and she ate a slice slathered in butter once a day. It was only a small slice and the battle with anorexia went on, but the cake reassured her that she was winning. Caryn was at pains to point out that her problems had started long before Bryn's faux pas. She had struggled with self-image as a teenager and, in spite of a previously close relationship with her dad, when she had found a reason to hate him, she hadn't been able to let it go.

Listening, Nina had seen parallels in her relationship with Scarlett, which made her more determined than ever to bring father and daughter back together again. If Bryn and Caryn could do it, there was hope for her and Scarlett too.

'Bryn explained how he felt about it once,' Nina had told her. 'He said it was like waking up one morning and discovering a brick wall standing between the two of you. You were talking at cross purposes and everything he said was misinterpreted. While he thought he was holding out an olive branch, you were fending off a sharpened spear.'

'Is that what it's like with you and Scarlett?'

'Yes, except I've given up on olive branches.'

'You shouldn't,' Caryn had said.

'I won't, and neither will your dad.'

That was when Caryn had decided to phone him. Nina had warned her that he would be driving, hoping to soften the blow if Bryn ignored her call, so they had both been surprised when he answered the call almost immediately. Parked in a layby, her beautiful, beautiful man was crying, and he was scared. He hadn't been able to say much but he had listened to Caryn and, to her surprise, he hadn't disconnected the call when Caryn passed the phone to Nina.

'I know you don't want to talk to me,' she had told him, 'and if I'm honest, I have nothing meaningful to say, no explanation and certainly no justification for treating you like I did. My belief in you should have been strong enough to withstand any doubts about us, about you, but to my shame, it wasn't.'

On the other end of the phone she could hear Bryn taking a juddering breath. He made no other response, but what had she expected? She had said nothing that he would disagree with.

'Maybe it was because we rushed into marriage before we got to know each other properly, but we did it for the right reasons, Bryn,' she had continued. 'I love you. You might be too good for me and I'm pretty sure I don't deserve you, but I want you in my life. I want to be your wife until my dying day. I want to love and honour you like I vowed I would, if only you'd give me a second chance.'

After such an outpouring of emotion, she had received no more than a mumbled promise that he would think about it. It wasn't much, but it was more than she deserved, and when she climbed out of bed the next morning there was hope warming her heart. She slipped on Bryn's dressing gown and imagined it was his arms wrapping around her.

'I'm sorry,' she whispered. 'Do you hear me, Bryn? I'm sorry. Please, come home.'

Knowing she wasn't going to receive an answer while hiding in her bedroom, Nina stepped on to the landing. She glanced at Scarlett's bedroom door and contemplated opening it. Her daughter had been noticeably subdued on the journey home from Wales and Nina's instinct, for what it was worth, told her that she was still in her room.

Liam's door was ajar and his bed empty. It was unusual for her son to be up and about so early, but today was not an ordinary day and she tracked him down in the darkened kitchen. He was sitting at the breakfast bar with his head in his hands which, in Nina's experience, was never a good sign.

Nina switched on the light and when Liam didn't look up, she asked, 'What's wrong, love?'

He rubbed his eyes with the balls of his hands and released a loud yawn as if he had just woken up. Nina wasn't fooled but pretended not to notice his damp cheeks. 'Sorry, I didn't hear you getting up. Do you want me to make you a coffee?'

'I won't say no,' Nina said, and as soon as she sat down, Liam got to his feet.

She waited patiently until the drinks were made and Liam had regained his composure sufficiently to tell her what was wrong. He sat down and pushed a steaming mug towards her before wrapping his broad hands around one for himself. He blew across the surface, took a sip, and said, 'Eva's mum is taking her to the clinic today.'

Nodding, Nina said, 'So she's going ahead with the abortion?'

'She messaged me this morning. Actually, we've been messaging each other all night. It might be the right thing to do, Mum, but for a while we had this picture of what it would be like. It's hard for her to do what she has to do, and for me to let her do it on her own.'

'You're not going? But I thought . . . '

'Her mum said I have to keep away.'

'Isn't it enough that she's got Eva to do what she wanted? Does she have to make it even more painful for you both?'

'Apparently, yes.'

After putting the world to rights the day before, Nina was more than ready for another fight. 'When are they leaving?'

Liam looked at the clock on the wall. 'In a couple of hours, I should think. Why?'

Nina grabbed the phone Liam had been keeping at arm's reach. She handed it to him and said, 'Phone Eva and tell her I want to speak to her mum. Now.'

The two mothers hadn't spoken since Nina had been unceremoniously kicked out of the McEldry house, but she didn't bother wasting time on pleasantries. 'I understand you're refusing to let Liam go with Eva to the clinic.'

'He's had more than enough involvement in my daughter's

381

life. He got her into this mess and we can do without his kind of help, thank you very much.'

'Isn't that the point?'

'Sorry?'

'You're right, Liam did get your daughter into this mess. He should have thought about the consequences before he became intimately involved with your daughter. He should have taken precautions, and the fact that he didn't means that he should bear the greater responsibility.'

'I agree,' Mrs McEldry said unhappily.

'Then perhaps you would also agree that today is going to be a difficult and unpleasant one. Why should Liam be excused? Why shouldn't he see the pain and discomfort that Eva's going to go through, physically and emotionally? Are you letting him off the hook?'

Mrs McEldry scoffed at the idea. 'No, certainly not.'

'In that case, he should be there.'

Liam was watching expectantly as Nina waited for an answer, which wasn't immediate.

'Fine, but tell him from me, I don't intend to make it easy on him.'

'Oh, believe me, I wouldn't want you to.'

When Nina put down the phone, she looked long and hard at her son. His eyes were bright with anticipation. 'She's agreed?'

'Yes.'

Liam went to high-five his mother. 'Good move, Mum.'

She waited until he let his arm drop back down. 'You think I said all of that just for effect?' she asked. 'You think you're not to blame for this? I meant every word I said, Liam. You got a sixteen-year-old girl pregnant and, maybe,

382

with everything that's been going on with Scarlett, I haven't had the time or the energy to be as mad at you as I should, but that doesn't mean you have my unquestioning support. You *will* go to that clinic and when you're there you can think about the life you created so casually, and the life you're destroying. It's the right thing to do, and you'll be there to reassure Eva of exactly that, but don't think for a minute that it's going to be an easy decision to live with. And next time you decide to have sex, you make absolutely sure you behave responsibly.'

Liam's cheeks were glowing with embarrassment, but she hadn't finished. 'You take proper precautions, Liam, or you leave your dick in your trousers.'

With his jaw clenched, he dropped his head and mumbled, 'OK, Mum, I get the message.'

Nina took a deep breath and her chest swelled. She had taken another step forward. 'Good,' she said.

And then there was a knock at the door.

'Do you want me to get it?' asked Liam.

A number of possibilities rushed through Nina's mind as to who might be calling at this hour. She questioned her earlier instincts and wished she had checked Scarlett's room. 'No, I'll go.'

Refusing to relinquish her buoyant mood quite so soon, Nina opened the door without hesitation.

'Hello,' Bryn said.

Nina froze, unsure how to react until she knew what Bryn's visit heralded. She could be about to mourn the breakdown of another marriage, or she could be getting her husband back. It was impossible to tell, because Bryn's expression was giving nothing away.

'Can I come in?'

Nina stepped to one side.

'Hello, son,' Bryn said to Liam, who had appeared in the hallway.

'Good to see you, Bryn,' Liam said. 'I'm so glad you're here.'

'Well, I'm relieved someone is.'

'I am too.'

Bryn raised his gaze to the top of the stairs where Scarlett was standing in nothing but an oversized T-shirt. He winked at her before turning his attention back to Nina. 'How about you?'

Refusing to let her emotions run free, she bit down hard on her lip. 'I suppose that depends on why you're here.'

Bryn rubbed the back of his neck. 'I think maybe we should talk – privately.'

On her way to the kitchen, Nina passed Liam. 'You'd better go and get ready. You don't want Eva leaving without you.'

'I was about to,' he said, and when Bryn walked past, he put his hand on his stepfather's shoulder. 'I hope you're here to stay. You wouldn't believe how hard a time Mum's been giving me.'

'From what I hear, it's probably deserved.'

Liam's cheeks glowed as he hurried away up the stairs.

Once they were alone in the kitchen, Nina was desperate to find out if she had a right to hope. 'Why are you here, Bryn?'

'It's not what you think,' he began, 'or at least not completely. I'm here because Vikki Swift has sent me. I have a message – technically, it's for Scarlett.'

'What did she say?'

Again, Scarlett's voice had appeared from nowhere. She had ignored Bryn's request to speak to Nina in private as if she had known it would be about her.

Scarlett

After that stupid, stupid phone call, I was just waiting for things to kick off. I actually threw up on the way home from Wales. I said I was car sick, but really it was because I was so scared, trapped in that car, waiting for Mum's phone to ring. And I wasn't being, like, completely selfish, I did think a bit about Vikki and how she must have felt, hearing me saying those things. If I'd been her, I would have phoned the police straight away and got Rob locked up for good, and probably found a way to lock me up too. But there was no phone call, and no sign of the police when we got home.

I didn't want to see or hear from anyone, not even Rob. I knew he'd be so angry. We were almost in the clear and I'd gone and wrecked everything. So I decided that if he was going to prison for years and years, I wanted the last memory he had of us to be a nice one; the one of me sneaking off to see him in the middle of the night. I wanted him to spend years longing for me, not hating me. That was what I wanted.

After I'd gone to bed and we still hadn't heard from

anyone, I started wondering if I might be worrying for nothing. Maybe Vikki wouldn't want Rob to go to prison. She had her little girl to think of and, you know, the baby.

Anyway, that seemed like the most obvious explanation for the police not showing up, which I suppose should have made me feel better, but then I got it into my head that maybe she still loved him. Rob had been telling me his marriage was pretty much over, but it must have been OK enough between them for her to get pregnant. He said it wasn't planned, but not everyone is as hopeless as Liam and Eva. I know you must think I'm stupid for not thinking of it before, but after lying awake all night, I finally realized that Rob had probably been lying to me as well as his wife.

You'd think that would be enough to knock some sense into me, but it wasn't like I could just switch off my feelings. It was still possible for him to be in love with two people at the same time. There are men in some countries who have more than one wife, and I wondered if that was an option. Seriously, that was what I was thinking. Vikki would get to keep the father of her children and I would get to keep my secret boyfriend.

And then Bryn showed up.

At first, I didn't think it had anything to do with what was happening with Rob and Vikki, and I was so happy to see him. Mum had been acting strange since meeting Caryn, like she didn't hate me so much any more, and if Bryn was back, it would put her in an even better mood.

It was obvious they wanted to talk alone, but I crept downstairs to listen anyway. I wanted to say sorry, and not only to Bryn but Mum too. It was only when Bryn mentioned Vikki had a message for me that I knew that *was it, my life was over. But that was when he told Mum how Vikki had been rushed into hospital and she'd lost the baby. That was why she hadn't gone to the police.*

I'd killed their baby.

I felt dizzy and sick just thinking about it, and I was waiting for Bryn to tell Mum how it was all my fault, but he obviously didn't know yet. He had been the one to bring Vikki home from hospital – apparently, she'd asked for him when she phoned for a cab. I couldn't believe she wanted to speak to me after what happened, I thought I'd be the last person she would want to see.

'I'm not going,' I told him.

The thing about Bryn is that he isn't someone who reacts straight away. It takes a while for him to get angry. Even when Mum had accused him of messing around with me, he'd been more sad than angry, but something had been building and building inside him, and there was no slow-burning reaction this time – it was like he exploded.

'You will go!' he roared at me. 'You might not think you owe me or your mum an apology, but you owe one to that poor woman.'

I wanted to tell him that I was sorry, but it was too late, wasn't it? I'd killed a baby and everyone was going to hate me even more, especially Vikki. I thought about locking myself in my room, but I couldn't hide away for ever so I decided I might as well get it over with. From the look on Bryn's face, I didn't really have a choice.

31

The doctor had seen no reason to keep Vikki in hospital once the ultrasound had confirmed there was no foetal heartbeat. Nature would take its course and there was nothing they could do to prevent the miscarriage now, but Vikki had known that the moment she had started bleeding. She had dragged herself out of the shower and phoned her mum, incoherent at first, saying over and over that Rob had been sleeping with Scarlett, and how much she hated him. Only when she mentioned that it was his fault she was losing the baby did her mum realize what was happening. Elaine had been out shopping and somehow had the presence of mind to drop Freya off with a family friend before coming home.

There had been plenty of missed calls on Vikki's phone while she was at the hospital. Some were from 'Home' and some from an unrecognized number, which she presumed was Rob's new mobile. That presumption was confirmed when she received a text message from the same number, then another, and another after that. They were pleas rather than messages. He wanted to speak to her; he wanted to explain; he loved her.

The drive home had been relatively calm, compared to the frantic ride to the hospital. Vikki had sent her mum ahead to pick up Freya, insisting that she would be fine taking a cab home. Elaine had refused at first and only agreed when Vikki reassured her that she would have a friendly face to drive her. She had considered telling Bryn everything when he picked her up, feeling duty-bound to do all she could to make things right between him and Nina, but there was someone else she had vowed to speak to first. In many respects, Scarlett was no different from Vikki, and it was time the two compared notes.

When Scarlett arrived with her mum the following morning, Vikki was downstairs. It had required a lot of effort to get ready, but she had taken her time with her appearance because, whether she liked it or not, she and Scarlett had been competitors for Rob's affections. While the prize was no longer worth the fight, she wanted to believe she still had some self-respect.

'She's in the kitchen,' she heard her mum saying at the front door. 'We were just on our way out to the park.'

Vikki could hear the pain scratching her mum's vocal cords. She was still reeling from the sight of seeing her daughter naked and bleeding, and would face more pain when she knew the full extent of what had happened and how far back it went.

'Don't let us stop you, we can find our own way,' Nina said.

There was a chorus of goodbyes as Elaine left the house with Freya, and a moment later Nina appeared in the kitchen.

'Hi,' Vikki said and made to stand.

'No, don't get up,' Nina said, going over to give Vikki a hug. 'I'm so sorry about the baby. How are you?'

'It could be worse,' Vikki said, and for a fleeting moment wondered if the miscarriage might be marginally better than still being pregnant, but before that wicked thought could settle into her consciousness, she added, 'Or maybe not.'

The room became crowded as Bryn and Scarlett joined them in the kitchen. It was clear from the way Bryn was holding up the rear that Scarlett would still be on the doorstep if she'd had her way. The two young women locked eyes briefly and said nothing.

'I'll leave you to it,' Bryn said.

Nina spun around. 'You're going?'

'I have a couple of errands to run,' he said. Turning to Vikki, he gave a more truthful answer. 'And I doubt you want an audience.'

Vikki smiled, grateful for this gentle man's insight. It was hard to imagine how anyone could have doubted his intentions, but as she knew from bitter experience, no one could be taken at face value. Rob being a case in point. 'Thank you, Bryn.'

Nina wasn't nearly as impressed by his valour. 'But I thought—'

'I'll come back,' he promised. 'Phone me when you're ready to be picked up.'

Still agitated, Nina asked, 'And you will answer your phone?'

'You could always go with him?' Vikki suggested. 'I was sort of assuming I'd be talking to Scarlett alone.'

In panic, Scarlett turned to Nina. 'Mum?'

Vikki had last seen Scarlett in Mrs Anwar's office, and

she looked almost as terrified about talking to Vikki as she had about being questioned by the police, if not more so. There had been an air of defiance back then, but not now. 'Why don't you sit down, Scarlett? Would you like a drink?'

'I can do that,' Nina said.

Vikki ignored the objections and stood this time. 'No, I can manage. I'm not as weak as I look,' she said for Scarlett's benefit.

'In that case, we'll be off,' Bryn said, pulling his wife away. 'And we can come back whenever you're ready.'

Nina scribbled down her mobile number and thrust it into Vikki's hand on the way out. Once they were alone, Vikki worked in silence as she made a cup of tea for herself and poured a glass of water for Scarlett, whose dry lips were sticking together.

Vikki's movements triggered a fresh wave of cramps that had been only one of many reasons she hadn't slept. 'I hope you're not going to waste time denying what happened yesterday,' she began as she joined Scarlett at the kitchen table.

'Have you told the police yet?'

'I haven't told anyone yet.'

'But you're going to.'

'One of us is.'

Scarlett was shaking her head. 'I won't do it. I can't. I'm really sorry about what happened to you, and I feel bad about the baby and all that, but you don't under-stand—'

Before she could finish, Vikki said, 'But that's the point, Scarlett. I think I do understand, or at least I'm starting to. I haven't brought you here to interrogate you, if that's what you're thinking. There are things I need to know, but mostly, all I want is for you to listen. And believe me, this is going to be hard for me too. OK?'

The girl with the violet eyes hunched her shoulders and dropped her gaze. 'I suppose.'

'You might think you're special, Scarlett,' she said to the crown of the young girl's head, 'but you're not. You're another version of me. I've been protecting Rob too, and in the space of twenty-four hours my whole life has been rewritten. The special relationship I thought I had has been replaced by another, seedier version that makes me sick even thinking about it.'

Vikki couldn't quite gauge Scarlett's reaction, until she saw the telltale shake of the head. She didn't want Vikki to continue, but nothing was going to stop her now.

'Did he ever talk about me?' she asked. 'I bet you didn't know we started dating when I was at school, did you? It turns out the only real difference between you and me is that I was in sixth form when I first slept with Rob, and he was a single man in those days.' She paused so her words could give Scarlett's conscience a nudge. 'I was over the age of consent, but it was still illegal. He was in a position of trust and I was under eighteen, so I had to swear not to tell anyone. That's what he asked you to do, isn't it? To take your secret to the grave?'

When Scarlett lowered her head further, Vikki said, 'Can't you at least look at me? I'm not asking you to talk, Scarlett. I'm only asking you to listen and I'd rather not talk to the top of your head.'

Scarlett lifted her head, but not her gaze; she looked everywhere except Vikki's face.

'You know, you might think I'm really sensible and mature, but I don't feel that much older than you. I went from living with my mum and dad to living with Rob, so I've always had someone looking after me and telling me what to do. I'm twenty-four and I still feel like a naughty child when I do something without asking Rob first – or at least, I did.' She stared at Scarlett until they finally locked eyes. 'The worst thing is, I never really noticed I didn't have a will of my own. I was happy to rely on Rob telling me what I wanted.'

'I wasn't forced into doing anything, if that's what you're saying.'

'Are you sure? I think I would have said the same thing not that long ago,' Vikki said as she sifted through the ravaged memories of her relationship. 'I became involved with Rob because my grades were slipping and he offered to give me extra lessons, and in those lessons we talked about anything except whatever paper I was supposedly struggling with. Is that how it started with you?'

Scarlett was reluctant to answer, but managed to give a tiny nod.

'When we were alone together, Rob kept telling me off for leading him into temptation. I thought I was so good at seduction that I could do it without even knowing and, stupidly, it's taken me until now to realize that simply being alone with him constituted enticement in his warped mind.' Vikki stopped and squeezed her eyes shut as a dull pain rippled across her abdomen. 'I can remember him pleading with me not to make him do it, as if I was pinning him against the wall and snogging his face off. I wasn't. I was sitting on the other side of the desk, in complete awe of him, not just because he was so attractive, but because I was shocked to have that power over him.'

Scarlett wiped the corner of her eye, but it was too late, the tear had fallen.

'When it came to sex,' Vikki said, 'I was insatiable. That's what he told me. I was adventurous and up for anything, so much so that I shocked him. And I shocked myself because I didn't know I was like that. "Don't hold back," he used to tell me, "play with me, play with yourself, make a noise, don't be shy".' Her cheeks felt warm; not with embarrassment but humiliation. 'And I believed him. I thought no one would ever know me as well as he did. How could they, when he knew me better than I knew myself? But it was all a lie and I went along with it because I didn't want to be a disappointment. He was putting his job on the line for me and I owed it to him to be worth the risk. I never saw it as abuse.'

'But you got married. How can you call it abuse if he married you?'

'How could *anyone* question it if we were married?' Vikki added, thinking how Rob had dodged an investigation from the school. 'And if the worst that had happened was that we fell in love and lived happily ever after, I'd happily agree with you. So what if he was my teacher? I was seventeen and he was twenty-three. We fell in love and it was only circumstance that made it a problem. His intentions were honourable, right? Except, they don't look honourable any more, do they? And what he did to me, he did to you too, Scarlett and that *is* abuse. And then there was Charlotte, and God knows who else.'

'Charlotte lied,' Rob said quietly.

Vikki gasped and there was the sound of chair legs

scraping across the floor as Scarlett's body jolted. For a moment Vikki thought Scarlett was about to leap into Rob's arms, but the schoolgirl had moved reflexively. Vikki hadn't moved at all except to turn her head towards the figure standing in the doorway that led out through the utility room. Her mum had left the back door unlocked.

'How long have you been standing there?'

'Long enough,' he said. His voice was soft and not in the least bit threatening. The man the police would soon label a predator sounded dejected and lost. 'You sound so different, Vikki.'

'I'm not your little girl any more,' she said. 'I've grown up a lot since I saw you yesterday, Rob. I've had to.'

'I'm sorry,' Scarlett said, directing her apology to Rob. 'About yesterday. About everything.'

He looked at her and smiled. 'I'm not here to blame anyone but myself. I'm weak and I allowed myself to be in love with two women at the same time.'

'She's fifteen,' Vikki reminded him. 'You might have used her as a woman, but she's still a child.'

'I know. I'm sorry.'

'You have to leave,' Vikki said. 'Mum's going to be back soon.'

'She's not long left.'

'You've been watching the house?'

Rob's face creased with pain. 'I've spent the last twenty-four hours waiting for a knock on the door and when it didn't come, I dared myself to hope. But listening to you now, Vikki, I know I have to face up to what I've done to you both. At least let me stay long enough so I can apologize.' He glanced at Scarlett and, choking on his words, added, 'All I ever wanted was to please you both, but I've ended up hurting you so much. I wanted to be everything to everyone and now . . . ' He put a hand briefly over his mouth as if he couldn't bring himself to admit it. 'Now I'm nothing.'

'You're not,' whispered Scarlett.

'You're better off without me, Scarlett. You both are.'

Vikki's tone was less conciliatory. 'Don't,' she warned him.

'Don't what?'

'Don't waste your time trying to make us feel sorry for you. Do you really think you can sneak in here to beg forgiveness and we'll agree to pretend none of this happened?' As she spoke, Vikki's words became louder and stronger. 'Do you think you're *so* good that you can handle the two of us at the same time?'

Rob took a step towards her. 'No, not at all.'

'Don't you come near me!' she yelled.

He stopped. 'I'm sorry. I'm so sorry, Vikki.' He held out a hand towards her in the vain hope that she might change her mind and reach out too. She didn't. 'I came here to tell you I'm going to make it easier for everyone. You don't have to testify against me, either of you.'

Scarlett stood up. 'You're going to the police? You can't!'

Taking a step back, he said, 'I just wanted to say goodbye. All I ask is that you don't hate me too much. I wasn't all bad, was I?'

The question was directed at Vikki. She didn't offer an answer, only a question. 'You're not going to the police, are you?'

'I love you, Vikki. I love our children. Remember that.'

He turned slowly, as if he were deliberately leaving enough time for someone to stop him.

'Wait!' Scarlett said and lunged forward in time to grab his coat sleeve and turn him around. 'If you're not going to the police, where are you going?'

He cupped her damp cheek in his hand. 'You really were my downfall, Scarlett.'

'No! You're not—' she started, but couldn't bear to complete the sentence. She swallowed hard and tried again. 'You're not thinking of killing yourself?'

'Forget me, Scarlett. Concentrate on your exams and prove to the world that I was a good thing in your life. Will you do that for me?'

'No,' she said and then louder, 'No! Don't leave.' But Rob was already pulling away from her.

Turning to Vikki, Scarlett demanded, 'Are you seriously going to let him go?'

When the house phone began to ring, Vikki ignored it. She was watching Rob and, as he prepared to walk out of her life for good, he stopped at the doorway so she could take one last look at him. He was waiting for his wife to save the day.

'Before you go,' she said softly, 'tell me that you still love me, Rob. Tell me that Scarlett meant nothing to you and you would never have left me for her. I need to know.'

'I love you, Vikki, I swear I always did and I always will.'

'And Scarlett was only a fling? She meant nothing?'

Tears welled in Rob's eyes. 'I love you both. I know that condemns me, but I won't lie to you, not any more.'

Scarlett let loose a sob and put her hand to her mouth. 'I love you too.'

From the kitchen counter, Vikki's mobile began to ring.

She ignored that too. 'If we were able to move forward from this,' she said, 'who would you choose, Rob?'

Rob scraped a hand over his face and his eyes fell on Scarlett. 'I've inflicted enough damage on you and your family. It would be better if we had a clean break so you can rebuild your life.'

Scarlett swallowed back a sob. 'No,' she said.

'It's the right thing to do, you see that, don't you? I know you had dreams, and for a while I was carried away by them too, but the sacrifice is too much, for both of us. Think of what you would be leaving behind, think of your mum.'

'I don't care, she hates me anyway!'

'So do it for me. I can't split myself in two, Scarlett, and I still want what's best for you. You're a clever girl, and I won't hold you back the way I did with Vikki. I was selfish, I should have tried harder to convince her go to university instead of staying in Sedgefield with me. I won't let my love stifle your potential too. And then,' he said, turning to Vikki, 'I can concentrate on making things right between us. I've lost my job, but I can still be a good husband and father.'

'And faithful?' Vikki asked.

Rob took a faltering step forward, but stopped. To reach Vikki he would have to step past Scarlett. 'God, yes, Vikki. I swear if we can all see a way past this, I'll never so much as look at another woman.'

'Do you swear? Like you did yesterday, when you swore on our baby's life that you hadn't slept with Scarlett?'

When Bryn had driven Nina into town, they had spied Elaine's car parked near the entrance to Victoria Park and had decided to stop at a nearby coffee shop in case they could catch her on her way back to the car. Nina was impatient for news and hoped that Elaine would at least know what Vikki had planned. All Vikki had told Bryn was that she knew Rob had been lying to all of them and she wanted to help put things right.

'What happens now?' she asked.

They were sitting outside the coffee shop, the sun glinting off the silver bistro table while the vapour from their breath mingled with the steam from their coffees.

'We wait until Vikki calls,' Bryn said. 'And hope by some miracle she's managed to succeed where everyone else has failed. Scarlett must see now that she has to start talking.'

'Actually, I wasn't even thinking about Scarlett,' Nina said. 'I meant, what happens with us? Do you think you could ever forgive me?'

'It's been a weird twelve months or so, don't you think?' he said. 'A year ago we were still getting to know each other and now . . . '

'And now we're still getting to know each other.'

They smiled politely at each other, as strangers might when they recognized a mutual attraction but didn't quite know what to do about it. 'I can't move back,' Bryn confessed, 'or at least not straight away. I think we need to take our time with this. Is that OK?'

Nina nodded, grateful for the shred of hope Bryn was offering. 'More than OK. And it's not like we haven't got our work cut out with other family relations. I think it's pretty obvious that I took my eye off the ball with Liam and Scarlett, and it's my job to fix things.'

Bryn didn't disagree. 'While I have the challenge of forging a new relationship with my daughter.'

'You'll be fine,' she said.

'Would you come with me, though?'

'To see Caryn?'

Bryn nodded. 'I'm scared of messing up again.'

'You won't. I don't think Caryn would let you.'

'Even so, I need you.'

'I like the sound of that,' Nina said. 'After weeks of feeling useless, it's so good to be needed for something.' Her voice cracked slightly, emotion and relief welling up in her like a tide.

Reaching out his hand, Bryn waited until Nina grasped it tightly. 'I need you for lots of things,' he said, 'and if it's not rushing you too much, do you fancy going out for dinner? Once you think it's safe to leave the kids home alone, that is.'

'Yes, oh please, yes, Bryn,' she said, gasping it out on a sob. 'I would love nothing better than to go on a date with you.'

He kissed her fingers and she warmed her hand against his lips.

'We're not disturbing you, are we?'

Nina had forgotten all about looking out for Elaine, but fortunately she had spotted them first. 'We went to the park, but Freya launched the entire bag of food at the ducks in one go and now she wants feeding too.'

'Me and Nanna gonna have chocolate cake.'

'I didn't want to take her home too soon,' Elaine continued. 'When do you think it'll be safe to go back?'

'I was hoping you would know,' Nina said, blinking her tears away and searching Elaine's face for answers.

Elaine shook her head. 'I'm afraid not. Vikki has barely spoken since yesterday, other than to say that Rob did, you know . . . ' she began but became flustered.

'I know,' Nina said so the poor woman wouldn't have to explain further. It was both sickening and reassuring to know that they had all reached the same conclusion. 'I only hope Vikki can talk my obstinate daughter into bringing this sorry mess to an end. Please, take a seat.'

Elaine released a heavy sigh as she sat down.

'Cake, Nanna!'

Rising quickly to his feet, Bryn towered over Elaine's granddaughter. 'And how about some hot chocolate to go with it?'

'OK. Can I come too?' Freya asked.

The trusting little girl reached up to take Bryn's hand without hesitation and they disappeared inside the cafe. Despite the chill in the air, Nina's insides glowed with love and pride for the man she wanted to spend the rest of her life with. It was only when her thoughts turned to Scarlett and what might be happening, that warm, fuzzy feeling disappeared and she leant over the table to give Elaine's hand a squeeze.

'I want to say how sorry I am for all the hurt we've caused.'

'It's not your fault, Nina.'

'Isn't it? Scarlett's my daughter, my responsibility. I thought I'd done a pretty good job bringing the two of them up on my own, but apparently not.'

'So what was my excuse?'

'Sorry?'

Elaine played with the sleeve of her coat and took a

while to answer. 'Scarlett isn't the only daughter who's been keeping secrets.'

'Vikki,' Nina presumed.

'I can't claim to know everything she and Rob got up to, but the story about not dating until she had left school is wearing thin, don't you think? More lies.'

'Did you know she was seeing him back then?'

Horrified, Elaine said, 'Good God, no. I didn't know she was seeing anyone but, with hindsight, maybe I should have picked up the changes in her behaviour. She started going out more, allegedly with her friends, and her grades were slipping. She had extra lessons, of course.'

Nina didn't need to ask who the lessons were with. 'Apparently, Rob downgraded Scarlett's tests so he could engineer their extra lessons.'

'Oh,' Elaine said, a blush rising in her cheeks, 'what an utter bastard my son-in-law is turning out to be. I've been such a fool, Nina. If only my husband and I had tried to stop Vikki taking a gap year, or talked her out of marrying so young and giving up on her plans to go away to university. If only she'd got away.'

'If only . . . ' Nina said. 'Why do we always blame ourselves instead of, and I quote, that bastard son-in-law of yours?'

'Oh, but I am guilty to some extent,' Elaine said. She had her head in her hands when she added, 'I think Vikki might have been persuaded to tell the police the truth about Rob when he was arrested, but I didn't want her to. I didn't even allow her to confess to me. I was too busy telling her she needed to salvage her marriage for the sake of the children. There would be all that horrible publicity and I'd . . . ' Again

Elaine's words failed her, but she wouldn't remain silent. 'I'd just got through cancer treatment and I thought I had a right to keep my family. I was scared that, if Rob was charged, Vikki might be forced to leave Sedgefield, and me. But what I came home to yesterday was the stuff of nightmares.' Her head sunk lower and whatever image came to mind caused her to shudder. 'I see him now for what he is, and what he's done to my family, and yours.'

'Why the hell don't these girls see him for what he is?' Nina muttered.

'I'm pretty sure Vikki does now, and I only hope she's strong enough to brave the storm that's coming. If it's not too much to ask, I hope our families can find a way to support each other.'

'Absolutely,' Nina assured her.

'And Sarah too, perhaps? She might be exactly the role model Vikki needs, unless of course she would rather distance herself from all the scandal.'

'I don't think that would stop her. Sarah phoned me as I was leaving the house this morning, and I hope you don't mind, but I told her what's happened. She wants to help all she can. Sarah can be a formidable ally, but I warn you now, she does like to interfere.'

Bryn arrived a moment later, with Freya in his arms and minus the chocolate cake. 'Sarah's just phoned me.'

Nina was about to make a quip about speaking of the devil, but the look on Bryn's face silenced her. She was rising to her feet as he continued.

'The security guard at the building site spotted someone hanging around your house earlier, Elaine. He was on foot so all we have is a description, but Sarah thinks it might have been Rob,' he said, mouthing the last word so that Freya didn't pick up on it.

Elaine grabbed the phone she had left on the table in front of her.

'Sarah's already tried,' he said, 'that's why she called me. I think she was hoping we were still at the house.'

Nina had that feeling again of having taken a step forward only to have Rob Swift push them back ten steps or more. There was no knowing how much advantage Rob could take of finding Scarlett and Vikki alone together. She dreaded to think, but she had a feeling she was about to find out.

'Let's get back,' she said, breaking into a run and leaving the others to catch up.

Vikki couldn't tear her eyes from Rob. His tears had quickly dried, leaving only a glint in his eye. He was waiting for Vikki to agree to the pact they were making, but the longer Vikki stared, the less she saw of the man she had married, the father of her daughter and the baby she had lost. The man in front of her was a liar and a cheat, and she hadn't been taken in by the way he had expertly answered her questions without alienating Scarlett. She was almost tempted to applaud.

'I thought I was doing the right thing. You were feeling vulnerable, I only wanted to make you feel better,' Rob explained.

'Oh my God, you swore on the baby's life,' Scarlett said. 'Is that why it died?'

Rob's face turned ashen. 'What do you mean? Vikki?'

'I lost the baby,' Vikki said. She had wanted to sound cold, but there was a sudden rush of emotion that she couldn't hold back. Her heart was full of horror and she wanted Rob to share the pain. 'I saw it, Rob. I knew I was miscarrying and then, in the middle of the night, I went to the toilet and it just fell away. I stood there, looking down, and I thought about the life you had sworn on, and I had to flush away.'

She stood up and her body burned while her eyes remained ice-cold. 'At first I was almost glad I was losing it. It was a part of you invading my body and I wanted it gone, but when it happened, there was no doubting it was a baby I'd lost. A tiny little thing that was being punished for your sins.'

Vikki walked past Scarlett to stand in front of Rob. She was reaching out her hand to him, precisely as he had wanted earlier, but she placed her palm firmly on his chest and pushed. 'So swear on *your* life this time, Rob. Swear you'll do the right thing,' she said, her voice growing louder and stronger. 'Swear you'll be true to me and leave schoolgirls like Scarlett alone.' She pushed hard enough this time for him to stumble back. 'And then fuck off out of my life.'

Rob's eyes flew to the schoolgirl standing behind his wife. 'Scarlett?' he asked.

Before Scarlett could answer, the back door burst open and in a blur of movement Bryn grabbed Rob's arm with one hand. The other was balled into a fist and struck Rob square on the jaw.

Scarlett

He didn't kill himself, and I know I should sound relieved,
but I sort of feel disappointed. He said he was nothing without
me and he said he loved us both. So when he lost us BOTH,
shouldn't that have been unbearable? And he'd lost the baby
too, after swearing on its life. If he was that heartbroken,
why didn't he jump in front of a bus or something?

I know that makes me sound like a right bitch, but that's
exactly what I am, and now I'm the one wishing I was dead.
Mum wouldn't care. I'm not saying she wouldn't be upset if
I died, but it would be so much easier for everyone. They
could all get back to normal a lot quicker without me.

Bryn stayed over last night. After punching Rob, he's
everyone's hero – mine too, if I'm honest, which is weird,
because that was always supposed to be Rob. When Bryn
knocked him down, I don't think he would have got up
again if Mum hadn't been holding Bryn back. No one
stopped Rob when he ran out of the house. I don't think
I was the only one who thought he would top himself, and
maybe that's why no one's phoned the police yet.

Or it could be that they're all waiting for me. Vikki said

I should think through what we talked about and I can go back and talk to her again if I want. I sort of do. I sort of get what she was saying about how Rob convinced her that she wanted things even when she didn't. I'm trying not to think about it though.

I have to go and speak to the police later, but I can't tell them all that stuff, can I? It's bad enough that they'll expect me to talk about sex, how do I admit that I didn't always want to do what Rob said I did? How stupid am I going to look? How can I explain that he had this way of making me do stuff, but not in an obvious way?

It was like what Vikki said about making a noise when they did it. He got me to do that too. He'd say how he could tell I was holding back and I should let myself go, so I'd be lying there making these stupid noises. And because I'd done it once, I couldn't admit that I didn't like doing it so I had to carry on. But how can you blame him for that when I was the one who was lying?

And yes, there was other stuff, stuff I actually hated, like, you know, putting it in places that hurt. But the next time, he'd say, 'You really liked that, didn't you?' Sometimes I wouldn't say anything, hoping he'd realize I didn't want to do it again, but he'd smile and say there was nothing wrong in being a bit kinky.

I'm so confused now. I think I still love him, sort of, but it's not fair. I was supposed to be special, but I'm not, am I? I was just there. Why are men so horrible? No way am I ever having sex again. How can I trust anyone that way? Not that I'll get the chance, not for years and years probably. Even if Mum did decide to let me out of the house, I don't have any friends left. There's still Eva I suppose, but she's

408

going to be practically under house arrest too, and anyway, if she carries on going out with Liam, she'll want to be with him, and if they do break up she'll keep away from both of us. See? Even if I don't kill myself, I'll be dead anyway.

I keep asking myself how this happened. I was like all my other mates once, but not any more and not ever again. I'm – I'm spoiled goods. Even I don't like me. I'm stupid, stupid, stupid. How could I not see how he was using me? All my life, Mum's told me how clever I am, but I'm not, am I? I hate myself. I really hate myself. And being stupid isn't the worst of it. I'm dirty and ugly and everyone hates me. I'm disgusting, and no, I won't calm down!

I hate myself!

And I hate Rob too!

I hate him for turning me into this horrible person who lied to everyone, who didn't care how much hurt I caused!

It's all a mess and I can't make things right. I can't make that baby not dead and I can't make my friends like me. I can't make anyone like me. Nothing is going to be the same again.

I don't know what to do.

'Don't you, Scarlett?'

Scarlett had drawn up her legs and curled herself into a tight ball on the padded chair. She had a box of tissues in one hand and a clump of damp used ones in the other.

'I can't,' she said.

'Can't what?'

Scarlett didn't answer immediately. It was the first time she had cried in front of her counsellor and now she didn't seem able to stop.

Her counselling sessions hadn't been what she had expected at all. There had been no cross-examination, no tricks to make her trip up like there were with the police. Mostly the counsellor let Scarlett do all the talking. At first, Scarlett had enjoyed shocking her by proving how worldly wise she was. The counsellor had never said she wasn't, it was a conclusion Scarlett had reached all on her own.

'I can't tell the police what he did. And no, I'm not trying to protect him any more. I just don't think I can do it.'

'What's stopping you?'

'Nothing, it's . . . it's because I'm so pathetic,' Scarlett said. She blew her nose, only to start crying again. She was looking past the counsellor to the closed door on the far side of the room. She wondered if her mum could hear her sobs.

'Why do you say that, Scarlett?'

'Because,' Scarlett cried. 'Because I'm scared. I'm scared that when everyone gets to hear what happened, no one will want anything to do with me ever again. I can't do it, please don't make me. Please.'

'You know that's not why I'm here. I won't make you do anything you don't want to.'

'I don't like this,' she said between sobs. 'I just want my mum.'

Scarlett released fresh howls, but she wasn't crying because she couldn't testify against Rob. She was crying because she knew she would.

Nina had been sitting outside the counsellor's office as usual. In recent weeks, there had been times when she had wanted to storm in there and push things along. She didn't know how these things worked, but if what had happened to

Vikki wasn't enough to persuade Scarlett to testify against Rob, no amount of talking to a counsellor was going to change anything.

In some ways, it was a moot point. If Scarlett wasn't prepared to give the police the evidence they needed to charge Rob, Vikki would be making a statement soon enough. Scarlett had one last chance to do the right thing and Nina was praying that she would.

Her daughter had been a beautiful baby with blonde curls and those startling eyes. As Nina had watched her grow into a young woman, she had presumed that they would remain best friends, and that Scarlett would always be able to share her deepest secrets with her. They had a bond, the kind that could never be broken and, despite everything, it was still there, or at least it was as far as Nina was concerned.

She didn't want to lose her daughter. She loved her so much and she wanted to undo all the harm Rob Swift had done to her, but she didn't know where to even begin.

'Would you like a glass of water?'

The receptionist had noticed Nina crying before she had realized it herself. She took the proffered tissue and said, 'No, I'll be fine.'

Nina blew her nose, and then her ears pricked as she heard the sound echoing in another room. Was that Scarlett crying? Nina's heart clenched when she recognized her daughter's distant sobs. She stood up and this time she didn't stop herself when she felt the urge to force open the door separating them. She walked straight into the counsellor's office and the moment she opened her arms, Scarlett rushed towards her. Nina took a deep, juddering breath. She was getting her daughter back.

ACKNOWLEDGEMENTS

I often have a personal connection to the subject matters I choose for my books, and that would usually be the first thing I'd mention in my acknowledgements. However, I'm pleased to say that the issues contained in *The Affair* couldn't be further from my own experiences; my main character Nina is simply living one of the many nightmares feared by any parent of teenagers. For me, those fears were never realized thanks in no small part to my daughter Jessica. I couldn't ask for a better daughter, friend and confidante.

As always, thank you to my mum Mary, Lynn, Chris, Jonathan, Mick and the wider family, and to all my friends. Despite my promises, I still don't meet up with you as often as I should, but I will do better – so no more surprise parties, Nee Parker! I would especially like to thank those friends who have helped with my research – by some strange coincidence, I've been introducing characters with jobs not dissimilar to the people I know (yes, that includes you Kathy Kelly). You have all been a part of my journey and I can't begin to tell you how much I appreciate your support.

Thank you to my agent Luigi Bonomi who has played

a key part in turning my love of writing into a career: my life continues to change in the most marvellous ways because of your guidance and support. I would also like to thank the fabulous team at HarperCollins including Kim Young, Jaime Frost and Katie Moss for their incredible support and belief, and I couldn't be more thrilled that we'll be publishing more books together in the coming years. There is one deliberate omission from that HarperCollins list and that's because I would like to pay special tribute to my amazing editor Martha Ashby who deserves much of the credit for *The Affair*. I can honestly say that writing this book was a team effort, and our long chats gave the story and characters new depths that I could dive straight into once I caught my breath.

Finally, I would like to say a big thank you to my readers. I feel privileged to have my books published and I couldn't do it without you.

A Q&A with Amanda Brooke

**1. Can you tell us a bit about your inspiration for
*The Affair?***

The Affair was one of those books that began with the germ
of an idea that mutated into something completely different.
I don't recall what triggered that first inkling of a story, but
I remember visualising a young teacher walking out on her
classroom and her career, leaving her students stunned.
She was meant to be my main character, but if you've read
The Affair, you'll realise that it's one of the schoolgirls I
imagined in my initial musings who becomes the focus of the
story. The book is unrecognisable from the original outline and
is the result of many interesting chats with my editor, Martha
Ashby, as we played with the lives of Scarlett, Nina and Vikki.

**2. Your books often centre around ideas of motherhood,
or parenthood, and then often on what could be termed 'a
parent's worst nightmare'. Is there anything in particular that
keeps you writing in this vein?**

We all take on different roles in our lives, both professionally
and personally, and for me, the most important role I've ever
had is that of a parent. It's a huge responsibility and not
without risk, and like many mothers, I started worrying about
my two children from the moment I discovered I was pregnant
with each of them. Unfortunately, no amount of worrying can
prepare you when bad things happen, and I had to endure
one of those 'worst nightmares,' when my young son died from
cancer. My experience has made me painfully aware

of how fragile the relationship between a parent and a child can be, and I think that translates into my writing as well as my everyday life. Having an overactive imagination is essential to being a writer, but from a parent's point of view, it can be curse. I have a beautiful, talented and amazing daughter who is in her twenties now, and writing *The Affair* allowed me to exorcise the ghost of one of those nightmare scenarios that my mind had conjured through her teenage years; which I'm pleased to report never came to pass.

3. And where do you get all your ideas from?

Writing two books a year means I have to be on constant alert for new ideas, and I wish I could say I've developed a special knack, but mostly it's a matter of waiting anxiously for inspiration to strike. The one thing I have trained myself to do is continuously ask those 'what if,' questions from everyday observations, and occasionally my answers transform into enough material for a full length novel. I have a little black book where I keep my half formed ideas, and while most will come to nothing, some manage to take on a life of their own. One recent idea that's starting to take shape came about while I was waiting in my car at traffic lights. I spotted a woman coming out of a nearby park and there was a man on the opposite side of the road who I was convinced was secretly watching her. That particular observation is about to become the opening scene in one of my next novels.

4. Tell us a bit about your usual writing day.

I've been asked this question so many times over the years and my stock answer would be to describe how I have to fit my writing around the day job, but since the release of my last novel, I've taken the bold decision to give up work and write full time. As a friend pointed out to me, I'm now doing my dream job and I don't have to squeeze my writing into every spare minute. These days, my writing day begins quite early because I prefer to write in the morning so I can spend the rest of the day thinking about what I've just written and where I need to take the story next. Working from home can be quite sedentary, but I have a very inventive brother-in-law who has made a desktop that sits on top of my treadmill, and my first hour of writing is spent walking and typing so I can wake up my body and brain at the same time. I then move into my office, which was my son's bedroom. I would never have become a writer if it wasn't for Nathan and it feels right to be in there. I love that, despite his short life, he has been such an inspiration.

5. In *The Affair*, you very cleverly play with the idea of how far we would go for love – parental love, marital love, forbidden love. Do you think there are limits to these kinds of love?

There are quite a lot of relationships that are examined in *The Affair*, including Nina's relationships with her children and her new husband, Vikki's relationships with her husband and her mum and, most challenging of all, Scarlett's relationship with her unnamed lover. Every one of these is tested in the course of the novel and my characters have to decide how far they're prepared to go for love, and what they're willing to sacrifice. I think by the end of the book, Nina, Vikki and Scarlett come to realise exactly where those limits are and that love isn't so blinding once doubt has taken hold.

6. Was it difficult writing about *The Affair* from fifteen-year-old Scarlett's perspective?

I had to think long and hard about how I was going to describe the affair using Scarlett's voice. Underage sex is a difficult and very emotive subject and I'm sure there are examples of fifteen-year-old girls who find the love of their life and go on to lead happy and fulfilling lives. That's certainly where Scarlett thinks her love affair is leading, and the challenge for me was to show how she was the victim even when she didn't recognise it herself. Although it's only ever Scarlett who describes her time alone with her lover, I hope the reader is under no illusion that this could be anything other than abuse.

7. Can you tell us a bit about your next book?

My next book has the working title of *The Truth* and my main character, Kate Harding, is a very confident and competent Neighbourhood Housing Officer. The story opens with Kate waiting to hear if she's been successful in a recent interview, only to discover that the job has been offered to an external candidate. When she hears who it is, Kate recognises the name, but she doesn't admit to anyone that she knows him, especially not her husband, because Thomas Moreton is a part of her life she would rather forget. When Thomas takes over as Team Leader, the past starts to catch up with Kate. For almost eight years she's been lying to herself about what happened one drunken night in a hotel room, but it's time for her to face the truth.

Reading Group Questions

1. Did *The Affair* keep you guessing about the identity of Scarlett's lover?

2. Who were the suspects to be the father of Scarlett's baby and why?

3. Who held the power in Vikki and Rob's relationship? How did their relationship change over the course of the book?

4. How much do you think Elaine, Vikki's mother, knew about Vikki and Rob's elationship? What did you think of her choices?

5. Nina and Scarlett's relationship evolves through many forms throughout the book. What were they and did you find anything relatable in the ways they interacted, articularly after you find out who the father of the baby is?

6. Are there any similarities between Vikki and Scarlett? What are they?

7. Do you think Nina and Scarlett have learned anything by the end of the book? What?

8. Did you find the characters likeable? Why? And do you think it is important for characters (particularly female characters) to be likeable in fiction?

9. How would you describe this book to another reader?

10. Did you enjoy the book? And would you recommend it?

Lucy has been desperate for a new heart for as long as she can remember. But getting the call to say a donor has been found will be a bittersweet relief: because for her to live, someone else must die.

Julia, Helen and Phoebe have been fast friends for all their lives, through Helen's unplanned pregnancy, the sudden death of Phoebe's mother, and Julia's desperation to conceive with her much younger husband. Yet a deep friendship can hide many secrets, and as their relationship reaches crisis point, what has long been buried is going to come bubbling to the surface.

With one tragic accident, these four lives will converge and Lucy will get her new heart. But who has made the ultimate sacrifice?

OUT NOW

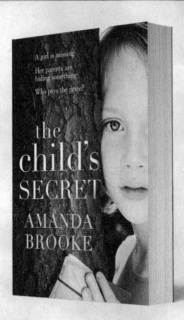

Everyone has secrets...

When eight-year-old Jasmine Peterson goes
missing, the police want to know everything.

What is the local park ranger, Sam McIntyre,
running away from and why did he go out
of his way to befriend a young girl?

Why can't Jasmine's mother and father
stand to be in the same room as each other?

With every passing minute, an unstoppable chain
of events hurtles towards a tragic conclusion.

*Everyone has secrets. The question is:
who will pay the price?*

OUT NOW